DREAD THE NIGHT

DEAR CELESTE

J.R. ERICKSON

For Ron. We'll see you on the other side.

1

____

Celeste crept slowly back up the stairs, grimacing when the floor creaked beneath her foot. She slipped into her office, eased open the closet door and stepped inside.

Why was she hiding? Why hadn't she confronted Jonathan during his phone call with Darlene Stiles—the woman who police believed had tried to kill her the year before?

She didn't have an answer. Her body wanted only to stand perfectly still in that quiet, dark place and wait. She checked her watch. Five minutes passed, then ten. Her hip began its low groan. Her leg tingled.

Celeste massaged her upper thigh, shifted from foot to foot. A sound in the room startled her, the office door creaking open. She didn't move, stared at the outline of the closed closet door, imagined Jonathan out there.

A shadow marred the light beneath the closet door. Four little obstructions. Romeo meowed.

Biting her lip, unsure if Jonathan was still in the house, Celeste eased open the door and stepped out. She knelt, lifted the kitten, and listened.

If Jonathan came upstairs, she'd play dumb, act like she hadn't heard the call. She sat at her desk, bare now that she'd packed her laptop and tucked away most of the documents from her search for River's birth family.

When another fifteen minutes passed, Celeste walked hesitantly downstairs. Jonathan had left.

Celeste called Harris.

"What's up?" he asked. He sounded distracted. In the background, she heard voices, suspected he was at the police station.

"Umm...do you have a minute to talk?"

The sound of a pencil scratching. "Uh, hold on one sec." She thought he set the phone down, heard a drawer opening, closing. "I can spare five minutes. I have a guy in interrogation, but he can sweat for a few more minutes. What's going on?"

"I was packing for West Virginia and Jonathan came home early. He must have thought I was out because my truck's parked in the garage. I overheard him on the phone. The conversation sounded pretty tense. He was telling someone not to say a word unless it was to her lawyer."

"He was talking to Darlene?"

Celeste sat heavily on a kitchen chair. A raven landed on the railing of the back deck. "Yes."

"Okay. Well, let me be totally honest with you. I've wondered if maybe...he was connected. What do you think's going on? An affair?"

"You were wondering if he was connected to Darlene? Why?"

"A hunch, sixth sense. You know how it works. It's hard to pinpoint where the feeling comes from. I haven't met the guy, but the detective on your hit-and-run mentioned a witness during the tire-slashing incident at his work. That witness called the detective and claimed he saw Jonathan in the parking lot a half hour before he reported his tires were slashed. He noted that Jonathan had put a big dark coat with a hood on over his lab coat, but he recognized him. He didn't see him slash the tires, but—"

"Bowman thinks Jonathan slashed his own tires? But why?"

"There are a number of possibilities, but Bowman wondered if Jonathan was trying to position himself as another victim. If police think the person who hit you is also targeting Jonathan, they'll assume he isn't a suspect. That's the reasoning anyway, though you'd be amazed at how many perpetrators actually do stuff like that. If anything, another lesser crime against the spouse or partner is often even more reason to focus on them."

"You believe Jonathan was involved in my hit-and-run? That he and Darlene planned it together? To kill me?"

Harris blew out a breath. "I'm not the guy working the case. As your friend, I'm going to be straight with you. I think Jonathan is dangerous and it's time to get out of that house. You already booked your place in West Virginia?"

"Yes. Well...I have hotel rooms. One tonight in Cleveland, Ohio, and another tomorrow in West Virginia. I figured once I got there, I'd decide on a more long-term option."

"Did you tell Jonathan what hotels you're staying at?"

"Yes."

"Okay. Cancel those reservations and make new ones under a different name."

"Jesus. Are you serious?"

"You know I am, Celeste. Just do it. Chances are he's not going to come after you. He doesn't want to get caught and he doesn't realize that anyone has uncovered his connection to Darlene."

"We're supposed to have an early dinner and say goodbye. If I just leave—"

"Make up an excuse. Write him a note. *It was too hard to say goodbye. I'll be in touch.* Leave it at that."

"And then when he starts calling?"

"Make sure he can't track your phone for starters. You might want to pick up a burner phone."

"A burner phone? Like a prepaid phone?"

"Yep. Write down your contacts, turn off your regular phone, and give out the new number only to people you trust completely."

"I feel like a fugitive."

"You're not. He is. He just doesn't know it yet."

After the call, Celeste wanted a drink. Instead, she returned to her packing.

Earlier that day she'd felt light, had been looking forward to going to West Virginia and beginning this new chapter. Now her mind was a hornet's nest. Her hands shook as she crammed clothes into her suitcase. She considered the box in Jonathan's closet. She couldn't take it because he'd realize what she'd uncovered.

She lifted it out, spread the contents across the bed and began to take photos. Celeste focused on the bottle of PX962, frowning and thinking back to the night before she'd visited Taylor, how groggy she'd been, how sensitive to sunlight. It was the drug Celeste's former co-workers had said they were testing at Dynamic Laboratories and it made no sense that Jonathan had brought a bottle home.

As she moved to the movie tickets, a door slammed on the first floor. She jumped and dropped her phone. It hit the bottle of pills and they skittered off the side of the bed.

"Celeste?" Jonathan's voice echoed up the stairs.

Celeste scrambled to gather everything and force it back into the box. She searched the floor for the bottle of pills, but couldn't find it. Out of time, she rushed the box back to the closet and shoved it into the corner just as the bedroom door swung open behind her. She emerged from Jonathan's closet to find him in the doorway staring at her.

2

―――――

"What are you doing?" he asked.

Celeste felt a bead of sweat slide from her forehead down the side of her face. It landed in her collarbone. Her heart thudded in her chest and she forced on a smile.

"Oh, uh..." She brushed a hand across her damp hairline. "I was trying to find my hooded sweatshirt. The gray one from work. I searched everywhere. I figured it ended up in your closet."

His eyes shifted to her empty hands. She held them up. "No luck." She looked at her watch then quickly dropped her arm when she realized how visibly it was shaking. "Is it already four? Gosh, where has the day gone?"

"It's two. I left early so we could spend an extra couple of hours together."

Harris had called half a dozen times during her afternoon with Jonathan, but she'd let his calls go to voicemail.

Celeste's hands shook as she fumbled her cell phone with one hand, her other hand on the wheel as she sped away from the house.

"Celeste?" he answered.

"It's me."

"Jesus." He released a loud breath. "Why haven't you answered your phone? I've been calling for three hours."

"Jonathan came home and wanted to spend the afternoon together."

"Shit. How'd that go?"

"I acted like everything was normal." She didn't offer details, that Jonathan had opened a bottle of wine and acted hurt when she hadn't indulged in a glass, so she'd forced a few sips. When he'd all but begged her to go to bed with him, she'd given in, though her reasonable brain screamed at her to just run out the door.

"And he believed it?" Harris asked.

"He seemed to."

"Where are you now?"

"Driving to buy a burner phone then getting on the highway and going south. I planned on staying tonight in Toledo, but I'll just drive until I'm too tired to keep going."

"That's probably not a good idea. You're running on adrenaline right now. You're going to crash—not literally, but obviously that can be an outcome of driving until you're exhausted."

"I'll know when to stop."

"Call me from the new phone so I have the number. And not to be paranoid, but I'd like you to text or email me your location every night. Just...in case."

"Sure. Okay. I have to call my brother now. He's supposed to keep my cats while I'm gone."

"All right. Drive safe."

Celeste hung up, and, hands still trembling, dialed Adam.

"Hey," her brother said.

"Adam, I need you to get the cats tonight. Now, if you can."

"Tonight? I'm supposed to meet a friend to see some live music. Is Jonathan really that pissed he can't keep the cats for one whole night without you?"

"No. It's..." She wanted to hold back, protect her brother from the sudden horror story of her life, but she couldn't protect him. She needed him now. "I overheard Jonathan on the phone today with the woman the police believe tried to kill me. I think they're having an affair."

She heard the sharp intake of his breath, a clatter as if he'd dropped something.

"No." His voice was small.

"Yes. My friend, the detective, said I need to get a burner phone, stay at different hotels. It may take days for the police to connect Jonathan, if he even is..." She didn't finish her sentence because who was she trying to convince? She'd heard him on the phone with Darlene. The writing was on the wall.

"Oh, God. Okay. I'll go right now. I'll just, umm...cancel. Wait! How will I get in touch with you if you buy a different phone?"

"I'll call you as soon as I have it. I'm driving to Walmart now. I'll touch base then."

"You could come here and stay with me."

"No. I'm going to West Virginia. Jonathan has no idea I realized anything is up. By the time he knows, I'll be far away and hopefully he'll be in custody." She'd spoken the words, but they rang hollow in her mind. How could she hope for Jonathan to be in custody? How could she possibly believe he'd conspired with Darlene to kill her?

"Custody." Adam echoed the word in disbelief.

"I know. I'll call you soon. Be careful when you go over there. Okay? He probably won't be home, but if he is you have to play dumb. Act like you're rushed, have to be somewhere for an appointment and are just stopping by quick to pick up the cats."

"Yeah. Good idea."

It was after eight by the time she had the new phone. She texted the number to Harris and her brother, then dialed Detective Bowman.

"Did you get the pictures I sent you?" Celeste asked when he answered the phone.

"I did. We haven't linked them to Darlene yet, but I suspect you're right. We're probably going to discover all of those ticket stubs et cetera were events Darlene and Jonathan attended together."

"When will you question him?"

"Soon. I was hoping to get a confession out of Darlene. If Jonathan is involved, the whole case will be stronger if Darlene agrees to testify against him. Unfortunately, right now, her lawyer is advising her not to talk."

"How can she do that? How is it okay to just not speak?"

"Whether or not she confesses, we have evidence she can't dodge. Once we lay it all out, she may be all the more compelled to give up Jonathan."

Celeste sagged in her seat, the road blurring for a moment behind tears. Despite overhearing the call between Jonathan and Darlene, she still struggled to reconcile his involvement in her hit-and-run. An affair was one thing, though even that seemed so unlike him, but attempted murder? At the same time, it was even harder to imagine Darlene had been the person who'd tried to kill her.

"And in the meantime, what am I supposed to do? I bought this disposable phone, but Jonathan is expecting me to call tonight, to check in. Do I just not?"

"That's your decision. Obviously, I wouldn't give him any specifics about where you're at and what you know. I understand it's frustrating," Bowman said. "I got used to the 'hurry up and wait' reality of arrests and prosecution a long time ago, but it's never easy when you're the victim of the crime."

After the call, she stared at the stretch of highway. The victim, Bowman had called her. It was an uncomfortable word, a label she didn't like or want. She hadn't felt like a victim after the hit-and-run. It had been a terrible accident—end of story. But now she knew there'd been intent. As she'd walked alone that morning, oblivious, safe in her little world, someone had been driving towards her with the intent to kill her, to erase her from the world.

Had Jonathan known? That was the question, the question that made her stomach squirm and her palms sweat.

A billboard on her right advertising a nearby church read: "God transforms messes into messages." Beneath the words was a dove, wings spread, backlit by a brilliant white light. During Celeste's near-death experience, she'd been there, been in that light. Why had she come back?

Despite Harris's warnings not to drive too long, Celeste didn't stop until she reached West Virginia. She'd grown tired a few times, but shook it off. She had a purpose now, a destination. A few stops for bathroom breaks, cups of silty gas station coffee and snacks and she arrived outside of Kingwood, West Virginia, just after seven in the morning.

Celeste pulled into the Micro Lodge. The two-story motel occupied a cracked asphalt lot across from a row of fast-food restaurants. She parked near the lobby and walked inside.

"How many nights?" the woman behind the faded counter asked.

"Let's start with two. I'd like to pay cash."

The woman raised an eyebrow, considered her, then shifted her gaze to her ancient-looking desktop computer. "Name?"

She almost said Celeste, but caught herself. "Umm... Juliet...Smith."

The woman's eyes again flicked up, and Celeste feared she'd ask for ID. She didn't.

Slowly the woman tapped on her keyboard, sighing several times. "Room 126. Can't miss it." She produced a key on a ring connected to a plastic tag with the '126' stamped in faded white letters.

"Thanks," Celeste told her, hurrying from the office. A burner phone, a false name—she was suddenly living like a fugitive, and that was how she felt: watched, hunted.

Like the rest of the motel, Room 126 did not appear to have been updated since its inception somewhere in the nineteen seventies or eighties. Thin brown carpeting, a sagging king bed covered by a plaid bedspread, and scratched wooden bureaus filled the space. The walls, once eggshell, had a yellowish-brown tinge. The television, a flat screen, appeared to be the only thing in the room bought in the last ten years.

Still, the room supplied the basics, and Celeste found comfort in her proximity to her childhood home. She had only vague memories of the place, didn't realize some piece of her had missed it, but now she jittered with excitement at the prospect of laying eyes on it for the first time in more than twenty-five years.

Despite the early morning, Celeste drew the curtains and crawled into bed. Her hip and leg ached from driving through the night and she stretched out long and wide, taking up as much space as she wanted.

She expected to get no sleep at all and, if she did, to have nightmares about Jonathan and Darlene—the two of them conspiring to murder her. Instead, she dreamed of West

Virginia. She stood in a stream, cool water rushing past her ankles, smooth river stones pressed against her bare feet. Dazzling sunlight cut through the heavy boughs of trees, and she watched the glistening black feathers of thousands of ravens perched on the branches, all of their eyes fixed upon her.

3

———

It was early afternoon when Celeste woke from her long nap in the hotel. Refreshed did not exactly describe her, but the exhaustion edging in during her last hours on the road had abated.

She poured a glass of Scotch and opened the envelope she'd carried for years—to college, to various apartments, eventually into the house she and Jonathan had bought. It was a scant snapshot of her once life in West Virginia. The envelope contained her birth certificate, a Kingwood library card, and a single photograph of Celeste's mother, Nettie.

In the image, Nettie, Celeste and Adam stood on a dock that jutted into a dark lake—Moon Lake. Nettie's smile appeared tight, and she had a baby Adam balanced on one hip and a toddler Celeste clinging to her leg, looking back at the camera shyly. On the back, someone, likely her mother, had written *Nettie, Celeste and Adam at the Kingwood House.*

Celeste had found the photo as a teenager in a green plastic tote of her dad's stuff—stuff he'd piled into attics or basements at the houses they'd lived over the years. Somewhere in adolescence, Celeste had taken to pawing through the items during afternoons when she and Adam were home alone after school. There were almost no pictures of their mother, but Celeste had found that one tucked into a faded paperback copy of *Romeo and Juliet*—an odd book for her father to own and keep. He was hardly a romantic.

She wasn't exactly sure where to begin in her search for her mother. Her dad had forever been mute on the topic and, when she'd pushed, he'd grown either defensive or irritable. She hadn't told him she was visiting West Virginia. In the previous weeks, it had all seemed so clear that she needed to go back, to return to where her life began. But now, as she sat miles from her childhood home, Celeste realized she hadn't really thought through what she'd do once she arrived, how she'd begin to make sense of where her mother had gone and why.

She'd been hopeful genetic genealogy could pinpoint her mother's family, but had been disappointed to discover her only genetic matches were distant cousins. Isolating closer relatives would involve a lengthy family tree process.

An old copy of the yellow pages, the front cover partially ripped off, sat in a bureau drawer. Celeste took it out and flipped to the residential listings. The book was old and out of date, but still, if her mother had once lived in the area, maybe she'd find her listed in the book. Next to the last name Harrington, she found two listings, one for a Paul S., and the other for Jim and Dana. No Nettie.

On Celeste's birth certificate, both her parents' full names were listed. *Father: Nathaniel Grant Harrington. Mother: Nettie Mae Caldwell.* Celeste flipped to the Cs in the phone book. No one at all was listed in the county with the last name Caldwell. Still, her mother could have returned to Kingwood, gotten remarried and been listed under a different surname.

Her burner phone rang, and Celeste dug it out of her bag: Harris.

"Hi," she answered.

"Hey. Just checking in. Did you make it to West Virginia?"

"I'm here."

"Where are you staying?"

"The Micro Lodge Motel just outside of Kingwood."

"Under a false name?"

"Yes. Juliet Smith."

"Okay. Good. Chances are those precautions aren't necessary, but better to be safe."

"What if Darlene hit me to have Jonathan all to herself and he was completely in the dark?" Celeste had ruminated on Jonathan's potential involvement during her drive to West Virginia. Ten hours had given her plenty of time to talk herself into and out of the belief he'd been involved several times.

"That's possible, but why was he telling her not to speak unless it's to her lawyer?" Harris countered.

Celeste sighed and shifted on the bed. It creaked beneath her, the soft mattress sunken near the middle. "Maybe he's in love with her too and doesn't believe she's involved."

"I told you what Bowman said about the tires."

"Yeah, but again, what if that was a cry for help? I was pulling away."

"So, he's having an affair and is in love with Darlene, but stages an elaborate slashing of his own tires at work as a subconscious tantrum because he doesn't want to lose you?"

It wasn't plausible, but her formerly organized life no longer adhered to rules of plausibility. She'd died and experienced the afterlife. She'd begun to see ghosts and have prophetic dreams, had stepped into the stories of two women who'd been touched by murder. The rules of reality had long since dissolved.

"I've given up expecting things to make sense."

"What is your gut telling you?" Harris asked.

Celeste scanned her body, searched for a clear response. "I don't know anymore."

"It's a lot to process. The last year has been a lot. How are you feeling, really?"

Celeste finished her Scotch. "Numb."

"Sometimes detachment is necessary."

"Yeah." Celeste had always been pretty good at compartmentalizing.

"What's happening down there? Do you have relatives you plan to visit or...?"

"No. If I have relatives around here, I've never heard of them."

"So what then?"

Celeste returned the phone book to the bureau. "I have this checklist from my genetic genealogy course for how to find a birth parent. I'm in a much better position than River because I actually know my mother's name and at least one address. I'm going to start feeding her name through the databases I have access to and see if anything comes up."

"That's a good plan. And if you can find out who her friends were in Kingwood, her employer, someone might know where she went."

"Fingers crossed I can track some of them down. I'm going to visit our childhood home tomorrow and visit other houses on the lake. Hopefully someone remembers her."

"Good luck, Celeste."

Celeste opened her laptop and started with a basic online search for Nettie Mae Caldwell. Not one single useful result. No birth records or death records. She thought there'd at least have been some obscure public notice regarding the birth of Celeste or Adam and listing Nettie as the mother, but there was none. A lot of old newspapers had never been digitized and, unfortunately, that appeared to be the case in Kingwood.

Celeste searched the tax records for the house she'd lived in as a child. She wanted to know who lived there now, how long they'd lived there. Celeste hoped they'd allow her to walk around the property, perhaps even go inside.

When the owner's name appeared, she frowned: Nathaniel Harrington. Her dad was listed as the owner of the house.

"That doesn't make sense," she murmured, scrolling to the sales history of the house. There'd been no change in ownership since he'd bought it.

She searched the MLS, wondered if he'd had it for sale for years, decades, and never been able to sell it. She couldn't find a listing anywhere. The county tax records listed a single payer: Nathaniel Harrington.

Celeste called Adam.

"Celeste! What's happening? Are you okay? I forgot about your new number and almost didn't pick up. Thank God I did. What's going on?"

"Nothing's happening. I'm fine. I just have a question for you. Did Dad ever tell you he still owned the West Virginia house?"

"The lake house from when we were kids?"

"Yeah."

"No. Of course he doesn't own it. He must have sold it twenty-some years ago."

"He's still listed as the owner on the tax records."

"Maybe they haven't been updated."

"They have. He paid taxes on it last year. He still owns it."

"But...why? I don't think he's been back to West Virginia since we moved. Right? How could he still own it and never tell us? Is he renting it?"

"I don't think so. I don't think anyone has lived there since us."

"Are you going to call Dad and ask him?"

"I think I have to."

"Good luck with that."

"How are Cash and Romeo?" she asked.

"Holy terrors."

"No. Really?"

He laughed. "No. They're great. I mean, they've only been here twenty-four hours, but Romeo thinks he owns the place and Cash has taken up residence in my bay window. So...have they arrested Jonathan?"

"No. Nothing has happened yet. Has he tried to call you?"

"Only about a dozen times. Maybe I should...I don't know, try to talk to him and record it. See if he'll admit to anything."

Celeste knew Adam was the last person Jonathan would confess to. "I think it's best to ignore his calls. He'll be trying hard to get information out of you."

"Have you talked to him?"

"No. Honestly, I don't want to. My head is full enough trying to make sense of Dad still owning the West Virginia house. I'm putting my attention on finding Mom now. All this stuff with Jonathan is just a distraction."

"Hmm...I hate to quote my therapist here, but I'm pretty sure she'd call that escapist behavior."

"I'm not jetting off to the Caribbean and sipping Mai Tais."

"Even so, I'm not sure you can outrun this thing with Jonathan."

"I don't intend to, but there's nothing I can do about it right now. The detectives in Grand Rapids have the power. I'm removing myself from the equation until I have more data."

"More data? Meaning what exactly?"

"Proof that he was or wasn't involved. Until then, I'm doing my best to stay out of it."

"All right. I'll stop badgering you. Tell me what you find out about Mom, okay?"

"I will."

After she ended the call, Celeste found her regular cell

phone in her purse. She hadn't used it since leaving Michigan, hadn't even turned it on, but she knew her dad wouldn't answer an unknown number. She powered on her cell, ignored the incessant pings as the flood of text and voicemail messages loaded, and called her dad.

The phone rang four times, five. She assumed he wouldn't answer and then, after the sixth ring—"Hello?"

"Hi, Dad. How are you?"

"I'm fine, Celeste. How are you?"

They hadn't spoken since their dinner weeks before. It wasn't unusual. In the past, they'd gone a month or more without so much as exchanging a text message.

"I'm all right, but...I'm in West Virginia. I want to visit our childhood home."

He said nothing, and she knew he would not offer her the truth unless she demanded it.

"I checked the tax records and found out you still own the house."

"And?"

"And why do you still own it? And why didn't you ever tell me and Adam?"

The silence stretched. In the background, she heard the muffled sounds of the television.

"What's there to tell? The market never made it worthwhile for me to sell, so I've hung onto it."

It was a stupid answer, a bullshit answer. Holding onto the house and letting it go to rot would only ensure it lost its value. Even if twenty-five years ago the market had been down, the house had surely doubled or even tripled in value since her parents bought it.

"I'd like to go inside."

"No."

"Why not?"

"Because there's nothing to see. It's an old house, and who knows? It might be invaded by rats now. It's not safe."

"Dad—"

"End of discussion. And anyway, the key is down here with me. There's no way for you to get inside without breaking in, and that is unacceptable."

"Mom never wanted her half of the house? Her share from the sale?"

"There was never a sale."

"But still, she never contacted you demanding half of everything so she could start her own life?"

"No. She didn't."

"What about her family or friends? Who could I reach out to around here who might know where she went after she left?"

Her dad released an exasperated sigh. "Celeste, your mother left over thirty years ago. Even if I remembered the name of her friends in Kingwood, which I don't, they're probably not even around there anymore."

"Family then? Her parents. Siblings."

"Her parents both died before we were even married. She was an only child."

"That's it? That's all you can give me?"

"I don't understand what you want from me, Celeste."

"Tell me about the last time you saw her."

"I have told you."

"No, actually you haven't. Just give me one image. The last moment you saw her, what was she doing?"

"She grabbed two suitcases and stomped out the door in a huff. That was it. I have to go. My...oven alarm is beeping."

A clear lie, but he left her no time to state the obvious. He hung up.

4

———————

N ettie

"Need a ride?"

Nettie looked up to see the new senior, Nathaniel Harrington, idling in his shiny white Pontiac Firebird. Her mouth went instantly dry and her eyes dropped to her tennis shoes, one side flapping thanks to the glue she'd added only the week before, already coming unstuck. She looked like a homeless girl. He was probably asking out of pity.

"No. I'm good. Thanks."

He raised an eyebrow. His blue eyes sparkled in the intense afternoon sun and a half smile played on his full lips. "You sure? I saw you at school. You're, what, a sophomore?"

"A junior."

He stuck his hand through the window. "I'm Nathaniel."

"Nettie." She shook his hand, aware that hers was slick and hot.

"Well, hop in, Nettie. Give those shoes a break. They look like they need it."

Warmth rushed into her face. She walked around the car and climbed into the passenger seat, instantly relieved as the cool air rushed from the dashboard vents.

"You moved here from Florida?" Nettie asked.

"Yep. Tampa. Ever been?"

She shook her head, dared not to tell him she'd never been more than ten miles outside of Davis, West Virginia.

Nettie caught sight of her face in the sideview mirror. Her nose and cheeks looked red, hair tangled. She finger-brushed her snarled dark hair and adjusted on the seat, her bare thighs sticking to the leather. She'd never ridden in a car with leather seats before.

"I'd like to see Florida," Nettie said. "Someday I'll go."

"Maybe we can go together," Nathaniel said.

Nettie looked at his profile, searched for the joke. Why was Nathaniel Harrington, basketball star and the new guy in school all the girls were whispering about, talking to her as if he were remotely interested? Likely because he hadn't been around long enough to realize Nettie lived in the Dogwood Estates trailer park and her mom had been picked up for shoplifting so many times, she'd been banned from the local grocery store.

"How do you like West Virginia?" Nettie asked.

"Pretty cool so far. Different from Florida, which is totally flat. My dad's afraid I'm going to send the Firebird off a mountain one of these mornings on my way to school."

"It's nice he's worried about you."

Nathaniel laughed, and looked at her sidelong. "I'm pretty sure he's worried about the Firebird."

5

____

Celeste spent the following morning at a diner in Kingwood. She downed two cups of strong French roast coffee, forced down a bagel despite her stomach feeling like a tiny acidic fireball, and attempted to organize her thoughts before heading to the house on Moon Lake.

She avoided thoughts of Jonathan, aware that her powered-off cell phone at the motel was likely filled with messages from him. Beyond the wall of numbness she'd erected since fleeing the Grand Rapids house, a space of despair hovered. The betrayal was so big and ugly, she didn't dare step into the room and look at it. Best to keep it shut away for now.

Celeste bought a bottle of water and left the coffee shop. The drive to Moon Lake took twenty-five minutes. The roads were winding and mountainous.

As she came upon the driveway to her childhood home, an insane thought popped into her mind. What if her mother was living there right at that moment? What if she and her dad had made some agreement—he could keep the kids and she'd keep the house and they'd part ways and never have contact again? It was ludicrous, and yet as Celeste turned off the road, her heart sped up.

She inched the truck down the tree-lined driveway. In summer, the thick foliage cast the driveway in shadow. The gravel ended at the back of the large Tudor-style house. The windows were dark and Celeste suspected no one had been there in a long time. The swell in her chest deflated.

She put the truck in park and stared at the house. She remembered the house and yet the memories had a hazy quality, more like remembering a very vivid dream than her actual life.

When she stepped from her truck, the smell jolted her, a faint mineral aroma combined with the dank earth. The air was filled with the hum of cicadas and the soft hush of water lapping the shore. For an instant, Celeste was a child again running across the yard, down the dock, plunging into the cool lake. The dark water closing around her.

Somewhere nearby a bird squawked and brought her back to the now. Celeste moved across the grass, high, but not so high that someone hadn't cut it in years. Her dad must have been paying someone to do at least basic maintenance on the property.

She stepped through the arched doorway and knocked on the heavy wood door. No sounds came from within the house. Celeste tried to turn the door knob. Locked.

An old wooden swing hung from a tree beside the house. Despite the weathered board, the swing and rope appeared sturdy. Celeste sank onto it, letting it sway gently beneath her weight. She looked at the house, framed now by the thick forest, and felt a hollow ache. She'd finally made it.

A raven swooped down and landed in the yard a few feet in front of her.

"Now what?" she murmured.

Faintly through the trees a boy's laughter rang out. The raven squawked and took flight.

It was possible the neighbors on either side of the Harringtons' house had lived there when Celeste was a girl. It was worth a shot. She couldn't see the houses that bordered her childhood home. Dense trees and wild foliage grew between them.

Celeste moved along the rocky shoreline toward the house where she'd heard the sound of the child. She frowned as she approached it. The house was modern, likely built in the previous decade, with enormous windows running the length of the dark, two-story structure. A tiered deck with a large copper fire pit adorned the front. No way it had been there when she was a little girl.

Celeste saw no sign of the child she'd heard and she flushed slightly as she navigated the lawn, aware the person inside had likely seen her through the front-facing windows as she walked to the door at the back of the house. She knocked and waited. A minute passed and then she heard movement inside.

The door swung open abruptly, revealing a woman who seemed more suited for California than rural West Virginia. Blonde hair piled into an elaborate updo, heavy makeup, and a silk robe—barely tied at the waist—revealing a glimpse of a zebra-print bikini beneath.

"Yes?" the woman demanded. She held a glass of white wine, her manicured fingers glittering with oversized rings.

Celeste blinked. "Hi. I'm sorry to bother you. I'm Cele—"

"Congratulations," the woman cut her off. "What do you want?"

Celeste swallowed her annoyance. "I grew up in the house next door. I'm back in town, trying to find out some things about my mom. She left when I was only a toddler and I thought maybe someone around here might have known her or—"

"Your mom?" The woman arched a penciled brow. Her gaze flicked over Celeste, evaluating her.

"Yes. Nettie Harrington. Have you been in this house long?"

The woman drained her wine and set the glass on a side table. She extended her hand. "My name is Rose. And no, I haven't been here long. This is my boyfriend's house."

Celeste, surprised by the sudden gesture, shook the woman's hand.

"What did you say your name was?" Rose asked.

"Celeste. Celeste Harrington."

"Rose?" A man's voice bellowed from the house.

Rose rolled her eyes. "Duty calls." She closed the door in Celeste's face without another word.

Celeste's face burned as she retreated up the driveway to the road. It would have been faster to walk the shoreline, but she abhorred the thought of the woman watching her clumsily make her way back across the yard. Celeste bypassed the driveway to her childhood home and continued in the opposite direction to the house on the other side. The driveway was steep and rocky and she stubbed her sandaled foot on a rock as she walked down it. She grimaced and peered down to see the nail on her big toe split and bleeding.

The sound of a vehicle rumbled towards her from the house and Celeste quickly stepped to the side of the driveway as a black convertible slid into view. The driver slowed. He was an elderly man, his scalp mottled with age spots, dark sunglasses obscuring his eyes.

"Hi." Celeste stepped closer. "I apologize for just walking up your driveway. My dad owns the house next door, and I was hoping to talk with some of the neighbors."

The man removed his sunglasses, revealing watery blue eyes. "The house next door?"

Celeste pointed through the trees. "The one through there. My dad is Nathaniel Harrington."

"Ah, I see. Huh. I remember Nate, sure. And you too, then. Hate to say your name has plumb slipped my mind. Sarah? Sandra?"

"Celeste."

He slapped the steering wheel. "Celeste. That's it. And you have a brother too, don't ya?"

"Adam."

"Okay, now it's coming back. Holy moly. It's been ages. Huh. What's brought you back? Is your dad here too?"

"Nope. Just, well...I actually...I'm"—Celeste stumbled over her words—"trying to find my mother."

He stared at her. "Is that so? Huh. So she came back then? She's living here in Kingwood?"

Celeste tucked a strand of hair behind her ear. "I don't know. I haven't seen her since she left when I was three."

Both his eyebrows shot to his hairline. "Never?"

"No."

He fixed his eyes forward for a moment as if deep in thought. Then he lifted his wrist and squinted at his watch. "Gotta get into town to see my doc. Already running behind, but you meet me back here in an hour. Hmm? We can have a talk."

"That'd be great. Thank you."

* * *

Celeste felt buoyant as she walked the shoreline back to her house. Already, she'd found someone who knew her family. As she studied the house where she'd lived the first eight years of her life, she wondered again why her dad hadn't sold it. They'd never once taken a family trip back to the house. He'd never mentioned it again after they moved to Michigan. But all that time, he must have paid someone to cut the grass, to check on it.

She had an hour to kill and she wanted inside the house. She walked the perimeter, double-checking the doors and trying unsuccessfully to push up the windows.

Her dad didn't want her in the house, had forbidden her from going inside, but she didn't care. She searched under pots that had once held plants and stuck her fingers into light fixtures above the deck and near the garage. When she didn't find a hidden key, she returned to the arched doorway at the back of the house.

The dark metal lock and door knob appeared sturdy, unlikely to be easily picked. A small arched window peered from the upper half of the door, but the wavy glass obscured the interior of the house. Likewise, at every window she'd attempted to look into, Celeste had been greeted by thick dark curtains.

On one side of the house, two steps led down to a door blocked by a screen. She opened the screen and wiggled the knob. Locked. But unlike the main door, this one was less solid. She returned to her truck and rifled through her wallet for an old gift card.

Celeste slid the card into the doorjamb down to the lock. She wriggled it furiously, but the lock stayed in place. As she angled the card and tried again, the card snapped.

"Damn it," she muttered, stuffing the broken card in her pocket.

The trees muted the sounds from the houses on either side. If she broke a window, likely no one would hear. She considered the rocks that lined the pathway toward the dock. She could try to kick the door, but that meant either balancing on her bad leg and risking a fall, or kicking with her bad leg and at the least being very sore if not causing an injury.

Biting her lip, she grabbed a rock. She peeled off her sweatshirt and wrapped it around the rock then smashed it hard against the window in the door. The glass spiderwebbed, but didn't break. She struck it again, losing her grip on the rock when the glass gave way. The rock skittered into the room and slid across the tile floor.

Celeste paused and looked around. No one emerged from the trees. Not that she expected anyone would.

She reached through the broken window, twisted the lock on the knob and pushed open the door. A faded yellow washer and dryer stood against one wall in the narrow laundry room.

Celeste stepped inside. She carefully swept the glass into a pile with her hand, pausing at a hairline crack that ran horizontal across one of the tiles. Had the broken glass done it?

A dark hallway opened beyond the laundry room. Celeste moved toward the front of her house. She passed an opening on her right, the kitchen, but bypassed it.

The house smelled of dust and mildew and was so dark Celeste walked directly into a side table and cracked her knee against the edge.

She hunched over and winced, but bit back the sound.

"No one's here," she reminded herself. Plus, this was her dad's house, her childhood house, and yet she felt criminal, a burglar creeping through a house she'd just broken into.

She rubbed her knee and straightened up.

Something creaked above her, the floorboards depressing as if beneath someone's feet.

Celeste froze and listened.

6

Maybe someone did live in the house, had been renting it for years and it only seemed like a tomb, a perception born of her own expectations rather than reality.

Celeste waited, counted the seconds, her eyes trained on the shadowy mantel in the living room. The longer she stared at the slab of dark wood, the more she noticed the layer of gray dust coating the surface. How could someone possibly live there? Their movements through the house alone should have disturbed the dust.

When no additional sounds arose, she straightened up, shook off the shudder running up her spine and stepped to a heavy curtain. She pulled it aside, releasing a flurry of dust and letting a stream of sunlight in.

Above the fireplace a pale rectangle, the bricks around it darker, stood out. A large photo had clearly once hung there.

As she retraced her steps into the hall, a soft noise stopped her in her tracks. It was faint, almost imperceptible—a whispering sigh, as if someone had exhaled right behind her. She turned sharply, her heart thudding in her chest.

No one stood behind her. She searched the gloomy corners for a shadow, an apparition perhaps, but nothing appeared.

The carpeted stairs leading to the second floor groaned beneath her. In the upstairs hallway, she was greeted again by pale rectangles where photos had once hung.

She paused at the closed door on her right—at the pretty cursive placard painted in white and yellow with bunches of flowers at either end. *Celeste*, it said.

This had been her bedroom and, though she hadn't thought about it in so long it hardly seemed real, she could already feel the soft give as she sat on her daybed as a child, the tickle of the ruffled dust skirt against her bare calves, could hear the sound of the water lapping stones through an open window.

They might have been distant, buried, but the memories of her childhood at Moon Lake had not vanished.

Celeste opened the door and stared into the shadowy interior, steeling herself against the tumult of emotion warring inside her. Celeste wanted to meet the house as a scientist, an indifferent observer, not swayed by the sadness the house itself seemed to exude. Could a house do that? Or was it merely Celeste projecting her own feelings onto the relic she'd once called home?

She crossed the room and peeled back the yellow curtains. Dust motes floated in the air, swirling in sparkling tendrils through the shaft of sunlight. The walls were painted a pale pink and trimmed with a wallpaper border of yellow flowers.

Again, memories surfaced, but they seemed to merge and bleed together. Playing a board game on the carpeted floor with Adam and another child, sitting on her bed and watching the small square TV that still sat on a dresser, a stack of DVDs beside it. She glanced at the one on top, *Labyrinth*—dust-covered like everything else in the house.

As she considered the bed, a twin daybed covered by an

ugly brown comforter, another memory swam up. Lying on her back and sliding beneath the bed, Adam already tucked into the darkness at the back, crying. Somewhere in the house the sound of yelling.

The next door in the upstairs hallway held a similar sign. Colorful little painted cars surrounded the name: *Adam*.

Adam's room, like hers, was an odd mishmash of tenderness and indifference. The walls were pale blue. Hand-painted clouds hovered near the top. Curtains, navy with images of colorful choo-choo trains, covered the single window. His bed, also a twin, held a plain gray blanket and a pillow with no case. A pile of toys lay in the corner of the room. A pretty wood toy box had a gaping hole in its side as if someone had kicked it.

Celeste understood why the walls and curtains appeared delicate and full of thought. Their mother had designed and decorated the rooms in preparation for her babies. And then she'd left and Celeste's father, who'd likely never thought of putting effort into a bedspread in his life, had taken over. The remnants of their mother's touch lingered, but the years of her absence had gradually replaced many of the pretty things with items he might have gotten from a thrift store—though she'd never known her dad to shop in those.

What bothered her even more than colorless bedspreads was the sheer quantity of what they'd left behind. Toys and books and clothes. Had they taken anything at all when they moved to Michigan?

She passed a bathroom, the door open, and peeked in. A bathtub, toilet and sink. Nothing extraordinary.

The door on the left at the end of the hall opened into a large master bedroom that faced the lake. As she walked into the room, a memory surfaced.

Child Celeste groping through the darkness into the master bedroom at night. She'd had a nightmare.

"Mama? Mama?" she'd been calling. Tears streamed down her face.

Rustling from the big bed, movements, the murmur of voices and then her father guiding her back out and away from the room, down the hall, to her bed.

How old had she been? Who had been in the bed with him? Was the memory even real?

In the dim light filtering through the curtain, she stared at the four-poster bed against the wall, bare of bedding though pillows remained. On either side of the bed sat matching end tables, each holding identical blue lamps with white shades.

She slipped out of the master bedroom and moved to the closed door on the opposite side of the hall. It was plain, unassuming, and yet Celeste paused and stared at it. She felt something, a reluctance to look in that room. She searched her memory. What had the room been when she was a child? She couldn't remember.

Shaking off her trepidation, she stepped forward and twisted the knob. Locked. She wiggled the knob a second time, thought it must be stuck, but realized after several hard twists it was definitely locked.

Something creaked inside the room, and she took a step back, stared hard at the door. She half-expected to hear the click of a lock, watch the knob twist and be standing face to face with her mother.

It didn't happen.

No noise accompanied the first creak.

She stepped forward and pressed her ear against the wood. No sounds except her breath.

***

Celeste wasn't sure how long she'd been in the house, but

imagined her hour had nearly passed. She was reluctant to leave, but wanted a chance to talk with the neighbor.

She made her way back downstairs and out through the side door. As Celeste rounded the corner of the house, she stopped. A little boy was running down the dock toward the stretch of dark water. He had a flop of red-brown hair, a t-shirt billowing behind him. His footfalls were silent as his tennis shoes hit the wooden dock and then he was gone. He didn't jump and disappear into the water with a splash. He was just...gone.

Celeste blinked at the glittering water. Had he too been a memory?

No.

He was a ghost.

7

————————

N ettie

Nettie sat cross-legged on the sunken couch in the tiny trailer. The hum of a distant train echoed through the air, mixing with the sound of her mother rifling through the medicine cabinet in the cramped bathroom.

Nathaniel would be there soon for their date and her stomach twisted at the thought of him seeing her trailer, the sparse burned grass lot, the broken-down, rusted-out Oldsmobile parked beside it. She'd tried to meet him in town, but he'd insisted on picking her up at home.

"Where are they?" Her mother's slurred voice cut through the room.

Nettie stood and paced to the window, pulled back the sheet that served as a curtain. The dusty road in front of the trailer lay empty. He probably wouldn't show up, had asked around about Nettie and learned she was one of those moun-tain girls with a dead father and a mother addicted to drugs. He was probably on his way to Jessica Marly's house, or Brenda Peters', one of the pretty, popular girls whose parents lived in the new houses by the river.

Suddenly her mother burst into the room and staggered toward Nettie. She grabbed a handful of her hair.

"Where are my pills?" she shrieked.

Nettie winced and wrenched away, leaving several strands of her long dark hair curled in her mother's fist. There were no drugs. Her mother had taken them all, but it wouldn't help for Nettie to say that. Her mother was in one of her moods, coming down from her latest bender, going out of her mind with desperation for a fix.

Nettie flung open the door and practically fell down the rickety wood steps into the dirt yard. Her mother chased after her, slurring and swinging.

Nettie ducked away and ran behind the Oldsmobile.

"Mom, stop!" she pleaded. "You used them. Okay. Don't you remember? Days ago."

"Liar!" Her mother lunged forward, grabbing Nettie's arm with surprising strength. "You're just like your father! Useless!"

Nettie heard the engine and saw Nathaniel's Firebird appear. Her stomach plunged as he stepped out, a yellow tissue-wrapped bouquet of roses in one hand. His smile faltered when he caught sight of Nettie and her wild-eyed mother.

"It's okay," Nettie called out to him. "I'm just...my mom is..."

Before Nettie could finish, her mother whirled to face Nathaniel. "Who are you?" she bellowed. "Get out of here. Go on." She whipped back around and darted toward Nettie, who tried to run, but her mother caught her high on her arm, finger-nails digging into her skin.

Nathaniel dropped the flowers and in three lunging steps closed the gap between them. He wrenched Nettie's mother away.

"What the hell's going on here?" he demanded, stepping in front of Nettie with a protective intensity that made her heart skip a beat.

Nettie's mother stumbled back. She glared up at Nathaniel. "I said to get off my property. You want a bullet between your eyes, boy?" She lurched toward the trailer, lost her footing and fell.

Nettie slipped past Nathaniel and, against his protests, helped her mother to her feet.

"Don't touch me," her mother screamed, batting her hands away.

Nettie stepped back, tears stinging her eyes. The shame burned white hot into her neck and face. She couldn't bring herself to turn around and face Nathaniel.

"Hey," he said, taking her hand and pulling her back toward him. "Come on. Let's get you out of here."

Nettie hesitated, cast a last glance at her retreating mother, and then allowed Nathaniel to guide her toward his car.

They drove in silence for five minutes. Nettie stared hard out the window, using her shirt sleeves to wipe away her falling tears.

Finally, Nathaniel maneuvered the car into a small over-look. A wooden guardrail was the only barrier between the nose of the Firebird and the sloping forest below.

"Nettie?"

She swiped a final time at her face, likely red and splotchy from her tears, and looked at him. She expected to see pity in his eyes, even disgust. It wouldn't be the first time a man had looked on such an exchange between her and her mother with disgust.

"I'm sorry," she whispered. "I didn't...want that to happen."

He took her hand, and she forced her eyes to his, saw there was no disgust at all, only kindness and something more... yearning that instantly caused the interior of the car to feel catastrophic and simultaneously too big.

He leaned forward, cupped her face and kissed her.

8

———————

Celeste found the neighbor sitting on his front porch. A large Great Dane lay stretched beside him.

"You're back," he said. "Half thought I imagined ya." He chuckled. "Though Doc said I haven't lost my mind just yet, and here you are."

"Here I am," she agreed, uneasy from the spirit of the boy she'd encountered moments before. As she'd picked her way along the lake toward the neighbor's house, she'd glanced repeatedly toward the water as if expecting the child to suddenly pop up.

"Can I get you something? I got soda pop in there and bottled water."

"No. I'm all set. Thank you. I forgot to ask your name earlier."

"Henry," he told her. "Henry Moser. Pull up a chair." He gestured at several white Adirondack chairs.

Celeste sat down, kneading her fingers together on her knees. "You knew us when we lived here? My family."

"Yep. Coach Harrington and his pretty little family."

"My dad was a coach?" Celeste asked, surprised. She'd never known her dad to play a sport, let alone coach one.

"Yep. Girls' basketball. And taught, too—chemistry, I believe."

"He was a teacher?" She couldn't keep the shock from her voice.

Henry raised an eyebrow. "You sure we're talking about the same man? You didn't know your dad was a teacher and coach?"

"No," she admitted. "For as long as I remember he worked in a plastics factory."

"Huh. I'll be darned," Henry said. "Must have decided to shift gears then."

"And did you know my mom?"

"Oh, yeah. We knew Nettie. My wife, Alma, spent quite a bit of time with your mom back when you were first born. Alma always wanted to have kids of our own, but not in God's plan apparently. She loved nothing more than rocking you to sleep to give your mom a little break now and then."

"Is your wife here?"

"Gone for six years. Cancer."

"I'm sorry."

"Thank you. In the end I was glad to see her go, to see an end to her suffering. Looking forward to joinin' her one of these days. But anyhow, she got pretty close with your mom for a few years and couldn't believe it when your mom left. Talked about it for ages."

"Did she know why my mom left?"

"Nobody did as far I can remember. I think her and your dad were having some marital problems and, from the way he told it, she had a bit of a breakdown and just left one day."

"And never came back? You guys never saw her even once?"

Henry gestured at the thick trees separating the houses. "Don't see much of anything from here. Part of why people like the houses on Moon Lake. Lots of privacy. We only ever saw your ma if she walked over or if she and your dad were out on the boats. Sometimes it'd just be her in the rowboat or her with you kids. She liked to fish. She'd go out in the boat real early in the morning sometimes."

"To fish?"

"Sometimes, yeah. And other times she just rowed for a while. It's real peaceful here in the morning. The big loud world doesn't even exist."

Celeste imagined her mother rowing alone on the lake early in the morning. What had been going through her mind? Had those solo trips been her time to contemplate leaving her family? "Did you see my mom before she left?"

"Afraid not. If memory serves, she left in the fall. Back in those days, Alma and I both still worked full time. We came here for weekends in the summer and might make it out a handful of times during the off season. We didn't know your mom had left until that next summer. Alma went over to see her and the babysitter told her she'd taken off the previous autumn. Alma was pretty upset."

"And you've never seen her there again? Not even someone who looked like her stopping by or—"

He shook his head, eyes sad. "I wish I could tell you different. I've seen your dad a couple times, but, gosh, it's been... years now. Couldn't even tell you how many. He'd stop in for a night or two and be gone. I never even had a chance to say hello."

"Did my mom have other friends around the lake? Or do you know who her friends in town were?"

Henry frowned. "Gosh, I wish I did. Your mom worked, I know, but for the life of me, I can't remember where at. Something with animals, I think. Maybe a vet's office?"

"Thanks, Henry."

"You betcha. I hope you find her. I head back to Morgantown tomorrow, but I'll be back and forth throughout the summer. If you're in the area, come say hi."

"I'll do that," she told him.

Celeste took the rocky driveway back to the road and started toward her childhood home. She called Adam.

"Everything okay?" he asked.

"Yeah. I just had a question for you. Did Dad ever tell you he was a teacher?"

"A teacher? Of what?"

"High school chemistry, and he coached the girls' basketball team."

"Umm, no. You're not trying to tell me Dad actually taught in a high school?"

"He did in Kingwood."

"I can't believe it. Are you sure? It's so...not his personality."

"I know. It's weird, and why didn't he ever tell us? Especially when you were getting your teaching degree?"

As she neared the mailbox that marked the entrance to her childhood home, a sound startled her. A man stood on the opposite side of the isolated road near a large black van. He tipped his ball cap up so she could see his face more clearly.

"Hi," he called out, waving.

Celeste frowned. "Adam, let me call you back later." She ended the call and slipped the cell into her pocket.

"You buy that place?" The man gestured at the gravel driveway leading to her former home.

"No. I don't think it's for sale."

"Me neither. Never seen a sign anyhow."

"I used to live here," Celeste admitted. "My dad still owns the house." It felt odd saying that out loud. Why did he still own the house? Why had he simply left it?

The guy in the ball cap nodded slowly. "That's interesting. I've been hoping to track down the owner of this house for years." He walked toward her and extended his hand. "I'm Spencer Ashman."

"Celeste," she told him, shaking his hand. Inwardly she chastised herself for giving her real name. What if this guy had been sent by Jonathan, was a private investigator tracking her whereabouts?

"Your dad owns this place, huh? How come he never visits?"

"He lives in Florida."

"Huh. All right."

"Why have you been looking for him?" she asked.

"Now that's a long story." He removed this ball cap to reveal dark thinning hair. "Maybe we could go inside and have a cup of coffee. I can fill you in."

"I don't think so." Celeste turned and started back toward the driveway.

"All right, hold on. It was just a suggestion. I'm a podcaster. My show is called *Dark Deeds*. Ever heard of it?"

Celeste paused and stared at him. "No."

His expression was an odd mixture of relief and disappointment. "Sure. It's kind of a niche thing. Long-form unsolved true crime. Used to be pretty popular, really popular, and then... well, things took a turn. That's part of me being here, really. It's a long story, but I'll give you the soundbite. Over twenty-five years ago a little boy came up missing. Elliot Thacker. His grandma lived about five miles thataway." He pointed into the trees on the opposite side of the road. "Five miles by car, three miles as the crow flies, and Elliot would come to this lake. Rumor has it he was here the day he disappeared, but the last confirmed sighting was his grandma, who watched him walk out the door with a fishing pole and a pocketful of pennies."

"Why do you want to talk to my dad then?"

"Tying up loose ends mostly. I've interviewed just about everyone who was around the lake when Elliot went missing.

Your dad was here. I reckon you were too. Remember a little boy going missing?"

Celeste shook her head. She didn't tell him she remembered almost nothing at all from her childhood in West Virginia.

"How about your mom? Is she in Florida too?"

"She left when I was three. That's part of the reason I'm here."

"Trying to find her, huh?"

Celeste nodded. "Are you from this area?" she asked.

"Oh, yeah. Got that Blue Ridge blood," he said.

Celeste considered him. He hadn't been sent by Jonathan. He might even be able to help her. He was from the area, had an investigative podcast. "I'll talk to you, but not at the house. Is there a place in town? A coffee shop or—"

"So long as you're not imagining a Starbucks, there are places that serve coffee. Frog's Diner's a nice joint. Twenty-minute drive from here."

"I'll meet you there."

9

Frog's Diner occupied a little stone building with a faded wooden sign painted with two frog legs jutting from a pot. Celeste parked beside Spencer and followed him to a booth.

"Amazing pizza rolls," he said, sliding a laminated menu toward her. "And if you're not hell bent on coffee, this place serves a mean ice cream soda."

The waitress, an older woman with gray curls tucked beneath a hair net, paused at their table. "Spencer, the usual?"

"Yep."

"And for you?"

Celeste's stomach growled. "Umm...pizza rolls, I guess, and an ice cream soda."

"That's what I get." Spencer winked at her.

"You were born and raised in Kingwood?" Celeste asked when the waitress walked away.

"In Clarksburg actually, not far away. I moved here to Kingwood nine, ten years ago. And you're from where?"

"Michigan."

"Ah yes, home of the Dogman, the Manistee Forest Witch,

that old asylum up north that had all kinds of madness going on—murders and whatnot. I've covered a lot of that on my other podcast."

"You have another podcast?"

"*Strictly Supernatural.* I've interviewed people from just about every state. You wouldn't believe the things people have seen. It's wild. I could have stuck with that, should have probably. True crime is a whole other animal. But you see, I was over in Point Pleasant at the Mothman festival about eight years ago and met a guy whose son had been murdered on the night of the Silver Bridge collapse. You hear about that one?"

Celeste shook her head.

"Well, it was a big deal in Point Pleasant. A suspension bridge full of cars collapsed. Forty-plus people ended up dead. And afterwards all these people started talking about seeing this winged monster with red eyes—the Mothman. Anyhoo, this fella I met at the festival, Roger Benson, had lost a son that very same night. Stabbed to death in downtown Point Pleasant right outside of his apartment.

"The case was unsolved in part because the bridge took all the time and resources the cops had. Piqued my interest. I started doing some digging and next thing you know I've got a six-episode series on the case, and I figured why not? Right? Might drum up some new leads for the poor guy. That's how *Dark Deeds* got started. And not three weeks after the podcast launched, tips started rollin' in and this girl Shaina Port ended up turning in her boyfriend, who'd confessed that he'd killed that kid to rob him all those years ago."

"So you solved the case?"

"That might be tootin' my own horn a bit. I got people talkin' about it again. Sometimes that's all it takes. But when you experience the rush of that, of helping resolve a fifty-year-old unsolved murder, justice for the dad who figured he'd die not knowing... Well, that's a feeling you get addicted to."

"That's what you're doing with this little boy's case? Chasing a feeling?" Celeste thought of the boy she'd watched running down the dock in front of her childhood home, disappearing into thin air.

"Chasing somethin' anyway. West Virginia is a strange place. I guess that's probably true about anywhere if you get in deep enough. Still, this place has a spook factor unrivaled in my humble opinion. I've only been lost in the mountains once —happened when I was a boy—and once was enough. It might have been that that got me going on Elliot's case. Lord knows it wasn't fame and fortune.

"You couldn't find a poorer, more down-and-out family than the Thackers. Like I said, it was Elliot's grandma, Sheila, who lived up by Moon Lake. She had a rundown little house up there. She's living in a nursing home now. Still has her wits about her, but the body isn't cooperating anymore, if you know what I mean. Elliot's mom and dad were both hooked on crack —both dead now. In a lot of ways, Elliot was another casualty of the drug epidemic. Once his parents got into drugs, Elliot got forgotten. Sheila Thacker, his dad's mom, started keeping him more and more, but she's an oddball herself. Never took him to school, let him run wild, barefoot and dirty most of the time, but at least at her place he had stew to eat and a bed to sleep in.

"Sheila told me he took to wandering down to the lake. Maybe 'wandering' is putting it lightly. He'd trek over there with a homemade fishing pole. People around the lake reported seeing him. One of 'em called me during the podcast —I think it was after the third episode, which was a long interview with his grandma, and she described how he had this raccoon hat he wore everywhere. He'd killed and skinned the coon himself, was real proud of it. Sheila said she'd sneak it off him when he was sleeping once in a while to shake out the dirt, 'cause in the daytime he wouldn't part with it.

"That's how somebody from the lake remembered him.

They sent me a message and said their family had a house on Moon Lake during the time Elliot went missing. This woman remembered seeing him. She thought she might have even seen him the day he disappeared, though she couldn't confirm that. Twenty-plus years ago is a long time to pinpoint specific days. But she said he was down there a lot that summer and fall, fishing and playing with other kids at the lake.

"Once I heard that I got some pictures around and took them to the lake, talked to neighbors. A few remembered him. Hobart Boggs, owner of Hobart's General Store, was the biggest help. He said Elliot came in every couple of days with a pocket full of pennies to buy a bit of fish line or a candy bar. His grandma assumed he'd headed to Moon Lake that day—a few people around the lake confirmed they saw him. And that's where the trail goes cold."

"And that's why you've wanted to talk to my dad?"

"Pretty much," Spencer confirmed. "Your mom took off, huh? That's interesting. When did that happen?"

Celeste saw the expression in Spencer's eyes. "She didn't take that kid, if that's what you're thinking."

He looked at her, startled, and quickly changed his expression. "Of course that's not what I'm thinking, but if I was...well, how would you know that? You said yourself she left when you were a toddler."

"I just know."

"All right. I'll take your word for it."

She suspected he had no such intention. She'd just given him a new lead. And the truth was she wanted him to look into it, to dig up the past. He was local. He'd have a much better chance of finding out where her mother had gone than she would, considering she only knew her mother's maiden name thanks to the birth certificate she'd ferreted out of her father's stuff years before.

"Her name was Nettie Harrington," Celeste offered. "Ever heard of her?"

"Nettie Harrington," Spencer murmured as if committing her name to memory. "Afraid I haven't."

The waitress returned with their ice cream sodas. Through the frosted glass Celeste could see the cola topped by vanilla ice cream, whipped cream and a cherry.

"When did your mom leave?" Spencer asked.

"1983."

He scratched his chin. "The timing doesn't work. Elliot vanished in 1988. No bueno. Still, maybe she came back looking for you and got confused." He shrugged. "Just spitballin' some theories."

Normally Celeste would have been annoyed at the suggestion, but she tried to imagine it. Could her mother have returned, spotted the little boy and confused him for her own child? But why hadn't she taken Celeste too, or at least looked for her?

Because, as her dad had said, she'd had a mental breakdown, lost it.

"You've searched for your mom?" Spencer asked. "Done a background check to see if anything comes up in terms of criminal activity, driving infractions?"

"No. I've searched for her with her name online. Haven't gotten any hits, but she probably changed it, right? Isn't that what people do when they start new lives?"

He scooped ice cream from his soda and slipped it in his mouth. "Maybe. I've investigated a lot of people who disappeared, but none of 'em got new names and started new lives. They were murdered."

10

Back at the motel, Celeste thought of the things Spencer had said about people going missing. *'None of 'em got new names and started new lives. They were murdered.'*

Was it possible her mother had left on a whim and run right into the hands of a killer? Her absence leading Celeste's father to conclude she'd abandoned them, so he'd never bothered to sound the alarm?

She wanted to ask him, to demand her dad tell her every detail of the months leading up to Nettie's alleged mental breakdown, but she knew he'd be frustratingly vague, if he agreed to answer her questions at all.

Celeste opened her laptop. She hadn't checked her Dear Celeste email since leaving Michigan. Amidst her Dear Celeste letters, she'd received several emails from Jonathan, the subject lines beginning simply enough—*Phone not working?*—and growing increasingly frantic, even hostile: *Where in the hell are you???*

She opened none of them and instead scrolled to an email from River that had come in the day before.

Dear Celeste,

Not much time to write this morning as I'm popping into the library before leaving on tour this afternoon, but I wanted to tell you we had a little reunion yesterday. It was a dream come true.

Thank you. For everything.

All my love,

River

Celeste clicked the attached image. A group of people stood in front of the chicken coop at River and Owen's farm. River stood snuggled against Owen, Hope balanced on his opposite hip, and beside them Cordelia and Clay, Frank Fulton, and Andrea 'Bowie' Ketchum. Celeste thought back to their sweet little farm with the chickens and goats and the rocking chairs, and the ache that had become her constant companion returned.

Her new cell phone rang. She looked at the screen and saw Detective Bowman's name.

"Hello?"

"Hi, Celeste, Detective Bowman. Have a minute?"

"Yeah. Of course."

"We brought Jonathan in for questioning yesterday afternoon."

"And?"

"And he played dumb. Said he was as shocked as everyone else over what Darlene had done, et cetera. He mentioned, a few times I might add, that you'd taken off and he wasn't convinced you hadn't intentionally stepped in front of the car that hit you."

Celeste picked at a bit of lint on the bedspread, unsurprised by the comment, but hurt anyway. "And did you show him the pictures?"

"No. We don't want to risk him destroying evidence, but we leaned hard on him about his affair. After about an hour, he was done talking without his lawyer."

Celeste wondered who his lawyer would be. Vaughn

Durham, who'd helped them with their wills? No. He was in family law, not criminal. Maybe Jonathan would get the same lawyer as Darlene, maybe he'd hired that person for Darlene to begin with. "What's happening with Darlene? Has she been arrested?"

"Not yet. No. The prosecutor is concerned about the case as it stands. He wants the Jeep, so we've got a team down in Ohio searching. We may never find it, but don't worry, the case is there without the vehicle. We just have to put it all together before the DA can go forward. You only get one shot at these things, so it's important we leave no stone unturned right now."

"Are you surveilling them? Are they together at all?"

"Unfortunately, we don't have the resources for constant surveillance. And it's best if I don't get into all the specifics of the case. Lie low and when I know more, you'll hear about it."

"Thanks, Detective."

She tried to read Dear Celeste letters, to focus on the words of strangers seeking her help: the woman in Texas who was considering calling off her wedding to the wealthy man she'd spent years trying to get a commitment from, the man in Florida who'd recently been diagnosed with cancer.

Each time she closed an email, her eyes drifted to the ones Jonathan had sent.

She bit her lip and opened the first message sent the night she'd left Michigan.

Are you aware that your phone is dead? You said you'd call me tonight. Not a word and now your phone is going straight to voicemail. I knew you'd changed after your accident, but I didn't realize you'd become cruel. Is that how you intended our separation to go? You disappear from our life completely? Reenacting your mother's choices perhaps?

The words stung, but more than that, they made her angry. He didn't realize she knew that he was the cruel one, the person having an affair, keeping secrets. The person who'd possibly been complicit or even an active participant in plotting her death.

She almost selected all of his messages and deleted them. Instead, she read each of them. The next three were variations on the first. The last one had a different tone.

Dear Celeste,

I don't know what the police told you, but it's all lies. They're trying to turn us against each other. You need to give me a chance to explain. Please. I'm going out of my mind here. I'm having the most terrible thoughts. Please. Call. Please please please!!!!

I love you.

Jonathan.

The final email had obviously been sent after Bowman questioned him. He sounded desperate in the message and a part of her did want to call him, hear his story, see if her newfound intuition might reveal to her if it was truth or lie. But she didn't.

It hurt not to call, to imagine him pacing the house, scared, in pain. But was that true? Or was his message a frantic scramble to hide his crimes, no more rooted in actual love or care for Celeste than when he'd been sneaking off to sleep with Darlene?

She pictured them tucked into a little booth whispering about plans to murder Celeste. No matter how she tried to frame it, it felt so impossible. Or maybe it just cut too deep, that kind of betrayal. Could she have lain next to the man night after night, made love to him, talked about the lab, eaten dinners, oblivious to his intention to murder her and live happily ever after with their co-worker?

Celeste stood and walked away from the laptop. She stepped into the bathroom and paused before the mirror. Shadows pooled beneath her eyes. Her hair, dyed months earlier, a vibrant red, now showed her dark roots. The woman before her was unfamiliar. This person had no home, no husband, no life beyond the transient world she'd built.

"Who am I?" she murmured.

No answer arose. She'd never felt so alone, so empty.

She poured a glass of Scotch and drank it quickly then poured another. She lay on the bed and closed her eyes.

* * *

Celeste walked the familiar road by her house, the road she'd walked every morning for years. The road where she'd nearly died. Her breath was shallow, each step hesitant, but she couldn't stop her legs from moving forward.

The road felt endless, stretching farther than it should. She wanted to turn around, to rush home, to not have ventured out that morning, but on she walked.

A cacophony of caws broke the silence. Dozens of ravens crowded the roadside ahead, their sleek black bodies heaving and twitching as they feasted on something hidden beneath their wings.

Celeste's skin crawled and her heartbeat quickened.

She tried to look away, but her feet dragged her closer, as if the road itself demanded her return to the scene.

The smell hit her next, acrid and metallic.

The ravens scattered as she approached, wings beating against the air in frantic bursts.

Celeste stared at the place in the road where she'd been hit.

Her own body lay there, bloody, unmoving.

Her twisted form was crumpled, arms bent at unnatural angles, shards of glass glittering in her matted hair.

Celeste's lifeless eyes stared back at her from the cold, bloodied face on the ground.

Celeste bolted upright in bed, gasping for air, drenched in sweat.

The room was still. Silent, but the phantom scent of blood lingered in the air.

11

N ettie

"I'm telling you, Luanne, I'm going to marry him," Nettie said.

Luanne pulled her gum out long, crossed her eyes at the pink glossy strand and popped it back between her teeth. "You remember you're seventeen, right?"

"It doesn't matter. I've found my Romeo."

Luanne rolled onto her side, smoothing the towel beneath her over the brittle sunburned grass. Her bikini strap had fallen over one bony shoulder and she pushed it back into place. "Romeo dies. So does Juliet. They hardly live happily ever after."

"It's not the ending I'm thinking about. It's the love. I'm serious. He's the one."

"Since when are you even into guys? I thought the plan was to become a vet and buy a big house for you and your thirty-six rescue pets."

"That's still the plan. But now I'll have someone to help me clean the kitty litter and scoop the dog poop."

Luanne propped her chin on her stacked hands.

Nettie followed her gaze toward the scorched grass. The summer had been dry, rain days few and far between. The plants had shriveled, the creek beds nearly dried up.

"Why don't you like him?" Nettie asked.

Luanne turned over, popped up onto her elbow and grabbed the bottle of baby oil. She squirted a glob into her hands and rubbed it across her stomach and chest. "'Cause he seems too good to be true. You know? Like nobody's that perfect."

"That's because we've lived in Davis our whole lives."

"Keith lived in Davis."

"Keith moved away, and plus we were friends, strictly friends."

Luanne gave her a knowing look. "If you wanted a man who was going to scoop the kitty litter, you should have stuck with Keith."

"Since when do you like Keith? You used to call him Crusty Keith."

Luanne laughed. "That's because he wore those dirty, ripped jeans twenty-four seven. I started to wonder if his family even owned a washing machine."

"They didn't. Him and his mom went to the laundromat."

"Oh." Luanne leaned her head back and closed her eyes. "I guess that's one thing Nathaniel has going for him. His clothes are clean."

Nettie didn't tell Luanne she secretly feared Nathaniel would one day grow tired of his new girlfriend. She was pretty enough for most of the Davis High boys to cast her an apprecia-tive glance, but she was also, in many ways, a typical poor Appalachian girl with a dead dad and an unhinged mom.

The saving grace in Nettie's life was her aunt Clementine—

Clem—who lived alone in a rustic mountain cabin. Clem did little to boost Nettie's reputation as an up-and-coming Davis girl, but she was a port in the storm of Nettie's life. Given the chance, Nettie would have moved in with Clem as a girl and never left.

"Listen, if you want to live happily ever after with the smooth-talking Romeo, be my guest. But remember, we're going to school in Morgantown and getting an apartment together our freshman year, and when you're a big vet and I'm an executive at some posh company, we're going to Paris on a girls' trip. No boys allowed."

Nettie laughed. "Deal."

12

———————

Celeste arrived at her childhood home early the next morning. She'd woken at dawn, the sheets sweaty and twisted around her legs, the previous night's dream sloshing through her mind. She'd bought coffee at a gas station, but couldn't stomach it.

Her cell phone, still off, sat in the glove box of her truck. She had nearly powered it on several times during the previous night. Jonathan's messages had gotten under her skin. She wanted to confront him, to demand he tell her the truth. At the heart of it, she wanted him to deny everything, and she wanted to believe him.

Celeste entered through the unlocked door at the side of the house, making a mental note to put some plastic and tape over the broken window to keep bugs out. As it had the day before, the utter quiet in the house unnerved her. It was as if the house were holding its breath.

She moved slowly from room to room, taking stock of the remaining furniture: the matching burgundy floral couches in the living room, the glass coffee table with a large hardcover copy of *Mountains of the United States*. She stared at the mantel. A stack of pennies sat on the wood. She stepped closer, frowning. Had they been there the day before? She didn't remember seeing them and, as she studied them, her unease grew. They looked clean, shiny even, unlike everything else in the house that was dust-covered.

The remaining art on the wall was scant—a watercolor of Moon Lake, some black and white photos of cities that Celeste thought might be Florida based on the palm trees. In the dining room downstairs, on a wall papered in contrasting blue and white stripes, hung a large, slightly askew photograph of an aerial view of the Kingwood High School.

The cupboards in the kitchen held dishes. Celeste reached for a plate, studied the edges rimmed with faded red and yellow flowers. A memory surfaced, blurry and indistinct, of one of the plates shattering on the kitchen's tile floor, splinters of glass spraying across the room to where Celeste and Adam had both stood barefoot, still in their pajamas as if they'd only just woken up.

She returned the plate and moved down the hallway, paused at the bathroom where dust-laden towels sat folded on an open shelf. When she opened a drawer, she saw toothbrushes and an old tube of toothpaste. She returned to the laundry room and opened the cupboards above the washer and dryer. Boxes of laundry soap and dryer sheets lined the bottom shelf. The upper was filled with folded blankets.

As she started to close the doors, a phone began to ring somewhere in the house.

She patted her pockets, but found her cell phone tucked in the back pocket of her shorts.

The sound didn't go away. It was far off, muffled and not the typical sound of a cell phone ring. It reminded her of an older phone, a landline phone. Had her dad left a phone line connected to the house? It seemed preposterous, and yet his keeping the house was bizarre. Leaving so many of their former belongings in the house was strange too. Why not one more oddity?

She stood and walked quietly down the hall and up the stairs. Cautious, she listened for any other sound. If it was the cell phone of a person hiding inside the house, they would have silenced the ringer.

Unless they were trying to lure her upstairs.

She paused and considered the discomfiting thought. Could someone have crept in and lain in wait?

Bracing for a sudden confrontation, she followed the ringing, which had gone on entirely too long now. Why hadn't the caller hung up?

It was coming from the locked bedroom.

Celeste put her hand on the knob and twisted. A part of her expected it to swing open, for someone to rush out. The paranoia was illogical. Clearly no one had lived in the house in decades.

As it had been the day before, the knob didn't turn. The ringing stopped, but she heard something else from behind the door now, a low creaking as if someone had sat on the bed.

"Hello?" she called, though her voice came out as little more than a croak.

She stepped back from the door, gooseflesh rippling along her arms. Was someone in there? Or was this part of her new reality? Something otherworldly reaching out, contacting her by whatever means necessary.

"Mom?" She felt foolish the instant the word left her lips.

Suddenly, a bang echoed from downstairs.

Celeste jumped back from the door. The banging came again. Someone was knocking on the front door.

Celeste hurried downstairs and wished she could discern the person through the frosted glass.

She could refuse to answer, pretend no one was home, but her truck sat in the driveway. Whoever was out there might have been sent by her dad or, worse, some concerned neighbor who'd sent the police to investigate a suspicious person at the long-abandoned house.

She opened the door slowly, surprised to see the neighbor, Rose.

The woman, dressed today in lace-trimmed black shorts and a white tube top, smiled. "I thought that might be you," she said. "I saw your truck." She gestured behind her.

"Yeah, it's me." Celeste stared at her coldly. She hadn't forgotten her rude reception the day before and had little interest in talking to her now.

Rose's eyes darted past her toward the glum interior. "I've always wondered what this place looked like inside. It's been dark as a tomb around here as long as I've lived next door."

Celeste moved, blocking her view into the house. "Did you need something?"

Rose laughed, though Celeste hadn't said anything funny. "Course I don't. But I thought I'd let you know I grew up in Kingwood and got to thinking after you stopped by that I knew your dad, Coach Harrington."

"You did?"

"Yep. I never had him myself, but I remember him."

"Did you know my mom? Nettie?"

Rose's mouth turned down. "I can't say I ever met her. But that's what brought you here? Your mom?" She'd forced sympathy into her voice, but Celeste didn't feel any warmth in the question.

"Yes. Do you know of anyone who might have known my parents? Friends of my dad at school or—"

Rose grimaced and pinched the bridge of her nose. "Migraine comin'. Great." She rubbed her temples and squinted. "I better get back to the house and lie down before this sets in good. You come by tomorrow, hmmm? Middle of the day. Carl leaves on business in the morning. I'll have time to talk and hopefully I'll have gotten in front of this headache."

Celeste watched the woman totter along the pathway, her black stiletto heels a ridiculous sight in the heavily forested driveway.

She closed the door and retreated into the house. There was a bureau in the living room with cabinets she hadn't opened. Celeste returned to those and pulled the top one open. Inside she found a mishmash of children's drawings, assignments from school with her name at the top. Kingwood Elementary. There were pictures of pumpkins. Halloween coloring pages and a small rectangular report card with a series of marks.

Celeste is a kind but quiet student, was the single note her teacher had written.

In the next drawer, she found her dad's teaching certificate. There were pictures of him standing with groups of girls on the Kingwood basketball team.

She stared at the image of her father flanking the group of smiling girls. He was obviously younger, but everything about him struck her as different, his wide easy smile, his sparkling blue eyes. He held a basketball under one arm, a whistle dangling from a string around his neck. He wore a white t-shirt, blue shorts, and white sneakers.

"Coach Harrington," she murmured.

Her father had been a teacher and a coach. She'd been so young in West Virginia that she'd never thought much about his job. But after they left, he'd worked at a plastics plant. Why had he given up teaching?

When Adam had declared his intention to become an elementary school teacher, their dad had been vocal about his opposition. *No money in it. Why not do something like Celeste? Get into the sciences or the medical field? Find a company with good benefits, a pension, paid time off.* But Adam had been insistent.

Had it been the stress of their mother leaving that had so dramatically changed their father? The pressure of raising two kids, a toddler and a baby, that had shifted his love of education, assuming he'd ever loved it to begin with? But they'd stayed in West Virginia for five years after Nettie walked out. Had he waited around hoping she'd return?

13

____

When Celeste returned to the motel, the dreariness of the space enveloped her. It seemed to symbolize the sudden turn of her life, the collapse of her former self, her marriage, her entire existence. This was the kind of place people retreated to when their dreams had died.

She didn't even close the door behind her, but left it open as she hurried to her bag, snatched a sweatshirt to shield against the cooling evening, and left. She had to find somewhere else to stay. It was a good idea, one Harris had recommended to begin with—move around. On the chance Jonathan came looking, she shouldn't make it easy for him to find her.

Down the block, she parked at a bar called the Lantern's Glow. The siding on the bar was warped and several pieces had fallen away. Despite its rundown exterior, the bar was warm and inviting. Soft yellow light shone from dusty stained-glass lamps. Knotty pine made up the floors and walls. A country song played from a jukebox in the corner. Celeste smelled traces of whiskey and bar food.

The bartender, a short grizzled man with a full beard, stood talking to several guys sitting at the long bar.

"What can I get ya?" he asked.

"Scotch on the rocks. A double, please."

He nodded and grabbed a bottle from the mirrored shelves behind him.

The men at the bar glanced her way then turned back to their conversation.

Drink in hand, Celeste found a booth and took out her laptop. She sipped her Scotch and opened a search engine.

"Having something for dinner, hon?" The waitress smiling down at her had long curly hair, gray at the roots. Her name tag read Sandy.

While Celeste had no appetite, she understood the need to eat something and didn't want to sit at one of Sandy's tables without placing an order. She glanced at the stained paper menu. "I'll take a basket of chicken strips and fries."

"Dipping sauce?"

"No. Thank you."

"All right. And can I get you a refill on your drink?"

Celeste looked at her glass, nearly empty. "That'd be great. Thanks."

Sandy disappeared into the back, and Celeste returned her attention to her computer. She searched for rentals in Kingwood. Halfway down the page she found a listing for a house on Moon Lake. Celeste clicked it and stared at the A-frame. She wasn't sure where on the lake it was located, but she didn't care. She opened the available dates and saw it was vacant for the next several weeks. She selected her dates, added two guests and requested the rental.

An odd tremor of excitement rippled through her at the thought of staying at Moon Lake. She'd have easy access to her childhood home. And she needed to get out of the motel.

She opened her Dear Celeste column and began to draft an answer to the woman considering backing out of her wedding.

"Fancy meeting you here."

The voice startled her. Celeste looked up to see Spencer, an enormous glass of beer in one hand, the thumb of his opposite hand hooked in the belt loop of his jeans.

"Want some company?"

"Oh...umm...sure." As he slid across from her, it struck her as it had on the road by the Moon Lake house that Spencer could have been hired by Jonathan. Maybe the podcast story was merely an elaborate ruse to throw her off the scent. It made little sense. Spencer struck her as the last person on earth Jonathan would hire as a private investigator, but she couldn't shake her misgivings.

"Do you have a card?" she demanded. "A business card?"

He sipped his beer, a foamy mustache lingering on his upper lip. "Do I have a card?" He beamed. "Wait till you see this thing. Had a buddy from high school design it for me." Spencer pulled out a Velcro wallet with *X-Files* printed in raised glowing blue letters on the surface. "Got this wallet on eBay for thirty-eight bucks," he said, tapping the wallet. "Quite a bargain." He fished out a card and handed it to her.

Celeste stared at the card. It was thick and glossy with an iridescent sheen. Around the name *Strictly Supernatural* was a forest scape with hulking Bigfoots and UFOs flying overhead.

On the back in blocky green letters was the name Spencer Ashman, a website and an email.

"Pretty neat, huh?"

"Yeah. Can I keep this?"

"You totally could"—he plucked it from her fingertips—"but I'm literally down to this one card and funds have been tight, so getting more printed is not exactly a priority." He returned the card to his wallet.

"No business card for the true crime podcast?" she asked, still suspicious.

"I have a box, but there was a printer error. Instead of Ashman, they printed Assman. I kid you not." He put a hand to his forehead. "Assman. That's a good way to get taken seriously."

"Why didn't you demand a refund?"

"I tried, but they said I typed it in wrong. We went back and forth for a few weeks and finally I threw my hands up and said screw it. Every now and then I fix one to look like an H and hand it out. Looks terrible, but better than nothing. So anyway, what brings you to the Lantern's Glow? Motel not up to par?"

She stared at him. "How do you know I'm staying in a motel?"

He took another sip of his beer and grinned. "There isn't anything but motels in this town. Now if you trek over to Morgantown, you can get yourself a hotel with a capital H. You seem a little jumpy. You runnin' from the law? And if so, can I get you on my podcast?" He laughed.

"Spencer." The waitress, Sandy, appeared a moment later with Celeste's chicken strips and another Scotch. "You're not bothering this poor woman, are ya?"

He gave her a 'who, me?' expression. "Course not, Sandy."

"Is he?" Sandy asked.

Celeste forced a smile and shook her head. This was the second waitress who'd called Spencer by his name.

"You eatin'?" Sandy asked him.

"I wasn't until I smelled those chicken strips. Damn if Jeremiah doesn't know his way around a deep-fat fryer. Better get me a basket of those, and onion rings instead of fries."

"All right, and the usual on the side?"

"Yep, barbecue and blue cheese. Thank you kindly."

Sandy walked away, and Celeste took a sip of her drink.

"Any luck tracking down your mom?" he asked.

Celeste shook her head. "My dad was a coach at the high school. Coach Harrington. Ever heard of him?"

"Nope. Like I said, I didn't grow up here. But I'd bet ya a twenty someone at the high school remembers him. Every high school has at least one teacher who's eighty-five years old and remembers all five generations of the Hatfields who passed through her class."

"Maybe I'll try that."

"How come you don't ask your dad outright, 'Where's Mom?'" Spencer took a sip of his beer and slopped a bit on his t-shirt, which read 'What Aren't They Telling Us?' above an image of a UFO sucking a dinosaur up through a beam of light.

"He doesn't know," Celeste said.

"In thirty years, he's never gotten a phone call? Never tried to get any child support out of her? Smells fishy."

Celeste suddenly didn't want to talk about her missing mother with Spencer. Not for the first time she tried to imagine what she thought she'd find in West Virginia.

"Your mom took off and then what? A few years later, you and your dad left?"

"Five years later, my dad, my brother, and I moved to Michigan."

"But your dad still owns the house."

Celeste nodded.

"And you've been in the house?"

"Yes."

"Ever see a raccoon-tail hat laying around?"

She frowned. "No. What are you trying to say?"

"Just askin' a question."

"Spencer, have you considered the possibility that Elliot drowned in this lake?" Celeste thought of the little boy she'd seen running down the dock. Maybe he'd drowned and appeared to Celeste so she would relay that bit of information to Spencer Ashman, one of the only people left still looking for him.

Spencer nodded. "I have, but it doesn't fit."

"Why not?"

"After a body starts to decompose, it floats. The gases push it up to the surface. He should have been found within a week."

"There's some marshy areas around the lake," Celeste countered. "Spots where there are no houses, high weeds, backed by woods. Maybe he got tangled up and..."

"I've been out there, walked those shores in my rubbers, ridden a boat back in those areas. I'm not saying it's impossible, but I don't buy it. His body would have turned up."

"What's your theory of what happened then?"

Sandy arrived with his food and Spencer popped an onion ring into his mouth only to immediately spit it back into the basket. "Holy shitbritches. That's hot. Ouch." He took a swig of his beer.

"I've got a couple theories." He held up a finger. "One, he got lost and succumbed to the elements. It's not impossible. The mountain woods at night get a little wonky in these parts. Like I mentioned, I've experienced it myself. He gets turned around, treks miles and miles the wrong way, ends up dying of thirst. I don't love it, but it's not impossible. Sheila didn't buy it because she said Elliot knew the woods better than the squirrels, but..." He shrugged. "There are skilled hunters and hikers who've gotten lost in the West Virginia forests."

He held up two fingers. "Theory two is what you just floated. He drowned in the lake and got caught up in brush, or an old tree, even did something insane like swam down deep into an old car and got trapped. But Moon Lake used to be a pretty popular swimming and boating lake. Not as many people head out there now that they did away with the public beach, but I still find it hard to believe that if it had been an accidental drowning he wouldn't have been found. But let's say somebody weighted him. Well, that might have kept his body from being found.

"Theory three, he got nabbed by some perv trying to hitch a ride home. He wasn't known for hitchin', but in those days it's not a crazy thing for an eight-year-old kid to do, especially a scrappy lad like Elliot who figured he could get himself out of any bind he got into. Even not hitchin', some douchebag mighta pulled up and offered him a ride or just hauled his ass into the vehicle and burned rubber. Again, I don't love the theory because there weren't any sightings of strange vehicles or guys lurking around that I could track down. Not to mention the roads out by Moon Lake are not exactly a child napper's playground. You're more likely to run across a cougar than a lone kid."

"But aren't most of those guys opportunistic? They're not necessarily out looking for a kid, but maybe they're driving to the store or to visit a friend and they see one."

"I'm not saying it's impossible, but I will say this, Sheila Thacker said Elliot could be a wild one, mean as a rooster when a fox sneaks into the hen house. He'd kick and bite and claw your eyes if had to. Did it once with some social worker when she tried to take him from his ma. Let's just say she never got that kid in her car. Makes me think if a napper had tried to grab him, they'd have left him on the side of the road once they realized what they'd gotten themselves into."

Celeste didn't remember ordering another drink, but suddenly Sandy slid one in front of her. Celeste stared at her empty glass, watched Sandy carry it away.

"Listen, I'll make you a deal," Spencer said, "a little quid pro quo. I'll lean on some of my contacts in the area and see what I can find out about your mom. You let me peek around your childhood house."

Celeste gazed at Spencer. "Why?" Her hand was on the drink, but suddenly she didn't want to take a sip. An image of the bottle of PX962 pills slid into her mind, the pills she suspected Jonathan had drugged her with.

The thought was absurd. Spencer had been sitting across from her, hadn't gotten up to use the bathroom, couldn't have ordered the drink without her knowing and obviously hadn't slipped anything into it.

"Why what?" he asked.

"Why do you want in my dad's house? I don't get it."

"I told you. Tying up loose ends."

"Did you go into every house on the lake?"

"Well, no." He shoved a chicken strip in his mouth. "But, you see, one of my witnesses placed Elliot around your house that day."

"What witness?"

"I can't divulge my sources."

Celeste rolled her eyes. She lifted the cocktail and swallowed a large gulp. She'd barely touched her food, and the alcohol had started to work its way through her limbs. Except rather than buzzed, she sensed she was teetering on drunk.

A cell phone rang, and Spencer stared at her expectantly.

"Oh." She fumbled it out of her purse and saw Harris's name on the screen.

"Hello?"

"Can you talk?"

"Umm..."

"Is everything okay, Celeste?"

"Yeah, I'm fine." She heard how the words ran together, realized she was, in fact, drunk. "I'll call you right back."

Celeste pulled a wad of cash from her wallet and squinted at it. She laid the crumpled bills on the table. "I have to go," she told Spencer.

"Hold on. I'll drive you." He started to stand, but she waved him back down.

"No," she said sharply.

Legs shaky, Celeste tottered from the bar and pushed through the door into the night.

14

———————

N ettie

"You'll have to park down here," Nettie told Nathaniel. "Your car will never make it up the hill."

He pulled the Firebird as far to the edge of the rugged mountain road as he could, glancing nervously out his window. "You sure it's safe here?"

"No one drives on this road. It'll be fine."

They climbed out and Nettie tried to settle the butterflies in her stomach. She wanted Nathaniel to like her aunt Clementine, but equally she wanted Clem's approval.

She watched Nathaniel eye the craggy trail that led up the mountain to Clementine's house.

As they ascended the rocky hill, Nettie tilted her head and gazed into the ancient trees. She loved Clem's forest more than any other place on earth and she tried now to ignore the uneasy expression on Nathaniel's face as he picked his way along the trail, slapping branches away as if they intended to bite him.

"She really lives out here?" he asked.

"For as long as I can remember."

The weathered, rustic cottage appeared before them. The stone foundation was mottled with moss, and its wooden walls were dark with age, the boards uneven and slightly warped. Smoke curled from the stone chimney, carrying the scent of woodsmoke and something faintly herbal. From behind the house, Burdock, the three-legged dog Nettie had found the year before half dead on the side of the road, limped toward them.

She squatted and folded him into her arms. He licked her face.

"Nathaniel, meet Burdock."

Nathaniel scratched the scruff of the dog's neck. "Quite a looker, isn't he?"

Nettie stood up and laughed. "Well, he's not winning any beauty contests, but we love him just the same."

The porch creaked under their weight, and before Nettie could knock, the door swung open. Clem stood there, barefoot as always, her long dark braid trailing over one shoulder. Her sharp green eyes moved swiftly from Nettie to Nathaniel.

"Come on then," she said, backing up and waving them in. "The stew is ready."

Nathaniel shot Nettie a slightly terrified look, but Nettie only smiled and nudged him forward. She tried not to betray that her own belly was a mess of fear.

"Nathaniel, ma'am. It's nice to meet you," he told Clem, extending his hand.

Clem's gaze dropped to his hand, then back to his face, her expression unreadable. Finally, she took it, her fingers curling around his in what looked more like a test than a handshake.

The inside of the cottage smelled like rosemary and something earthy. The walls were lined with shelves full of books, jars of herbs, and strange trinkets. Mingus, a black and white cat with one yellow eye and one cloudy blue, watched them from the rafters. He was one of three that lived at Clem's cottage, from a litter that had been born in Nettie's trailer park. The owner of the kittens had mentioned taking them for a drive and dumping them in the woods, so Nettie had crept over one night and smuggled them from beneath the man's rickety little porch. She'd driven them to Clem's the next day.

Nathaniel's eyes drifted up to the cat and he shrank back as if afraid it might pounce on him.

"Don't worry." Nettie put a hand on his arm. "That's Mingus, sweet as a lamb."

"Ha!" Clem laughed. "A rabid one."

"Clem," Nettie said, exasperated.

"What? Look here." Clem held out her arm to reveal two long red scratches. "He did that to me just this morning."

"You were probably teasing him," Nettie said. "Come here, Mingus. Was Aunt Clem teasing you again?" Nettie coaxed the cat from the wooden beam and nestled him close. The cat began a loud purr.

Nathaniel looked at the cat uncertainly but then brushed his fingers over his sleek head.

"See? Sweet as pie."

Clem poured steaming stew into three mismatched mugs. She handed one to Nathaniel, her eyes boring into his. "Scared of cats, are ya? Nettie's the Pied Piper of cats. Best you start gettin' comfortable with 'em real quick."

Nathaniel leaned down as if to smell the stew, but when Clem narrowed her eyes at him and thrust a spoon into his hand, he scooped a large bite into his mouth.

"Mmm..." he mumbled.

Nettie set Mingus down and picked up her own mug, inhaling the aroma of wild mushroom stew.

"This is really good," he said as if surprised.

"Clem's stew is the best," Nettie said.

A tapping sound came from the window and all three turned to where a raven sat on the sill pecking at the glass.

"Is that a pet too?" Nathaniel asked.

Clem frowned. "No. It ain't, but there are those who say a visit from a raven warns something dark is comin' our way."

"Like a storm?" he asked.

"Like a death," Clem muttered. She walked toward the bird, but before she reached the glass, it flew away.

15

———————

Celeste bypassed her truck and made the short walk back to the motel, her vision swimming from the Scotch. The room was hot, stuffy, as if the heat had been cranked to a hundred. Something seemed different, but she couldn't discern what had changed.

Had housekeeping been in?

No. The bed was unmade. Her towel still hung draped over the back of the wood chair in the corner.

She searched unsuccessfully for her cell phone. "No," she groaned. Had she left it on the table in the bar? Before she finished the thought, it rang in her pocket.

"Harris?"

"They're searching your house right now. They got the warrant this afternoon."

Dizziness made her legs unsteady, and the room became suddenly claustrophobic. She needed air that hadn't been drifting in the dust particles from the old carpet, that didn't smell of long-stubbed-out cigarettes and floral perfume. Booze sloshed in her stomach, but more so in her brain. She imagined her brain bobbing up and down in the pool of cerebrospinal fluid in her skull.

Celeste pushed through the door and outside. The iron rail was painted white. Bits of paint had chipped away, revealing the rusted metal beneath. She gripped the rail with one hand, wanted to lean against it, but didn't trust it to hold her.

"Did you hear me?" Harris asked.

"Yes, I...How did Jonathan react?" she croaked.

"I don't know. Bowman texted me on his way to the house."

Celeste tried to imagine it. Jonathan pulling open the door to find the detective, warrant in hand, a line of police cars on their quiet suburban street. He'd be humiliated, furious. "They're looking for the stuff I found?"

"Probably. Bowman can't give me details on what they hope to find, but he couldn't have gotten the warrant without probable cause. I'm guessing either Darlene talked or they've found something to connect Jonathan to your hit-and-run."

Celeste stared into the cracked parking lot, her head swimming.

"Celeste?"

"I'm here."

"You sound...Are you all right?"

"Mmm-hmmm..." She walked back into the room and sat on the edge of the bed. "I'm tired. Can I call you tomorrow?"

"Of course. Celeste—"

She ended the call, kicked off her shoes and shuffled out of her jeans. She pulled the blanket up and turned on her side. The bed tilted beneath her, the room whirling as though she were on a carousel that wouldn't stop.

Celeste groaned, trying to steady herself, but the alcohol had her in its grip. The cheap floral wallpaper rippled, its faded roses crawling toward her like something alive.

Something...no, someone moved the long dark curtains near the window. She struggled to lift her head and look that way. They moved again. As the fabric flicked apart, she caught a glimpse of a person there, a child in a strange white Halloween mask.

"Not real..." she muttered.

She threw an arm over her face and clenched her eyes shut.

Celeste walked barefoot across the cool grass at the lake's edge. The moon hung big and white above the thick pines and distant mountains. Behind her, a child laughed. Celeste spun and searched the trees, glimpsed a flash of white.

She moved toward it, listening. Above her the trees rustled and murmured, the voices of thousands of ravens, their dark eyes fixed on Celeste.

The laugh came again, and Celeste picked up her pace. She knew that laugh, needed to get to him, to warn him.

She started to run, branches and stones digging into the soft soles of her feet. As she weaved between the trees, her gaze caught another flicker of white. Her foot caught on a rotted tree stump. She sprawled forward on the ground.

In front of her, a child stepped into view, his face obscured by a white Halloween mask with hollow eyes and a faint, unsettling smile. He stood motionless and watched her.

Celeste opened her mouth to tell him to run away, to hide, but no sound came out.

The boy tilted his head, the motion sharp and unnatural. Then he turned and sprinted deeper into the woods, his laughter ringing out again.

"Wait!" Celeste called, her voice suddenly emerging, but only as a whisper.

She stood and ran after him, branches tearing at her sleeves and whipping her face. Every few seconds, she caught glimpses of him—

his small frame slipping between the towering trees, the mask glowing faintly in the moonlight.

The woods grew darker, the ravens louder as she ran, the boy always just out of reach.

Finally, she stumbled from the woods into the gravel driveway at the back of her childhood home. All the sounds—the boy's laughter, the muttering ravens, the rustling of leaves—ceased.

In the center of the driveway something pale caught the moonlight. Celeste took a step and then another, until she was close enough to see.

The boy's mask, blood-spattered, lay in the gravel, its empty eyes staring up at her.

Celeste woke from the terrible dream and lurched to the bathroom, barely made it to the toilet before the alcohol ejected violently from her body. She threw up until her stomach was empty. As she rested her forehead against the cool lip of the toilet edge, she tried not to imagine the colonies of thriving bacteria on and around the toilet.

For a while, she sat perfectly still, willing the turbulent sea that was the bathroom floor to grow steady and calm. When the nausea subsided enough for her to stand, Celeste staggered to the sink. She rinsed her face with cold water, then filled a little plastic cup from the faucet and drank it quickly.

Back at the bed, she sat for a while and blinked at the dark television across the room, waiting to see if the sickness would strike again.

When it didn't, she lifted her laptop from the bedside table, hoping she'd heard from the rental house owner at Moon Lake. She needed somewhere else to stay, could not stand another night in the motel room.

She let out a rush of breath when she saw she'd received an

email from the owner of the A-frame approving her for the rental with a request to meet the following evening to give her the keys once she'd paid the rental amount in full. She paid the invoice and confirmed the next day's meeting.

A half-dozen new emails from Jonathan populated her inbox, but she scanned past them.

On the search bar, Celeste typed in 'Dark Deeds' and 'Spencer Ashman.' A slew of articles appeared.

'Amateur Detective Podcaster Proves Yet Again Why Investigations Should be Left to the Police.'

'Disgraced Podcaster's Murder Theory Debunked.'

'Spencer Ashman's Fall From Grace: The Woman in the River.'

'True Crime or Pure Fiction? The Scandal Surrounding *Dark Deeds*.'

Celeste scanned the articles that detailed how Spencer, on his true crime podcast, had claimed a young woman who'd vanished had been murdered by her stepdad. When police had discovered the woman had actually run off the road in her vehicle into a river, Spencer had been crucified.

When her eyes grew tired from reading, Celeste closed the browser window. Her stomach still sloshed uncomfortably. She forced herself up and started packing her few belongings. The following day she'd be moving into the A-frame. She couldn't vacate the dreary little motel room fast enough.

16

Celeste's face burned the following morning as she walked back to the Lantern's Glow to get her truck. The parking lot stood empty, a small mercy.

She'd forgotten to lock the truck the night before and, when she climbed behind the wheel, she detected a change in the interior. She'd carried her purse back to the motel the previous night. There'd been no valuables to steal, but had someone been inside her vehicle? She opened the glove box and stared at the papers there—her registration and insurance, the truck's owner's manual and a vet bill from Romeo's first appointment. Nothing missing. In her center console, she had a handful of change, a pack of gum and a few pens. Again, nothing had been taken and yet she had the distinct impression someone had pawed through the contents.

Spencer? Celeste had found him online. His podcasts were real, so he clearly had not been hired by Jonathan.

"You're being paranoid," she muttered. And she was, but her distrust felt justified. In the previous weeks, she'd discovered the man she'd been married to for years had been cheating on her. A co-worker she'd thought she'd known had tried to kill her.

Celeste drove back to the motel, quickly loaded her bags and checked out.

School at Kingwood High had let out for the summer, but a handful of cars occupied the lot outside the long brick building. Celeste parked and tilted the rearview mirror. Her face still looked pale, eyes slightly bloodshot, but better than she had two hours before when she'd woken from the bits of remaining sleep she'd gotten and forced herself into the shower.

She walked toward the double glass doors, the memory flashing through her mind of a similar walk from the previous January when she'd gone into Katie Ellis's high school and discovered the video footage of her search for the killer of a girl in Graves, Michigan. Katie's own investigation had sealed the teenager's tragic fate.

The front hall was large and shone as if it had recently been cleaned. The scent of bleach lingered in the air. She turned into a glass-walled office, but no one sat behind the large reception desk. There was no bell, no way to summon a person from an interior office, but she heard voices behind a closed door. She waited, moving to a huge bulletin board where someone had posted a school calendar and photos from various sports events and school activities. Celeste's eye caught a photo of the girls' basketball team. That was what her dad had coached. The current coach was a petite woman with a serious expression.

"Can I help you?" A woman's voice startled Celeste. She hadn't heard the office door open.

"Hi. Yes. I hope so anyway. Have you worked here for a long time?"

The woman looked slightly annoyed by the question. "Five years, but I'd imagine that's long enough to answer any questions you have."

"Well, it's actually about a teacher and coach who worked here over twenty years ago. Nathaniel Harrington."

"Oh. Hmm...Well, I'm not a Kingwood native, so I can't assist you with that. Principal Morrison has only been here for two years, so he will also be unable to assist you. Why are you asking?"

Celeste tucked a strand of hair behind her ear. "He's actually my dad and I'm...working on a family...time capsule," she lied, not having a clue what a family time capsule actually entailed. "and I hoped to get some quotes from people who used to work with him here or students he taught."

"Oh. I see. How thoughtful. My advice is to go see Garth Durand. He teaches history and English here at Kingwood and has done for thirty years, maybe even forty. In the summer, he works at the Children's Museum."

* * *

The Children's Museum occupied a red building, a colorful mountain scape painted on the side. Celeste walked through the glass door into a gift shop of toys and games. The buttery aroma of popcorn wafted from a popcorn machine in the corner.

She spotted Garth immediately by his name tag. He looked to be in his fifties, maybe early sixties. He was bald except for a patch of blond hair encircling the crown of his skull. He sat on a stool, attaching Lego pieces to a pirate ship. He looked up when she entered and smiled.

"Let me just get this cannon locked in and I'll help you," he called.

Celeste walked over. "No need to get up. I'm here because the receptionist at the Kingwood High School gave me your name. I was hoping to ask you a few questions about my dad. He taught at Kingwood in the eighties."

Garth had narrowed his eyes at the little cannon and fixed his lower lip between his teeth. After a quiet moment, he leaned back and grinned. "Got it. These fingers are getting more and more reluctant to put these Legos back together. I keep telling Catherine, the museum director, we're going to have to switch to Duplo blocks or hire some teenager to come in here and piece these things together after the kids leave." He stood and patted himself on the head as if for a job well done. "Sorry for my distraction. What were you saying? You used to be a student?"

"No, my dad used to be a teacher at Kingwood. I thought you might have known him."

"Probably I did. What's his name?"

"Nathaniel Harrington."

"Harrington..." the man murmured, nodding slowly. An odd expression crossed his features. "Sure. Coach Harrington. He taught chemistry, I believe."

"Yeah. And coached girls' basketball."

"That's right."

"I'm curious if you knew my mom. Nettie Harrington?"

The man scratched his jaw. "I met her once. Gosh, was it her? Yeah, it must have been. It was on Moon Lake. Your dad had a fancy little speedboat. My wife and I were out there on a pontoon with friends fishing and your dad came zipping along scattering our fish." The man laughed. "Except it wasn't him driving. It was your mom, dark hair blowing back, belly out to here." He held his hand in front of him. "Must have been pregnant with you, maybe."

"Or my brother," Celeste murmured, trying to imagine that moment. "Were you and my dad friends at all?"

"Oh, no," he said quickly, as if to backtrack from the suggestion. "We didn't really run in the same circles."

"Was he a good teacher?"

Garth scratched his jaw. "I wouldn't be the one to ask that. I never took a class with him."

"Were you aware my mom left us?"

Garth returned his gaze to the Lego as if searching for another piece to fix. "Umm...I do remember hearing something like that."

"Were there ever rumors about where she went? Or..."

Garth shook his head. "No. No. I wasn't involved in any conversations like that. Obviously, your dad would be the one to ask—"

"I have. He has no idea, and she never came back. Never. Not once."

Garth's mouth turned down. "That's unfortunate. I didn't know her or...even your dad all that well."

"Okay. Thanks." Celeste was nearly at the door when Garth spoke again.

"Nicole Veen. She owns the dog grooming place right downtown, Dapper Doggies. She was a student. Talk to her. She can tell you a lot more, I'm sure."

It struck Celeste as strange that Garth insisted a student would know more about her father than he, a fellow teacher, would, but she got the distinct impression he did not want to talk to her about her dad.

"Nicole Veen," she repeated. "Thanks, Garth."

***

Dapper Doggies occupied a bright store in the middle of a strip mall. The walls were a cheery yellow and decorated in framed pictures of dogs caught wearing goofy grins. The space smelled of wet fur and a coconut-scented shampoo.

A woman emerged from the back. She wore a paw-printed smock and had rubber gloves to her elbows.

"Help ya?" she asked.

"Are you Nicole?"

"Yep. Did you call to schedule? I don't have any walk-in space today."

"No, actually. I just spoke with Garth at the Children's Museum. He said you attended Kingwood High in the eighties."

"And?" Nicole glanced back and Celeste suspected she had a dog waiting on her.

"My dad was a teacher at Kingwood. Nathaniel Harrington."

"Okay."

"Do you remember him?"

"Yeah."

"Can I ask you some questions about him?"

Nicole's lips thinned and she again looked behind her. Celeste feared she'd say no, but her face softened. "All right. Fine. But you'll have to come back here. I've just gotten Brutus in the sink for his bath. We can talk while I wash him."

Celeste hurried around the counter and followed Nicole through a beaded curtain into a large room with several stainless-steel sinks and a matching table.

Brutus was a large fluffy dog that appeared to be a mix of Siberian husky and chow.

"Brutus has got fur for days," Nicole said. "Don't ya, buddy? At least he likes the water. Goodness, some of the dogs that come in here act like the water is a rattlesnake rearing up to attack." Nicole turned on the faucet and sprayed the nozzle into her hand. "I'd say that's just right. What do you think, Brutus?" she asked, directing the spray at the dog, who wagged his tail and turned to bite at the water.

"Did you have my dad as a teacher?" Celeste asked.

"Hannah and I both did."

"Hannah?"

Nicole gave her a strange look. "Yeah. Hannah Hawley. Your dad's girlfriend."

Celeste stared at the woman, the name suddenly ringing familiar in her thoughts. "Hannah," she whispered. The memories tumbled blurry and indistinct through her mind. A young woman with long golden hair and big brown eyes. She'd been their babysitter and then something more...their father's girlfriend.

"I'm embarrassed to admit it now," Nicole went on, "but I was jealous of her. Your dad was larger than life. Handsome, funny. He drove this black convertible sports car."

"He dated a student..." Celeste breathed. The nausea from the night before surged back in and she put a hand on the metal table to steady herself.

17

———————

N ettie

Nettie stood at the edge of her mother's freshly dug grave, her black dress clinging to her in the damp spring air. The rain had stopped, leaving the cemetery soaked, the ground muddy and soft.

She hadn't said a word since they'd arrived, her chest too heavy to catch a deep breath, her mind a blur of grief and confusion.

She'd received her acceptance letter to West Virginia University that morning and should have been excited, but as she'd read the words, the tears she'd not yet shed over her mother's death had poured out of her. For a half hour she'd stood in the little trailer, now hers alone, gasping for breath and crushing the letter against her chest.

When Nathaniel had arrived to pick her up, she'd almost

refused to answer the door. Puffy, mascara smeared beneath her eyes, she'd forced herself out and into the Firebird.

The priest droned on in the background, speaking about forgiveness and eternal peace. Nettie struggled to focus on the words and to believe them. Her mother had surely never experienced peace in life. It was a small reassurance to think she might have it in the afterlife.

"You okay?" Nathaniel's voice broke through her fog.

Nettie forced a nod. In addition to them, only twelve other people had attended the funeral: Clem, Luanne, a few neighbors from the trailer park and a handful of people Nettie's mother, Gina, had met at AA meetings during the times she'd tried to get clean. Nettie suspected those people were there less to mourn the loss of their friend than as a reminder for how their lives too might end if they ever started using again.

Luanne stood crying, arms across her chest. Clem stood beside her, stoic, the only person in the group not dressed in black but in her signature patchwork jeans and a deerskin vest. Rather than watching the priest, Clem had her gaze fixed on Nathaniel. He didn't seem to notice.

Nathaniel's perfect black suit looked like something out of a catalog, sharp and precise, like the boy himself. His blond hair was neatly combed, his features set in an expression of earnest concern. Nettie suspected he would rather have been anywhere else on earth. She would have too.

They were two years into undergrad at West Virginia University when Nettie woke with a quiver of nausea rolling through her belly. She lurched to the bathroom, barely yanked the toilet seat up in time to the spew the meager contents of her stomach.

"Oh, no," she whispered, leaning her forehead against the

cool lip of the toilet seat. She had a calculus exam at noon, an exam worth thirty percent of her final grade.

"Nettie, have you seen my keys?" Nathaniel called from somewhere in the apartment.

Nettie sat back and wiped her mouth on a washcloth. The nausea had slightly subsided. She stood and made her way into the tiny living room where Nathaniel stood rifling through a laundry basket.

"In the bedroom," she told him. "On your nightstand."

He stood up and hurried to the bedroom, emerging a moment later, keys in hand. "You're a lifesaver." He kissed her on the cheek and paused. "Feel okay? You look pale."

"I'm fine." She waved him toward the door. "Don't be late."

He kissed her again and ran out the door.

Nathaniel was a year ahead of her at the university and had taken an accelerated program to get his teaching degree. Just that week, he'd started student teaching at a high school on the other side of town.

Nettie showered, dressed and met Luanne at her apartment to walk to campus.

"How does this look?" Luanne asked, twirling in her doorway. She wore a blue and white striped leotard beneath a jean skirt.

"Don't you have an English class?"

"Exactly. And I told you about that guy Greg who's been checking me out. I want him to take notice."

"That outfit should do the job then."

Luanne grinned. "Good."

They were halfway to school when Nettie had to run to a bush and throw up.

Luanne brushed Nettie's long hair away from her face. "Don't tell me you guys went to the Underground Railroad last night without me," Luanne said.

Nettie shook her head and tucked her hair behind her ears. "We didn't go to the bar. I must have the flu."

"Fever?" Luanne rested a palm on Nettie's forehead. "Not too warm."

"No fever. I just feel pukey."

Luanne's eyes widened.

"What?" Nettie asked.

"Holy shit. Are you pregnant?"

***

"This is ours," Nettie murmured, standing on the dock and staring at the Tudor-style house on Moon Lake. It defied belief. Even when she'd dreamed of the future, of one day becoming a vet and making a decent living, she'd never envisioned a big two-story house on a lake, a handsome husband, a baby girl on the way. She rested a hand on her belly, on the growing mound beneath her t-shirt.

"It's all ours," Nathaniel agreed, wrapping an arm around her waist and kissing her temple. He tucked something into her hand.

"What's this?" Nettie looked down at the blue velvet box.

"Open it."

She lifted the top. Inside lay a gold necklace with a delicate golden key and taped beside it a regular door key.

"The key to my heart and a key to our house," he said, kissing her.

"I love them both."

Nathaniel clasped the necklace around her neck. "Let's christen this place."

Nettie laughed, grateful there'd been no morning sickness that day. It had been a perfect day, marred only by the encounter with Nathaniel's mother that morning. His parents had cosigned on the house and helped with the down payment as a wedding gift. The wedding—hardly a wedding really—had happened the week before and had included Nathaniel, Nettie, Nathaniel's best friend Drew, who'd flown up from Florida, and Luanne. They'd gotten married at the courthouse and gone out for dinner afterwards at a steakhouse.

Nathaniel's parents had been upset by their choice to opt for a civil ceremony and had showed their disfavor by not attending the small wedding. Still, they'd not withdrawn their offer to help them buy their dream home, and for that Nettie was grateful. They'd met at the closing office that morning. Nathaniel's mother, Bianca, had been especially nasty, commenting multiple times that Nettie appeared to already be putting on too much weight during her pregnancy.

After a miserable hour of completing paperwork, Nathaniel had turned down his parents' offer of lunch and he and Nettie had driven straight to the house on Moon Lake.

Nathaniel picked Nettie up and carried her into their new house.

"Why is there a slice of bread on my dresser?" Nathaniel asked.

Nettie, settled in the chair with a blanket on her lap, smiled. "Piece of bread and pinch of salt in every room. To invite prosperity and stave off hunger."

He chuckled. "Ah, my little backwoods girl." He kissed her head. "I brought you a blueberry donut."

She squealed and held out her hands. "I'm starving!" She took the paper bag and inhaled the sweet scent. "God knows where I'm gonna put it, though." She patted her enormous belly.

Nathaniel kneeled and leaned his face against her stomach. "Celeste says don't worry, she'll make room."

18

———————

"Everyone in school knew," Nicole said matter-of-factly.

"The students knew about my dad and Hannah?" Celeste asked.

Nicole, who'd paused to squirt a blob of shampoo onto Brutus's back, glanced at her, surprised. "Oh, yeah, and the faculty, at least some of them. I'm sure because I overheard the principal snap at him one time for being in his office with Hannah with the door closed. I look back now and it's disturbing, but I hate to admit as a sixteen-year-old girl I didn't realize how wrong it was."

"She was sixteen?"

"When it started."

"How long did it go on?"

"Years," Nicole said.

"Did their relationship start when, umm...when my mom was still around?"

Nicole bit her lip and scrubbed the shampoo into the nape of Brutus's neck. "I'm not sure."

"Are you and Hannah still friends? Is she in town?"

"I haven't seen her in years," Nicole admitted. "I don't have a clue where she's at."

As Celeste drove toward Moon Lake, she dialed Adam.

"Hey," he answered.

"Do you remember Dad's girlfriend?"

"His girlfriend..." Adam repeated. "Oh...gosh, yeah. Huh. I haven't thought about her in forever. What was her name?"

"Hannah Hawley."

"Hannah, that's right. Hannah the Hag." He laughed. "Remember we called her that?"

Celeste had forgotten, but now that he mentioned the nickname, she did remember. A particular memory in fact rose up of Celeste bounding upstairs into Adam's room to tell him Hannah the Hag wanted to see him in the kitchen. She didn't realize Hannah had followed her. At the mention of the mean nickname, Hannah had walked to Celeste's room, picked up her favorite stuffed bear, ripped its head off and walked back down the stairs.

"She was a student at Dad's school. She was sixteen."

"What? No. Are you sure?"

"Yeah. Apparently, the whole school knew."

"But...when did it start? Like was it after Mom left or—"

"I'm not sure."

"Holy crap. Do you think that's why...she left?"

"Maybe."

"Have you asked Dad?"

"No. He'll just be evasive, as usual. When I called and confronted him about still owning the house, he acted like I was out of line for even asking."

Adam sighed. "Shocker."

"I broke into the house. I've gone back every day since I've been down here."

"No way. Really? What's in there?"

"Everything. Our old furniture, toys, clothes. Everything, Adam. It's weird."

"That is weird." He said something in the background. "Celeste, can I call you later? I'm at the dentist and they're just taking me back."

"Yeah. Bye."

As Celeste drove and parked near the house, she looked up at the second story and froze. The window in the back corner of the house, the window belonging to the room with the locked door, was open. The curtain fluttered softly out. She searched her memory. Had the window been open? She thought back to days before, walking the perimeter of the house searching for a way to get in.

No way. There'd been no windows open, she was sure of it.

Had someone broken in? It wouldn't take much. She'd already done the hard part. They had only to open the door she'd broken into and walk inside.

She was being paranoid, just as she'd been paranoid about Spencer the night before. Something else had opened the window. Something that wanted her to get inside.

Celeste studied the roof line and tried to figure out how to get up there.

The house had no garage, but a small white shed, paint chipped and faded, sat at the edge of the woods. It was locked, but the lock was flimsy and rusted. Inside the house, she found a hammer in a laundry room utility drawer. She returned to the shed and swung the hammer until the lock broke free and fell to the ground.

The shed was a mess of stuff. Mildewed lifejackets, deflated lake toys, rusted tools. No ladder.

She'd have to go through another upstairs window and

across the roof. She gazed at the steep roof line, the narrow ledge that jutted from the house, and wished for her old body, the body before the accident that could walk miles, run them even, without so much as a cramp.

Celeste unlocked the window in Adam's childhood bedroom. The curtains moved, brushed her face, and the sensation of the fabric against her cheek brought a memory back. Her and Adam hiding behind the curtains, a woman calling out to them. Not a woman, a girl. The girl who had replaced their mother when she left. The student at her father's school.

She blinked away the memory and focused on the window.

At first it wouldn't budge, and she struggled to push it up. Finally, the pane of glass lifted with a shriek.

Celeste kicked off her shoes and went onto the roof barefoot, not wanting to risk climbing across the roof in sandals. The roof was even steeper than she'd noticed from the ground. She clutched to the window frame as long as she could, then flattened herself against the house and shuffled forward.

Almost there.

She stretched her leg forward, testing the next foothold. As she inched ahead, her foot slipped on a patch of moss. Her body pitched backwards, and for one terrifying moment, she felt the pull of gravity seize her. Celeste flailed and cried out.

As she started to fall back, a hand snaked from the open window of the locked room and gripped her arm, jerking her back toward the house. She locked both hands on the window ledge and searched for the face of the person who'd saved her. There was no one there.

The hand—if it had been a hand—was gone, replaced by a faint shimmer of warmth along her skin. Celeste steadied herself, her breath coming in shallow bursts.

She climbed into the room, still shaky, still aware of the

invisible touch that had gripped her arm moments before. She rubbed her skin. The sensation was fading.

Celeste gazed around, slightly disappointed. It was an ordinary room with a full bed stacked with cardboard boxes. More boxes and several totes were stacked on the floor next to the bed. In the corner sat a tall dresser, two more boxes on top, squeezed next to a white lamp.

As she opened the flaps on the first box, the window slammed behind her.

Celeste jumped and spun to face it. The room was empty, the curtains still waving from the force of the window.

"Is there someone here with me?" she asked.

She did not believe a person occupied the room, had darted into the closet, but she was not alone.

No answer.

After another moment, Celeste returned her attention to the box. It was stuffed with a mishmash of items. Clothing, books, pairs of shoes. Celeste lifted a shoe up, a woman's weathered cowboy boot, soft and faded. She frowned and set the boot aside, sensed she'd just discovered all that her mother had left behind when she'd abandoned the Moon Lake house.

When she opened the next box, her heart sank. On the top, the glass frame cracked, the intricate webbing obscuring her mother's face, was a large family photo of Nathaniel, Nettie, Adam and Celeste. Celeste stood beside her mother, clutching her hand. Adam was cradled in her opposite arm, his eyes cast upward. Nathaniel's smile looked tight, unhappy. Celeste turned the photo over, allowing the glass to shake loose on the little wood end table. When she flipped it back, she could see her mother's face. Nettie's smile, like Nathaniel's, appeared forced and Celeste detected something in her eyes. Sadness maybe.

Beneath the cracked photo, a Polaroid lay. The picture was blurry and taken from a distance. The girl stood on the end of the dock in front of the house, long blonde hair falling over her tanned shoulders. She was in profile, a smile on her lips. This was Hannah Hawley, the student her father had been involved with.

In another box, Celeste found mail, heaps of it, all addressed to Nettie Harrington. Celeste dropped the photo of Hannah into the box and carried it to her truck.

She returned to the room and opened the closet door. The deep, narrow walk-in closet was stuffed with totes wedged so tight she nearly fell over trying to haul the first one off the stack. When she peeled off the lid, she discovered a menagerie of stuff from crumpled papers to wrinkled and balled-up clothes. There'd seemingly been no rhyme or reason to the packing. It was as if someone had grabbed handfuls of stuff and shoved it into the tote.

Celeste checked her watch. She had less than an hour before her meeting with the owner at the A-frame and she wanted to talk to the neighbor, Rose. She'd return and search the totes the following day. Before she left the room, she angled a box in front of it to ensure it could not again close and lock.

Celeste found Rose lying out on a lounge chair on her deck, a bright red towel beneath her. She wore a black one-piece swimsuit cut low to reveal her ample cleavage. A large gold necklace with a diamond rose pendant rested between her breasts.

"I wondered if you'd come back," Rose said. She held a cigarette between her red-painted nails. Large mirrored sunglasses reflected the lake beyond.

"Is your headache better?" Celeste asked.

"It's not worse."

"Do you mind if I sit?"

"Nope. But don't pick the blue chair, the back's broken,

you'll fall right out. Carl did it on a drunken rampage a few months back." She shook her head. "Men."

"Is Carl here?"

"Gone on business. Comes about every other weekend. Used to be every weekend, but you know how that goes."

"Is he from this area?"

"Nope. Morgantown. He bought this place as a vacation house. Not that he can rest to save his life."

A disgusted look darkened Rose's face and Celeste followed her gaze to where a raven had flown down and landed on the deck rail.

"Ugh." She leaned to the side and picked up her sandal, flinging it at the bird. "Go away," she shouted.

The bird squawked and took flight.

"I hate those damn birds," she muttered. "They shit on everything."

Celeste watched the raven disappear into the trees. "What do you remember about my dad, about Coach Harrington?"

"Coach Harrington," Rose murmured, pushing down the cuticle on her thumb. "I remember his pretty little car. A Camaro. Nobody in Kingwood drove a car like that. Had every girl in school panting when he parked in the morning."

Celeste wrinkled her nose. The last thing she wanted to envision was a group of high school girls lusting after her dad. "Were you at Kingwood High School when my dad got involved with Hannah?"

"Yep."

"And how did things get started between them?"

"Beats me. How do such things start? He probably cornered her alone in the locker room."

"You think he pressured her?"

Rose ashed her cigarette on the ground. "Isn't that what most men do?"

"Yes, certain kinds of men." Celeste struggled to put her dad in that role, not because he lived on some moral high ground, but because she'd never seen him flirt, date, nothing. "What was Hannah like in high school?"

"Oh, you know, a girl you loved to hate. Pretty and blonde and skinny."

"Popular?"

"With the boys. Most of the girls hated her. She wasn't a homecoming queen, that's for sure."

"Did you have any contact with her after high school?"

"Nope. Though I heard she was living out here with your dad. I didn't stay in Kingwood. Only came back a few years ago."

"What brought you back?"

"Carl. I met him at a casino in Morgantown. When he told me he lived here, I about ended things then and there. Over my dead body was I moving back to Kingwood, but he wore me down. And frankly when I saw this house." She gestured at the enormous windows reflecting the lake. "How could I say no?"

"And he wasn't here when my parents were?"

Rose's eyes narrowed in a mix of skepticism and annoyance. "Does this house look like it's been around since the eighties? No, he wasn't here."

"Do you know who else around the lake has lived here a long time?"

"I'm not exactly Mr. Rogers, Celeste. Most of the folks out here are new, I'd say."

"My mom left in 1983. I really don't have any memories of her, so I'm not sure if Hannah was in our lives before my mom left or—"

"Spend too much time in the past and you might die there."

Celeste looked at Rose sharply. "Excuse me?"

Rose laughed. "That's what my mom used to say. Basically her way of making me feel ashamed any time I missed my dad." She grabbed a spray bottle and misted her chest and face. "Not terrible advice now that I think about it, even if her intention was shit. I can't tell you when Hannah and your dad started getting hot and heavy. After high school, I split. Never thought I'd come back, but then I met Carl and he lured me to this house in the middle of nowhere."

"So you have no idea where Hannah is now?"

Rose lit another cigarette. "Dead for all I know."

19

The rental house, with a small dock jutting into Moon Lake, sat almost directly across the lake from her childhood home.

"We just started renting it last year," the owner, a middle-aged man with buzzed dark hair, explained. "It's been a pain. We live in Morgantown and we've tried a few management companies but then get reviews of the house being dirty, the doors unlocked." The man rolled his eyes. "Is it just you, or do you have family coming?"

"My husband is coming," she lied. "Sometime in the next few days." She didn't feel comfortable with anyone, including the owner of the house, knowing she'd be there alone.

"Gotcha. Well, the binder on the coffee table tells you everything you need to know about the house. Trash pickup is on Mondays. The bin needs to get dragged to the end of the driveway. Wifi password, the key code to the shed, and instructions for how to work the whole-house fan are all in there. Hobart's General Store is maybe a half mile from here. Neat little place and has the basics—bread, eggs, milk. There are a couple kayaks with paddles down by the water. Life jackets and whatnot are in the little shed outside. My cell is listed and so is my wife's. We have a guy in town we can call to swing by if you have appliance issues or any other problems."

"Thanks," Celeste told the man, following him toward his car. "Before you go, how long have you owned this house?"

He opened his door and climbed in. "Seven years, maybe eight. Bought it for a summer place, then my kids decided to join every sport known to man, so we spend most of our weekends at soccer and basketball tournaments all over the country. Never thought I'd look forward to them going off to college." He smiled. "Call me if you need anything."

***

That evening, Celeste settled into the house.

She put her clothes in the dresser and closet, her toiletries on the upstairs bathroom counter. Next to the master bedroom was a smaller room with a twin bed and a short dresser. This would be her research space. She hauled her corkboards from the truck, but only hung one. She labeled it: *Where is Nettie Harrington?*

Last known whereabouts. Celeste tacked a photo of the Moon Lake House with the address on a Post-it note.

Last confirmed sighting by Nathaniel Harrington as Nettie walked from the house with two suitcases.

She stared at the little note and a knot formed in her stomach. What had she been doing when her mother walked out the door? Had she been watching through a window, crying, calling out to her mother? Had Nettie experienced even a moment's hesitation at leaving her two small children? Or had Celeste been oblivious to her mother leaving? Had she been taking a nap or sitting on the floor playing with toys, unaware that her mother had just walked out of their lives forever?

Celeste opened the box of mail addressed to her mother. On the top sat the picture of Hannah. Celeste tacked it to the bulletin board and studied the teenager. She suspected Nettie had taken the photo. Hannah appeared unaware that someone was photographing her.

More memories of Hannah had begun to emerge. Celeste remembered Hannah screaming at Nathaniel then storming up the stairs and slamming a bedroom door. In another memory, Hannah dropped Celeste and Adam off at school when they missed the bus. As Celeste started to climb from the car, Hannah had grabbed her ponytail and yanked it hard. "Next time you miss the bus, you'll walk," she'd spat.

The memories were dark and yet a few lighter ones filtered through. Hannah taking them to someone's house to play with a litter of kittens. Hannah making them Valentine cupcakes shaped like hearts. Hannah and Nathaniel sitting together on the couch, snuggling as they watched a movie.

How had she forgotten so much about her childhood, as if someone had reached into her brain with a giant eraser and scrubbed out the years in West Virginia? Except the smudges remained. It wasn't all gone.

Amid the mail, Celeste found an envelope from Kingwood Animal Control and opened it. A check for Nettie Harrington lay inside. It was a paycheck. Her mother had worked at the animal control.

Inside was a small handwritten note.

Nettie,

Is everything okay? Please call us or stop in soon.

Tabby

In her notebook, Celeste wrote: *Tabby, Kingwood animal control.*

In the stack of mail, she saw a square pink envelope. It had never been opened. Celeste slid her finger beneath the flap and drew out the small hot pink card stock.

You're Invited to Luanne's 25th Birthday!

A date and time were listed as well as an address in Morgantown, West Virginia.

On the bottom was a handwritten note in sloppy cursive.

You better be there, Nettie! Leave those little ones with Nathaniel and come kick your feet up with your very best friend. Miss you! Xoxo

—Lulu

Celeste added Luanne's name to her notebook.

Her cell phone rang. Harris.

"Hi," she answered.

"Hey," he said. "Just wanted to check in."

"Did they find anything last night?"

"I don't know. Bowman's kept me in the loop, but there are things he's not going to share and that's one of them."

"He hasn't called me."

"That's not unusual and he knows I'm keeping you informed. Jonathan hasn't tried to make contact?"

"He's sent me a lot of emails. I haven't used my regular cell other than to make a quick call to my dad the other day."

"You haven't spoken with him then?"

"No. Why?"

"I'd imagine he's feeling the pressure now that they've secured a warrant, interrogated him. He's aware that they know about the affair. Just be alert."

"He doesn't know where I'm at."

"How many motels are in Kingwood?"

"I moved into a house rental tonight, a place right on Moon Lake."

"Okay. That's good. Text me the address when we're off the phone."

"All right."

"What are you up to?" he asked. "You sound distracted."

"I'm elbow deep in a box of mail that my mom never opened."

"Anything helpful?"

"Maybe. I found out she worked at the Kingwood animal control, so I'll go in there tomorrow."

"Good. I'm happy you're staying busy."

After the call, Celeste took out her computer. She searched first for Tabby at the Kingwood animal control, but she wasn't listed on the 'Our Team' page on their website. Next, Celeste typed in 'Luanne Oswald,' the name listed on the return address for the birthday party invitation. She found a LinkedIn profile for a Luanne (Oswald) Boden and opened it.

The listing showed Luanne as a manager at a credit union. Celeste maneuvered to the company website and searched for Luanne Boden in the directory. She found her and quickly typed her an email.

Luanne—

My name is Celeste and my mother was Nettie Harrington. I believe the two of you were friends. Please call me at your earliest convenience.

Celeste added her phone number and email and hit send.

She returned to the search bar and typed in 'Hannah Hawley.' A few results came back, but nothing recent. No social media profiles populated the results. Celeste's dad had left West Virginia more than twenty-seven years before. Hannah could be anywhere, had likely gotten married and changed her name.

Two kayaks sat on the weedy beach in front of the rental house. Celeste made her way across the spongy ground, grabbed a yellow kayak, and dragged it into the lake. The cool water soothed her aching feet and the tall weeds tickled her shins.

She climbed into the boat. It wobbled, and she nearly flipped, but managed to steady it by poking the oar into the soft sand.

Celeste dipped the paddle on one side, then the other, savoring the quiet rhythm. The warmth of the evening air wrapped around her and she inhaled the earthy scent of damp wood and pine. Nostalgia hovered just over her shoulder. She had longed for this place in the years after leaving, but had never really known it.

She thought again of her mother—of Nettie. Henry said she'd take a rowboat out to fish or just to be alone. Had she ever taken her little daughter along? Celeste almost had a memory of clutching the aluminum side of a rowboat, peering into the lake as a silver fish darted by. Had it happened?

Nearly half of the lake was wooded and weedy. She floated in front of a stretch of dense forest. The water's edge appeared swampy, clearly why it was undeveloped. Nearly swallowed by the encroaching forest lay the remnants of a mostly collapsed boathouse. The roof had caved in and the side boards had rotted. Ravens flanked the old structure, lined the crooked dock and chattered from the surrounding trees.

As Celeste's rowboat drifted closer, a hush fell over the birds.

She squinted into the shadows of the boathouse. The darkness seemed thicker there, almost solid. Then it shifted.

Celeste's breath caught, her paddle suspended in midair. Within the boathouse, a figure took shape—human, female, she thought. Its outline was fluid, the edges feathering into the gloom as though it were part of the shadows themselves.

As she stared at the figure in the boathouse, she had the distinct feeling it stared back at her. The hair rose on her neck and arms.

The ravens stirred, wings rustling.

A sudden cacophony broke the spell. The ravens erupted into flight, their wings slashing the air with a thunderous flurry.

Celeste shielded her face, the kayak rocking beneath her as the birds swarmed overhead.

When the chaos subsided and the last raven vanished into the tree line, Celeste lowered her arm and looked back at the boathouse. The figure was gone. The shadows had returned to their ordinary stillness, as if nothing had ever been there.

20

N ettie

Nettie filled the little porcelain bowl with water and held it near her lips. "Protect her," she whispered and placed it next to Celeste's crib.

She stared at her daughter, at her perfect rosebud mouth and her green eyes. Celeste was in a deep sleep, her fingers twitching. Nettie wanted to wake her, to draw her from sleep in case whatever dream had taken her was a bad one, but she quelled the urge. Nathaniel would be home in an hour, and it was their anniversary. She wanted to make chicken cacciatore.

She turned the dial on the baby monitor to high and reached into the crib, rested a hand on Celeste's chest and felt the rapid flutter of her heartbeat. "Sleep tight, my angel."

"Did we get a cat?" Nathaniel asked, settling in front of his plate at the kitchen table.

Nettie offered him a perplexed expression. "A cat?"

"There's a bowl of water next to Celeste's crib. I'd imagine we're not expecting her to drink out of it."

Nettie smiled and returned the casserole to the oven to keep warm. "Protects the baby from wandering spirits."

He raised an eyebrow. "Seems a bit childish, doesn't it? Or redneck? Are you going to tell my parents that if they come over to meet the baby? They'll be on the first plane out of here."

The comment stung, but she forced a smile and carried her plate to the table. She sat slowly, still healing from the birth, still sore. "If you think it would bother them, we'll remove it when they visit."

He nodded, but turned his attention to his food, dropping the subject.

"Do you mind holding her for a bit, Alma? I need to put in a load of laundry." Nettie handed Celeste to her neighbor Alma, who'd come over that morning.

"Do I mind holding her?" Alma cooed at Celeste. "I can't imagine anything in the whole world I'd rather do than rock this sweet girl."

"Thank you," Nettie told her, pushing her sweaty hair off her forehead. She'd been sick most of the week, with sudden violent bouts of vomiting, and had neglected the housecleaning and laundry.

"Not feeling well, honey?" Alma asked. "You look as white as that swan out there." She gestured at a swan floating in the center of the lake.

"No. I must have a stomach bug."

"Feeling achy too then?"

"No. Not really, mostly just sick to my stomach."

"When was your last period?"

Nettie paused, her stomach plunging. "Oh, my God." She sat heavily in a kitchen chair.

Alma grinned and kissed the top of Celeste's head. "You're going to be a big sister," she whispered.

Nettie stared out at the lake. "Don't mention this to anyone, okay? I'd like to be sure first."

"Heavens, no. I'd never do that. Our talks are just between you and me." Alma dropped her voice, eyes twinkling. "And between you and me, I'm over the moon excited."

Nettie stood on the dock, the wood damp beneath her bare feet from last night's rain. The lake stretched before her, a mirror of muted gray beneath the fog, rippling with a faint breeze.

She'd told Nathaniel the night before about the pregnancy and, though he'd grinned and hugged her, there'd been a tightness around his jaw, a stiffness in his body. They'd never talked about how many children they'd have, and Nettie had assumed they'd eventually give Celeste a sibling, but perhaps it was the timing. In the previous few years, they'd gone from college kids living in an apartment to owning a house with bills and maintenance needs, taking care of a baby daughter, both working. Nathaniel had the stress of school and coaching basketball. Nettie had taken the job at animal control. Moments together were stolen and sporadic.

"It's going to be okay," she murmured. "Better than okay, amazing."

Nettie untied the rowboat. The mist on the lake was thick and cool. It hovered ghostlike over the flat water beneath. She stepped into the boat, steadied her hand against the dock as the bottom wobbled beneath her. She sat, grabbed the oars and arced them back, gliding away from the dock.

She watched the house as she rowed away. The lights were out. On Saturdays, Nathaniel liked to sleep in. Nettie rarely left on the chance that Celeste would wake up and start to cry, waking Nathaniel as well, but that morning as she'd walked onto the porch with her coffee, decaf now that another life had moved into her womb, she yearned to drift in the little rowboat, to be entirely alone with her thoughts.

She rowed around the lake, gazing at the other dark houses, their occupants sound asleep or far away. Few people lived on the lake year-round and summer had given way to fall. It was still warm, but for most people, school was back in session and lake life had been set aside.

As she drifted along a stretch of forest, she squinted toward a dark shape flopping on the ground. She angled the boat toward the disturbance and drifted onto the stony shore. The pebbles were cool against her bare feet as she climbed out and made her way to the trees.

Four baby birds, their glossy dark feathers in disarray, flapped on the ground. Around them lay the shattered remains of their nest—twigs and moss scattered among the fallen leaves.

Nettie crouched, her heart tightening at the sight. The nest must have tumbled from the towering oak above, its branches barely visible in the thick fog. She glanced up, but the mother bird was nowhere to be seen, her absence an aching silence.

She studied the birds—ravens, she thought, based on their size.

The birds seemed ravenous, snapping and closing their soft beaks, their pink mouths open and desperate.

Nettie peeled off her sweatshirt, folded the little birds inside, and returned them to the bow of the little boat. She shivered when she began to row back across the lake. The day would grow warm, but not for hours.

At home, she searched the garage for a lamp and slipped into the house for a heated blanket. Once she settled the babies into a cardboard box, Nettie grabbed a can of wet cat food, items she always kept in her truck for animal control runs, and fed each of the birds. They nipped and squawked at her, but eventually calmed down.

"What is in the garage, Nettie?" Nathaniel stood staring at her, hands on his hips.

Celeste, sleeping fitfully in her vibrating chair, gurgled and a bubble of spit popped on her lip.

"They're baby birds. I found them across the lake yesterday. The wind or some animal knocked their nest out of the tree, so…"

"So, you moved them into our garage rather than let nature takes its course?"

Nettie tucked a wisp of hair behind Celeste's ear, her own baby so fragile, so beautiful. "Why should they die if I can save them?"

All but one of the baby birds survived. They began to fly just as Celeste's first tooth punched through her bottom gums.

Nettie grabbed the bag of birdseed and settled onto the porch. Within minutes, her birds arrived and then others joined them as if they'd gone out and told their friends.

Nettie tossed a handful of seeds into the yard, watched the birds pluck it from the grass, squabbling and flapping at each other.

The runt of the litter—Popeye, she'd named him after his one bulging eye—hopped across the porch toward her. She threw him some birdseed, which drew five more ravens onto the deck. Popeye flew over and landed on the arm of her chair.

"Good morning," she told him, slowly reaching to slide a hand over his sleek feathers. He shuddered, but allowed her touch.

Celeste, who sat nestled in her lap, squealed and reached for the bird. He squawked and took flight.

Nettie rocked in her glider chair, stroking Adam's wispy hair as he nursed. He held the golden key on her necklace in his tiny fist. Celeste sat in her playpen, studiously marching her My Little Ponies back and forth across her blanket.

The front door opened and Nettie smiled. She'd put chicken cacciatore in the slow cooker, Nathaniel's favorite, and knew he'd be excited. Adam had fallen asleep, so she gently pulled him away. Milk bubbled on his lips.

Nathaniel appeared in the hallway.

"I'm making chicken cacciatore," she told him.

Nathaniel stepped aside and a teenaged girl shuffled in front of him. "This is Hannah. She plays on the basketball team and is in my fourth period chemistry class. She offered to babysit for us."

Nettie, breast still exposed, quickly covered herself and, flustered, shifted Adam to her chest and patted his back, ensuring a burp. Hannah was petite and slender, with blonde hair cascading over her shoulders. She wore pink shorts and a Kingwood Basketball t-shirt.

"Nice to meet you, Hannah. You play, umm...basketball on Nathaniel's team?"

Hannah, whose eyes had wandered past Nettie to the sparkling lake beyond the front windows, nodded. "Yeah."

"I figured you could use the help," Nathaniel said. "Since you want more hours at the animal control. Hannah's available after school and on weekends when the daycare's closed."

"Oh...thank you. That's great." Nettie had not asked Nathaniel to find a babysitter. She worked two days a week and once in a while those hours ran into the evening and Nathaniel had to do pickups, but it worked. It irritated her he hadn't talked to her before offering his student a babysitting job.

Nathaniel picked Celeste up from her playpen and blew a strawberry against the side of her neck. She laughed and kicked her legs. He turned her to face Hannah. "Look, Celeste. I brought you a new friend."

Hannah stepped over and shook Celeste's little hand. "Nice to meet you," she said.

Nettie set Adam down in the bassinet and mopped the spit-up from her shirt. "Hannah, are you staying for dinner?" she asked.

"If that's okay?" Hannah cast her eyes first at Nettie and then Nathaniel. "I'd love to."

21

____

Celeste slept fitfully during her first night in the A-frame, followed into sleep by the strange spectral figure from the boathouse. In her fragmented dreams, the figure turned into a giant raven that swooped down and attacked her in the kayak, its massive black eyes boring into her as its sharp beak drew blood from her hands thrown up to protect her face.

A small pantry in the rental house contained a few basics, so Celeste managed a cup of coffee and a granola bar for breakfast, but by midday, she needed to run to the store.

She drove to Hobart's, the general store the house owner had mentioned, and parked in the dirt lot, empty except for one other truck and a few bicycles propped against the wooden ramp. The general store had first opened in 1872, according to the painted wood sign near the entrance.

Spencer too had mentioned the store and how Hobart had remembered Elliot Thacker visiting the store the summer he disappeared. If he'd been around then, more than twenty-five years before, he might also have known Nettie Harrington.

A man stood behind the register fiddling with tape for the credit card machine. He wore a blue shirt, Junior embroidered in red above the breast pocket.

"Hiya," he said. "Don't mind me. Gotta stay with the times," he grumbled. "Credit cards and cryptoid cash and Penpal."

"Are you the owner?" Celeste asked.

He flicked his eyes up and then back to the credit card machine. "I am. Bought it from my uncle five years ago. What are you looking for?"

"Actually, I had a quick question about someone who used to live on Moon Lake. Nettie Harrington."

The man shook his head. "Never heard of her. How long ago did she live here?"

"Over thirty years."

He looked up again, considered her. "Probably won't be of much help to ya. I've only been in these parts for about thirteen years. Started out as a prep cook over in Charleston, then bought a deli in Elkins and eventually landed here in Kingwood. Kept heading east for some reason or another."

"Is Hobart your uncle?"

"Sure is. The second Hobart, that is. The first who originally opened the store is long dead."

"Is your uncle still alive?"

"Not sure if 'alive' is the word I'd use. He's still breathing. Lives in a nursing home in Morgantown, but the dementia has taken what's left of his brain."

"I'm sorry."

Junior shrugged. "We're all just possums in the headlights of life."

Celeste smiled in spite of herself. "True enough. Thank you."

She picked up a basket and filled it with a loaf of bread, butter, coffee, a few bags of salad, and several cans of soup. She'd been surviving on bar food and takeout, but now that she'd moved into the A-frame, she looked forward to some normalcy in her diet.

Junior rang each item up, turning it over in his hands and commenting. "This soup's pretty good. Prefer the rye bread myself. You see you got the salted butter here, not the unsalted?"

"Yeah. I like the salted for toast."

"Ah, I see. I like a good toast now and again. Now my wife eats her toast untoasted and slathered with mayonnaise. Ever heard of such a thing?"

"I can't say I have."

"Well, I recommend you don't try it."

A woman bustled from the back carrying a crate. She was red-faced and shot Celeste an irritable look. She dropped the crate with a huff and disappeared into the back room.

Junior watched her go and scowled. "My pa always said marriage was a marathon. He didn't tell me I'd be runnin' barefoot on a road full of tacks."

"It's not easy, that's for sure," Celeste agreed.

Large bags of birdseed sat piled on a pallet near the door.

"I'll also take one of those," Celeste said, gesturing at the bags. She thought of the ravens watching her each time she went to her childhood home.

As Celeste walked to her car, she heard voices from the side of the store.

A girl's voice said, "I bet it was the Phantom of Moon Lake."

Another voice scoffed.

Celeste moved closer and peered around the store to see three teenaged girls sitting on a picnic table eating ice cream cones.

"It for sure was," said a girl in an oversized SpongeBob t-shirt, her ice cream cone nearly gone. She popped the remaining cone in her mouth.

A girl in pigtail braids shook her head. "There's no phantom. That's total bullshit. Upperclassmen just started that rumor to keep us off the lake."

"No way," SpongeBob T-Shirt argued. "It's totally real. My cousin Jane said her older sister saw it like ten years ago."

"Whatever," the girl in pigtails said, standing and walking the remainder of her cone to a green trash bin. As she moved back toward the table, she spotted Celeste and stopped, staring her down.

"Sorry," Celeste called, moving into view around the side of the store. "I didn't mean to eavesdrop—well, I guess I did mean to. I heard what you guys were talking about. Is there a rumor there's a phantom at Moon Lake?"

The girls stared at her. The one in the SpongeBob t-shirt bobbed her head. "Yep."

Pigtails rolled her eyes. "It's an urban legend—aka BS."

"All legends start somewhere," SpongeBob T-Shirt snapped.

Celeste walked toward them. "Can you tell me about it? I'm renting a house on the lake. I actually lived here when I was young."

The third girl, who'd not spoken since Celeste appeared, said, "I think it's real too." Celeste stared at her. She resembled Katie Ellis. Her hair was long and straight, parted in the middle.

Pigtails gave the girl an annoyed look. "That's because you're backwoods."

"What's your name?" the girl in the SpongeBob shirt asked. "My dad probably knows you. He grew up here too. Not on the lake. Hardly any locals live on Moon Lake."

"Celeste Cleary. My maiden name is Harrington."

"Huh," she said. "I'll ask him."

"What are your names?" Celeste asked.

"Serena," the girl in pigtails said.

"I'm Rachel." SpongeBob T-Shirt pointed at herself.

"Amy," the third girl, who resembled Katie, offered.

"Can you tell me the phantom story?" Celeste asked.

Rachel shrugged. "Sure. So, let's see. I've heard a few different stories about her."

"And him," Amy murmured.

"Oh, yeah. The kid. There aren't as many stories about him."

"A woman and a child?" Celeste asked.

"Yep," Rachel confirmed. "Most of the stories are about seeing her in the lake, not all of 'em, but most of 'em. My cousin Jane said her older sister, Bernie, was swimmin' in Moon Lake ages ago. She's a lot older than Jane, has a whole different dad and stuff. She came to the lake with a bunch of friends and they were jumping off the raft. Apparently, Bernie's hat flew out of the little fishing boat they rode out in, so she swam after it. All of a sudden, the hat stopped dead still in the water even though the wind and the current were still moving. She thought maybe it got caught on a branch, which doesn't make a whole lotta sense cuz it's pretty deep out there.

"Bernie got to her hat and, floating just beneath, staring up from these fish-eaten eyeballs, was a dead woman. She had one of her hands up and she was holding that hat perfectly still for Bernie. Well, Bernie didn't even get the hat. She screamed bloody murder and about drowned, filled her mouth full of water and went thrashing back to her friends. She was so scared they had a mind to believe her and they all piled in the boat thinkin' there was a dead body in the lake. As soon as they untied from the raft, Bernie's hat took off again, getting blown across the water. They tried to motor to the spot Bernie saw the woman, but they didn't find nothin'. And that was that. They eventually caught up with her hat stuck over in the cattails by that old boathouse."

"What did she look like?" Celeste thought of the shape amongst the ravens at the boathouse.

Serena sneered. "Like a ghost. Duh."

Rachel rolled her eyes. "I've heard different stuff from different people. Someone said she had black hair down to her feet that wrapped around her ankles and legs like snakes."

Celeste imagined the thing in the boathouse. There'd been nothing distinguishing about it at all and yet it had scared her.

22

"I heard she was pretty, angelic even," Amy offered.

Serena yawned, appearing bored.

"What about the boy? What have people seen?" Celeste asked.

Amy's face had gone pale. Celeste sensed Amy had seen the boy herself, but suspected she was too embarrassed to admit it in front of her friends.

"The only story I've ever heard about him," Rachel explained, "is that a few people say they hear a boy laughing or crying in the woods by the lake, sometimes they even see one, but then he's never there."

Celeste focused on Amy. "Is that what you've heard?"

Amy tugged on a strand of her long hair. "Umm...that and... I think someone said...that sometimes he has a mask on."

"A mask?" Celeste asked.

Serena snorted.

"I've never heard the mask thing," Rachel said.

"What kind of mask?" Celeste asked Amy, her dream of the boy in the mask filtering in.

Amy let her hair fall to cover one eye. "Oh...I guess kind of an old-timey, like plastic, kid's Halloween mask. You know, the masks they used to wear with the strap on the back." She shrugged. "It's just something I heard."

Serena pulled a cell phone from her pocket and stared at it. "We've got to go, you guys. My mom's on her way to get me at Rachel's."

"Thanks," Celeste told them. She watched them ride away on their bikes.

Celeste dropped her groceries at the A-frame and drove around the lake to her childhood home. As she parked, she looked up at the window that had been open the day before. It was closed. The memory of the grip on her arm lingered. She'd nearly fallen and been badly injured, if not worse. Who had saved her? The Phantom of Moon Lake?

Celeste took the bag of birdseed to the front porch and ripped it open. Before she even tossed the first handful into the grass, the ravens arrived. They landed in the yard and on the deck. One perched on the rail so close to Celeste she could have reached out and touched it.

"You guys are pretty friendly, aren't you?" she asked, watching the birds peck at the seeds. The one on the rail beside her didn't join the others. It stood and watched her.

She took a step toward it, reached out her arm, but before she could brush her fingers along its sleek feathers, the bird flapped and flew away.

Celeste put the rest of the birdseed in the shed and returned to the house. Back upstairs in the spare bedroom, she hoisted one of the totes from the closet.

Celeste smoothed out a piece of light green paper. It was a college transcript with a list of classes for student Nettie Caldwell. Also in the box, she found old receipts, greeting cards, and near the bottom a baby book—her baby book. On the front someone, likely Nettie, had slipped a newborn photo behind the plastic case. The title at the top said *My*

Baby Book and beneath that, in black marker, *Celeste (Ceecee) Harrington.*

Celeste flipped it open. Another newborn picture occupied the first page, along with a list of stats, including her birth weight and time.

She flipped past to where questions prompted the family to write about baby's first word, food, toys.

The first half of the book was filled out, but the rest had been left blank.

First word: Mama.

First toy: A stuffed bear.

In another of the chaotic totes, she found Nettie's high school diploma, several cookbooks, and a variety of women's clothes. A balled-up t-shirt lay in the bottom, soft and gray. Celeste smoothed it out and read the words on the front: *Be Kind to Animals.* As Celeste stared at it, a memory swam up. A young Celeste had been holding the t-shirt in bed, gripping it tightly, and crying as someone wrenched it away.

Celeste set the t-shirt aside to take back to the A-frame.

She found a box filled with photo albums and carried it downstairs, wanting a comfortable seat as she paged through the old photos.

She sat on the couch and opened the first album. The plastic covering the pages crackled and her breath caught as she took in the first photo. It was her mother, smiling brightly, perched on the edge of a picnic blanket. Her dark hair cascaded over her shoulders, glowing with the golden hue of the sun. The next photo showed both her parents, Nettie and Nathaniel, young, wearing matching West Virginia University t-shirts and standing in front of a tall brick building.

On the following page there was a candid photo of her mother sitting on a park bench, holding a book in one hand and shielding her eyes from the sun with the other. The book was *Romeo and Juliet.* It looked like the same copy her dad still kept in the green tote where she'd found all the other remnants of their mysterious life in West Virginia. More photos of her parents. On her mother's ring finger was a gold band with a heart-shaped diamond in the center. Several of her dad holding up his degree, then his teaching certificate, then pictures of her mother pregnant, hands resting on her belly.

In the next album, there was a photo of Nettie holding an infant Celeste, standing in front of Moon Lake. Celeste's chubby hand reached for her mother's face in the picture, and she could almost hear her mother's laugh frozen in time. What struck her most was the expression in her mother's eyes—pride and love. Had so much changed after Celeste's birth that her mother had walked away from their life? She struggled to believe it, looking at the woman staring with such adoration at her baby girl.

Celeste continued through the albums and noticed the change in both of her parents. After Adam's arrival, her mother looked pale, tired. Her father appeared leaner, stronger, as if he'd started lifting weights. In many of the photos, they no longer embraced or touched in the images, but stood inches or even feet apart. Their smiles looked forced. As she neared the end of the album in her lap, most of the pictures were of a toddler, Celeste, and a baby, Adam. Few included her parents at all.

In the last album, the only one that included pictures of Adam and Celeste as young children rather than a baby and toddler, at least half of the photos were missing from the slots. There were photos of Celeste waiting for the school bus. Celeste stared hard at herself, her wrinkled t-shirt, an obvious brown stain, likely chocolate, above the pink hearts in the center. Her tennis shoes were faded, the laces untied. Had this been her first day of school? And if so, had nobody put any effort at all into making her look presentable?

She flipped further into the album. Christmas with a barely

decorated tree, a handful of unwrapped presents in the large living room. In a mirror, she caught the reflections of two people in the background, but their images were too blurry to distinguish. Adam, probably five, and Celeste, around seven or eight, sat on the floor, their smiles pinched, their eyes wary.

Sun streamed through the window and warmed the house. Celeste took off her sweatshirt and draped it over the back of the couch. The heat had begun to lull her. Her eyelids grew heavy. She leaned back on the couch and closed her eyes.

Something shifted in the living room, a rustling like footsteps on the carpet. She opened her eyes.

In front of her, steps away, stood a little boy. The right side of his head was crushed. He stared at her from a single blood-curdled eye.

"It should have been you!" he hissed.

23

Celeste's eyes snapped open to the empty living room. No dead boy. Her heart hammered against her breastbone, her breath came in shallow bursts.

She'd fallen asleep, and the sun was lower in the sky. Dark clouds moved across the lake. She must have slept for hours.

"It was a nightmare," she murmured, "just a nightmare." A thought that might have settled the Celeste she'd been before the accident, but dreams, she now understood, held messages, warnings, premonitions.

Her mouth tasted dry, sticky, and she wanted out of the house.

By the time she parked next to the rental house, the sky had opened up, and the rain had started.

She hurried inside and stripped off her wet clothes, took a hot shower and changed into flannel pants and a t-shirt. She made toast and sat on the living room couch.

Rain pounded the roof. The lake beyond the window was little more than a gray blur.

Celeste nibbled her toast, feeling suddenly lonely. Her cell phone had been off for days and, though she'd spoken with plenty of people, they were all strangers.

The intensity of discovering Jonathan's secrets followed by her swift departure had left her little time to sit with the stark reality of her new life. Her marriage was over. Life as she knew it had imploded.

She called Joanna, unsure if the woman would pick up with her unfamiliar number.

"Hello?" Joanna answered on the second ring.

"Joanna, it's Celeste."

"Celeste? Oh, my gosh, I was just thinking about you. I'm completely serious. I was out on my balcony and this raven swooped down and landed on the rail not two feet away from me. I instantly thought of your beautiful cane and then, of course, you."

"That's amazing." Celeste imagined the line of ravens at her childhood home that day. Celeste didn't tell Joanna she no longer had the cane, that it had burned in the fire in Wisconsin, the fire that had taken the life of Kurtis Peters and revealed the body of River's long-buried mother.

"Is this a new number?" Joanna asked. "I didn't recognize it when I answered and it didn't show up with your name."

"Yes. It is. It's a long story, but I'm using a temporary phone for a bit."

"A temporary phone? Is everything okay?"

A bubble lodged in Celeste's throat. She wanted to tell Joanna, felt an intense urge to spill everything, but in the background, she heard a bellowing laugh—Floyd.

"Is that Floyd?"

"It sure is. He's here because Brandon," Joanna dropped her voice, "my boyfriend"—she laughed—"it still feels weird calling him that—insisted Floyd and Camile come over so he could cook them his famous short rib tacos. It smells pretty darn great."

"That's really fantastic, Joanna. All of it. I'm so glad you've found someone, and that Arizona is working out."

"Thanks, Celeste. I hope you know it was all thanks to you."

"Not at all."

"No. It's true," Joanna insisted. "If you hadn't found out what happened to Katie, I don't think I could have ever left Graves. I'm still surprised most days that I did. It wasn't easy at first. The heat here is bonkers. It's supposed to be one hundred and eight degrees tomorrow. But there's so much to love and the truth is, without Katie, Michigan wasn't home anymore."

"Was there anything that helped in those early days? Anything that helped you get through the hard times? The lonely times?"

The background sounds faded as if Joanna had gone into another room. "Are you sure everything is okay, Celeste? Has something happened?"

"I'm fine, really. Just curious."

"All right." Joanna didn't sound convinced. "I sat in a lot of coffee shops and restaurants. Pretty sage advice, huh? It helped though because it reminded me of the Sidewinder and it kept me from sitting home feeling sad. And then I started working at Brandon's coffee shop and now...I've found my place here. We all have. Obviously, Floyd and Camile already had friends here, so that helped—plugging into their community—but honestly it was just taking it a day at a time. Some of those days, the early ones especially, I just lay in bed and cried all day." She sniffled. "It's been a while since I had one of those, but...I try to let it happen. I think that's the only way to heal, you know? To feel it."

Celeste's call waiting beeped, and she saw Detective Bowman's name appear. "Joanna, I have to go. I have an important call coming in."

"Absolutely. So good to hear your voice, Celeste. You should come for a visit sometime. Call me again. Okay?"

"I will. Bye, Joanna." Celeste ended the call and answered Bowman's.

"Celeste?"

"I'm here," she said.

"We searched your house."

"Harris told me. Did you find anything?"

"The box of stuff you found in Jonathan's closet was gone. No sign of it."

Celeste sighed, unsurprised.

"The search is actually not why I'm calling. I don't want to alarm you, but Jonathan was MIA at work today. I sent someone by the house and no one answered. The garage is empty. We've tried multiple times to get in contact and he's not answered nor returned our calls."

Celeste's heart sped up. "You think he ran?"

"I don't know. He hasn't technically committed a crime by leaving. He isn't under arrest yet, but it's possible. Does he know where you are?"

"He knows I'm in West Virginia."

"But not your exact location?"

"No."

"Okay. There's likely no reason for alarm, but I wanted you to be aware."

"Thank you. If you find him, will you call me?"

"Yes. And it's entirely possible his being off our radar is completely innocent."

"I'm sure it is," Celeste said, and she meant it. Jonathan was not the type of person to flee from the police. If anything, she imagined him meeting with attorneys or scouring the internet in search of laws to prevent his arrest. Running from the law was the kind of thing Jonathan would look at with absolute disdain.

You didn't really know him.

The thought popped into her mind and hung there, a neon

sign pointing toward what the police and Harris believed. Celeste could barely comprehend he'd had an affair. The leap to attempted murder had left her reeling. Not once in the discovery of his transgressions had it aligned with the man she'd believed she knew, had once loved, had married.

Celeste listened to the relentless rain drum against the slanted roof. Beyond the picture windows, the droplets slammed into the dark lake, causing the surface to ripple and explode. It wasn't yet dark, but the mass of gray clouds sucked the light from the trees and lake—they all seemed dipped in charcoal.

A flash of lightning split the sky and the lights flickered.

"Please, no," she murmured. She did not want to spend the evening in a pitch-black house. She hadn't even bothered to look for candles or flashlights—had no clue if there even were any.

Quickly, she stood and hurried into the kitchen, opening drawers. She found a box of votive candles and a lighter and set them on the counter. In a utility closet, she found a flashlight and added that next to the candles. She might not need them, but just in case.

She plugged her cell phone into the charger and then made her way to the second floor to do the same with her laptop. On the stairs, the lights flickered again and went out. Thick darkness fell over the house. Clutching the rail, she returned to the first floor, feeling her way to the kitchen. She lit four votive candles and carried them one by one to the coffee table in the living room.

Celeste sat on the couch, tucked her knees beneath her, and wrapped a blanket around her shoulders. She'd never minded rain storms, power outages, but this one set her nerves humming. Jonathan was unaccounted for.

She shook her head as if she might fling off the idea in much the same way a dog shakes off droplets of water. It was absurd, ridiculous to think Jonathan had fled Michigan and stalked her to West Virginia. It was not in his personality.

Still, she stood and, carrying a little candle, checked the doors and windows were all locked. She grabbed a knife from the butcher block and returned to the couch.

Firelight danced off the metallic blade. Why had she retrieved it? Did she genuinely believe she could thrust a blade into Jonathan's body if he did show up?

"No," she whispered. She grabbed a magazine and slid it over the knife so she didn't have to look at it.

Stretched out, an itchy embroidered pillow behind her head, Celeste drifted into a fitful sleep.

"Ready or not here, I come!"

The voice startled Celeste awake. She sat up and twisted around on the couch. The power still hadn't come back on. The candles she lit on the table, now burned down, flickered as if a breeze had passed by.

Had she dreamed the words? A child had spoken them. It was the call at the beginning of a game of hide and seek.

Above her, she heard the sound of feet running fast across the floor from one end of the house to the other.

She stood quickly and stared at the beamed ceiling.

Celeste did not want to go upstairs and yet sitting on the couch pretending she'd heard nothing was out of the question. She picked up one of the little candles and hissed when the flimsy alumina burned her fingertips. She dropped it, splattering wax across the glass-topped table.

"Just breathe," she murmured, but her lungs did not expand. She sucked in shallow breaths as she walked to the kitchen and found the flashlight. Gripping it so tight her fingers ached, she ascended the stairs.

The beam of her light captured a cylinder of the darkly carpeted stairs. Halfway up one step creaked and she paused for a moment, listening. The house had gone quiet, the only sounds the steady patter of rain.

The nightmare boy she'd dreamed of earlier in the day floated behind her eyes, his head smashed.

Dead. He was dead and he was angry.

At the top, she turned into the long dark hallway and shone the flashlight over empty floor and walls. As she twisted to face the other direction, a jagged streak of lightning lit the sky through a window at the end of the opposite hall.

It illuminated a figure standing there.

A little boy in a white Halloween mask.

24

Nettie

Nettie arrived home from work just after four in the afternoon. She slipped into the house and found it quiet. In the living room, Celeste lay on a blanket on the floor asleep, her heart-shaped pillow that Nettie had sewn during her pregnancy beneath her cheek, a line of drool clinging to her pink lips. Adam was in his playpen, also asleep, a discarded bottle near his outstretched hand.

Nettie brushed her fingers across his dark hair and felt the swell of love for her children that often assailed her as she watched them sleep. It seemed impossible to love someone so much, as if her body could hardly contain it. Sometimes she pondered that love, which had been so instant and instinctual, and wondered if her mother had ever felt it at all.

Her gaze drifted to the front window, where the dock stretched into the calm lake. Nathaniel stood at the end. The familiar sight of him in swim shorts and a faded navy t-shirt should have been comforting, but something in his body language set her on edge.

Hannah, the babysitter, was there too. The teenager's golden hair shimmered in the sunlight, and she was climbing onto the dock, her lean body glistening from the water.

As she walked up the dock, Nathaniel playfully bumped into Hannah, nearly sending her sprawling back into the lake. She clutched his arm.

Nettie blinked at them, at the playfulness between them.

Nathaniel said something, and Hannah threw her head back in a laugh, the sound muted by the glass.

Hannah adjusted the strap of her bikini, the gesture slow and deliberate. Nathaniel's gaze flicked briefly to her shoulder before he looked away.

Nettie had told herself she was imagining things—the fleeting touches, the exaggerated smiles. Now she stepped back from the window, the room suddenly feeling too small, the walls closing in. Her heart thudded in her chest and her mind raced. Was she overreacting? Was this just harmless fun?

Nettie wrapped her arms around herself and turned away from the window. She forced her gaze down to her two beautiful sleeping children. Celeste had woken and watched Nettie, her bright green eyes fixed on hers.

Nathaniel pulled ground beef from the refrigerator. "I'm going to grill burgers. You could make some of that macaroni salad that's so good?" Nathaniel suggested, kissing Nettie on her temple.

"Sure. I think I have the ingredients." She moved past him to the cupboard in search of a box of macaroni. Through the front window she heard Hannah laugh.

"Where are Hannah and Celeste?" Nettie asked.

"Hannah's pushing Celeste on the swing."

"Oh. Do you think we should run her home before you start the burgers? Or is she staying for dinner?"

"I offered her the spare room tonight. We have the basketball tournament early. She can just ride to the school with me."

"Is that really appropriate? Having a student stay at our house?" Nettie asked, a little knot forming in her stomach.

"I've told you about her mom. Drug problems, her and the stepdad both. If anything, I'm sure the school would appreciate our offering to help Hannah. You of all people know how nice it is to have a safe place."

Nettie didn't look at him, kept her eyes focused on the cupboard, though she'd stopped registering the contents. "That's true," she said, finally.

They ate dinner on the patio, Celeste toddling through the yard after the ravens that landed every few minutes, cast an expectant eye at Nettie, and then flew away.

"They do that because you're feeding them all the time," Nathaniel said, watching the birds, annoyed.

"What's wrong with that? A lot of people feed birds."

"Pretty birds," Nathaniel quipped. "Cardinals, robins, not" —he scowled and flicked his hands at the dark birds—"crows."

"They're ravens," Nettie said.

"They're kind of creepy," Hannah murmured, taking a bite of her cheeseburger.

"Celeste likes them," Nettie pointed out as a giggling Celeste chased after Popeye, who seemed to be playing a game with her, hopping only a foot away each time she chased him.

Nathaniel disappeared into the house for several minutes.

He returned with a beer for himself, a bottle of Coke for Hannah, and a drink for Nettie.

"I made you an old-fashioned," he said handing it to her.

"Thank you," she said, surprised. Old-fashioned had always been Nettie's drink of choice, but Nathaniel harbored a certain disdain for alcohol. Beer was okay, wine acceptable, but hard liquor was the stuff of drunks and bums.

Nettie woke disoriented. She reached across the bed, but Nathaniel's space was cold beside her. Her eyelids drooped, sleep calling her back down, but something flickered on the ceiling of the room. Her eyelids fluttered back open. She dragged herself, heavy as if her blankets were the weighted kind the dentist laid across her for an x-ray, out of the bed, to her feet.

Orange light glowed beyond the windows.

Nettie walked forward, teetered for a moment, then steadied. She pulled aside the curtain and blinked down at the front lawn. A fire burned in the stone fire pit. People sat around it, their faces lit by firelight—Nathaniel, and another teacher from the school, and two teenage girls. Hannah and a girl Nettie didn't recognize.

Orange cinders fled toward the black sky and Nettie stood transfixed. Hannah stood and twirled near the fire, her long blonde hair fanning out. Nathaniel watched her.

25

———————

Celeste woke to discover the power had been restored. After her encounter the night before with the little boy, she'd returned to the couch and lain awake for hours.

She sensed the boy was Elliot Thacker. Which meant what? He had died near the lake? Or had some other preternatural force drawn him to Celeste?

Celeste made coffee and carried a towel to the damp porch, dried off a folding chair and sat down.

Her phone rang, and she stared at the unfamiliar number, considering what Bowman had said about Jonathan. It rang again and then a third time.

She snatched it up and answered it.

"Hello?"

"Celeste, it's Spencer. Wasn't sure if you were an early bird, but figured I'd take a chance. You're up?"

"How'd you get this number?"

"Uh, you gave it to me, remember? At Frog's diner the first day we met?"

She frowned. She'd forgotten. "Oh...yeah."

"You all right? Ran out of the Lantern's Glow like you'd gotten a call your house was on fire."

"Everything's fine. I just...never mind. What do you need, Spencer?"

"I did a bit of sleuthing on your mom. Figured I'd pass along what I found out."

Celeste's heart quickened. "Do you know where she is?"

"I'll come to you? Are you at the Moon Lake house?"

Celeste stood and walked into the house, dumped the remainder of her coffee in the sink. "No. I'm in town," she lied. "Why don't I come to you?"

Celeste parked in front of the road at the address Spencer had given her. The single-story house looked like it had seen better days. The blue paint was cracked and peeling. The roof was so moss-covered she couldn't distinguish the color of the shingles beneath it. A UFO birdfeeder on a pole, leaning dangerously to the side, jutted from the overgrown grass in the front yard.

Celeste rang the doorbell and, a moment later, Spencer pulled open the door.

Spencer wore jersey shorts and a white t-shirt with a noticeable coffee stain above the words *Ghost Hunters Get All the Girls*.

He looked down at his shirt. "Like that? I got it from a paranormal investigator I interviewed a couple of years back. Man, did he have some stories." He chuckled. "Welcome to my palace. Had to let the maid service go, as you can see."

Celeste stepped inside, instantly hit by the scent of man sweat, coffee, and something faintly earthy that she hoped wasn't coming from the carpet. The living room was a kaleidoscope of chaos: shelves crammed with books on everything from unsolved murders to alien abductions, an array of Bigfoot figurines lining the windowsill, and a UFO-shaped lamp balanced on a stack of newspapers.

"It's a lifestyle," Spencer said, closing the door with his foot. "Some people collect stamps. I collect evidence of the unexplained and also, apparently, mugs." He gestured to a corner table where a tower of coffee mugs threatened to topple. Each one bore a conspiracy-themed slogan like "Bigfoot Believes in Me" and "Aliens Stole My Homework."

A battered couch covered in mismatched throw blankets faced a large wall-mounted television. On the coffee table, she saw stacks of notebooks, a few mismatched socks and a half-eaten bagel.

"Let's talk in my office," he said. "Can I get you a coffee first?"

"No, thanks." Celeste would have liked another cup of coffee, but wasn't sure she trusted anything produced in Spencer's kitchen. She followed him into another room.

Like the living room, Spencer's office was a disaster. The focal point was a desk and a laptop computer. Every surface was a jumble of stuff. Framed posters of Bigfoot, Mothman, and the Dogman covered one wall. On another wall, he'd tacked dozens of missing person posters, many with notes scrawled in the margins.

He opened a small door. "This here is where the magic happens. My recording studio."

Celeste leaned toward the tiny, cramped space. The walls were obscured by thick black foam. Two stools sat behind microphones with wires trailing to a laptop perched on an unstable-looking shelf. "Is this a closet?" she asked.

He chuckled. "It used to be. It's easier to handle the acoustics in a small space. When the podcast was at its peak, I had my sights set on this office downtown in a basement. It was already soundproofed because some musicians used to lease it." He sighed wistfully. "A man can dream." He closed the door. "Anyway. This is my place."

"And this is all your material?" Celeste frowned at the piles of paperwork stacked haphazardly on surfaces around the room. Sticky notes, scraps of paper, napkins scrawled with words. A tower of papers rested against the side of a worn, cat-hair-covered black chair. A whiteboard covered in half-erased notes sat angled against the wall on top of a desk with not a single bit of clean surface.

"Yep."

"And is there a method to the madness? How do you keep track of anything in here?"

He grinned and moved one of several coffee mugs off of a spiral-bound notebook. "I keep it all in here. My trusty notebook or notebooks. I've got about fifty of these things, but I transcribe what I find." He gestured at the stacks of looseleaf paper.

"I'd have a panic attack just opening the door every morning."

Spencer plopped into the rolling chair in front of the desk and swiveled toward her. He propped his feet on a crate table stacked with notebooks and she lurched forward ready to catch the half-full coffee mug teetering perilously on the end. Somehow, it stayed put.

As Celeste eyed the missing posters, one near the center caught her eye. She stepped closer and stared at the picture of the little boy.

Have You Seen Me?

Name: Elliot Thacker.

As Celeste studied the photo, something skittered up her spine, a wink of recognition, a memory.

"I knew him," she whispered.

Spencer spun around, followed her gaze. "You knew Elliot? Are you sure?"

Celeste frowned, tried to get more of the memory. She almost grasped it, like reaching for a leaf as it fell from the tree and moments before contact suddenly caught a breeze and darted away.

"Yes. I'm sure, but..." She shook her head. "The memory is vague."

It *was* vague, a whisper of her and Elliot in the woods near the lake, him crouched low and then holding up a perfectly flat gray stone. "Perfect for skipping," he'd announced.

The boy who was haunting Moon Lake, the boy Spencer had been searching for, had been her friend.

"You remember him from when you were a little kid?" Spencer asked, eyes bright.

"I think so."

"The timing is right." He nodded and drummed his fingers on his chin. "You said you left West Virginia when you were eight?"

Celeste nodded, straining to bring more memories to the surface. She felt them, a lake of memories trapped beneath the ice, so close.

He stood and paced away from the desk. "When were you born?"

"1980."

He rubbed his hands together. "Elliot vanished in 1988. It all lines up. You knew him. He probably used to visit you at the lake. Holy shit."

"That doesn't exactly get you any closer to finding out what happened to him."

"It might. What do you think about setting up a phone meeting with your dad? I could just ask him a few questions."

Celeste shook her head. "He'll never go for that."

"Why not?"

"Because he won't. He's a very...closed-off person."

Spencer dropped back into his chair, clearly deep in thought.

"What about the Moon Lake Phantom? Ever heard of her?" Celeste asked.

Spencer gnawed his lower lip and then, after a moment, nodded. "Oh, yeah. All kinds of ghosts haunting the holler. I tried to do a deep dive into her ages ago back when *Strictly Supernatural* was in its heyday. I interviewed a guy who saw her. You should listen to the episode. It was wild."

"What did he say?"

Spencer closed his eyes for a moment. "Let me see...Okay, yep, I've got it. There used to be a camping spot on the east side of Moon Lake. It was rustic. No facilities, but you could pitch a tent and have a gorgeous view and access to the lake. So that guy spent a weekend there. It was fall, and he'd brought a little boat to do some fishing. First morning he woke up to the sounds of birds. He said it sounded like a thousand birds were right outside of his tent and it spooked him because he saw that Hitchcock movie *The Birds* as a boy. So, he said he lay real still and he could see their shapes outside the tent—hundreds of the birds walking and flying and squawking.

"Eventually he dozed back off and when he woke up they were gone, but he walked out to find his camp pretty trashed. Cooler tipped on its side, had some clothes on a camp chair and those were strewn about, his sweatshirt was gone, never did find it. Anyway, he got his fishing gear around and went out in his boat. It was still pretty early, maybe seven or eight in the morning and, again, it was fall, so he said the lake was quiet as a graveyard. He found a spot near the woody shoreline on the north side of the lake where the fish were biting.

"Probably a half hour into fishing, everything got real quiet and when he looked up, he saw hundreds of birds sitting in the trees watching him. Black crows or ravens or something. He started to feel panicky and went to pull his line, but he'd caught a big one and it was tugging hard. He leaned over to peer into the water as he was reeling it in and suddenly there's a hand holding his fishing line coming up out of the water, then a head, the skin all mottled and eaten away, the long hair sticking in strips to this woman's mostly bare skull.

"He screamed, stumbled backward and fell off the back of the boat. The water was ice cold, sucked the air right from his lungs. And then..." Spencer, who'd been talking with his hands, showed her both palms. "Nothing. He has no memory of what happened next. He woke up in his boat, goose egg on the back of his head where he smacked the side of the boat going overboard, soaking wet and cold as a popsicle. No recollection of how he got back into the boat, but he rowed like the Devil was chasing him and got the hell out of there. Never went back to Moon Lake."

26

"How did you find him to get his story?" Celeste asked.

"Well, after every episode of *Strictly Supernatural*, I'd put a call out to listeners and ask if they'd had any strange experiences. Mothman sightings, Bigfoot, Nessie, you know the drill. He sent me an email."

Celeste thought of the ravens that had first appeared in her near-death experience. Their presence had become even more prevalent since her arrival in West Virginia. They'd covered the boathouse where she'd seen a shadowy figure, a female presence, she was sure. Harris's friend Lena had called the ravens Celeste's guardian angels, but the story Spencer had shared left her uneasy.

Spencer continued. "The guy said he walked on eggshells for weeks after the incident at Moon Lake. Apparently, he mentioned something to his mother and she, a superstitious woman, insisted the black birds were harbingers of death. So, he's thinking at any moment he's going to drop dead from a heart attack. He even went to his doctor and had a full work-up done, stress test, blood work. He sent me a copy of the medical records. He didn't have any proof from the weekend except one black feather he found later wedged in the bed of his truck."

"Did you believe him?"

Spencer furrowed his brow, then nodded slowly. "I've got a pretty reliable bullshit detector. I've done a lot of interviews about unusual sightings. When somebody's yanking my chain, I get a little tickle right back here." He tapped the back of his neck. "But even without that, there's a certain quality to people who are telling the truth. It's embarrassment or shame, and they spend half the conversation trying to justify what they saw while simultaneously acknowledging that no logical explanation exists on God's green earth. I get the sense from those, like this fisherman, that they're calling me with the hope that I'm going to offer the logical explanation, unveil Scooby Doo's monster, so to speak. I can't do that, but I can usually tell 'em they're not the only one who's witnessed what they saw and that, on its own, is a bit of reassurance. A 'you're not crazy' card, if you will."

"You've heard of other people who've witnessed the phantom woman."

"Oh, yeah. Urban legends don't get started from nowhere. I've talked to five people at least who've seen her, but the only one I could get on the record was the fisherman and even he wouldn't let me use his real name."

"How far back do they go? The stories?"

"Hmm...hard to say. Urban legends rarely have a clear date of inception. I'd never heard of her until that guy sent me the email. Here. This might help." He opened his laptop and squinted at the screen for several minutes. When he turned the screen to face her, Celeste stared at a web page called 'I Know What I Saw.'

"What is this?" She asked.

"It's a forum. You can search for folklore, strange experiences by state and even the name of the monster. When I first heard the phantom woman story, I hopped right in here. I'd been reading people's stories of West Virginia encounters for ages. I figured someone might have shared a Moon Lake story. Sure enough, that's the thread right there. Last post is from about four years ago, thread has pretty much gone dead, but if you scroll back," he moved the cursor up the page, "Dirty-Bird365 shared a story he says happened in 1992."

Celeste pulled the laptop closer to read the story.

This happened when I was only seven years old. I've never shared this story. All my life I thought it was a dream, but it felt real.

In 1992, my family and I visited a great-aunt who had a house on Moon Lake in Kingwood, West Virginia. One morning, I woke up before the whole family and wanted to swim. I knew if I asked my mother, she'd say no. There was a swim raft a way offshore and I decided I'd swim out, jump off a couple times and swim back before they woke up. It was spring, and the water was still pretty cold.

I made it about halfway to the raft and got a cramp. I'd heard of the usual 'don't swim after you eat' thing, but I'd never experienced a genuinely debilitating cramp. I tried to turn back, but my whole side seized and I couldn't kick that leg. I started going under, swallowing water. There was no way I could get back to the shore, so I tried to keep going for the raft, but soon I was under and I stopped swimming because it hurt too bad.

I knew I was going to drown. Everything went dark. I don't know how long I was under, but all of a sudden, I feel sand under me. I pop my eyes open and I spit out about a gallon of water. I'm on my side on the shore and when I look up, I see this woman wading back into the lake. She's wearing something long, like a nightgown, but it was all tattered and green-tinged. She looked scary and yet I knew she'd just saved me. She'd dragged me to the shore.

She never turned around. I didn't see her face. Maybe she didn't even have a face. I found this forum a few weeks ago. This is the first time I've let myself believe she was real. I think the Phantom of Moon Lake saved my life.

Celeste sat back and crossed her arms over her chest. 1992. She'd have been twelve, gone from West Virginia for four years by then.

"Why so keen to know about this, anyway?" Spencer asked. "You seen something at the lake? Remember something from when you were a kid?"

She didn't say anything. She was thinking of her mother. Had she died at the lake and rescued the little boy who'd attempted that ill-fated morning swim, or was Celeste searching for some answer to why her mother had left? Easier to accept she was a spirit than that she'd chosen to abandon them. She thought again of slipping on the roof, that hand grabbing her.

Understanding dawned on Spencer's face. "Wait. Do you think the Moon Lake Phantom is your mom?"

She shrugged. "It's not any more farfetched than the other theories rotting my brain lately."

"You think she's dead, then? I mean, like I said before, I haven't found too many people who"—he made air quotes—"*took off* who weren't dead, but still..."

"I read about you online." Celeste moved away from Spencer and sat on the edge of a small couch. Something shifted beside her and she jumped. A white cat, previously blending into the menagerie of papers around it, stood and stretched, then padded over and settled on her lap.

"I see Noodle likes you. That's a good sign." He winked at her. "What'd you read? Nothing good, I'm sure."

Celeste scratched Noodle's neck, and he purred and turned slightly to reveal his belly. "Aren't you sweet?" she told him, missing her own kitties. She felt better knowing they were likely getting spoiled by Adam back in Michigan. "It wasn't all bad. It wasn't all good either."

Spencer leaned back and stared at the ceiling. "Anyone who ever said 'there's no bad publicity' hasn't lived through the shit-show I experienced. I couldn't go to the grocery store for months without getting evil looks. Someone keyed my car. My house got egged eight times—seriously, eight times. Throw in burning bags of dog shit, soap on my windshield, and I won't even tell you about the online trolls. In some ways it was the perfect example of 'be careful what you wish for.' I used to lie in bed and think, 'I want people to know about *Dark Deeds*. I want them to talk about Spencer Ashman.' Well, they did." He rubbed his face. "Not my finest hour."

"What happened?" she asked.

"When the podcast took off, it was like I had the Midas touch. I'd found my path. My whole life I'd been that guy in the broom cupboard scribbling theories, stories, musings. This time, the time of podcasts and YouTube and self-publishing, blogs—shit, the internet, period—this was my time. Suddenly I could be myself, do what I loved, and make a living at it. Then came the scandal."

He pointed to a missing person's poster off to the side on the wall. A pretty teenager with a gap-toothed smile and short curly hair.

"Addy Sadler. She was the one who ruined me. Not her, obviously, but her case. I went deep on that one. Got a little obsessed, though I didn't see it that way at the time. I was sure her stepfather killed her. She was nineteen. They'd been having problems, and she was telling friends she wanted to get out. When she disappeared, police called her a runaway, but a bunch of people thought it didn't add up. She had a hundred bucks in her sock drawer, left her journal, pretty much all her stuff. I started lookin' into the stepdad, Martin, pretty heavy. Found out Martin's father was in prison for murder. Thought it must run in the family. So then I got convinced Martin not only killed Addy but her mother, too. I floated some idea he pushed the mother down the stairs because that's how she died, from a fall down the stairs. The podcast got shared on a couple of social media platforms, went viral. Overnight, I went from a thousand subscribers to a hundred thousand. Had a book deal lined up if I could make a strong enough case that the stepdad did it.

"Well, then they found Addy's car submerged in a quarry with her skeleton in it right on the route she'd have taken that night back from the party she was last seen at. She must have missed the curve. She'd been drinking and went right off the edge into the ravine. It was pretty clear Martin hadn't killed her. He sued me. And that's when a rival podcast did a big segment on the whole thing, including how Martin was out of state the day the mother died in the fall down the stairs. They crucified me. Within two weeks, I was cancelled. My book deal got dropped, advertisers pulled out of my podcast, my subscribers cancelled in droves. Maybe I deserved it. Who knows? My ma told me I was getting too big for my britches not a week before the whole thing went down. Guess she was right.

"But that's why I need to make some headway on Elliot's disappearance. This is the case that's going to bring me back from the dead. It's the longest unsolved missing person case in the county. If I could crack this one..." He gazed toward Elliot's missing person flier, his eyes gleaming.

"Why are you so desperate to get inside my dad's house? What does that have to do with finding Elliot Thacker?"

27

Nettie

"What's goin' on here, doll?"

Nettie winced when Tabby touched her upper arm, tender and bruised. When she looked at it, the outlines of Nathaniel's fingers remained. "Oh, it's nothin'. Bumped into the doorframe."

"Ain't ever seen a doorframe with five fingers on it." Tabby put her hands on her hips.

"It's nothin', Tabs, let's get this done."

As Nettie followed Tabby to the van, she thought of the night before. She'd woken again to an empty bed and couldn't find Nathaniel. After checking on Celeste and Adam, she'd walked outside and startled Nathaniel on the cordless phone. He'd jumped and grabbed her hard before realizing it was only Nettie. When she'd asked who he was talking to, he claimed it was a fellow teacher at school.

Nettie had lain awake most of the night, watching shadows cast by the moonlight on the ceiling and trying to imagine what teacher at school he'd be talking to after midnight.

The house was rundown, and as Tabby pulled into the dirt driveway, a prickle of unease lifted the hairs on Nettie's neck.

"Deputy said this guy's got ten dogs at least in there. Poor animals. Apparently half of 'em looked starved." Tabby reached for her door handle, but Nettie put a hand on her arm.

"Not yet."

"What is it? You got one of those funny feelings?"

"Mmm-hmm." Nettie stared at the front door. No one opened it and yet she sensed a person just behind it, watching them. "Back up. There's someone in that house."

"The sheriff said they hauled the guy who lives here off to jail. I hate to leave all those animals."

"So do I, but there's someone in there."

Tabby frowned, put the van in reverse and backed down the driveway.

At the office, Nettie called the sheriff, Theon Flores. "Hi, Theon. I wanted to ask about a house we were sent out to today. According to your deputy, there's a whole mess of dogs in the house that need to be taken out. House is listed as empty, but when we went by, someone was inside."

"George Newton's the owner," Theon said. "And he's locked up in county. No way Newton will post bail. Barely has a pot to piss in as it is."

"Does he have a son? Anyone else who might live there?"

"He's got a brother who blows through now and then. Brice. Meaner than a two-headed snake."

"He might be at George's house. We can't go get those animals on our own."

"All right. I'll round up a deputy to come by and go with ya."

It was after six when Nettie got home. They'd managed to return to Newton's now empty house and rescued fifteen dogs, some of them so emaciated they could barely walk. The day had been draining, and she went straight upstairs to run a bath.

Nettie paused in the master bedroom. She'd made the bed that morning, smoothed the khaki-colored comforter to the edges and propped the pillows at the top. The bed was made, but now appeared rumpled, as if someone had lain on it. A slight indent in one of the pillows, a ripple across the center of the bedspread.

Nettie walked downstairs. Adam was asleep in the playpen. Celeste sat on the couch watching *Fraggle Rock*.

"Everything go okay when you picked them up from daycare?" Nettie asked Nathaniel, who stood in the kitchen frying ground beef.

"No issues. How was your day?"

"Stressful. We had to rescue a houseful of neglected dogs."

Nathaniel nodded, but didn't ask for details. "I'm making spaghetti."

"Smells good." She started from the kitchen and paused. "Did you come home today?"

He glanced at her. "No. Why?"

"The bed looks weird, like someone slept on it."

Nathaniel shrugged. "I probably sat on it this morning to put my socks on."

Nettie frowned and thought back to that morning. She'd made the bed after Nathaniel had left for school, hadn't she?

"Are you worried someone is breaking in now and taking naps in our bed?" It was a joke, but his tone held an underlying edge.

"No. It's just...weird. I'm going to have a bath."

"Make sure to clean your hair out of the tub," he said, shuddering. "I hate when it clogs up the drain."

The phone rang, and Nettie hurried to answer it. Both Celeste and Adam had fallen asleep, and she didn't want the ringing to wake them. Adam was teething and had been a grump all day. Celeste, apparently sensitive to the moodiness in the house, had followed suit by flinging her SpaghettiOs across the kitchen at lunchtime.

"Hello?" Nettie answered.

"It's about time I hear your voice," Luanne laughed. "I feel like we've been playing phone tag for a month."

Nettie softened into the couch and smiled. "Maybe longer than that."

"No. Really? Gosh. I've been busier than a bee in a flower shop. Ugh! I can't believe I just said that, taken straight from my grandmother's mouth." She snorted. "I have though. I've been dating Troy. I told you about him, right?"

"The plumber?"

"Yes. Exactly. But not one of those beer-bellied plumbers with a mile of butt crack sticking out of his pants. This guy is hot. He could be in one of those working man calendars, I swear. Anyway, that was going pretty well until Ryan started work at the bank and asked me on a date. He's a mortgage guy and, I kid you not, he looks just like David Cassidy from the *Partridge Family*. Remember how I had the biggest crush on him?"

Nettie watched a boat pass by on the lake outside. Sunlight filtered through the open blinds and made the room warm. She yawned, tried to stifle it with her hand.

"I heard that," Luanne said. "Have I bored you to sleep already?"

"Not at all. I haven't been sleeping great."

"How come? The baby? Is Adam keeping you up?"

Nettie thought of the previous nights. Waking up oddly disoriented, disjointed voices in the house, Nathaniel rarely in bed beside her. "No. He's been okay. It's more...do you remember I told you Nathaniel hired a babysitter, a girl from the high school?"

"Yeah."

"Well...she comes over a lot."

"Huh. I'd think that'd make you less tired, having help with the kids. What aren't you telling me?"

"I don't know, to be honest. I don't want to jump to conclusions, but the girl, Hannah, she's very comfortable with Nathaniel, almost...flirty."

"Get rid of her."

Nettie laughed.

"I'm dead serious, Nettie. A sixteen-year-old girl coming on to your husband is not good. Kick her to the curb."

"It's not that simple."

"Why not?"

Nettie chewed her bottom lip. "I don't think he'd let me."

Luanne didn't speak, and Nettie imagined her sitting in her apartment, ankles crossed on the coffee table, traffic from Morgantown passing on the street outside. Her best friend was living a whole other life, juggling two boyfriends, going on dates, working at a bank. Nettie suddenly felt as if she lived a reality that was light years away. The Moon Lake house was beautiful, but also isolated, its own secret little world.

"Do you think he's sleeping with her?" Luanne, never one to mince words, asked.

The question did not startle Nettie so much as cause an

instant sharp nausea to roll through her stomach. She sat up and clenched her eyes shut.

"Nettie?"

"No...I mean...of course not. No. Never. He'd never do something like that. She's a student, practically a child."

"She's sixteen," Luanne said, a bit more gently now. "Listen, why don't you come here for a weekend? Get out of there for a couple days. You need a break. Nathaniel can watch the kids and—"

"She'll be here if I leave. She'll be here alone with them."

Behind Nettie, the front door opened.

"Nathaniel is just getting home. Let me call you back."

"Nettie—"

Before Luanne could finish, Nettie hung up the phone.

28

———

Spencer picked up a coffee mug, started to take a drink, then squinted into the cup and made a face. "Old yogurt. Or ice cream." He shuddered and set the cup back on his desk. "Call it a hunch. And while we're on hunches, I have a question for you, Celeste. What brought you back to West Virginia in search of your mother now? Hmm...? I think you have a story. I have a nose for these things. I'm getting murder house energy from you."

She raised an eyebrow, glancing again at the mug she was sure would tumble sideways at any moment. "Murder house energy?"

"Yeah. You know, innocent Cape Cod on the outside, but filled with blood-splattered walls and a sinister backstory. Basically, another way to say layers, more going on than meets the eye."

"That's a disturbing way to phrase it."

He grinned. "It's true though, right? What are you, thirty? And you're just now coming back to West Virginia to find your mom? What's up with that?"

"I'm thirty-five, thirty-six in November, and...well..." She stared again at the mug, could suddenly relate to it sitting there, the mess pushing ever closer, ready to tip it off the edge. "It's a long story."

"I love those."

"I'm going through a divorce."

"Ah, I see. I've been through two myself. Is that it? I don't think that's it."

"I nearly died last year. I was hit by a car, an SUV."

"Crikey. And that got you pondering the past? About the mother who left?"

"Sort of." She couldn't tell him about Katie Ellis and Joanna, and finally River. She couldn't tell him about the ghosts and the nightmares and knowing things she shouldn't know, knowing things that got people killed, like Dee Simmons, who had been murdered after Celeste's premonitions sent her into the truck of her killer. All of that had to stay separate, in its own little room, and the closer stuff—Jonathan and Darlene, the affairs, the search warrants—that too had a little room. And another for the Dear Celeste letters piling up and another for all those West Virginia memories that she both wanted to surface and wanted to stay buried.

"All right," he said. "I get it. You're a fortress with no drawbridge, eh? I'm not afraid to swim the moat. I see you don't trust me and that's okay. Let me make it a little easier. Let me tell you what I found out about your mom."

Celeste sat forward, braced for the news. Maybe Nettie had used her social security number, had been living a new life somewhere else.

"Last legal job that I could find was at the animal control right here in Kingwood. No traceable job since that point. No criminal record. No driving infractions. She attended two years at West Virginia University back in the late seventies. Major was animal science. I've got her childhood address. She grew up in Davis, West Virginia, a little town about forty miles from here. Feel like taking a road trip?"

Celeste frowned. "You found her home address?"

"Yep, and a few other things, and I'm familiar with Davis. I dated a girl from there. I can drive. Be your tour guide."

Celeste stared at him. She didn't have any reason not to trust him. "Okay. But tomorrow. I have something I want to do today."

* * *

The animal control building was plain and squat. Its cinderblock walls were beige. A wooden sign that read 'County Animal Control' marked the entrance. A tattered American flag hung from a tall metal pole rustling in the morning breeze. A chain-link kennel enclosure sprawled to one side of the building. Two large dogs, both pitbull mixes, watched Celeste as she strode to the front door.

The inside was dimly lit, with a flickering fluorescent light buzzing overhead. Outdated flyers for spay-and-neuter programs and lost pet notices, their edges curling and yellowed, adorned a large board. The office smelled of wet dog and disinfectant. This was the place her mother had worked.

A narrow counter divided the small lobby from the back area, where muffled animal sounds, barks and the mewing of cats, drifted out. A man stood behind the counter holding a small watery-eyed Chihuahua, its once-dark muzzle flecked with gray.

"Help ya with something?" he asked. "Two-for-one special on cats today. Not kittens, only cats."

"Actually, I'm looking for someone who used to work here. Maybe she still does. Tabitha?"

"Tabby Cat!" he said, grinning. "She hasn't worked here in ten years. Still comes in now and again to socialize the animals, though."

"Any idea where I could find her?"

"At her house, I reckon."

"And where is that?"

He patted the head of the little dog, which closed its eyes. "May I ask why you're looking for her?"

"Yes. She worked with my mom, here actually, a long time ago."

"Huh. And who's your mom?"

"Nettie Harrington."

He stared at her blankly. "Never heard of her. Must have been before my time. Tabby lives on Old Mill Road. Head east out front here." He pointed toward the door she'd just walked through. "Drive for about five miles. Take a left on Taylor Pass. Down another mile, mile and a half. Right on Old Mill. Little yellow house. She's got a mailbox shaped like a rooster. Can't miss it."

Celeste didn't know if she'd find Tabitha at home, but figured it was worth a try. She slowed the truck to a crawl on Old Mill Road, searching for the rooster mailbox. She found it just under two miles down on the left. It sat at the end of a short gravel driveway. The yellow house behind it was worn, but well kept. Purple flowers bloomed in large bushes on either side of the front stoop.

Celeste walked up to the front door and knocked. A minute later, a woman appeared. She was short and slender, her thin frame swimming in a pink t-shirt and baggy gray shorts. She smiled at Celeste and searched her face as if trying to place her.

"Are you Tabitha?" Celeste asked.

"You found her. What can I do for you?"

"My name is Celeste..." She started to say Cleary, but suddenly didn't want to. "Harrington. I think you used to work with my mom, Nettie."

Tabitha's mouth fell open. Her eyes brimmed with tears. "Good heavens, I knew you looked familiar. You're Nettie's girl." Tabitha grabbed Celeste and pulled her into a hug. "Lord almighty, you're purdy! And you're a spittin' image of your mama too."

"It's good to meet you, Tabitha," Celeste said, flushed from the stranger's hug.

"Tabby, please. Only one who ever called me Tabitha was mean old Miss Boyles from second grade and when she spoke it, she had a face on her like she ate a spoonful of rotten fish. And you're Celeste, but you know how I remember you? As Ceecee. That's what your mama called you. Little Ceecee, and Adam was Duckie because he followed your mama and you like a baby duck the second he started crawling. Come on. Get in here. Let's catch up."

Celeste followed Tabby into the house, down a hall filled with paintings of dogs and cats, and into a sunny kitchen with daisy wallpaper. "Have a seat." Tabby pointed at a round table with four chairs. "What can I get ya? Sweet tea? Ice water?"

"Nothing for me. Thank you."

"Oh, come on now. That sun is declaring war on us today. You need to stay hydrated."

"Water then. Thank you."

Tabby filled them each a glass of ice water. Her cups were painted in little blue kittens.

"You worked with my mom at the animal control?"

"I surely did," Tabby said, staring at Celeste as if she'd never seen anything quite like her. "And your mama was just the sweetest thing. My gosh, she had a way with God's four-legged critters. I once watched her lure a pitbull that had been beaten every way but Sunday and left to die chained to this post out in the mountains. That dog was as scared as a shadow at sunrise and spitting mad if you got near him. Nettie went out there three straight days and sat a little way off and tossed chicken to that dog and talked to him, sang to him. By the end of the third day, he was eatin' out of her hand. A week after he came to the shelter, he was sittin' in her lap. I'm tellin' you she was so special."

"Do you have any idea where she's at?"

Tabby's eyes popped wide. "No. I haven't seen her since... well, not for a very long time. When did you last see her?"

"She left when I was three. I barely remember her."

Tabby's face drained of color. She picked up a scarf on the table, a knitting needle dangling from the fabric. "I knew it," she muttered.

"You knew what?"

Tabby, frazzled, jabbed the long needle into the fabric. "I knew something terrible happened. When she didn't come back to work..." She blinked, eyes welling with tears. She set down her knitting and pressed her fingertips against her closed eyelids.

"My dad said she left us. That she had a mental breakdown and left."

Tabby's eyes popped open.

"Did she ever confide in you she was thinking of leaving?" Celeste asked.

"Of course not. On account of she ain't ever planned to leave."

"What does that mean?"

"It means that if she did pack up and leave, which I find near to impossible to believe, it happened on the spot. Prolly walked in on 'em, I reckon. But if you want my gut on this one, and I said it back then just as I'm sayin' it now, your mama became inconvenient for your daddy. And us women know that nobody is more likely to disappear than an inconvenient woman."

"Wait, walked in on who?"

"Who else? Your dad and his little schoolgirl."

29

"Your mama never picked up her last check, never came in to collect her stuff," Tabby continued. "Wasn't worth much, but your ma had this coffee mug she'd bought at some garage sale she just loved. I still have it, believe it or not. I've moved twice since your mama went missing and both times, I didn't blink an eye at takin' that mug with me. You sit tight." Tabby stood, set her knitting on the table, and moved to the cupboard.

She handed Celeste a white mug rimmed in gold. In the crackled image, a woman in an old-fashioned dress with cascading hair leaned over a flowered balcony towards the man climbing the trellis below. In gold calligraphy, Celeste read *Romeo and Juliet*.

Celeste turned the mug in her hands. Romeo. The name she'd given to her new kitten.

"You keep that," Tabby said.

Celeste stared for another moment at the image, her heart heavy at the two lovers staring in adoration at one another. "You think my mom caught my dad and Hannah? That they were having an affair?"

"Yes. I do. Nettie was protective of your dad and she was not the kind of woman to speak ill of her man. In the beginning when that girl showed up, Nettie talked about how kind it was for Nathaniel to help her—broken home and all that—but my Spidey sense went up straight away. I could tell your mama was uneasy about the whole charade, but didn't want to overreact.

"And at first, your ma appreciated having her around. The job at animal control wasn't full time. The city didn't have the budget for that, which was fine by me and Nettie. She had two babies at home and a house to keep up, a husband to feed. But she also wanted to go back to school and get her vet's degree. So, Hannah coming into the picture was a blessing for all of about two weeks."

"And then what?"

"And then Nettie started feeling strange about Hannah's relationship with your daddy. They were a bit too comfortable with one another."

"You think she found them in bed and left us?"

"No. I don't think that," Tabby said, fixing her with a serious look. "Maybe a week before your daddy called to say she'd taken off, your mama got in a bad accident. And I'll tell it to ya straight. She thought someone tried to run her off the road. Her truck got totaled and, frankly, she was lucky to have lived. She hurt her ankle pretty bad. It swelled right up. They put her in one of those little boot things, so she was off work."

"Someone ran her off the road? Who?"

"That's the mystery. She didn't know. Somebody in a big ol' pickup. She was scared, and she half-thought it mighta been one of the Newton boys. George or Brice. We'd taken a whole mess of George's animals after the sheriff got called for neglect. George got arrested and his brother, Brice, started making threats on Nettie."

Celeste took out her notebook and wrote their names down

—Brice and George Newton. "Do the brothers still live in Kingwood?"

"Beats me. I've been out of the loop for eons. Nettie told the sheriff about the accident, I do know that. A week or so went by and outta the blue, your daddy telephoned the office and said, 'Nettie left me.' I said, 'Come again?' I'd sooner have believed a frog sprouted feathers than Nettie walked out on your dad. Then he said, 'She left me and the kids.' I was reeling around the office like I just drunk a bottle of tequila. I could not believe it.

"I figured she walked in on him and that girl and took off. I was thinking a day or two would go by and she'd be back. She'd pack up you and your brother and tell Nathaniel to take a flying leap. I even got my guest room all ready. Washed the sheets, put some fresh flowers on the dresser. I was thinkin' she'd need a place and anything I could do to brighten her spirits, because Lord knew she was gonna be heartbroken. But then days went by and a week. I called your daddy. 'Nope, she's still not back.' And then I started to get this sinking feeling, this feeling that something terrible had happened."

"Did anyone tell the police?"

"I called your daddy every few days and when two weeks had passed, I said, 'You need to report her missing,' and he said, 'She called me last night, she's off with friends,' said she told him it's his turn to know what's it like to take care of a house and two little kids. I wanted to believe him, but I didn't. So, I tried calling the sheriff myself.

"But see, it was an election year, and the sheriff we'd had for years, Theon Flores, who Nettie and I both knew personally on account of our dealings with the animals, lost his post a few weeks after your mama went missing. I heard later it was his choice, really. His mother was sick out in Texas and he wanted to be with her. Put the word out in town that he backed Jerome Shoup, this other guy who'd been a deputy in another county.

Well, wouldn't you know that guy, Shoup, was a close friend of your daddy's? Your daddy coached his daughter, who was workin' on a scholarship to some big university. Let's just say when I dropped a hint or two that I thought somethin' bad mighta happened to your mama, he looked at me like I was nuttier than squirrel shit.

"It was months before Theon came back from Texas. Ended up having to bury his mama. I went right over to his house and told him, 'Nettie's gone missin' and I think...well, I think something happened and that Coach Harrington had a hand in whatever it was.' He listened to me, said he'd talk to the new sheriff and to your dad."

"And then what happened?"

"Not a darn tootin' thing. Crickets. I finally went back over to his place and he gave me the brushoff, said Nettie had been in touch with your dad, she'd left of her own free will, was a grown woman, and that was that."

"You never heard from her again?"

"Never."

"Did she have friends in town? Anyone else who she might have contacted?"

Tabby shook her head. "When she and your daddy moved here, she was pregnant with you. She didn't have a whole lot of time to make friends and, to be frank with ya, she preferred animals to most of the folks she met. Now your daddy had all kinds of friends being a teacher and a coach, but it was different for your mama. I know she had a girlfriend up in Morgantown, she talked about her now and then, but I couldn't tell you her name."

"Luanne?" Celeste thought about the birthday invitation.

Tabby nodded slowly. "I think so. Yeah. That name rings a bell."

"Do you have any idea where she'd go if she did leave? Family? Her parents? A sibling?"

Tabby's face fell. "I don't know much about your mama's life before Kingwood, but both her parents were gone, and I never got a real fuzzy feeling when she did talk about them. I think things at home were less than peachy. There was an aunt she mentioned once, but"—Tabby shook her head—"I couldn't tell ya a thing about her. She was somewhere in West Virginia, maybe back by your mama's hometown. I wish I could offer ya more, honey. I really do."

"Okay. Well, thanks, Tabby. Can I have your phone number? Just in case I have other questions."

"You absolutely can." Tabby stood and pulled a little notebook from a kitchen drawer. She scrawled her name and number on it and handed it to Celeste. "You find anything out, you call me or just stop by. I'm retired now, so I'm always up for a visit."

Celeste drove to her childhood home and parked the truck. She stared at the house through the windshield. The windows were dark, the sun glinting off the glass.

Since her arrival days before, the house had felt heavy, weighted with the mystery of Celeste's childhood and the abandonment by her mother. Now it felt unbelievably sad. Her father had been having an affair with a student, a child. What had that felt like for Nettie? Watching the man she loved, whom she'd staked her future on, turn his attention to a younger, newer model? Rage at her father for his betrayal burned hot beneath her skin. Celeste wanted to call him, scream into his ear that she knew what he'd done to drive their mother away.

She climbed from the truck and walked to the house. The humidity had become oppressive. Tabby had been right. It was a scorcher. Beyond the house, the lake reflected an unsettling calm. Seconds later, the quiet was shattered when a speedboat roared by on the lake, two children clutching inner tubes behind it.

Celeste entered the house and walked upstairs. She'd spent little time in the master bedroom, but she went there now and began to open drawers in the bureau. They were largely empty. Nettie's stuff, as Celeste had already learned, had been crammed into boxes and locked in the spare bedroom—out of sight, out of mind. Apparently, Nathaniel had wanted a clean slate when he moved his teenaged girlfriend into the house, and he *had* moved her in. Celeste was positive about that.

More memories had begun to surface. Memories of Hannah and her dad sitting at the kitchen table eating buttered saltine crackers, something Celeste's dad still liked and that Jonathan had once called disgusting. Memories of Hannah watching television and the sense that Celeste and Adam were not allowed to make a sound when her shows were on.

There was a Christmas memory of Hannah screaming with glee when she opened a little box wrapped in red and green striped paper. A gold bracelet lay inside.

And then there was the time Hannah intentionally dropped an expensive glass vase and blamed it on Celeste. Celeste had stood in the kitchen sobbing, her dad berating her while Hannah, a glint of evil glee in her eyes, made a show of sweeping the glass into a dustpan.

No wonder Celeste had blocked it out. Her loving mother had been replaced by a teenager who hated her. The house seemed pregnant with the pain it had witnessed—Nettie's pain, Celeste's and Adam's. Perhaps the house had had its own pain as it watched the once-happy family fracture and break apart.

Next to a large closet with sliding mirrored doors stood a tall bureau. Trophies lined the top. They were her dad's high school basketball trophies. Celeste seized one and hurled it at the full-length mirror. The glass cracked and several pieces fell away. For a moment, in the undulating glass, Celeste glimpsed a woman behind her.

Her mother, Nettie, pale and translucent, her eyes dark pits of sorrow. Her hair hung in wet strands, and her lips moved, though no sound came out.

Celeste spun around and faced the empty room.

"Mom?" she whispered.

She turned back to the glass, searched the broken shards for a glimpse of the woman who'd been there seconds before.

There was none.

30

Harris called during Celeste's drive to Spencer's house the following morning. She'd stopped at a gas station to buy a cup of to-go coffee and had just climbed back in her truck when the phone rang.

"Hi," she answered.

"Hey. Just checking in. Everything all right?"

"That's one way to put it."

"Why? What's happened? Has Jonathan made contact?"

"No. I mean...well, he's probably emailed, but I haven't checked it. I've just been finding out stuff about my dad. It's been a lot."

"What kind of stuff?"

"Oh, that he was cheating on my mom with a teenaged student."

Harris didn't speak for a moment. "That's unfortunate."

"Yeah."

"Do you think that's why she left?"

"I'm starting to think she didn't leave."

"Meaning what? That she took her own life? Was killed?"

"I don't know. I met a woman who used to work with my mom and she said my dad wanted her out of the picture. That she'd become inconvenient."

Harris blew out a breath. "Did the police ever investigate him?"

"No. He never even filed a missing person's report."

"You're kidding me."

Celeste turned onto Spencer's road. "I have to go. I'm meeting this podcaster today and we're going to visit the place my mom grew up."

"A podcaster, huh? What's his podcast about?"

"True crime. He's been doing a show about this little boy who disappeared by Moon Lake. Elliot Thacker." Celeste almost added that she'd been seeing Elliot, was convinced he was haunting her.

"So how can the podcaster help?"

"Well, he's lived here for a long time, has a lot of connections, though some of those have gotten frayed. Apparently, he accused an innocent person of murder on his podcast, and the community turned on him. This is his way of coming back from the dead, as he calls it. Anyway, he found out where my mom grew up and offered to drive, so—"

"You trust this guy?"

"I'm trying."

"It never hurts to err on the side of caution."

"Thanks, Harris."

"If you have time, call me tonight," he said. "I want to hear more about what's going on with your mom. I'll be with the others—the Memento Mori group."

"Lovely. I can share my childhood trauma with the whole gang."

He chuckled. "I'm happy to step away so we can talk in private."

Spencer wasn't ready. Celeste stood on his stoop and rang the doorbell three times before he finally jerked the door open, bleary-eyed, wearing flannel pajama pants and a rumpled Dogman t-shirt.

"Alarm clocks," he grumbled. "Worthless. Give me five minutes." He waved her in.

Celeste reluctantly stepped back into the madness of Spencer's living room. She eyed his bookshelf again, scanning the titles, then stepped closer to the coffee table where new papers had appeared, papers with notes scrawled about her mother: Nettie Harrington.

He raced through the room a moment later, a new t-shirt half on, his chest hair flaked with what looked like food crumbs. A steady beep sounded in the kitchen. "Coffee's done. Want a cup?"

"No, I got some on the way." Celeste stared at the notes. They were as chaotic as everything else in Spencer's house and barely legible.

Nettie's date of birth was listed, and the approximate date she'd left the family. There was a crudely drawn map of Moon Lake with an X where Celeste's childhood home was. She saw Elliot's name written in several notes as well.

Spencer bustled back through the room, a cup of coffee sloshing in one hand. "Two minutes," he told her.

Through a tiny square of glass not covered on the coffee table, Celeste saw two glowing eyes peering up at her as she strained toward Spencer's notes. She jumped, startled.

The cat, Noodle, emerged from beneath the coffee table and coiled around her legs.

"Good morning, Noodle." She ran her hand down his back. "Thanks for the jumpstart."

The cat purred and flopped on his side.

"Ready to rumble?" Spencer careened from his office, a notebook rolled in one hand. The t-shirt he'd put on read *I Work Hard so My Cat Can Have a Better Life.*

Celeste gave Noodle a final tummy pat and stood. "I'm ready."

"This is where she grew up?" Celeste's heart sank when Spencer turned into the old trailer park. The sign at the entrance read *Welcome to Dogwood Estates,* though most of the paint from the sign had peeled away.

The unrelenting sun highlighted every rusted panel and sagging roof on the rows of drab trailers. Celeste had seen plenty of trailer parks, but this one conjured a flurry of thoughts—despair, destitution, darkness. Junk lay strewn on most of the scorched lawns. Laundry flapped limply on lines stretched between skeletal trees.

Celeste and Spencer climbed from his van. The air was thick with humidity and sticky like syrup.

"According to my research, your ma lived in that one there. 209 Magnolia."

The once-white trailer was mostly gray. Its roof had been patched with mismatched pieces of metal and duct tape. A sagging porch held an assortment of cracked lawn chairs and empty beer bottles.

"Who lives there now?" she asked.

"Vacant, according to the Dogwood Estates website."

"I can't imagine why," Celeste murmured.

"Looks like a place someone might want to leave behind," Spencer said.

Not for the first time, Celeste questioned why she'd felt

compelled to come to this place, to dig up her mother's past. Nettie had worked hard to escape this reality. Maybe she'd hoped her children would never know it even existed.

They climbed back into Spencer's van and Celeste was grateful for the rush of icy air.

Spencer handed her his notebook. "Pulled an all-nighter researching your mom. Not much of an online footprint, but if you know where to look, you can find a few things."

Celeste opened the notebook to find a stack of folded printed sheets of paper. The first was an article about a drunk driving death.

"That was your granddad," Spencer said. "Jerry Caldwell."

The article was short. *Jerry Caldwell died Friday after wrapping his pickup truck around a tree at the corner of Forest and Kent Roads in Tucker County. Alcohol is believed to be a factor. There were no other vehicles involved in the crash.*

"This was my mom's dad?"

"Yep."

"She would have been..."

"Thirteen," Spencer finished for her.

The next was an obituary for Gina Caldwell.

Gina Caldwell, 38, of Davis, West Virginia, died unexpectedly Saturday.

She is survived by her daughter Nettie Caldwell. She is preceded in death by her husband Jerry Caldwell and her parents.

There are no services scheduled at this time.

Gina's death had come four years after Jerry's. Nettie had lost both her parents while she was still a teenager.

"I found an article that didn't name her, but reported death by drug overdose in the Dogwood Estates on the same day Gina died. I'm guessing that was her," Spencer said.

"A drug overdose," Celeste murmured.

"Yep. I don't get the feeling your mom was living the dream, that's for sure."

Celeste's eyes pricked with tears as Spencer drove out of the dreary trailer park.

"Where to now?" she asked, forcing the tremble from her voice.

"I found a record for an old address for Grant and Bianca Harrington. Any chance those are your dad's parents?"

"That's them," Celeste confirmed. "My grandfather died a few years ago. Bianca lives in Florida, not far from my dad."

"I saw that," Spencer said. "I figured it was the same Harringtons."

Celeste thought of Grant and Bianca. They were grandparents in name only. They'd never been kind to Celeste or Adam. The few times their grandkids had visited, the trips had been awkward. Grant had grilled Adam about his grades, his interest in art rather than sports. Bianca had criticized everything about Celeste, from the books she read to the color of her backpack. Celeste hadn't seen her grandparents since her wedding to Jonathan. When her grandfather had died, she'd intended to go to the funeral, but her grandmother had called her and said it was a small affair and only she and Celeste's dad would be in attendance.

"I've never been close with them," Celeste admitted.

"No? I'm close with my grandparents on my mom's side. My dad's parents are both dead and have been since I was a kid, so..." He shrugged. "But my mom's mom, Gerdie, she could get a grandmother of the year award. Still bakes me a tray of cookies for every holiday, sends me chocolate-dipped strawberries on Valentine's Day, even knitted a sweater for Noodles this last Christmas." He chuckled. "That woman's got a heart of gold."

They drove for several minutes in silence. Celeste watched the steep slope of trees.

"Do you know a woman named Hannah Hawley?" Celeste asked.

Spencer flipped on his blinker, turned down the winding mountain road. "Can't say the name's familiar. Who is she?"

"She dated my dad after my mom left. She was…a student of his at the high school."

Spencer whistled. "Cradle robber, huh?"

Celeste shifted uncomfortably, her hip suddenly grumbling. She pressed her fingers hard into the bone. "She lived with us at the Moon Lake house. I'd like to talk to her. Find out what she knows about my mom."

"I'll do some digging," Spencer offered.

***

The Harringtons' former home in Davis was a massive mountainside chalet with floor-to-ceiling windows and a wraparound deck. A three-car garage faced the road. An Escalade and a shiny yellow Corvette were parked in the driveway.

Spencer slowed to a stop. "I think it's safe to say your mom married up."

Celeste thought of her father. A cold, emotionally distant man who was a mirror of his mother. A man who'd begun an affair while Nettie was home raising two young children. And yet Tabby had described how protective Nettie was of Nathaniel, how she envisioned him as a sort of Romeo.

Had the fear of returning to her former life blinded Nettie to Nathaniel's true nature? Had she been so desperate to escape the trailer park she'd ignored the signs that she'd made a terrible mistake in marrying him?

"We can drive by the high school where your mom went? Check out the library? I'd bet money they have yearbook pictures of both your parents."

Celeste shook her head. "Let's go back to Kingwood. I've seen enough."

Celeste watched the trees whiz by. Her mother had grown

up in a dilapidated trailer park with a mother addicted to drugs. She'd lost her father to drunk driving at thirteen, her mother to drugs at seventeen. No wonder she'd fallen so hard for Nathaniel—her knight in shining armor, her ticket to freedom.

31

N ettie

"Got something for us, Sheriff?" Nettie asked when Theon Flores walked into the animal control.

He stopped at the counter, hands shoved in his pockets. "Not exactly. Had a gal come in this morning who was at Skinny's Tavern last night and overheard Brice Newton running his mouth about whoever took all his brother's animals. Guess he was pretty fixated on you, Nettie. Seems to think you masterminded the whole thing. Probably just blowin' off steam, but I wanted you to be aware just the same."

"Why is he focused on me?" Nettie asked. A flicker of discomfort moved through her as she thought of visiting the Newton property days before. She'd felt a presence in the house, a malicious one, and wondered if it had been Brice Newton.

"Again," Theon assured her, "it's likely nothing to lose sleep over. I'm trying to track him down, make sure he realizes we're aware of what he's saying."

"Thanks for letting me know, Theon."

"You bet. Give me a call if anything feels off, okay?"

"I will."

"Nettie?"

Nettie looked up from the shelves of crackers she'd been considering.

"Keith? My gosh, it's been..." She shook her head. He stepped forward and hugged her, caught her off guard. He smelled like he'd always smelled—pine woods and grass—and the scent pushed her back into high school, evenings stretched out on slabs of rock still hot from baking in the sun, staring at the stars, talking about getting out of Davis.

"Do you live in Kingwood?" he asked.

"I do. We have a house on Moon Lake."

He whistled. "Living on a lake, huh? Moving up in the world."

"How come you're in town?"

"My job brought me to Kingwood for the month. I've been working as a lineman for the last six years."

"A good fit. You always could scamper right up the face of a rock like some kind of mountain goat."

He laughed. "It does come in handy now and then. How about you, Net? I swear I heard through the grapevine you got hitched."

She nodded, rubbed her thumb over her heart-shaped diamond ring. "Yeah. Nathaniel Harrington. He's a teacher here in Kingwood and coaches the girls' basketball team."

"A teacher, huh? You basically married the Man."

She smiled. "All adults were the Man when we were young.

Sort of narrows the dating pool after a certain age. How about you? Married? Kids?"

"No such luck. Been busy workin' and daydreaming about the one who got away." He winked at her.

"Very funny."

He shrugged. "Funny as a heart attack. You want to grab a soda?"

"A soda? That stuff rots your teeth."

He groaned. "You've even become the Man!" He clutched his heart.

"Shut up," she laughed, shoving him playfully. "You're making a scene."

"Not a scene, another nail in the coffin of young, rebellious Nettie Mae Caldwell."

"Young, rebellious Nettie Mae Caldwell has two kids and a job."

"Two kids." He whistled. "You've been busy."

"Good God, Keith."

"Come on, you can have coffee or tea or whatever grownups drink."

She rolled her eyes. "Fine. But I can only stay about fifteen minutes. I have a babysitter at home and..." She thought of Hannah alone at her house, how Nathaniel would come home soon.

They walked across the parking lot to a deli.

"Coffee, huh?" Keith said after Nettie ordered. "I remember the time you had a cup of that at my ma's house and spit it all over the table. Said it tasted like pig shit."

Nettie laughed and flushed at the memory of Keith's mom shaking her head in irritation and flinging a rag at Nettie to wipe up the mess she'd made. "In my defense, it was more chicory root than coffee."

He tapped his cup of Mountain Dew. "That's why I stick with the Dew. Ain't nobody slippin' chicory root in here."

She eyed the cup and frowned. "I doubt we can even pronounce what they're slipping in there."

"So catch me up. Two kids, huh? And you married Nathaniel Harrington! That guy was slicker than a boiled onion."

"Gee, thanks, Keith."

He chuckled and took a sip of soda. "I'm only kidding—half-kidding anyhow. I moved, what, two months after he started school in Davis? Hardly had any time to get to know the guy. Tell me about the kids, then."

Nettie rifled through her bag and found her wallet. She opened it and took out a photo they'd had done months before when JCPenney in Morgantown was running a special on family portraits. She handed Keith the picture. "Celeste and Adam."

"My gosh, they're the cutest critters I've seen lately. Can't say I'm surprised you'd make pretty babies. How old are they?"

"Celeste is three, she'll be four in November, and Adam is one and a half."

"And how about vet school? Still doin' that?"

"I dropped out when I got pregnant with Celeste. I'm working at the animal control here in town. It's a pretty good gig and I figure once the kids are a bit older, I'll go back, get my degree." She didn't mention that Nathaniel did not like the idea of Nettie returning to school. It was expensive, and it'd mean more daycare costs. Still, it had been months since they'd discussed it.

"I'm sorry to hear you had to put it on hold, but I get it. I'm sure you've got your hands full with these two. But you're happy? Things are good?"

Keith locked her with his imploring, earnest eyes. He'd been one of her closest friends in elementary and middle school, but he'd also had a crush on her, a thinly veiled secret she'd known for years. Clem had loved Keith and often joked that someday, Nettie and Keith would have an old-fashioned Appalachian wedding at her property in the woods. As she stared at him now, a part of her wondered why she'd never considered him as more than a friend. He was definitely easy on the eyes. In high school he'd been on the skinny side, but he'd filled out, his shoulders broad, his arms muscled.

"Yeah." Warmth filled her face, and she looked down, tucked a strand of hair behind one ear. "Things are good."

He raised an eyebrow. "Bit of a pause there."

She shrugged and in the back of her mind a hundred dreadful moments from the previous months jostled for her attention. Hannah tossing her long blonde hair and smiling at Nathaniel, the weird hazy nights, the man in town spreading rumors he wanted payback for her taking his brother's dogs.

"It's been a long week," she murmured. "I've had some issues with a couple of guys in town. We took a whole heap of neglected dogs out of this guy's house. The sheriff threw him in jail. His brother is a menace too and apparently has me in his sights."

Keith frowned. "That's no good. Does Nathaniel know? Are you guys armed?"

She thought of Nathaniel's reaction when she'd told him; he'd barely looked up from his newspaper. "Yeah. Nate has a gun in a safe."

"One?"

She laughed. "Remember, he's not a West Virginia native; he didn't get his first gun when he was three."

"I was five. And even so, why don't you have a gun?"

Nettie shook her head. "I never enjoyed shooting and now,

with Celeste and Adam, I don't like the idea of guns in the house. One is fine, but…"

"Nettie." He fixed her with a serious gaze. "I'm not gonna lecture you, because I remember that time you kicked Mr. Ratcliffe in the shins for telling you to brush your hair more…"

Nettie groaned. "He deserved it. That guy was a total asshole."

"Agreed, though you weren't brushing your hair much in those days."

Nettie flicked him.

"But still," he went on. "If I were you, I'd get a concealed permit and a little gun to keep in the glove box."

"I'll think about it."

"Do. And if those guys give you trouble, call me. I'm staying at Sanders Motel until the end of the month. I'll have a talk with 'em."

Nettie laughed. "Who are you? I remember when we spent two hours hiding in a tree because that goon Buster happened to be fishing in the pond we were at."

Keith made a face. "Why do you think I had to hit the gym?" He grinned and flexed his biceps. "Needed to put some weight on my scrawny ass so the Busters of the world would stop kicking it all the time."

Nettie laughed. "I think we could have taken him."

"With wits anyhow."

Nettie glanced at her watch and took a final sip of her coffee. "I've gotta go."

"Don't forget Sanders Motel, Room 107. Call me or stop by." He took her hand, squeezed. "It was good to see you, Nettie."

32

As they drove back to Kingwood, Celeste took out her own notebook, flipped through the pages. "Do you happen to know a George or Brice Newton?"

Spencer, who'd been humming along to *What a Girl Wants* on the radio, turned down the volume and nodded. "I sure do. Bought a generator off of Brice two years ago. Might as well have walked outside and lit my five hundred bucks on fire. Total piece of crap. Never worked once."

"Did you get your money back?"

Spencer scoffed. "I tried once, drove up to his little compound, and he came strollin' out with a shotgun. That was the end of our business dealings. How come? Do you know him?"

Celeste shook her head. "Tabby, the woman my mom used to work with at the animal control, said she and my mom confiscated a bunch of dogs from one of their properties. Apparently, they were pretty mad and not long after my mom got run off the road. That was like a week before she..." The word *left* was on the tip of her tongue. "Disappeared."

"Huh. I don't know George, but Brice is a fiery old goat. Let's pay 'em a visit."

"Are you sure? What if..."

"What if what? He shoots us? I doubt he will."

Spencer parked the van on a dirt lot speckled with two rundown houses, a trailer and four rusted-out vehicles on blocks.

"Welcome to the Newton Manor, where luxury goes to die," Spencer announced.

They climbed from the van. Celeste stared at the dark windows in the houses, wondering if anyone was home.

"Gotta take a quick piss," Spencer told her, shuffling toward the trees.

Before she could argue, a girl emerged from behind the trailer.

"What you want?" The girl eyed Celeste meanly, thumbs hooked in the loops of her dirty jean shorts.

"I'm looking for George Newton, or maybe Brice. Either would be fine."

"Well, if it's George you want, best get you a shovel and dig him up."

"Oh. I'm sorry. How about Brice? Is he around?"

"Uncle Brice!" the girl shouted. "Got some lady here for ya." The girl walked back behind the trailer.

A minute later, a man, Brice apparently, emerged from one of the houses. He had a weathered face with bloodshot eyes crusted at the corners. A scrawny dog followed him, and he kicked a foot out, missing its spindly ribcage by mere centimeters.

Celeste paused, suddenly unsure what they were doing

there. If this guy did have a hand in her mother's disappearance, she was putting herself and Spencer both in danger.

As she started to turn away, Spencer appeared, zipping his fly. She turned back and saw Brice's eyes narrowed on the two of them.

"How you doin', Brice?" Spencer asked.

Brice fixed him with beady brown eyes. "Do I know you?" he demanded.

Spencer shot her a look. "I guess not."

"Do you remember a woman named Nettie Harrington?" Celeste asked.

Brice shifted his attention to her, darting his tongue over his lower lip. Celeste tried to hide the shudder that rolled up her spine.

"Ned Harrington?" He asked, spitting on the ground.

"Nettie," Spencer shouted, though Celeste suspected he'd heard her perfectly fine the first time.

"Nettie...Nettie..." Brice repeated, rolling his eyes high in his head. "Nope."

Shadows moved behind Brice near the second house. An old woman came into focus with one cloudy eye and the other a bright blue. She was there and not there, a shadow flickering, then gone.

"Do you bury your dead here?" Celeste asked.

Spencer shot her a questioning gaze, but she ignored him.

Brice's eyes went wide and then slitted. "Ain't no business of yours what we do here. We own this place. We've owned this place for a hundred years and—"

"Your, umm...your grandmother..." The name Bethel appeared in Celeste's mind. "Bethel..." A stream of images appeared. Bethel hunched over a stove, stirring something in a rusted pot. Bethel thrusting a chicken onto a slab of wood and chopping its head off. Bethel buried in a stark grave, her once headstone cracked and fallen. "She's upset about her head-stone. She wants you to fix it."

Brice's mouth fell open, and he spun to look behind him as if he thought she might be able to see the graves from where she stood. She couldn't, suspected they were tucked deep in the woods on the property.

"And..." Celeste continued, lying now, "she wants you to tell me about my mom, Nettie. If you know anything at all about what happened to her."

Celeste sensed Spencer's eyes boring into her, but she kept her gaze on Brice.

Brice closed his mouth, then opened it again. He pulled a flask from his pants pocket and took a swig, then turned back a second time as if to confirm the graves weren't visible.

"How do you know?" he demanded. "How do know about Bethel's headstone?"

"She showed it to me."

He shook his head, spit again. "Ain't no way. She's been dead fer...a long time."

"Lightning struck a tree, right? And the tree split and fell on her headstone?"

He glared at her, blinked. "This some kind of voodoo you're doin'? Huh. Some backwoods black magic?" He reached into his mouth as if he suspected his teeth might suddenly come loose and fall out.

"No," Celeste said. "We'll leave as soon as you tell me about my mom."

"Your mom. Who was your mom?"

"Nettie Harrington."

"Ain't nothin' to tell."

"Do you remember her?" Celeste asked.

"Sure. Had eyes on her a couple times on account of her stealin' my brother's dogs. He wanted me to rough her up a bit."

"And did you?" Spencer asked, still casting probing glances at Celeste.

"Nah." Brice shook his head. "Too busy in them days. No time for slappin' around some broad. And George had too many goddamned dogs to begin with."

Celeste searched the man's face, tried to gauge if he was lying. She honestly didn't know.

"Okay." She turned to Spencer. "We can go."

33

———

Silence filled the van as they drove away. Spencer glanced at her repeatedly.

"Well?" he said finally.

"Well, what?"

"Oh, come on. Don't leave me hanging in suspense. How'd you do that? That thing with his grandma and the headstone. I couldn't see shit. Could you see those graves?"

Celeste leaned her head against the seat and closed her eyes. "After my accident, the hit-and-run, I came back with some..." She opened her eyes to see Spencer staring at her. "Can you watch the road, please?"

He jerked his gaze forward.

"Heightened abilities, I guess. Sometimes I see people who have died."

"You're shittin' me."

"I'm not."

He grinned and slapped the steering wheel. "Can we do an interview? Get you on *Strictly Supernatural*?"

"No."

"I've interviewed other mediums, Celeste. Lots of 'em. Those episodes are dynamite. People love ghost whisperers."

"I'm not interested, Spencer."

He frowned. "All right. I'll drop it for now. But I'm gonna ask again."

"I don't doubt it," she murmured.

As they drove toward Spencer's house, Celeste spotted a large grocery store ahead.

"Can you pull in there?" She pointed at it. "I need a few things."

"Hobart's General Store isn't as well stocked as you'd like?"

Celeste glanced sidelong at him. "How did you know I've been there?"

He chuckled and parked the van. "And I thought I was a card-carrying member of the tinfoil hat club. Maybe I better give my spot to you. It's the only store within five miles of the lake. Everyone at Moon Lake goes there."

"Oh." It made sense, and she did feel slightly embarrassed at her overreaction, but since arriving in West Virginia, she'd felt on edge and her logical mind had a litany of reasons to feel wary of people. In the previous months, she'd discovered her husband had been having an affair, her co-worker had tried to kill her, and she'd come face to face with two murderers who'd had every intention of silencing Celeste forever. Celeste's faith in humanity had been solidly rocked.

"I know how you can make it up to me." Spencer beamed. "Come on *Strictly Supernatural*."

Celeste rolled her eyes and pushed open the door. "No."

They walked through the double doors into the brightly lit grocery store. A cashier near the end of the row waved. He looked to be in his twenties, thin, with a mop of curly red hair.

"Spence. What's up, man?" the cashier called.

"Not much, Tyler. What's new with you?" Spencer started toward him, then turned back to Celeste. "I'll catch up with you."

Celeste nodded and grabbed a shopping basket. Reading the guides above each aisle, she made a mental list of what she needed: razors, shampoo, and sandwich fixings. At the wall of liquor bottles, she grabbed another bottle of Scotch, though she had plenty at the A-frame and frankly hadn't had much of a stomach for it in the previous days.

She found the aisle for condiments and grabbed a jar of honey mustard. Behind her, someone cleared their throat loudly.

"Oh, sorry." Celeste stepped aside, assuming the person wanted access to the condiments.

"Hello, Celeste," Rose said, when Celeste turned around.

Rose wore a nearly sheer black beach cover-up with a leopard-print bikini beneath. Her hair was pinned up by a black butterfly clip.

"Rose, hi. How are you?"

"Dreadful. I ran out of painkillers." She held up a box of migraine relief tablets. "Figured I might as well restock on wine if I had to drag myself into this godawful town. Looks like you prefer something a little harder."

Celeste's face flushed.

"How's the search going? Find Mommy dearest yet?"

Celeste stiffened. "No."

Rose pressed her finger against a diamond stud piercing in the center of her ear. "Got this damn daith piercing last year to help with the migraines. Hasn't done jack shit and it hurt like hell. That's what I get for listening to Carl." She gestured at Celeste's basket. "Come by if you don't feel like drinking alone."

"Sure," Celeste murmured, though she had no intention of a social visit with the rude neighbor from Moon Lake.

"Adios," Rose said, walking away.

Celeste watched her continue down the aisle.

"I see you've met Rose." Spencer stopped next to Celeste.

Together, they watched the woman sashay around the corner.

"You know her?" Celeste asked.

"I've met her. Interviewed her a couple of times during the podcast, or tried to, anyway. Slippier than an eel, that woman. The first time I showed up at her house for an appointment, I about fell over dead when she opened the door. She looked like a Barbie doll who'd been left on the radiator."

"I don't get it."

"Plastic surgery. Face all"—he wiggled his fingers in front of his face and made a ghoulish expression—"shiny and tight and weird-looking. Anyway, said she had to reschedule for obvious reasons. Next time I come back she's sitting on the porch topless, I kid you not. Just letting 'em blow in the wind. Clearly, she's had some work done in that region too." He gestured at his chest.

Celeste wasn't surprised. Rose did have the look of a woman who'd been modified. "She can't be very old, right? I mean, forties, maybe fifty, though I doubt that."

"Who knows? Might be seventy for all the work she's had done. I wouldn't be surprised to find out she's the Crypt Keeper."

Celeste burst out laughing, a deep, unrestrained laugh that surprised even her.

Spencer grinned, clearly pleased with himself. "See? You get it."

"Want to grab some lunch?" Celeste asked. The laugh had softened something inside of her. She couldn't remember the last time she'd laughed about anything.

"Does a duck have feathers? Of course I want to."

They ate lunch at a pizza place on the outskirts of town. Spencer ordered a strange combination of pickles, bacon, and banana peppers. Celeste opted for the more classic pepperoni.

For an hour, they didn't talk about Celeste's mother and Celeste didn't think about her.

Celeste sipped her lemonade, eyeing Spencer over the top of her glass as he gestured wildly with a slice of pizza in hand. "This guy is convinced the Mothman is coming to his house every night and sitting out on his roof. He finally sets this trap to catch it." Spencer lowered his voice dramatically. "So he buys this huge net and lies in wait on the roof, ends up nodding off, as one does, and wakes up to see those two glowing orange eyes. He jumps up and tosses the net over the Mothman, but suddenly he's hearing these screams and realizes it's his teenaged daughter and her little friend from next door. They'd been sneaking onto the roof to smoke cigarettes every night." Spencer guffawed. "He's seeing the orange embers through his window and thinking it's the Mothman." He shook his head. "I'm telling ya, the stories I've heard."

Celeste laughed and took another bite of her pizza.

"As much as I want to regale you with stories of the Mothman all afternoon, I found out a few other things when I was sleuthing about your mom." Spencer took a notebook out of his worn leather satchel. He thumbed through, found the page he wanted and spread it open on the table.

"Elliot disappeared on October eighth, 1988, a Saturday. Sheila, the grandma, said he left first thing in the morning. She barely saw him. Your dad, Nathaniel Harrington, chemistry teacher at Kingwood High and girls' basketball coach, resigned on Monday, October tenth. He formally withdrew you and your brother from the school the following day, Tuesday the eleventh."

Celeste blinked at the dates, the light mood instantly extinguished.

"Two days," Spencer clarified. "Two days after Elliot Thacker left his grandma's house headed for Moon Lake, your dad resigned. He withdrew you guys from school and, though I can't say when he moved you to Michigan, he started a job at a plastics factory in Michigan in mid-November."

Celeste's mouth had gone dry. She pushed her pizza away. "What...? You think he did something to Elliot?"

"I told you, I pulled an all-nighter, right? Around midnight, I go off on this tangent thinking, what if your brother is actually Elliot? Maybe your real brother died and your dad in his grief kidnapped Elliot and plugged him into your lives." Spencer shook his head. "Can't be. I found your brother online, good-looking guy. Blue eyes, not brown. Looks a lot like your dad, actually, not that I found many pictures of him.

"Anyway, that was a dead end and probably more of a soap opera theory, anyway. You spend enough time listening to Bigfoot stories and you start thinking the craziest notion is the right one. So then I back up and think about what I told you before. Your mom, unhinged, comes back into town and snatches Elliot, thinking it's her Adam. Is it full of holes? Sure. Like she didn't remember her own kid had blue eyes, not brown? But again, we're looking at the insane mother theory, so who gets to decide how crazy she is, right? I've heard stories of women stealing dolls from departments stores because they thought it was their dead baby. Still, it feels like I'm straining at the waistband of belief on that one. My third theory, the most plausible one"—Spencer tapped his fingers on the table and looked at her—"is an accident."

Celeste said nothing, was still reeling from his initial findings. Her dad had fled with his children only days after Elliot Thacker vanished.

"Elliot's playing with you at the house," Spencer explained, "and he drowns in the lake. Your dad panics, hides the body and erases his and your life in West Virginia. Poof. Gone. It's like you've never been there."

"That's crazy. He'd never..." But she didn't finish the sentence. She didn't know the first thing about what her father would never do. Since coming to West Virginia, she'd begun to realize she didn't know the man at all.

"Not only do I think he hid Elliot's body, I think he hid him in the house. An attic, a crawl space, under the deck. Why else hasn't he sold the place? Right? Who holds onto a lake house for decades? He's sitting on half a million dollars, probably more, and just letting it collect dust. Why? You guys struggled a bit after you went to Michigan. For the first ten years, he was barely making ends meet. You got evicted twice."

"How do you know all that?"

"I have my ways. It's not important. Listen." He sat forward in his seat. "I can see it in your eyes, Celeste. You think I might be right, don't you? Are you getting a weird feeling in that house?" His eyes went wide. "Have you seen Elliot's ghost?"

34

———

Nettie

Nettie left the office and drove to the daycare to collect Celeste and Adam. She was running a few minutes late and found herself repeatedly glancing in her rearview mirror. Had the dark pickup behind her followed her from the animal control?

Her grip on the wheel tightened as she turned onto the narrow road leading to the daycare. The truck turned too, maintaining its distance but never fading from view. As the daycare slid into view, Nettie's pulse quickened.

If the person was following her, she didn't want to lead them to her children. But she was also late. She glanced at the clock and eased off the gas. She slowed and rolled onto the shoulder. The truck seemed to slow too and then it picked up speed and roared past her. Nettie turned, tried to get a look at the driver, but they were going too fast. She waited until they disappeared from view, then, shaking, eased back onto the road and pulled into the daycare.

Inside, the front desk was empty. She rang the bell twice before the manager finally appeared, looking annoyed. "Can I help you, Nettie?"

"I'm here for Celeste and Adam," Nettie said, irritated the woman even needed to ask. She'd dropped them off and picked them up dozens of times.

"They've already been collected."

"Excuse me?" Nettie's heart leapt into her throat. "Who picked them up?" Her thoughts instantly veered to Brice Newton. "I didn't say anyone else could pick them up."

"Whoa," the manager said, holding up her hands. "You need to calm down."

"I need to calm down?" Nettie stepped toward her, was ready to grab the woman by her shirt and drag her across the counter.

"It was your babysitter, Hannah. Your husband called and approved it."

Nettie blinked at her, heart hammering in her chest. "I need to use your phone."

The woman narrowed her eyes at Nettie then gestured at the phone on the desk.

Nettie snatched it up and dialed the home phone. After two rings, Nathaniel answered.

"Did Hannah pick up the kids?" she demanded.

"Yes. You thought you might have a late night at the animal control. I told you this morning Hannah was picking them up. Why do you sound hysterical, Nettie?"

Nettie clutched the phone tight. Tears blurred her vision and she shook her head slowly. "No, you did not. I would have remembered."

"I most certainly did," he snapped. "Nettie, I don't have time for this right now. I only stopped home to grab a sandwich. Conferences start in thirty minutes back at the school."

"Where are they then? Where are Hannah and the kids?"

"They're here. They're fine. Goodbye."

He hung up before she could say more. The daycare manager watched her from the hallway. Nettie, hand shaking, hung up the phone.

She hurried from the little building across the parking lot to her truck. From behind the wheel, she watched the manager step outside the building. She continued watching Nettie, a wary expression on her long face as if she feared Nettie might floor it and drive into the building.

Nettie blinked and looked down, still kept the tears at bay, but they were roiling hot behind her eyes.

As she drove from the parking lot, she searched her memory for Nathaniel telling her Hannah would pick up the kids. He'd come in when she'd been in the shower the night before, said something while she was sudsing her hair. Had that been when? Or that morning when she'd been rushing around trying to drink a cup of coffee, get Celeste to eat her scrambled eggs, and convince Adam to stop taking off his diaper—before rushing all of them out the door?

35

———————

Celeste stared across the table at Spencer, the revelations burrowing into her thoughts.

"I'd like you to take me to my truck," she murmured.

Spencer's face fell, and he sagged back in the booth. "That's it? No curiosity? You're just shutting it down? You recognized Elliot from the missing person's poster, Celeste." He sat up, opened his Velcro wallet and fished out a photo, plopped it in front of her. Elliot in his raccoon-tail hat sitting on a stump, a bullfrog resting on his open palm. "Sheila's eighty-nine. You know what she told me? That her one dying wish is to bury Elliot in the cemetery where she has a plot. That's it. She gave me all the information so if she dies before we find him, I can make sure his remains end up next to her."

The pizza curdled in Celeste's stomach. Elliot's face, the nightmare face of a child, a dead child, flashed in her mind.

It should have been you.

"Can you just take me to my truck, please?"

They drove in silence back to Spencer's house. As Celeste

climbed from the van, she glanced at Spencer, staring straight ahead.

"I'm not saying no. I need some time to think," she told him.

He turned to look at her slowly, and then his serious expression fell away, replaced by an enormous grin. "We're back in business!"

As Celeste drove toward Moon Lake, her cell phone rang with a number she didn't recognize.

"Hello?" she answered.

"Celeste?" a woman with a slight Southern accent asked.

"Yes. This is her."

"Wow. Goodness me. This is Luanne Boden, formerly Oswald."

"Luanne," Celeste breathed. "You knew my mom."

"She was my best friend. We grew up together."

Celeste clutched the wheel harder, sudden relief loosening the tension in her shoulders. "That's so good to hear. I've been searching, trying to find people who knew her."

"That's me. I'd love to meet you, Celeste. Can we do that? Where are you?"

"I'm in Kingwood, actually."

"That's such good news. When I saw your email, I figured I'd be booking a trip to Florida. That's where your dad grew up. I assumed when he left, he prolly took you and your brother down there."

"To Michigan actually."

"Michigan? Why in the world did he go there?"

"For work apparently."

"Huh. A teaching job, then?"

"No. I never knew he was a teacher at all until I came down here and started looking for my mom."

"Looking for her? Does that mean that...you've never found her?"

"No. No one in our family has spoken to her since she left when I was three."

Luanne drew in a sharp breath. "Can we meet today?" Luanne asked. "I'm in Morgantown. Or I'm happy to come to you. You tell me what's better."

"Let's meet in the middle."

Celeste arrived at the coffee shop Luanne had suggested just after three o'clock.

It occupied a row of weathered brick buildings. Above the door, a hand-painted sign read 'Clara's Coffee and Antiques.' The large front windows were crowded with a chaotic array of items: a copper tea kettle, a stack of vintage books, and a porcelain doll with glassy blue eyes. Celeste stared at the doll and shuddered momentarily, back in the house with the serial killer, Kurtis Peters, a porcelain doll hanging from a noose in the center of the room.

"Celeste?"

Celeste turned to see a tall, slender woman in white shorts and a sleeveless teal blouse. Short blonde hair framed her angular face. Her smile lit up her gray eyes, and she pulled Celeste into a hug.

"Oh, my God, you look like her." She drew Celeste away and studied her face. "So much like her." Tears welled in Luanne's eyes. "I told myself the whole way here I wasn't gonna cry, and wouldn't ya know?" She swiped her cheeks. "Well, come on. Let's get out of this heat."

Celeste followed Luanne into the shop. The air was cool and smelled of coffee, old wood and furniture polish. Worn wooden shelves lined the walls, crammed with antiques of every kind: ceramic figurines, tarnished silver candlesticks, and old postcards stacked in neat bundles tied with twine.

"Sensory overload, I know," Luanne said, leading the way toward a seating area with a coffee bar in a back nook of the store. "My husband thinks I'm mad, but I love places like this." She rang the little bell on the counter and then turned again to stare at Celeste. "I can't get over how much you look like her."

"I only had one picture of her growing up," Celeste admitted. "I found it buried in my dad's stuff. He never talked about her."

Luanne sucked in her cheeks and shook her head. "What a rat! I mean no offense, he is your dad, but, well, actually, I do mean offense. What a scoundrel. He never showed you pictures? Your mom had albums of pictures. She captured everything. And a video camera. Oh, my gosh. I wonder what happened to all the videos."

An older woman emerged from deeper in the store carrying a brass pot she was polishing with a cloth. She stopped behind the counter. "What can I get y'all?" she asked.

"It's too damn hot for regular coffee, but do you still have iced coffee? Or those old-fashioned sodas?"

"I got both," the woman said.

"Celeste?" Luanne asked.

"Iced coffee, please," Celeste told her.

"Make it two," Luanne added.

Luanne led them to a small table with a delicate floral tablecloth. Celeste took a seat, and the chair wobbled slightly beneath her. The store seemed to go on and on. She took in a wall of antique clocks, tables heaped with fine china and a row of antique mirrors reflecting fractured glimpses of the room.

"Did my mom tell you she planned to leave him?" Celeste asked.

Luanne's mouth turned down as if the memory tasted bad.

"No, but I wasn't surprised when she left. Nathaniel hung the moon. To discover that betrayal must have shattered her."

"His relationship with the babysitter, with Hannah?"

Luanne nodded. "The writing was on the wall, but Nettie was in absolute denial. I don't blame her."

The woman delivered their iced coffees. "Ring the bell if you need anything else, ladies," she told them.

"But she didn't mention that she'd decided to leave?" Celeste asked.

"No. From what I heard, she didn't tell anyone. Just packed a bag and left. The truth is, our lives had taken such different paths. At twenty-five, she was a married woman with two babies. I was more of a party girl. Two or three boyfriends, out every night.

"Looking back, I realize I wasn't there for her. When she'd call, I'd be going on and on about this guy or that, some new bar opening up, some girls' night out I had planned. When she talked, I didn't listen, didn't hear her. My existence was superficial. I'd stopped putting our friendship first. I really feel terrible about it now. We talked about the babysitter. Your mom said she worried she and your dad were too close. It was making her uncomfortable. I told her to get rid of her."

36

"And that was the last time you spoke to her?" Celeste asked.

Luanne nodded, eyes misting. "When I was in my early thirties, I had a new baby. Roger. He never slept for more than an hour his first year. I'd been awake with him around the clock, had dozed off on the couch with him screaming from his bassinet. I had the most vivid dream that Nettie walked in, picked him up and rocked him to sleep. It was the most real dream I've ever had and what's even crazier is when I woke up, Roger was sound asleep and he slept for about five hours straight after that. The first time he'd ever done it." A tear leaked from Luanne's eye and she brushed it away. "I should have been a better friend. She should have been able to come to me."

Celeste tried to imagine what her mother had gone through, how alone she'd likely felt.

Luanne reached across the table and took one of Celeste's hands. "Tell me about you, Celeste. Are you married? Do you have kids? Has your life been...okay?"

Celeste's gaze drifted to one of the mirrors, the frosted glass reflecting a hazy, disjointed image of her. Celeste forced on a smile. She didn't want to unload the trauma of the previous year on this former friend of her mom's. "I'm married, no kids, two cats."

Luanne grinned. "An animal lover like your mom. I'm not surprised. And your husband? What's he like?"

"He's a scientist, we both are," Celeste lied. For the longest time, those had been her answers, her truth. It had been so much easier.

"Oh, my. That's your dad coming through. He taught chemistry, was very smart. Obnoxiously so sometimes." Luanne rolled her eyes. "You're happy? Life is good?"

"Yeah." Celeste broke eye contact, pulled her coffee closer and took a long drink. "Can you tell me about my mom? What she was like?"

A bittersweet smile curved her lips. "Nettie was an outdoors girl all the way, a bit of a tomboy. She'd scale rocks barefoot. I can still see her crawling up the mountains with no shoes on." Luanne's eyes widened. "She loved animals. She wanted to be a vet, and she'd have been great. And Nettie wasn't one of those girls who just wanted to get married and pop out a few kids. Not that there's anything wrong with that, more power to 'em, but Nettie never had much time for boys.

"At least she didn't until she met Nathaniel. It really was love at first sight for her. She'd never even seriously dated anyone before him. She'd had an occasional date, but..." Luanne shook her head. "I don't even understand it now. I'm fifty-three and still have never experienced it. I guess we're not all meant to. I was so happy for her, a little envious too. She'd found the one, fallen madly in love like a fairy-tale princess. And she deserved it. I'm not sure how much your dad has told you, but Nettie had a difficult life. Her dad was a heavy drinker, her mom was on drugs. They both died before Nettie graduated from high school.

"When she and Nathaniel got married and bought the lake house, it was proof positive you can rise up from all that. Your life doesn't have to be defined by your parents, your childhood. But as time went on, I saw they were not living happily ever after, not at all. I only went to their house a few times. My jaw about hit the ground when I pulled up for the first time. It was a dream and right on Moon Lake, and Nathaniel was all tan and driving his little convertible sports car, and Nettie was pregnant with Adam then and glowing with her long dark hair. My first thought was she'd really done it, achieved the big dream.

"She had her Romeo—that's what she called him when we were young—and her beautiful house. But then we went for a ride in the speedboat, just tooling around the lake mostly, and she admitted Nathaniel had started to change. He was teaching and coaching, and it took up all of his time. He was out late every night, at sports tournaments on the weekends. Nettie had made friends with an older couple next door, but they were summer people and she hated the thought of cold weather because then the few people who did live on the lake would mostly leave.

"I started to get a sense of how cut off she felt from the world. Her job at the animal control helped, but her pregnancy with Adam was difficult. She was sick a lot early in the pregnancy and later the doctor ordered her off her feet for the last month. We talked on the phone once a week, or every other week, when she was home."

"Did my dad call you after my mom left?"

Luanne took a sip of her coffee. "Nope. I didn't know for months. I called the house a few times and left messages, but she never called me back. I figured she had her hands full with you and your brother. Then one day Clem showed up on my doorstep. That was a shocker. Clem rarely left the mountain. She used to say, 'If I can't get it right here, I don't need it.'

Food, medicine, firewood, you name it, she found it in the woods."

"Wait. Who's Clem?"

"She's your great-aunt. She was more like a mom to Nettie than her own mom ever was. You've never heard of Aunt Clementine?"

Celeste shook her head.

Luanne's nostrils flared. "What a piece of work he turned out to be. Prince Charming my ass," she muttered. "Aunt Clementine was your grandma's sister who lived up in the mountains on the outskirts of Davis. When your mom left, I was living in a house in Morgantown with two other girls. We were all still in bed, and my roommate Jamie yelled down the hall that someone was at the door for me. I walked out and there was Clem in her deerskin vest and jeans she must have patched up about fifty times. No greeting, no 'how are ya,' she said, 'Have you seen Nettie?'

"Could have knocked me over with a feather, I was so surprised. Clem rarely left the mountain and I'm pretty sure she considered Morgantown hell on earth. And to be honest, I was a little annoyed, mostly because the night before it had been half off at the wine bar and we'd been up till about two in the morning. I had a hangover, and I gave her a bit of an attitude, but that died the instant she told me Nettie hadn't been seen for two months. Nathaniel said she'd left him."

"Her aunt didn't know where she was either?"

"No, and it was pretty clear to me Clem was suspicious of your dad's story. The bottom line was Clem could not believe for a second your mom left you kids, and I have to say I could hardly believe it too. After Clem went home, the whole thing bothered me for days. I finally drove over to Kingwood and confronted your dad. He said your mom had suffered pretty bad postpartum depression after Adam and things had been strained for a while and one day she took a bunch of money out of their bank account and said she needed some time away, packed a bag and left. And that girl was at the house, Hannah. He'd moved her right in and I thought, 'No wonder she left.'"

"You never questioned his story that she just took off?"

Luanne frowned. "Why shouldn't I believe him? You know? I never had any reason not to, and like I said, Nettie and I had grown apart. I wasn't close enough anymore to know what was happening in her mind."

"But you never heard from her again?"

"No." Luanne wrung her hands. "I should have gone to the police, insisted he report her missing. I'm sorry, Celeste. I was such a self-absorbed little shit. I'm embarrassed now how I just let her slip away."

"What do you think happened to my mom?"

Luanne pulled a little package of tissue from her purse and dabbed at her tear-stained face. "I honestly don't know."

"Do you think my dad hurt her?"

"It breaks my heart to think that, Celeste. I almost can't bear it. She loved him so much. The person you need to talk to is Nettie's Aunt Clem. I'm sure Nettie was confiding in her at that time."

"Clem. Okay. And where can I find her?"

Luanne took out her cell phone. "I haven't spoken to Clem in twenty years at least, but I can't imagine she'd ever move. GPS isn't going to take you to her house and even if it would, I'm not sure she has any kind of listed address. You can get there from here on your way back to Kingwood or, and this is the better choice, go during the day tomorrow. Those mountain roads can get confusing at night."

Celeste listened as Luanne described how to find Clem's isolated mountain cabin.

37

N ettie

"Aunt Clem?"

Clem looked up from the table where she sat with Celeste, peeling wild leeks into a bowl. Celeste was doing a lot more playing than peeling. Adam lay asleep in the wood bassinet that Clem had hand-carved.

"What is it, Nettie?"

"Do you remember, umm...years ago, you helped my mom with a...spell, a banishing jar?"

"I remember." Clem reached for Celeste's hands and showed her how to snap off the remaining roots.

"Could you help me make one?"

"I could."

"Would you?"

"This is for the girl who's come into your home?"

Nettie nodded.

Clem stood and plopped Celeste in the corner to play with the litter of kittens Nettie had brought to Clem's weeks before. They'd been abandoned outside the animal control in a cardboard box and she'd been unable to find anyone to foster them.

Clem stopped in front of Nettie. "You are a smart young woman. Do not ignore what is right in front of you."

"I'm not. That's why—"

Clem lifted her finger to her lips. "You can make that girl go away. But if Nathaniel has chosen to stray, banishing the girl will not contain his wandering heart."

"I know that."

"You can stay here with me, Nettie. You and the babies."

"I appreciate that, Clem, but..."

"But you cannot bear to leave him?"

Nettie shook her head. "I love him. We love each other. This is a speed bump, but we're going to get over it."

Clem supplied the brown glass jar, but told Nettie she had to collect the rest of the items and perform the ritual alone—black thread to bind Hannah, a thorn to puncture her intentions, red pepper to build heat and make her uncomfortable, vinegar to sour her relationship with Nathaniel, a bit of Hannah—hair preferably, but clothing, a fingernail, those would do.

"This banishing is best done when the moon is full," Clem explained. "That's when the moon is wild. She's stirring things up, revealing what's hidden. Once you place the girl's hair in this jar, write her name backward on a slip of paper. Bury the jar where it will not be discovered."

Nettie sat at the kitchen table, her hands trembling slightly as she worked. The sun had begun to lower in the sky, filling the house with afternoon light. On the table before her lay the items for the banishing spell: a spool of black thread, a jagged thorn from a bouquet of roses Nathaniel had bought for their anniversary, a small jar of red pepper flakes, a bottle of vinegar, and a plastic sandwich bag containing strands of Hannah's hair, lifted from her brush earlier that day.

Nettie had waited until Celeste and Adam were down for their naps upstairs. The basketball team had a game that night and Nathaniel wouldn't be home until late.

Nettie added each of the items to the brown glass jar, imagining each piece cutting Hannah's connection to Nathaniel and driving her out of their lives. On a slip of paper, she wrote Hannah's name backward, pausing when she realized Hannah's name came out the same whether written backwards or forwards. It caused a sinking feeling in Nettie's stomach, but she pushed it away, then dropped the paper in the jar and tightened the lid, sealing it with a determined twist. She sat back, exhaling shakily, and placed her hand over the cool glass surface.

She intended to take the jar to the lake and bury it deep in the stones along the shore, but she wanted to wait until dark. The moon was full that night and Clem had said full moons were the ideal time to perform a ritual of release.

Just as she was about to hide the jar in a laundry room cupboard, she heard a knock at the door. The sound so startled her, she dropped the jar, and it smashed on the tiled laundry room floor. Glass skittered across the floor and the scent of vinegar rose into the air.

Nettie grabbed a towel from a hamper, dropped to her knees and quickly wiped the mess into a pile. She frowned at a crack in the tile, hoping Nathaniel wouldn't notice it when he returned later that night.

The knock came again.

She opened the door to a woman with a long, lined face, brown hair tucked beneath a ball cap. A child, maybe three, barefoot with a Kool Aid-ringed mouth, stood beside her wearing only a sagging diaper and a t-shirt.

"Sorry to bother ya," the woman said. "My truck broke down up on the road. Thought I might use yer phone."

Nettie hesitated, imagining the smashed jar in the laundry room, then overrode her misgivings as she considered the exhausted-looking woman and the sweaty child beside her. "Yes, of course." Nettie opened the door and led the woman and the child to the kitchen. She pointed at the phone hanging from the wall.

As the woman dialed a number, Nettie squatted down.

"What's your name?" she asked the little boy.

"Enyit."

"Enyit?"

"Elliot," the woman on the phone corrected. She didn't seem annoyed so much as exhausted. She pressed to end the call and dialed another number. "He's my daughter's boy, but wouldn't you know, she's not home and neither's his daddy. Jesus H. And it's hotter than the devil's armpits today." She hung up the phone, her face growing red. "Thanks, ma'am," she told Nettie. She grasped Elliot's hand and tugged him toward the door.

"You didn't get ahold of anyone?" Nettie asked.

The woman shook her head no, but didn't turn back. Nettie followed her, caught her as they were stepping outside. "Then what will you do?"

The woman forced a brittle smile, but her eyes had begun to mist. "We'll walk. Ain't nothin' we haven't done before. Right, Elliot?"

He didn't respond, but his lower lip quivered.

"Let me drive you. Where do you live?"

"We'll be just fine." The woman hoisted the little boy onto her hip. Tears rolled down his face, cutting paths in his dirty cheeks.

"No, please," Nettie called out. She strode to the woman and offered her hand. "I'm Nettie Harrington."

The woman shook it. Her hand was hot and trembling. "Sheila Thacker. We'd appreciate the ride."

"Give me two minutes. My little ones are down for a nap. They love a drive." Not entirely true. Celeste liked to ride. Adam hated it and he'd be as mad as a wet hornet when she woke him from his nap and thrust him into the car seat.

Two minutes turned into fifteen, but eventually Nettie wrangled both children into the truck, Elliot buckled in the backseat beside them. Nettie turned the air conditioner on high as they pulled from the driveway. A half mile down the road they passed a broken-down blue pickup, the tire wells nearly rusted to nothing.

As they drove, Elliot and Celeste began to babble together like old friends. Nettie smiled and tilted the rearview mirror to watch them.

"How old is she?" the woman asked.

"Three in the October."

"She's got your eyes."

"Thank you. Do you watch your grandson often?" Nettie asked, following Sheila's directions onto the dirt mountain road.

"Yes. His ma is...well, she ain't around much. Got sober for about a year after she had him, then got a new boyfriend and started taking pills. Been the same story since she was fifteen, makes it a few months, then disappears." Sheila shook her head. "Can't say I blame her. Life ain't exactly sunny lake houses for her."

Nettie ignored the comment. "My mom took drugs. She died when I was seventeen."

The woman sighed and reached back a hand to pat Elliot's skinned knee. "His mama is far from perfect, but this guy's pretty special."

Nettie pulled into the dirt drive at the woman's house. It was rundown, slightly lopsided, the once-white paint all flaked away.

"Thanks for the ride," Sheila said. She opened the back door and hoisted Elliot, who began to cry, from the seat. Celeste cried as well, reaching for him.

Nettie stepped out and grabbed a paper bag from the back of the truck. "I put a few things in here. Diapers, some snacks. Just in case you need it."

"I don't need charity," Sheila grumbled, but she took the bag.

"If you ever...need help with him," Nettie started, but Sheila turned away and started toward the shack, Elliot crying in her arms.

38

Celeste had been lost for nearly an hour, searching for Clem's house. The narrow two-tracks, more trails than roads, wound through the mountain in jagged, almost forgotten grooves. Some had been overtaken completely by the forest. The ones that remained zigzagged as if the person who'd cut them had been delirious, lost himself, hacking at anything and everything in his bid to escape the mountains.

A fog had begun to creep up the mountainside. Low and slow at first, but gaining as Celeste maneuvered the truck up a steep path and turned around again. Luanne's directions no longer assisted her. She'd lost track of the rough description and now drove aimlessly, praying to find a paved road and make her way back to Kingwood. Any hope of finding Clem had been replaced by a desperation to get out of the mountains before night fell.

As Celeste climbed yet another steep hill, her truck suddenly jolted and stopped. The engine died, leaving her in the quiet of the cab. Celeste blinked through the windshield, her body a live wire of anxiety. She took a breath, shifted into park, and turned the key. Nothing. The engine didn't so much as sputter.

She'd already checked her cell phone twenty times, but she took it out again. No service.

Celeste climbed out and stared at the overgrown dirt road in either direction. Somewhere off to her right, a raven's caw cut through the muted forest.

She turned right and began to walk.

Celeste had lost track of time. Her hip and leg had gone from muttering to wailing. She hadn't brought any water. Her mouth was dry and gluey.

She should have stayed with the truck. Maybe it had overheated and just needed to sit. Twice she'd almost turned back to it, but the sudden fear she'd get more lost had urged her on.

A rustling sound came from beside her and she squinted into the trees, the fog nearly obscuring the forest floor. She couldn't make out what had made the noise. Celeste was not familiar with the West Virginia wildlife. What might she encounter if night fell and she was still scrambling through the mountain forest?

As if to ramp up her growing fear, a gunshot echoed from somewhere on the mountain. Celeste stopped walking, heart doing double time, and tried not to imagine what kind of person she might stumble upon in the isolated mountain woods. Why hadn't she taken Luanne's advice and set out the following day? She could have taken Spencer, someone with knowledge of the area.

Somewhere in front of her, she heard a soft tinkling sound. She started to walk again, slowly, straining toward the noise. Through the fog, she caught sight of an off color against the green and brown of the trees. The setting sun poked through the dense canopy and lit a bit of colored glass. Celeste inched forward, aware of the steep embankment beside her. It took a moment to recognize the bits of color were dozens of glass bottles hanging from the branches of a tree. They clinked in the wind.

A rugged path cut into the forest behind the bottles and Celeste saw an old wood sign nailed to a tree. She recognized a crude C and L carved into the wood.

Had she found Clem's property?

By the time she crested the hill at the top of the path and the cabin slid into view, a stitch had embedded in Celeste's side and sweat slid between her shoulder blades. She tried to slow her rapid breaths as she approached the old rustic structure. The weathered cabin was nestled against the shadowed mountainside, its roof sagging under the weight of years. The sight was almost spectral in the muted light, as though the house had grown from the ground rather than been built upon it.

A woman emerged from the forest to Celeste's right and beckoned her toward the cabin. The woman's face was a map of deep-set lines, skin tanned and leathery. Her steel-gray hair was tied back in a braid. Her clothes looked handmade—animal skin pants and a tattered green shirt. She stared at Celeste, her green eyes sharp, assessing.

"Come on then," she demanded.

"Are you Clem?" Celeste choked, voice hoarse.

"Clem's right," the woman told her. "Come on."

"I'm—"

"I know who you are," Clem snapped. "You're Nettie's girl. You think I don't recognize my own kin?"

"Oh." Celeste stared at her, unnerved by the woman with her weathered face and sharp tongue. "But how?"

"Same way you knew I lived here."

"I got lost trying to find your house."

Clem raised an eyebrow. "Looks like you ended up right where you intended. What's lost about that?"

Celeste followed Clem into the rustic cabin. The interior smelled of earth, with a faint metallic tang beneath it, like rust or blood. Mismatched furniture faced a dark hearth. The kitchen was little more than a slab of sealed wood atop stumps and an iron basin for a sink. Shelves crammed with jars of who knew what lined the walls.

"Sit," Clem ordered, gesturing toward a threadbare armchair. "You look like you're about to keel over."

Grateful, Celeste sank into the chair, moaning as the pressure finally eased off her hip and leg.

Clem moved into the kitchen, took down an earthenware mug hanging from a hook and dunked it in a metal basin. She walked over and thrust it at Celeste.

Celeste slurped it, gasping as she spilled some down the front of her shirt. "Thank you," she whispered.

Clem nodded. She returned to the kitchen, pulled a dusty bottle filled with a dark liquid from the shelf. She filled two additional mugs and returned one to Celeste.

"What's this?" Celeste asked, setting her water mug on the floor.

"Spring tonic. Drink up." Clem swallowed hers in a single gulp.

Celeste sniffed the dark liquid and then, as Clem had done, she opened her mouth and drank it. The liquid was bitter and vinegary, but she managed to swallow it. She tried to keep the disgust from her face. Celeste picked her water back up and drank the rest, erasing the taste of the tonic.

"Do you know where my mom is?" she asked.

Clem stared at her. The hardness had gone from her eyes. She appeared sad. "We both know where your mom is, don't we?"

"Dead."

Clem nodded. "But that's not so bad, is it? Just leavin' one world for another. Course"—she gestured at Celeste—"it ain't easy when you're still in this one."

"Did you ever speak to her after she left us?"

"No one ever spoke to her."

"But how do you know that? Maybe she had a secret boyfriend or a friend who helped her or—"

Clem held up a hand. "I'm not in the business of tellin' lies —not to another and not to myself. When you do that"—she wiggled her fingers—"that thing you're doin' just now with the 'maybe this' an' 'maybe that,' what you're really doin' is tellin' your knowin' to go on, git out of here. You're cuttin' off the piece of you that don't need no facts to get to the truth. I told your ma that when she came up here cryin' because Nathaniel had all but moved that girl into the house, the babysitter. Your ma knew...she knew it here"—Clem rested a hand on her bony chest—"what he was up to with that girl, but my Gawd did she rattle off the excuses. The girl came from a bad home, her stepdad was mean, her mom was into the pills. Nathaniel would never do that, would never betray her. On and on it went.

"I told her right then, 'Pack up those babies and get outta town.' I offered her to come here." Clem smiled wryly. "A downgrade for some, but Nettie loved this place. She understood real wealth didn't lie in those fancy lake houses and fat bank accounts. But it wasn't the lifestyle she clung to. It was Nathaniel. She loved him blindly. She could not see what he was up to, even when she saw it with her own two eyes. And for that, she paid the ultimate price."

39

———————

A sudden fluttering noise drew Celeste's attention to the open window. A large raven stood on the windowsill, its inky feathers gleaming. It tilted its head, fixing her with a beady stare.

"The raven knows," Clem said.

"Knows what?" Celeste asked. "You believe my dad murdered my mom?"

Celeste had accepted her mother was dead, but her logical mind had offered up a laundry list of how that could have happened. She'd had a mental breakdown, like Celeste's dad had said, and eventually committed suicide after abandoning her family, or the breakdown had caused a drug addiction and subsequent overdose. Or the breakdown had led her into the hands of sinister people, and they'd taken Nettie's life. Or there'd been an accident somewhere in the months or years after Nettie left. The list was endless. People died every day.

"Somebody did."

"How do you know that?"

"Same way I know a rattlesnake in the grass when I see one. Same way I know sun's gonna rise over there"—Clem pointed toward one end of the cabin—"and set over there." She swept her gnarled finger toward the opposite end.

Tears welled in Celeste's eyes. Was she as blind as her mother had been? Willfully ignorant to who her father truly was, so much so that even as the evidence piled up, she clung to any theory that pointed another direction?

"Come on then," Clem said, waving her up.

Celeste stood and followed Clem from the cabin. The old woman led her off the porch to the edge of the woods. A dozen or more wooden crosses made from two sticks and wound together with twine stuck from the ground.

"Those are Nettie's dogs and cats. They came from her shelter. We called my place the mountain of last resort. Most of 'em ran wild here, but Nettie and I built dog houses, cat houses. There were summers my whole porch'd be covered in animals. After she'd been gone for a few years, I started breaking the houses down, using 'em for firewood. Two of the critters lasted a good ten years after Nettie went missing—a cat we called Mad Mingus 'cause he'd tangle with any animal that crossed his path and a three-legged dog named Burdock because he was constantly full of burrs. I got to shaving him each year, or he'd just turn into one giant burr. That's them there." She pointed at two crosses that were larger than the others and off to the side.

Clem moved toward a third large cross, this one scattered with dead wildflowers. "I planted this here the night Nettie came to me. She stood at the foot of my bed and didn't say a word, but I knew."

Celeste stared at the crosses. Her body had begun to feel light, buoyant. She wondered what was in Clem's tonic. She followed the old woman back into the cottage, watched her build a fire in the stone hearth despite the warm evening.

"Get close now." Clem waved Celeste over. "Get close so you can remember."

Celeste sat down on a threadbare rug in front of the fire. Her limbs had grown heavy and her head swam as she looked into the flickering flames. She'd never noticed how many colors fire contained. Red, orange, yellow, green, blue.

Clem was talking, but she could no longer make out the words. They sounded far away.

Celeste leaned forward, catching a glimpse of something in the flames. She blinked and stared, eyes growing unfocused, the object becoming clear. It was a telephone, and it was off its base, the wire coiled between the receiver and the clunky white base, and on the carpet beneath a stain was growing, darkening the beige carpet. The steady beep-beep-beep of the dial tone filled the air. A red stain marred the white receiver. A toddler Celeste padded down the stairs, calling out for her mama, but there were no sounds except the beep of the phone in that bedroom. Out the door she went and around the house, and the birds were there, the ravens surrounding something in the grass.

"Celeste!" Her dad's voice broke the quiet. She was lifted up, carried back into the house.

And now Celeste was running through the woods, older, branches and leaves brushing her face and arms. He was behind her, laughing. *Ready or not, here I come.* She doubled back, saw the car and quietly slipped into the trunk, pulled it almost closed, peered through the crack in the back. He wore her Halloween mask, came barreling from the woods looking for her.

Heat from Clem's fire surrounded Celeste. A trickle of sweat slipped down her face, pooled in the hollow of her throat. The gold and orange flames swirled, seemed to reach out and pull her closer.

"Time to go."

Celeste looked up, startled. The hearth had gone cold and dark. Had Celeste fallen asleep? The memories, visions, receded into the shadows of her mind.

Now Clem stood in front of her, waiting.

Night had fallen. A luminous white moon peered through the dense canopy of leaves. As they walked down the steep path, cicadas humming, Celeste seemed to float. Her leg didn't ache. Her whole body bobbed along behind Clem as if they were riding an invisible wave down the mountain. The sound of birds replaced the cicadas, and she looked up to see ravens, dozens of them—no, more than that, hundreds of them—perched in the branches of the trees watching them, their black eyes glittering in the moonlight.

When they arrived at the truck, Celeste stared at it, confused. They'd only just left the cabin. The truck had been miles away, at least. But maybe she'd gotten so turned around she'd doubled back and not realized it.

When Celeste climbed into the truck and turned the key, the truck started right up as if it had never died at all.

Clem patted the hood, then reached through the window, folded something into Celeste's hand. A glossy black raven's feather.

"Look where the light don't reach," Clem said.

40

Celeste woke in the queen bed at the A-frame. Light poured through the triangular window. She sat up, groggy, the night before playing in her mind like a dream. She had no memory of driving out of the mountains and returning to the rental house.

How had she possibly done it at night? And yet she had.

Celeste made coffee and poured it into her mother's *Romeo and Juliet* mug. It sent a pang through her chest each time her eyes drifted to the image. On the porch, she stopped and studied the wooden deck. Pennies, twenty at least, lay strewn across the wood. She crouched and picked one up, and tried to imagine if she'd walked out there the night before, possibly spilled her purse on the deck.

She thought of her conversation with Clem and then of the visions as she'd stared into the fire. Were they memories? Actual moments in Celeste's young life she'd forgotten?

She tried to bring them into focus—a phone off the hook and lying on the floor, then wandering outside in search of her mother, seeing the birds. In the second vision, she'd climbed into the trunk of a car. Why would she have done that?

"We were playing," she murmured. Who had been playing? Her and Adam?

At the truck, Clem had told Celeste, 'Look where the light don't reach.'

Across the lake, her childhood home sat hulking and quiet.

She showered, put on clean clothes, and drove to the house.

Spencer had mentioned the crawl space at lunch and then Clem, hours later, had offered her cryptic advice. Was she, too, referring to the crawl space within the house? Was there even a crawl space in the house?

The house was silent when she walked inside, but the moment she closed the door, a phone began to ring. Celeste looked at the ceiling.

The house released its usual series of groans and sighs as she walked slowly up the stairs and down the hall. She stared at the closed bedroom door that she knew she'd left open. The ringing continued, setting her teeth on edge, and after a moment's hesitation, she reached forward and twisted the knob. The door swung in.

A white landline phone sat on the floor beside the bed. Had it been there previously? She didn't think so.

Mouth dry, stomach knotted, Celeste edged into the room, bent down and picked up the receiver.

"Hello?" she answered.

Nothing at first and then breath, shallow, raspy, as if the person calling struggled to take a breath.

"Is there someone there? Do you need help?"

A gurgling exhale. Then silence.

"Hello?" she repeated.

The phone suddenly began to release a shrill beep-beep-beep. Celeste jerked the phone away from her ear and dropped it. Immediately the beeping stopped.

As Celeste's gaze drifted down to the base of the phone, the hair on her arms prickled.

The cord lay coiled against the carpet, the end completely frayed.

Still, she bent and lifted the limp cord, then searched for an additional cord plugged in, but found nothing. As she studied the phone, she noticed the stain in the carpet beneath it. It had been cleaned, but a section of the beige carpet remained darker than the surrounding area.

Outside Celeste crossed the yard and paused at the lake edge. She gulped the air, thick and wet, not unlike the breaths on the phone she'd just heard. She rubbed her face, pressing hard into the hollows of her eyes. The vision of the phone at Clem's danced at the periphery, merging with the phone upstairs.

It took Celeste a half hour to feel ready to walk back inside the house. The moment she stepped through the door, she expected to hear the phone ringing once again. All was silent.

She moved from room to room, gazing at the floor in search of the outline for a crawl space that might not exist.

She almost missed it, had done a cursory check of the slanted closet beneath the stairs, but as she started to close the door, a bump on the rug caught her eye. When she pulled the rug away, she spotted the square outline of an opening in the floor. The panel resisted her efforts to tug it loose. Celeste braced herself and yanked hard, the aged wood giving way with a groan.

A dark opening yawned before her. She crouched down and peered inside. The space smelled of damp earth and the brackish tang of the nearby lake. A chill ran through Celeste as she thought of the walled-up staircase at the stone schoolhouse in Graves, Michigan, the place where she'd discovered Katie Ellis's body.

As she'd experienced so many times in life when confronted with entering a confined space, a cold sweat broke out on her skin. She didn't want to go down there.

Was Spencer right? Was the body of Elliot Thacker down there? Or her mother's? Or both?

She stood up and left the closet, walked into the front room, and braced both hands on the back of a chair. The thought of entering that dark hole and finding one or both of their bodies made her sick to her stomach. She should stop now, call Harris or the local police. Let someone else make the grisly discovery, if there was one to be made.

She returned to the closet and stared again into the opening. With a deep breath, she dropped into the darkness, the earth soft beneath her feet. As she hunched down and shined her light through the space, she caught gossamer cobwebs and tiny black spiders fleeing from the bright orb. Her flashlight's beam swept across the small chamber, landing on a large, dark object in the far corner.

Fighting panic, she crawled on hands and knees to reach it, clenching her mouth against the webs that tickled her face.

A rust-streaked safe sat in the corner. Nearly as tall as the cramped ceiling, the safe must have been almost impossible to maneuver into the crawl space.

Nettie stared at it, mouth going dry.

A body could fit inside the old safe.

Clearly father had taken pains to hide it. A combination dial and keyhole were affixed to the front of the safe. Above the lock, a symbol of a three-pronged spear was etched into the metal beneath the word 'Trident.'

As Celeste studied the face of the safe, a memory surfaced. A key with the same insignia she stared at now. The key had been tucked into the green tote their father carted from house to house, the scant evidence of their former life in West

Virginia. The single photo of Nettie that Celeste had stolen years before. The place he'd gone to get her birth certificate when she needed it for her driver's license. The box he'd dug Adam's social security card out of.

The key had been in a velvet box along with a gold band she suspected had been her father's wedding ring.

41

N ettie

Nettie stared at the little black tube of lipstick sitting on the table next to her bed. She picked it up, didn't need to read the shade to know it belonged to Hannah. Nettie had never worn lipstick, very little makeup at all, but Hannah was never far from her cosmetic bag.

Nettie found Hannah in the kitchen, feeding Adam in his highchair. Her eyes narrowed on the bowl of Cocoa Puffs. "Why are you giving him that when I asked you two days ago not to?"

Hannah started and turned. "Nate said it was okay, so I figured..."

Nettie held up the lipstick. "Why was this sitting on the table next to my bed, Hannah?" Nettie's eyes bore into the younger woman's.

Hannah stared at it, frowned and shook her head. "I guess Celeste carried it in there." She plucked it from Nettie's hand

and stuck it in the pocket of her cut-off jean shorts. "You know how excited she gets over my makeup." Hannah laughed. "Maybe for her birthday I should get her one of the makeup kits for little girls. My friend Loretta works at Polly's and can get me the discount."

"Absolutely not."

Hannah glanced back at her as if surprised, then her face turned placid. "Okay. Whatever you say, Mrs. Harrington."

The way she said the name 'Mrs. Harrington' bothered Nettie. Nathaniel was Nate, but she was Mrs. Harrington. Nettie had never invited Hannah to call her Nettie, but it bothered her anyway. Hannah said it as if Nettie was old and Nate was young. As if Nettie were the authority figure Hannah and Nate rebelled against.

"I'm going to take a quick swim," Hannah said, disappearing down the hall.

Nettie thought of the smashed banishing jar. She'd intended to make another one, but there'd been no time and she knew what Clem would say if she'd told her she dropped the jar.

'Fate's got steady hands, even when you think she's fumbling.'

Hannah climbed out of the lake and shook out her long hair. Water ran down her shapely body, her hips beginning to widen. She was in the space between girl and woman, the woman beginning to take over.

Nettie watched her, suddenly sensitive to her own body, the ten pounds she'd not lost since having Adam, the stretch marks that now marred her once-smooth hips and stomach.

As Hannah walked up the dock, a raven swooped from a tree and dove at her. Another joined and then a third. Hannah screamed and swung her arms wildly, trying to beat the birds away as she sprinted toward the house.

Nettie hurried to the side door, but as she put her hand on the knob, she had a moment's hesitation. What if she didn't help, instead locked the door and let Hannah fend for herself against the birds?

Hannah's scream split through her thoughts and Nettie jerked the door open and ran onto the deck, yelling at the birds and waving her arms. They instantly lifted up and scattered back to the trees.

Blood trickled from Hannah's hairline. Her face was red and splotchy, and tears streamed over her cheeks. She ran full speed into Nettie, nearly knocking her over.

"Oh, my God, oh, my God," she cried, hands still covering her head. "I have to get inside. They're after me."

Nettie wrapped her arms around Hannah. Her skin was damp and clammy and her entire body shook. In that instant, Hannah was only a child, and Nettie felt ashamed for her indecision moments before.

"It's okay. Shh...they're gone." Nettie led Hannah into the house. The girl continued shaking. When she touched a trembling hand to her head and came away with blood, she screamed and startled Nettie.

"It's okay, Hannah," she said again, grabbing a rag from the edge of the sink. "It's just a little scratch."

"But what if..." Hannah struggled to get her words out. "What if they had rabies?"

"They didn't have rabies."

"How do you know?" Hannah snapped, jerking the rag from Nettie's hand.

Hannah pressed it to her head. From the front of the house, the door opened. Hannah glared at Nettie and ran down the hall.

"Nate!" she called out. "Nate. The birds...they attacked me."

Nettie could not hear Nathaniel. His voice had dropped, low and soothing. He seemed to be consoling her.

Nettie stepped into the hallway and froze. Hannah's head was buried in his chest. His arms were around her, his large hands sliding up and down her goose-pimpled skin.

He looked up, neck flushing, and put his hands on Hannah's shoulders, gently pushing her away.

"What happened, Nettie?" His voice was accusatory.

Nettie wanted to bite back, to ask why the hell Hannah was at their house in the first place, why he'd practically moved a student in. "She was swimming, and some birds dive-bombed her. They must have a nest nearby."

"Was it those giant black birds you're always feeding? Jesus. What if this happens to one of the kids?"

"They're ravens," Nettie said. "And they'd never attack the kids."

Nathaniel took the rag from Hannah's hand and dabbed at the cut on her head. "I don't care what they are. It's time for them to learn to stay away from our house."

Upstairs, Adam started to cry. Hannah started toward the stairs, but Nettie brushed past her. "I'm home, Hannah. I can take care of my own children." As she started up the stairs, she stopped and looked back down at them. "It's probably time for you to drive her home, Nathaniel."

Nettie grabbed the bag of birdseed and slipped onto the porch. The dregs of night had mostly filtered out of the morning sky, and the humidity already shimmered in the air. As she started toward the yard, she froze. Her fingers loosened and her coffee mug fell from her hand, splattering hot coffee against her bare legs. The pain barely registered.

The front yard and dock were littered with dead ravens.

Their glossy black feathers held the sheen of the previous night's dew. Their beady eyes, glazed over, seemed to watch her. The lake, so calm it could have been a mirror, cradled the floating remains of more ravens.

Nettie began to tremble all over. For several minutes she blinked at the ravens, willing them to stir, to reveal it was all an elaborate hoax.

"What did you do?" Nettie hissed.

Nathaniel looked up from his oatmeal, startled. "What?"

She thrust the plastic garbage bag toward him. He glanced down and recoiled. "Jesus. Get that thing out of the house. Are you trying to infect us all with some bird disease?"

"You poisoned them."

He didn't look at her, but dipped his spoon in his oatmeal and slid it between his lips. "They're a nuisance. You saw what they did to Hannah. You have only yourself to blame, Nettie. Keeping the baby birds in the garage, feeding them every day. This isn't a zoo."

42

———

Celeste turned into the long-term parking at the Morgantown airport.

Her cell phone rang. Harris.

"Hi," she answered.

"Decided not to call and have the Memento Mori group offer life advice?"

"Yeah. Sorry. Yesterday was a blur. I'll fill you in soon, but right now, I can only talk for a minute. I'm about to catch a plane."

"A plane to where?"

"To Florida. I'm going to see my dad."

"All right. That's probably a good idea. Still no sign of Jonathan in Grand Rapids. Has Bowman called you?"

"He left me a voicemail yesterday. I haven't gotten back to him."

"I'd imagine he's just warning you. Going to your dad's is probably the safest bet right now. Though I'm guessing Jonathan knows where he lives?"

"Yeah." Celeste didn't tell him she intended the trip to be

short and, if she were running for safety, the last place she'd choose was her dad's.

"Hmm...again, Jonathan probably won't try anything, but—"

"Be vigilant. I get it. I'll talk to you soon."

***

Celeste arrived in Florida just after one p.m.

She picked up her rental car and drove to her dad's condo. When she knocked, no one answered. She had no idea what her dad's day-to-day life consisted of. He rarely talked about it, mentioned friends or golf outings or much of anything. It wasn't anything new, but she realized as she stood there he could be out of town, out of the country for all she knew, and she would be totally unaware.

She called him, but his cell went straight to voicemail. She hadn't contacted him ahead of time because she wanted the element of surprise. Now she wondered if that had been a mistake.

Celeste's grandma, Bianca, her dad's mom, lived only a few miles away.

***

Her grandma, Bianca, gazed at her for a long moment after Celeste knocked on her door. "What is it then? Something happen to your dad?" she demanded.

"No. I flew down to visit him and he wasn't home, so I figured I'd come say hi."

"Did you now. Well, I hope you're not thinking he's here. Only visits me about once every three months and even then he's in and out of here so fast he doesn't get a crease in his pants from sitting."

"Can I come in?"

Her grandmother frowned, but opened the door and retreated into the house. Celeste followed. It smelled as it had in their youth. Mothballs and potpourri. Thick, sheer plastic covered all the furniture, the same furniture that had been in the house since Celeste was a little girl.

"Do you still have your cat?" Celeste asked, sitting opposite her grandma on a chair. The plastic crinkled beneath her.

"Dead."

"Oh. I'm sorry."

Bianca sat in a chair and eyed Celeste. She didn't offer her a drink. Not that Celeste wanted one, but it struck her as it had every time she'd visited her grandparents' house how cold her grandmother was. She watched Celeste as if she suspected her granddaughter would steal something if she glanced away for even a moment.

"I wanted to ask you about my mom," Celeste said.

Bianca said nothing.

"Umm..." Celeste fiddled with the sleeve on her shirt, felt that old weird shame despite not having done anything wrong. "Do you remember when she left?"

Bianca pursed her thin lips. "I remember your dad flying you and Adam down and dumping you on our doorstep for a week with hardly a phone call."

"He did?"

"Yes. Probably running around trying to find your mom. A lot of good that did."

"Were you surprised my mom left?"

"Hardly. She was a wild animal. Why Nathaniel thought he'd civilize her is beyond me. She was one of them mountain people, you know? Can't change those people."

Celeste bristled at the comment, but tried to keep her expression neutral. "Did you have a relationship with my mom at all? Did she ever confide in you that she was having a hard time?" The question was absurd. Celeste doubted anyone had ever confided a secret to the woman in front of her.

"No. I'm sure she thought we were up in our airs. That's why we moved out of there. Stupidest thing Grant ever talked me into, moving to West Virginia. He had some big real estate development plans." Bianca scoffed. "We barely lasted three years in that hellhole. Of course, that was plenty long enough for a mountain girl to sink her teeth into Nathaniel. Now he was a catch. If we'd have stayed here in Florida, he'd have married the daughter of a big insurance guy. That's who he dated early in high school, and her dad had real money. Now we had money of our own, but nothing like the Vanderhoff family. But oh, no, Grant drags us off to flea-bitten Davis, West Virginia, and enrolls Nathaniel at the godawful school."

Celeste tried to keep her expression measured as Bianca spit her hatred. Not for the first time, she realized it was no wonder her father was emotionally void. This was supposed to be his nurturing parent.

"You guys moved back to Florida after only three years? But my dad stayed?" Celeste asked.

"Of course he did. He was enrolled at college and had started dating your mother. Nathaniel was not a quitter. And I'm sure he felt bad for her. It was like adopting a stray cat. How do you shove 'em back out the door once they've gotten used to three meals a day and a warm fire to sleep beside? Hmm...? And conveniently, she got pregnant right away. Not a wonder he never remarried after that fiasco."

It was everything Celeste could do to not slap the smug expression off her grandmother's face. She took a deep breath and gazed at the floor for a moment, gathering herself.

Celeste glared at her grandmother. "Did you know my dad was sleeping with our babysitter? A student at his high school?"

Bianca's eyes narrowed on Celeste's and she lifted her thin wrist to squint at the gold watch there. "My show is coming on. You'll have to leave."

43

———

"Celeste, what are you doing here?"

Her dad blinked at her almost as if he thought her standing on his doorstep was an illusion and at any moment she'd disappear.

"I flew down this morning."

He reached into his pocket and took out his key, inserted it into the condo door lock and twisted it. "You might have called."

"It was a spontaneous thing, and I tried to call a little while ago. You didn't answer."

He frowned. "I was at pickleball. Are you staying here with me?" It was clear from his tone he hoped the answer was no.

"No. I booked a hotel room."

"Where's Jonathan?"

She had no intention of filling her dad in on what was happening with Jonathan. Even if he did feign concern, he'd insist on talking about that instead of why she'd come—to confront him about Hannah Hawley and find the key to the safe.

He set about making coffee in the kitchen, turning on the

percolator and then pouring them each a cup. "Cream or sugar?" he asked.

"Both. Thank you."

He slid a cup to her.

"You had a girlfriend after Mom left," Celeste said.

He clinked his spoon on the edge of the coffee cup. She thought she detected a slight tremor in his hand. "I'm sure I dated several women after your mom left."

"I only remember one, and I'm not sure I'd call her a woman. More like a girl."

He frowned, but said nothing.

"She was your student and our babysitter. Hannah Hawley."

"And?"

"And how could you get involved with a student? How could you move her into our house right after our mother left? If you did that today, you'd go to prison."

He pursed his lips. "I was in a very difficult position, Celeste. I was a working father with two young children and Hannah was already helping so much. You both knew and loved her. She'd been babysitting for the two of you for a year. It just...evolved."

"A sexual relationship with a teenager just evolved?" Celeste demanded. "What if Mom had come home and found her sleeping in your bed? Or weren't you worried about that?"

"It crossed my mind. Of course it did, but frankly, your mother left. End of story. If she came back and was...was angry about my relationship with Hannah, well then, so be it. I was angry she'd abandoned me with two small children."

"So you inserted a mean teenage girl who hated us into the house?"

"That's not true. Hannah loved you both. She was...well, she was young, but—"

"She hated us," Celeste interrupted him. "No one thinks

Mom left. No one who knew her in West Virginia believes she left us."

"Well, she did." He stood and walked stiffly toward the sliding glass door, unlocked and opened it. "It's stuffy in here. I need some air."

Celeste followed him out. It was hot and muggy, hardly a space for fresh air. "I want to see the letter she sent you. You said Mom mailed a letter after she left. Where is it?"

His eyes widened. Sweat had broken out on his hairline. The humidity on the balcony was thick, suffocating. "I threw that out years ago. When we were still in West Virginia, I'm sure."

"You didn't think you should save it for our sakes? Mine and Adam's?"

"No, because I assumed your mother would eventually come back. It wasn't important, a few lines about needing more time, more space."

"You never reported her missing."

He braced his hands against the rail and squinted down at the courtyard. "It's too hot out here," he huffed, walking back into the condo. Again, Celeste followed him. "I did not report her missing because she wasn't missing. She left of her own free will. She was an adult woman. People are allowed to leave, Celeste."

"She loved us. Her world revolved around us. Everyone said so. You expect me to believe she walked out one day and never came back? Never so much as called to check in on us, never sent a birthday card?"

"I don't care what you believe." He wiped the sweat from his brow and walked to the thermostat, cranked the air conditioner higher.

"Her friend Luanne asked you to report her missing."

"I don't remember that."

"And her aunt Clementine told me she believes you did something to her. That you...hurt her."

His jaw tensed and something flickered in his eyes. "What do you mean her aunt Clementine told you? Clem is dead. She's been dead for years."

Celeste stared at him, tried to understand why he'd lie about such a thing. "No, she's not. I visited her cabin in the mountains. She was very much alive."

"I was in West Virginia when she died. I'd gone back to check on the house. The police called me. Nettie and I were her only next of kin. She's dead, Celeste."

Celeste blinked at him, marched back through her memory of that night, getting lost in the woods, sitting mesmerized in front of Clem's fire. It had been real. And yet...

Nathaniel's stomach growled loudly. He winced, eyes narrowing on Celeste. "Good grief. What are you thinking, Celeste? Dredging all this up now." He rubbed his stomach and closed his eyes. "I need to use the bathroom," he murmured.

Her dad disappeared into the bathroom and a part of her wondered if he'd hide inside until she left, anything to avoid the difficult conversation.

His condo wasn't big, and she knew what she was looking for. She slipped down the hall and into his bedroom, hurrying to the closet. The doors squeaked when she opened them and she cringed, but did not hear her father emerge from the bathroom.

She quickly scanned the top shelf. There were three shoe-boxes and a stack of blankets. She pushed his clothes apart and checked the floor. Nothing. Biting her lip and listening for sounds of her father exiting the bathroom, she hurried to the bed and hunched down. A pair of slippers beneath his side of the bed.

Celeste ran lightly to the guest bedroom. It was plain, with no pictures on the walls, a basic white bedspread covering the full bed. Again, the closet doors squeaked when she opened them, but she ignored it and pushed on. This closet was much fuller. Clothes crowded the rack. Golf clubs sat at an angle. In the corner behind a pair of rollerblades she could hardly believe her father had ever worn, she saw the green tote. It was the same one he'd moved from house to house for years.

Celeste yanked off the top, grimacing at the loud sharp pop as it unsealed. She glanced at the doorway, empty.

Focus.

She thrust her hands into the box, pushed aside the tattered *Romeo and Juliet* novel, the folder of personal paperwork, pulled out two Polaroids, both of Celeste and Adam. At the bottom, her fingers brushed the velvet corner of the box. She didn't open it, just shoved the whole box into her pocket, closed the lid on the tote and thrust it back into the closet as she heard the toilet flush across the condo.

She stood and ran on the pads of her feet back to the kitchen. As the door to the bathroom opened, she withdrew the box from her pocket and shoved it deep in her purse.

When her dad emerged from the bathroom, he looked pale.

"Are you okay?" Celeste asked.

He filled a glass of water and drank it quickly. "I'm fine. Might be...catching a bit of a cold." He wiped a hand across his forehead.

"Why did we leave West Virginia?"

He rubbed his temples. "Celeste, I'm not feeling well."

"I won't ask anything else. I'll leave and you can take a nap, but tell me this last thing. Why did we move to Michigan?"

He shook his head. "A job offer."

"A job in a plastics plant. Not a teaching job."

"I'd had enough teaching. It was time for a new beginning."

44

Nettie

"I made you an old-fashioned." Nathaniel carried the drink to where Nettie sat on the porch and handed it to her.

She took it. "You used to get mad at me when I drank these. Now you're feeding them to me."

He stared at her, eyes hard. "If you don't want it—" He reached for the glass.

"No. I do." She sipped the drink and patted the chair. "Come sit with me. I feel like we haven't had a good talk in weeks."

Adam and Celeste were both asleep in the playpen, wisps of Celeste's hair fluttering from Adam's breath.

Nathaniel perched on the edge of the chair, stare fixed on the lake, eyes far away. "What do you want to talk about?"

"Anything. How's school going?"

"Good. Typical end-of-year stuff. Students and teachers, all ready to clock out for the summer."

"And you too?"

"Of course." He appeared agitated, stiff.

"Relax. Why do you look so edgy?"

He glanced at her as if surprised. "I'm not. I'm just…" He shrugged and eased back into the chair, but the tightness didn't fall away from his body. He looked ready to spring out in an instant.

After a dinner of leftover meatloaf, Nettie went upstairs and put the kids to bed. She'd suggested to Nathaniel they watch a movie, but he'd shaken his head, wanted to go for an evening run. He'd never been a runner, but now he planned to train for a 5K.

He'd pecked Nettie on the cheek and walked out the door.

When had the erosion of their love begun? With her second surprise pregnancy? Weeks where Nettie struggled to hold down so much as a piece of dry toast? Or in the days after Adam came into the world and they both moved through the house like two strangers, their interaction little more than transactions as they juggled a baby and an infant and collapsed each night to catch a few hours of sleep?

Busyness had thrown a cloak over the fraying threads of their marriage. Him at school and her tending to the children, working at animal control. Both of them mired in the details of the house, the bills and their growing family.

She stared at his loafers tossed haphazard near the door. He'd always been meticulous about putting his stuff away. It had sometimes annoyed her. Nettie had not been raised in a clean house and Nathaniel's desire for order at times felt oppressive, but now his lack of care provoked another type of distress in her. As if the carelessness of the shoes represented his feelings toward her and the marriage. It had been months since he'd touched her with intent, with desire.

"I'm just tired," she murmured.

Her period was days away and like clockwork she'd slipped into the throes of premenstrual angst—achy back, cramps, bloating. Tiredness, hormones, overwhelm. The list that might justify her feelings of loneliness, her fear that he might suddenly leave, was endless. It could easily be written off as the thoughts that arise during PMS and yet each time her eyes landed on those askew shoes, a jolt of fear snaked up her body.

Upstairs, Nettie changed into her nightgown and lay on the bed. She began to cry, but soon her eyelids were heavy and she slipped away.

Nettie woke disoriented and dry-mouthed. A slight ache pulsed behind her eyes. She stood and made her way to the bathroom, grasping the side table, then trailing a hand along the wall in her unsteadiness. She took a sip of water, blinking against the fuzziness in her brain.

As she made her way back to bed, she realized Nathaniel's side of the bed lay empty. She leaned toward the alarm clock. The numbers blurred, then focused.

1:32 am.

Why was he still awake? Had he come to bed and, like her, woken back up?

Nettie moved toward the doorway and paused. Somewhere in the house, she caught a snatch of voices. She couldn't make them out, though she thought one belonged to Nathaniel. Had Celeste woken?

As if in response to the thought, Celeste cried out. "Mommy!" The call had come from Celeste's room just feet away. She was not downstairs with Nathaniel.

Nettie, still foggy, hurried to Celeste's room and cracked the door. Her daughter stood in her crib gripping the side, her big green eyes watching Nettie.

"Hi, Ceecee. Did you wake up?"

"Up. Up!" Celeste said, waving her arms.

As Nettie carried Celeste down the stairs, she encountered Nathaniel coming up.

"Is there someone here?" Nettie asked. "I heard voices."

He stared at her, then shook his head. "It must have been the television. Celeste woke up?"

"Yeah. I'm going to get her a bottle."

"Let me. I'll bring it up in a minute."

Nettie yawned and nodded. Grogginess pulled at her like a mental undertow. "Okay," she murmured. "Thank you."

Nettie returned Celeste to her room and sat in the rocking chair next to the window. She hummed *Rock-a-bye Baby* and nestled her daughter against her chest. Celeste began to curl her fingers into Nettie's hair. Nettie's eyelids fluttered and refused to stay open.

She couldn't pinpoint the source of her tiredness. Had her single cocktail from the night before caused the sedating effect? She didn't drink often, but in previous years, she'd never had trouble putting away three or four old-fashioneds in a night and waking up perfectly fine.

"Here you go," Nathaniel said, startling Nettie, who'd begun to doze.

"Thanks," she mumbled.

45

———————

Celeste caught the six a.m. flight out of Tampa and was back in Kingwood, West Virginia, by noon. She didn't bother going to the A-frame, but drove straight to her childhood home.

She walked in through the side door, made her way into the hall, and paused. The house smelled, as it had before, of mildew and dust, but there was a new smell, a faint cologne smell. Celeste sniffed the air, tried to follow it deeper into the house. Where was it coming from? Had she disturbed something that had released the scent? Perhaps something in the totes in the upper bedroom. Celeste walked quickly through the house, peering into the rooms. The scent was stronger upstairs. In the master bedroom, she stopped and stared at the shelf near the closet. The trophy she'd thrown at the mirror had been returned to its place on the shelf.

Celeste searched her memory. Had she put it back?

No.

Someone else had been in the house.

Celeste pulled her cell phone from her bag and called Harris.

"Hey, Celeste," Harris answered.

"Hi. Sorry to bother you. Are you working?"

"I am, but I can take five minutes. What's happening?"

"Probably nothing. I'm back in West Virginia and just walked into my childhood house and...I smell cologne, something that wasn't here before."

"Cologne?"

"Yes."

"Anything else disturbed?"

"I think so. There's a trophy that was on the floor and now it's on the shelf."

"Leave."

"Has there been any sign of Jonathan?" Celeste asked.

"No. He's still missing. Celeste, just get out of the house, okay? Just in case."

"Maybe it's..." She thought of what her dad said. *Clem is dead.* And the ringing phone, the boy in the mask, the phantom of Moon Lake.

"Maybe it's what?" he asked.

"The other stuff. The paranormal stuff."

"Do you think it's that?"

She bit her lip. "It's lingering, and it's quite strong."

"Whatever it is," Harris said, "it's making you feel uncomfortable. Follow that feeling and leave."

"All right," she agreed.

"Call me as soon as you're back at the A-frame," he said.

"Sure."

Celeste walked back downstairs. As she passed the closet with the crawl space, she paused. She wanted to open the safe, had flown all the way to Florida for the key. But what if someone was already down there? Waiting?

"No." She shook her head. There was no reason to think that. If anything, the person she needed to worry about was her dad and he was in Florida. She doubted he could even get into the crawl space.

"Five minutes," she whispered.

Celeste slipped into the closet. The rug was still bunched to the side, the crawl space door standing open as she'd left it. She dropped into the hole, shining her cell light around the space, prepared to discover someone hunched in a far corner watching her. The space was empty.

She shuffled to the safe, inserted the key in the lock, and hesitated. Again, the potential of discovering something terrible assailed her. The boy's face, the bloody Halloween mask, twisted through her thoughts.

The safe was big enough for a body, a child's body. Elliot Thacker's body.

Celeste bit her lip and turned the key. She swung open the heavy door, shining her flashlight over the contents. An immediate breath of relief whooshed from her lungs. No skeleton. No long-ago-decomposed corpse.

Photographs and videotapes. That was it.

Celeste's crouched position was causing a cramp in her left hip. She shifted onto her knees and flinched when her fingers brushed something furry in the dirt. She shined her light down. A tuft of dark animal fur stuck from the soil. An animal must have died in the crawl space.

She shuddered and returned her attention to the contents of the safe.

Celeste lifted the first Polaroid out and recoiled.

It was Hannah Hawley, wearing only a pair of red under-pants, tiny breasts exposed. She knelt on the bed in the master bedroom.

Stomach clenched, Celeste flipped through the others, stared at more half-naked photos of Hannah. As she flipped, she discovered a second teenager, also in various stages of undress with a man who was not Celeste's dad.

Celeste studied the man. He looked vaguely familiar, but she couldn't place him. In some of the picture the second girl was straddling the man. In others, Hannah was kneeling over her dad, long blonde hair brushing his chest.

Celeste looked away, the photos so disturbing she wanted to lock them back inside the safe.

There were ten videotapes, none of them labeled. She gathered all the photos and videotapes. As she started to close the safe, her eyes landed on a single piece of jewelry in the bottom of the box. A ring.

Celeste picked it up and, for a moment, the ground tilted beneath her. Her eyes blurred and when she focused them again, she understood what she held in her fingers. Her mother's wedding ring. The gold band with the heart-shaped diamond in the center.

What did it mean that it was tucked here in this safe? That her mother had left it behind?

She shined her light once more into the safe and saw she'd missed a notebook towards the back. She pulled it out, gathered it with the box of videotapes, the Polaroids stacked on top, and crouch-walked back to the trapdoor.

She shoved everything through the opening and crawled up after it.

In the living room, she deposited the photos and videos on the coffee table and sat down on the couch with the notebook. When she flipped it open, she saw it was a handwritten planner, a seven-day grid drawn onto each page with dates in the corners. On the inside cover, it read: *Property of Nettie Harrington.*

Celeste stared at the writing, small and messy, but legible. Her mother had written appointments, grocery lists and, at times, a few scrawled sentences. Why was Nettie's old planner in the safe?

She flipped through it, scanning doctor and dentist

appointments. Reminders to call Luanne, to take pet food to Clem, to get Adam a teething toy.

On some of the dates, Nettie had written little notes.

Celeste had a fever this morning. 102. Nathaniel says it's allergies.

Nathaniel basketball tournament Saturday and Sunday.

Hannah watching kids from 4-7 p.m.

Nathaniel extra basketball practices on Tuesday and Thursdays.

Ask Clem for spring tonic recipe.

Celeste stopped at a note written about a month before Nettie disappeared.

Found Hannah's clothes in the dryer this morning, shorts, t-shirt and underwear too. (Frowning face.)

The next note was written on a date several days later.

Met Sheila. Her truck broke down. Drove her and Elliot (grandson) home.

Celeste's eyes lingered on the name Elliot. Her mother had met Sheila and Elliot Thacker, but that was years before Elliot had disappeared. She thought again of the notion of her mother returning, half mad, snatching Elliot up and carrying him away. The Phantom of Moon Lake, but real, a flesh-and-blood woman haunting the holler, as Spencer called it.

On several dates, Nettie had noted her alcoholic drinks. *Nathaniel made me an old-fashioned tonight—groggy.*

The same note was on two dates in the next week.

Another note less than a week before she went missing.

Got in an accident last night. Run off the road by large truck. Scary. Sheriff said lucky to be alive.

Two days before Nathaniel claimed Nettie had stomped from the house:

I've begun to dread the night.

46

———————

Celeste hunted through a house for a camcorder to play the tapes on. She didn't find one.

She called Spencer. "Spencer?"

"Yep." He sounded like he had a mouthful of food.

"You don't own an old video camera, do you? The kind that recorded on little cassettes?"

"I'm old school, but not that old school. Why do you need one?"

Celeste thought about the tapes, about whether she wanted to share what she'd found.

"Celeste?"

"I found a box of old videos at my dad's. I want to watch them." Her phone beeped low battery.

"I could probably track one down and bring it by. We could watch them together. Maybe I'll get lucky and catch a glimpse of Elliot somewhere in the footage. Shoot, we could even poke around the house a bit. See if—"

Celeste shook her head. "Maybe," she cut him off. "I'll call you back later."

She hung up before he could reply.

———

In Kingwood, she found the only pawnshop and hurried to the aisle filled with old, dusty electronics. Large stereos, VCRs and boxed TVs lined the shelves. No camcorders.

At the long glass counter, she waited for the guy working to notice her. He was staring at his phone, whispering urgently. She glanced down and saw a soccer game.

"No!" he shouted and slapped his hand on the glass, startling Celeste.

He looked up and blinked. "Shit. Sorry. You been there long?"

"No. Just a couple of minutes. I'm looking for a camcorder. Something that could play one of these."

He sent a longing glance at the sports game on his phone, then set it aside and took the tape from her hand and turned it over. A woman emerged from a back room and set a dusty DVD player on the counter.

"Nope," he said. "Don't have one in the store. Call over to King Pawn in Morgantown. They've got every gadget that's ever existed. Prices are highway robbery, but if people'll pay it." He shrugged and returned his eyes to his phone.

"Thanks," Celeste told him.

As she started leaving the store, she spotted a cane leaning against a glass-topped bureau. It was knobby and appeared hand-carved.

Celeste picked it up. It was priced at forty dollars.

She returned to the counter. "I'll take this."

The guy rang her up, and she paid cash.

As she started to climb into her truck, a woman emerged from a side door in the store. She waved at Celeste and jogged over.

"Hey, are you looking for a camcorder?"

"Yes."

"I've got one. It's in a storage unit we just bought. If you can hang around for half an hour, I'll run and get it. Probably cost ya fifty dollars?"

"That'd be great. Thank you."

As Celeste waited for the woman to return with the camcorder, a large white SUV pulled into the lot and parked. A woman got out and started toward the store. It took Celeste a moment to place her.

"Nicole!" she called when the name returned.

The woman removed her sunglasses. She walked to Celeste. "Hello again," she said.

"Do you have a minute?" Celeste asked.

Nicole glanced at the pawnshop door. Celeste sensed she had no interest in talking, but she sighed and nodded. "Just a few. I have a Bernese Mountain Dog getting dropped at the salon for a bath in a half hour."

"When I asked you the other day if my dad was with Hannah before my mom left, you hesitated."

Nicole chewed her bottom lip. "I honestly don't know. I mean...I suspected, I think a lot of us at school did. When rumors started that Coach Harrington's wife had abandoned the family, I figured she found out or...something worse."

"Something worse?"

"Ever see that movie *Poison Ivy?* The one where the wife is sick, and the girl moves in to take care of her, but ends up killing her to get the husband? That's Hannah. Not literally, but I swear the first time I saw that movie, I nudged my husband, pointed at the screen, and said, 'That's Hannah Hawley.'"

"Are you saying you believe Hannah killed my mother?" It hadn't crossed Celeste's mind that rather than her dad, it might have been his young girlfriend behind her mother's disappearance.

Nicole's face darkened. "I don't have any proof of that. None. And maybe it's a totally insane idea. But Hannah got what she wanted. I mean, obviously your dad was in the wrong. She was a student, a teenager, but if you knew Hannah, she didn't back down when she went after something.

"She liked this guy our freshman year in high school. Danny Frisk. He was a senior, had a girlfriend, but Hannah was mad for him and wanted him to date her and ask her to prom. She started bumping into him everywhere, on purpose, obviously. And when she saw him, she'd pour on the compliments —'you played so great Saturday night, you're the hottest guy in school,' on and on. Then she began the attack on Shelby, his girlfriend. First, she dug up some ugly picture of Shelby from middle school and had like a hundred copies printed at the library and hung them on the lockers. Then she started spreading rumors about her. That Shelby was easy and had been sleeping with two or three other guys on the football team. She even planted used condoms in Shelby's car."

Celeste frowned. "Really?" A part of her wondered if she was hearing the type of wild rumors that infested high schools, spreading like a virus and mutating into ever stranger, more exaggerated forms. Yet in the back of her mind, the young woman from her memories, cruel in hidden, underhanded ways, fit the personality of the girl Nicole described.

"Yes. Honest to God. I was with her. She stole the condoms from her mom and squirted some hand soap in them. I don't know exactly what happened, but within two days, Danny had broken up with Shelby and started dating Hannah. And let me add, this wasn't the first time something like this happened. There was even a rumor in middle school she burned down the house of some boy who rejected her. Now I don't have firsthand knowledge of that, but I wouldn't put it past her."

"In middle school? That sounds a little farfetched."

Nicole shrugged. "Maybe, but like I said, Hannah got what

she wanted. Once she got interested in your dad, well...look at how that turned out."

"You think Hannah pursued my dad?"

"I know she did. I was in the same chemistry class. She started wearing these tiny skirts, asking him for help after class, asking him for rides home after basketball practice. It was obvious what she was doing."

"How long after my mom left did Hannah move in?"

"Soon. I can't say how soon, but I'd say weeks after, maybe only days. Hannah couldn't get out of her house fast enough."

Celeste rubbed the hollows beneath her eyes. A headache had begun to seep in. "My dad moved her in while she was still a student, and no one confronted him? Called the police or anything? He didn't lose his job?"

"Times were different back then. There was kind of a 'don't ask, don't tell' policy, you know? And Mr. Harrington was a star in Kingwood. He'd coached the girls' basketball team to the championship. No one wanted to see him leave the school. She was more than happy to take your mom's place, but the shimmer wore off real quick. Diapers and cooking and cleaning. She didn't know how to do any of it. I remember her and I changing one of your brother's diapers. It was the blind leading the blind. It fell off three times before we finally figured it out. Honestly, I was afraid you and your brother might have an accident."

A memory surfaced of Hannah and her dad fighting in the kitchen. Celeste didn't know how old she'd been, four or five maybe. Her dad was furious because he'd come home to find Celeste and Adam out on the deck unattended. *They could have drowned,* he'd yelled at her.

"Do you remember any rumors at all that something bad might have happened to my mom?" Celeste asked.

"No. He sold the story your mom left, abandoned him with two kids, and everyone bought it. No questions asked."

"What about someone running my mom off the road? Ever hear anything about that?"

Nicole shook her head. "No, and Hannah didn't have a car, but I will say this, she could get people to do what she wanted. Guys especially, and there were more than a handful in school during those days who would have happily done it if they thought they could get in her pants."

"But no one ever said they did it?"

"Not to me."

"How long was Hannah living with us? I have memories of her, but for some reason, it's like my whole childhood in West Virginia is a blur."

"Hannah didn't leave the Moon Lake house until your dad left. She acted real weird about the whole thing. I hadn't talked to her in months then. She was playing house, and I'd already started workin' at a department store in town.

"One day she shows up at the store looking for a job. I was like, 'Come again? What happened to the golden boy?' That's what we called him. Even though he wasn't a boy, he was a grown man. Anyway, she shrugged it off and said they'd broken up and he'd moved and taken his kids. End of story. I mean, we literally never talked about it again. It was like those years disappeared into a hole. I tried to get it out of her a few times, but she'd get pretty defensive and either change the subject or just leave. So after a while, I stopped. I figured he must have dumped her, and she was feeling sour about it."

"When did you lose contact with her?"

"Oh, gosh, twenty years ago probably. She stayed in Kingwood for a few years after your dad moved away and then she left. I couldn't tell you where." Nicole looked at her watch. "I really have to go."

"One more thing, please." Celeste took out the Polaroid that showed the second man and the other teen girl. Celeste carefully positioned her fingers over the image to hide their nakedness. "Do you recognize them?"

Nicole looked at it, frowned, then nodded. "That's Loretta Boggs. She's married to Junior, the guy who owns Hobart's General store. And you've met this guy. It's the teacher, Garth Durand."

47

Celeste drove back toward Moon Lake beneath a bruised sky. Heavy dark clouds were gathering.

Rain began to fall, softly at first, then harder, drumming against the windshield. By the time she arrived at her childhood home, it was a downpour.

She'd half-considered driving to the Children's Museum to confront Garth, but her desperation to watch the videos had won out. Celeste tucked the box with the camcorder under her arm and ran into the house.

Rain pounded on the roof as Celeste settled on the sofa and loaded the first tape. The tiny screen flickered to life, its grainy image adjusting and stabilizing to reveal a moment frozen in time.

The video began with a shaky close-up of her mother's face. Celeste sucked in a breath. Nettie, young and vibrant, laughed into the lens, her dark hair framing her face in soft waves. "Is this thing on?" her mother asked. Celeste had no living memory of her mother's voice, but now it existed. She literally held it in her hands, and the sound tugged at the rope of some deep yearning she'd dropped into a dark hole a long time ago, meant never to retrieve.

The camera tilted, then steadied, as her father's voice responded off-screen, "Yeah, it's on. Say something to future Celeste."

Her mother's smile widened, and she came fully into frame, her pregnant belly beginning to show pressed against a green and white striped dress.

"Hi, Ceecee," Nettie said, resting her hands on her belly and tilting her face down. "Mama wants you to know she loves you so much and your daddy and I are so excited to meet you!"

"We sure are," Nathaniel said. The video wobbled and Celeste realized her dad had set the camera down. He moved into the frame and wrapped his arms around Nettie, kissing her.

Young and in love. That was how they looked. No cracks in the façade, worry lines at the mouth, dark circles beneath the eyes. Nothing at all in their demeanors that foreshadowed the grim future awaiting them.

In the next clip, the camera ascended the upstairs hallway and into the open doorway of Celeste's bedroom. The walls were painted a fresh pink with bright yellow daisies. In place of the daybed stood a crib, a mobile of colorful dogs and cats dangling above it. The image panned to Nettie in a white rocking chair, a pink-wrapped bundle pressed tight against her. She was humming a song. It sounded like *Unchained Melody*.

"There are my girls," Nathaniel whispered.

Nettie's eyes drifted up, sleepy, but happy. She looked so happy.

The clip ended.

On the couch, Celeste shifted, the ache deeper than her body.

The footage shifted to a sunny day by the lake. Celeste recognized the dock out front, though it looked newer and sturdier than it did now. Her father stood waist-deep in the water, a baby tucked in his arms.

"How's my little Ceecee?" her mother called.

Nathaniel dipped Celeste's feet in the water. She squealed and laughed, kicking her legs.

Celeste made it through two entire video cassettes, watching glimpses of her infancy and baby years with her mom and dad. Tense, she studied each video, searching for the moment it all began to change, but had yet to witness the fracture.

It dawned on her as she slid the next tape into the camcorder that she'd likely not find one. No earth-shattering moment, no sudden rip in their once-happy lives. Like her marriage to Jonathan, the disease would be invisible and insidious—a latent virus, lying dormant until conditions favored its emergence. For her dad, those emerging conditions had been Hannah Hawley.

As she slid the next cassette in, a red battery blinked on the screen. The video died. Celeste would have to watch the rest of the videos back at the A-frame, where she could charge the camcorder.

She gathered up the tapes and loaded them into her passenger seat. When she turned the key in her truck's ignition. It didn't start—didn't even make a sound.

"Shit." It had been pouring rain when she'd arrived. Had she forgotten to turn off the lights and drained the battery? The truck had also died on her way to see Clem. There might be some other issue with the engine, which meant she'd have to call a tow truck, take it to a mechanic and get a rental car. The whole process sounded daunting.

She rested her head against the seat and closed her eyes. Tiredness gnawed at her. The walk around the lake back to the A-frame was at least three or four miles. The sky looked dark and green and there'd likely be more rain. She could sleep in the truck, a thought that instantly caused her hip to start grumbling.

"Okay," she muttered. She stepped from the truck, locked it, and returned to the house.

It was a perfectly good house, still almost entirely furnished. There was no reason not to sleep inside.

With no power in the house or in her truck, Celeste could not charge her cell phone. She considered walking next door to Rose's house, asking to use a plug for an hour, but mostly she wanted to lie down, close her eyes and capture a six-hour reprieve from the ugly truths she'd been discovering.

She found a set of bedding in the master bedroom closet, shook it out and made the bed. The humidity transformed the already stuffy house into a sauna. Celeste opened the windows, lay down and closed her eyes.

Sharp fingernails dug into Celeste's forearm.

'Get back in your own bed!' the girl hissed. She dragged a groggy Celeste from the bed and marched her down the hall, shoved her into the twin bed and slipped from the room, a whoosh of blonde hair before the door slammed.

Celeste startled awake, one foot in the dream. As her eyes adjusted to the wall opposite her, she realized she had woken in her childhood bedroom—the curtain swaying lazily through the open window.

The dream hovered, the sting of the girl's fingernails as she'd dragged Celeste out of the master bedroom. Had Celeste acted the dream out and sleepwalked to her childhood room?

A window next to the bed stood open. She blinked at it, aware she had not opened the window. As she studied the darkness, two black eyes watched her from the ledge. She jumped from the bed, heart thumping, her left leg spasming, then righting itself.

The creature's head turned, and the mouth opened, releasing a scratchy caw—a raven.

The bird shuddered, then flapped its wings and flew into the night.

From downstairs, she heard the moan of a floorboard. Celeste tilted her head and listened. The house was old, had been abandoned for years. Humidity from the lake and hot summers combined with cold winters had likely warped boards, caused the entire place to grumble more than a newer house might.

Another sound—soft, deliberate—footsteps climbing the staircase this time. Her breath caught, and she froze, straining her ears.

One step. Pause.

Another.

On tiptoe, Celeste moved to the closet, eased open the door and slipped inside. She shuffled behind the hanging clothes, biting her lip as she angled a hamper full of stuffed animals in front of her.

Her vision tunneled and her mind raced as she tried to put together who might be in the house. Jonathan? Had he followed her from Michigan after all? It didn't fit the Jonathan in her mind.

Who then? Her dad? She could not picture him creeping around at night. If he were afraid of what she might uncover in the house, would he send someone? Someone to retrieve evidence? Someone to silence her?

She imagined what Nicole had said about Hannah Hawley. *She gets what she wants.* But Hannah no longer lived in the area. She couldn't possibly know that Nettie Harrington's daughter had returned to Moon Lake searching for her mother. Unless

Nicole had lied about knowing where Hannah lived and had tipped her off.

The bedroom door groaned open. Celeste stared at the closed closet door, little more than a black silhouette. Sweat rolled between her shoulder blades.

The temperature in the closet began to drop. As the chill seeped in, the sweat coating Celeste's body turned icy.

A faint beam of light flickered under the closet door. A flashlight.

Celeste pressed her back against the closet wall, her knees drawn to her chest. Her hip burned from the tension, but she didn't move, didn't breathe.

To her right, she heard a tinny sound like change clinking together. The sound had come from within the closet.

Claustrophobia pushed in. She had the sudden dangerous impulse to scream, to claw the clothes away from her face and lunge from the closet. She was going to panic and give herself away.

The beam swept back and forth. She waited for the closet door to swing open, the beam to illuminate her hiding place.

She turned her head, blinked into the gloom and saw in the far corner, only partly visible behind hanging clothes, the face of the boy in the Halloween mask.

His eyes were two dark pits in the pale plastic face. They had no distinguishable characteristic and yet she felt them boring into her, angry, hostile.

Celeste forced her eyes forward, watched the beam of the flashlight disappear from the room.

Total darkness now.

48

———

Nettie

"Have you seen my necklace?" Nettie asked Nathaniel.

"What necklace?" He didn't bother looking up from the newspaper.

Nettie tried to keep the irritation from her face. She wore no jewelry besides her wedding ring and the gold key necklace. "The gold necklace you gave me when we moved in. The only necklace I ever wear."

He glanced up. "No. Where do you usually put it?"

"I thought I left it by the bathroom sink when I showered yesterday, but it's not there."

"Did you look on the floor? It probably fell." He returned to the paper.

Nettie had looked on the floor and behind the toilet and in all the bathroom drawers. She'd checked dresser tops and windowsills and every foreseeable place she might have set it down. It was nowhere.

That afternoon, Nettie eyed Hannah's purple backpack. The girl took it with her everywhere. She thought of her necklace, the tube of lipstick by her bed, the rumpled comforter from days before. Was Hannah going into her room when she was gone? Had she taken the necklace?

Nettie quickly unzipped the bag, eyes darting repeatedly to the front window, where Hannah played in the yard with Celeste. She dug past schoolbooks, a tattered notebook, a bunched-up sweatshirt. Her fingers hit something hard at the bottom of the bag. She gripped it and lifted it out, her stomach plunging.

It was a sterling silver framed wedding photo of her and Nathaniel. It usually sat on his desk at school, but now it lay at the bottom of Hannah's backpack. Nettie's face had been scratched out.

Nettie marched outside to where Hannah stood blowing bubbles with Celeste. Adam laughed and pointed at the bubbles from his playpen.

"Hannah, I need to talk to you," Nettie said, trying to steady her voice.

Hannah handed the bubbles to Celeste, her long blonde hair cascading over her shoulders. She wore cut-off white shorts and a bikini top.

Nettie said nothing. She held out the photo to Hannah.

The color drained from Hannah's face.

"We no longer need your babysitting services, Hannah. Get your stuff together. I'm taking you home."

Hannah's mouth opened as if she wanted to argue, but after a moment she said nothing, only dropped her head and rushed into the house. Nettie followed her, wanting to make sure she didn't stuff anything into her backpack.

During the drive to Hannah's house, Celeste chattered in the backseat, holding up a series of little plastic animals and showing them to Adam.

In the passenger seat, Hannah began to cry. "I'm...I'm sorry, Mrs. Harrington," she whispered. "I...that happened ages ago and I shouldn't have. Please."

"Mommy, Hannah's crying," Celeste shouted from the backseat, alarmed.

"That's okay, Ceecee," Nettie told her, reaching an arm back and patting her leg. "Sometimes we all need a good cry."

Nettie ignored Hannah's pleading. When she parked her truck in front of Hannah's mom's trailer, the teenager grew hysterical.

"Please, please, don't make me go. I love Celeste and Adam and—"

Celeste and Adam started to cry as well.

"Hannah, get out of my truck." Nettie fought to keep her voice measured, to withhold the rage she'd felt toward Hannah for months.

Hannah, as if sensing Nettie's fury, closed her mouth and stepped from the truck. Tears streamed down her face as she ran to the trailer and disappeared inside.

When Nathaniel returned that night, he said nothing. Nettie understood that somehow, he knew she'd fired Hannah.

They ate takeout pizza he'd picked up and took the kids out on the boat.

As they got ready for bed, Nettie watched Nathaniel walking around in his underwear. He'd gotten leaner that summer, stronger. He and Garth had been working out at the high school gym doing weight training. He ran nearly five days a week and had largely stopped eating sugar.

"Nathaniel?"

"Hmm...?" He picked up a trophy from his shelf, licked his thumb and rubbed it across the face.

"Has something been going on with you and Hannah?"

He looked up, startled. "You're joking, right?"

She stared at him. "No."

He raised an eyebrow and returned to the trophy to the shelf. "No. That's a ridiculous thing to ask me."

"Is it?"

He frowned and climbed into bed. "Yes, it is." He pulled the blankets up and rolled on his side, facing away from her.

49

Despite her terror, Celeste sat in the closet for nearly an hour. When she finally crawled out, she could hardly bear weight on her left leg and had to limp painfully down the stairs and out to her truck. She didn't have a plan, but wanted to get away from the house. She had no idea what time it was, suspected daylight was still several hours away.

She unlocked her truck and climbed inside. When she turned the key, just like at Clem's, the truck started right up.

"Oh, thank God," she murmured.

As Celeste pulled from the drive, wind rushed through the open passenger window. She slowed, but didn't stop. Her passenger window had been smashed out. Glass glittered on the empty passenger seat. The box of videotapes was gone.

When Celeste parked at the rental house, she reached for her new cell phone, but discovered the cupholder where'd she left it empty. Whoever had taken the videotapes also had her cell. She searched the glove box for her old cell phone. Also gone.

She was unsure what to do. Drive to the police station? If she did, she'd have to tell them everything. Her missing mom, the safe in the crawl space, Jonathan.

She needed time to process all that had happened. She limped into the rental house, locked the door behind her, poured a glass of Scotch and walked upstairs.

The thief hadn't gotten the Polaroids or her mom's planner, which she'd put in her purse the day before. Celeste flipped through the planner and made sticky notes for each of the strange comments her mother had written in the weeks leading up to her disappearance.

Everything she'd discovered pointed to a terrible likelihood that her mother had never left the Moon Lake house. She'd been murdered.

But by who?

Celeste's father? The man who gazed out from the photo albums, cupping his baby daughter in his large hands, smiling? Or Hannah Hawley, the girl from the Polaroids, the student her father had moved into the house days after her mother vanished, who Nicole described as the type of person who 'gets what she wants?'

A couple of weeks before her mother vanished, she'd written a note in her planner. *Ran into Keith Albright.*

Celeste opened her laptop and searched for his name. No results appeared for a Keith Albright in Kingwood, but she found a social media profile for a Keith Albright in Clarksburg, which wasn't far away. He looked to be about the same age her mother would have been now, and his childhood home was listed as Davis, where Nettie had grown up. As Celeste clicked around his profile, she saw hundreds of pictures with Keith and his wife, children, and grandchildren. It might not have been the same man Nettie had mentioned in her planner, but still, it made Celeste sad to look at the man's large, happy family.

She logged off and closed the laptop. Her mind swam and her body ached with each movement. She abandoned the corkboards and went into the upstairs bathroom.

Celeste ran a bath and settled into the large jacuzzi tub, releasing a deep sigh as the hot water climbed to her neck. She hadn't taken a bath since leaving Michigan, and the water instantly soothed her. The aching muscles of her hips and leg softened. A full glass of Scotch sat on the rim of the tub, but as she eyed it, her stomach squirmed. Perhaps from getting sick on it days before, the mere sight of it made her queasy.

Celeste closed her eyes, letting all the revelations of the day slip down, as she focused on the water lapping against the sides of the tub and did her best to melt. She didn't want to think about her next steps: calling the police, confronting her dad, revealing all that she'd discovered.

Most of all, she didn't want to think about that little boy in the Halloween mask.

Something creaked outside the door. Celeste's eyes snapped open. She sat up and gripped the bathtub edge and listened.

Another sound, muffled. Celeste's skin prickled. She waited, ears straining to catch any hint of movement. The house was too quiet. Her breath sounded too loud.

Celeste stood and stepped quickly from the bath, toweled off and hurried back into her clothes. The door to the bathroom was closed, but unlocked—the lock seemed to be broken —and she kept her eyes fixed on the handle.

The noises might have come from a spirit, a visitor from the other side. She'd not figured out how to discern the uncanny from the real, but the events of that night pointed to a very real predator lurking nearby.

As if in response to her thoughts, a door clicked closed somewhere in the house.

She searched the bathroom for a weapon. A rack held towels. A bottle of hand soap sat on the sink's edge. Biting her lip at the sound, she eased open the cupboard beneath the sink. A stack of washcloths, extra shampoo, conditioner and bar soap. Nothing to defend herself with.

She had to leave the bathroom. There was no window, no way to escape if someone burst through the door.

Celeste opened the door and tiptoed into the hall. She didn't wait, but hurried toward the stairs, took them lightly and veered into the kitchen, where she grabbed a butcher knife from the wood block.

Celeste slipped down the hall, craning to discern where the person might have moved to inside the house.

A sudden flurry of footsteps sounded from above her.

Celeste sprinted to the glass patio door and twisted the knob, her heart thumping a quickstep behind her ribs. She pushed the door closed and grimaced at the loud click, but she didn't have time to worry about whether they'd heard her. She ran across the porch and headed for the stairs when a man came around from the shadows at the side of the house.

Celeste screamed, bare feet sliding on the slick wood as she tried to change directions.

"Celeste?" The man spoke and her brain took an agonizing moment to register the voice: Harris.

She hadn't moved, stood with her legs splayed apart, her right hand clutching the kitchen knife.

"Are you okay? Jesus. My heart jumped out of my chest when I saw you."

Celeste's own heart had done the same, was still running down the street screaming. Steadying her breath, she walked the knife to the patio table and dropped it with a clatter. She rested a hand against her breastbone. Apparently, her heart was still in there after all, thudding madly.

"Holy shit, Harris," she muttered.

"I knocked on the front door."

"You did?"

"Yeah. For about a solid minute. Scared the daylights out of me when you didn't answer. Yesterday, when you didn't call me back and your phone started going to voicemail, I decided I better just drive down."

"Just a quick nine- or ten-hour drive to check on me?" She rubbed her face. "Thank you. My phone died and then my truck. I'm sorry I didn't call you back. I ended up having to sleep at my childhood home and there's no power. Someone broke in last night. I hid in the closet. After they left, I went to my truck and it started, but...but they smashed the window out and took all the videos." She was talking too fast, needed to slow down, take a breath.

"Someone broke into the house while you were in it?"

She nodded, then shook her head. "I broke a window out in a door downstairs. That's probably how they got in, but yeah, someone was in there with me."

"You didn't see who it was?"

She blew out a breath and sat in one of the chairs and then immediately stood back up and looked at the enormous glass window into the A-frame. "And just now I heard someone in there." She gestured at the house. "I was in the bath and—"

"Inside the house? Right now?" His hand flicked to his hip. She saw the gun there now, hadn't registered it when she first saw him. The strap hung loose. "What did you hear? Are you sure it wasn't me knocking?"

She watched the interior of the house, largely dark, as she'd extinguished most of the lights before her bath. "Footsteps and a door closing, but inside the house. I'm sure of it. Except..."

"Except what?" Harris didn't look at her. He, too, stared into the murky interior as if searching for movement.

"I've seen things since I came here. Spirits."

He glanced at her and nodded. "But for some reason, what you heard tonight struck you differently than those sounds?"

She frowned, thought of the sounds. "I don't know, but after what happened across the lake, I assumed it was the same person."

"Go sit in my car." Harris handed her the keys. "Lock the doors. I'm going to search the house."

50

After Harris searched the house and confirmed no one was inside, he and Celeste settled in the guest bedroom. She showed him her corkboards and told him what she'd discovered since coming to West Virginia, ending with the intruder in her childhood home and the stolen tapes.

"Who knew you found those videotapes?"

"No one. Well...Spencer, the podcaster. I told him because I needed a camcorder. He didn't have one."

"Remind me how you met him."

Celeste frowned. "He was standing on the road in front of my dad's house. He asked me if it was for sale, said he was a podcaster looking into a little boy's disappearance."

"Huh. Are you sure he's who he says he is?"

"Pretty sure. I've been to his house. He lives in town, half the waitstaff greet him by name. He's drowning in folklore memorabilia. And he's not exactly a James Bond."

"Could it have been Jonathan at the house?"

"It's so unlike him. And he doesn't know where my childhood home is. Plus, why would he steal the videotapes?"

"And you didn't manage to watch all of them?"

"No." Celeste wished she'd not put the videos in her truck to begin with, or that she'd taken them straight to the A-frame and not gone back to her childhood home at all. Now they were gone.

"But you found them in a safe in your dad's crawl space?"

"Yeah. Twisted, right?"

Harris rubbed his jaw and shook his head slowly. "It doesn't look good."

"No," Celeste agreed.

"If Hannah killed your mom, it seems difficult to believe your dad wasn't aware, either before or after the fact. He's the one who maintained the story of her taking off, claimed she contacted him afterwards, insisted she had a mental breakdown. Not to mention he moved the babysitter in almost immediately, strongly implying he knew your mother wasn't coming back."

Celeste sagged onto the bed. "Yeah. That's what I've thought too. What do I do now? Go to the police?"

"Yes. But you may find yourself with some resistance. You're dealing with a cold case—no, worse. A case that was never even opened. Thirty years of dust, no official missing person report, no body..." He blew out a breath. "But obviously someone is still trying to cover it up. Breaking into your truck brings the case into the present, so that helps."

He eyed the planner lying open on the small dresser. That and some of the Polaroids had been missed by whoever had broken into her truck because they'd been in her purse.

Harris studied her notes on the board. "Did your mom suspect your dad was drugging her?"

"She wrote several notes about him making her a cocktail, then feeling groggy afterwards."

"And what's this? 'I've begun to dread the night?'" He pointed at one of Celeste's sticky notes.

"She wrote that in her planner too, just a few days before she disappeared."

Harris paced away. "I can reach out to the sheriff's office for you or we can go in there together. You haven't been able to find Hannah Hawley?"

"No. I've searched for her online. No social media accounts, but maybe she's married, has a different last name."

"And here I figured you were down here getting away from all the danger."

"I don't think I'm in danger. I mean, weird stuff is going on, but, well, I think it's my mom and also...there's a little boy who disappeared from this lake. The podcaster I told you about has been working on his case for years. I keep dreaming about him and I knew him. The memories, like most of my memories here, are fuzzy, but I remember him and look at this." She flipped through her mom's planner. "A few weeks before she disappeared, she mentioned meeting Sheila and Elliot Thacker. That's the little boy, but what's strange is he went missing five years after my mom."

Harris stared at the entry. "Strange, but..." He shook his head. "If they both lived in this area, it's hard to imagine they wouldn't have met at some point. It's pretty isolated around here."

"Yeah. That's true."

"When she disappeared, your mom didn't have a vehicle?"

"No. She wrecked it before she went missing."

"And your dad claims someone picked her up, but he didn't say who."

"Yep."

"Any idea what your dad was driving at the time?"

"A convertible sports car."

"You're sure?"

Celeste nodded. "Why does that matter?"

"Because that's not a vehicle you could easily move a body in. Not impossible, but not likely, which implies she wasn't taken far."

"I think she's in the lake."

"Why?"

"Because there's a ghost, the Phantom of Moon Lake, they call her. I think it's my mother."

"Have you seen her?"

"I think so."

He nodded. "That's complicated in terms of evidence. If she was put in the lake, weighted down and hasn't floated up, any evidence on her body is long gone. Cause of death, unless she was shot or stabbed, will be impossible to determine." His eyes flicked up to her as if realizing who he spoke to. "I'm sorry. I shouldn't discuss it like this. She's your mom—"

"I barely remember her, Harris. Does it make me sick to think she didn't leave and my dad murdered her? Yes. But I'm not going to find out the truth by dissolving into some emotional mud puddle. You're right. Physical evidence is long gone. The case against him will mostly be circumstantial."

"And you're okay with that? The police opening an investigation into your dad?"

"I don't know if 'okay' is the word. Either they prove he murdered her and now my dad is a murderer and spends the last years of his life in prison, or they can't build a strong enough case against him and he's free. None of it is a happy ending."

"No. Well, death is. For all of us, we have that to look forward to."

Celeste smiled sadly. "What happens exactly if we go right now to the sheriff's office and tell them everything?"

"A lot of possible answers to that one. What's happening in the present takes precedence, but ideally, we'd talk to either the sheriff or a detective and lay out everything—your missing mother, the little boy, the timeline of events, you coming back, the escalation of vandalism, stalking, whatever it is. The fact that someone in real time is trying to shut you up or prevent you from finding something is obviously significant. If law enforcement actually hears the story and is willing to entertain that it's all connected, they assign an investigator and start trying to get warrants. Your dad owns the house. If he'll agree to a search, they don't need warrants, but—"

"That's unlikely."

"Yeah. A crime was committed there, someone broke into your truck, broke into the house. That could be deemed probable cause to enter, except you also broke into the house after your dad told you he did not want you inside. Anything they find without a warrant is liable to be tossed out in a future trial if they enter without his consent. Another issue is that your dad could press charges against you for breaking and entering, which adds another layer of legal tape to the whole ordeal."

"A legal nightmare, in other words."

"Without your mother's remains, a criminal case may never go forward."

"But there's so much evidence. The Polaroids, her planner, his keeping the house, and..." Celeste thought of the ringing phone, the spreading stain from her vision. "There might be physical evidence. There's a stain on the carpet in an upstairs bedroom."

"Forensic evidence would help, assuming there's enough left to test and get DNA. A lot of the circumstantial evidence is flimsy. Allegedly, you found those photos in a safe in the crawl space. Allegedly, that was your mother's planner. A good defense attorney will cast doubt on every single thing you've found. The most solid proof of a crime right now is that someone is trying to scare you away. And they're doing things that can get them in trouble today."

"Which strongly implies my dad didn't kill my mom."

"Unless it's Jonathan."

She blinked at him. "Why would Jonathan be trying to scare me out of my dad's house? And why would he steal videos he knows nothing about?"

"I'm not saying he is, but let's consider why he might do that. The primary reason I can think of is to send you back to Michigan, where he has control over the situation. By leaving the house, coming to West Virginia, you took away Jonathan's control. If he was involved with trying to kill you, and I think he was, keeping you close is in his best interests. Far away, you're unpredictable.

"Another element best not to ignore is that Jonathan, based on what you've said, has floated the theory of you intentionally stepping in front of that vehicle. That claim might be bolstered if suddenly you're here in West Virginia breaking into your dad's house, then saying someone is following you, smashed out your truck window. It's a way to undermine your credibility."

"But it's actually happening."

"I know that and you know that, but you'd be amazed at how many manipulative partners twist everything around to look like their unstable spouse is doing it all. It's gaslighting and people do it because it works. The person being manipulated starts to get emotional, erratic. They're so frustrated they lash out. Meanwhile, the partner pulling the strings plays it cool, seems like the sane one. If nothing else, it throws a lot of dirt on the credibility of a victim, so if a case ever reaches court, the defendant can offer their attorney a mountain of completely fabricated proof that the spouse was nuts."

"You think Jonathan is down here doing all this?" Celeste leaned back.

"I don't know, but I don't think it's impossible. He's clearly an intelligent man, and he's now backed into a corner. Police are onto him. He's scrambling. If it is him, he's a very unsafe person to be around right now."

"What do you think I should do?"

"I think *we* should set a trap."

51

Nettie

It was dark by the time Nettie left the office.

As she drove home, the rain that had been a steady drizzle all day swelled into a downpour. She turned her wipers to full speed, but their frantic tempo did little to wick away the pelting rain.

As she drove the twisty mountain roads toward home, headlights appeared behind her in the mirror. The vehicle, large based on the height of the lights, bore down on her.

"Back off," she muttered, clutching the wheel tighter and forcing her eyes back to the road. There were too many curves, too many sharp drop-offs to be distracted on this drive.

The headlights filled her cab and their reflection in the mirror pierced her eyes and gave her an instant headache. She tilted the rearview mirror down and wished there was a passing lane or even a pull-off so she could let the truck go by. There wasn't. For the next five miles, there was nothing but narrow winding roads.

The truck drew nearer.

She glanced at the dial to her radio, wanted to turn it on, find some music to calm her jittery nerves, but they were on a steep section of road and she didn't dare take even one hand off the wheel.

As she rounded an especially tight curve, her tires skidded slightly and her stomach plunged. For an instant she thought her vehicle would keep sliding, but the tires found grip and she made the curve.

Now her heart thundered with the pounding rain. Her hands had grown clammy on the wheel. Despite the slick roads, the truck following her had not fallen back.

Suddenly, the truck bumped her.

Nettie cried out and clutched the wheel. Had it been an accident? No. The truck hit her a second time, this time harder. Nettie pressed on the gas pedal and shot forward. As she came to the next curve, she knew she had to slow. It was tight, practically ninety degrees, and as she sped into it, the truck bumped her again.

There was no time to right herself. The wheel spun as her truck fishtailed and slid off the road toward the steep slope of trees.

For an instant, her truck went airborne and then gravity took hold once more and she was crashing through bushes and trees. She came to a violent stop when the front bumper rammed into an enormous pine tree crumpling the hood.

Nettie jolted forward in her seat, slammed against the wheel. The breath was sucked from her lungs. The windshield was shattered. Her bag had flown to the floor of the passenger footwell and the contents lay strewn about.

Nettie drew in a shaky, painful breath. Dazed, she unbuckled her seat belt and flung open her door. It released a metallic shriek. When she started to step out, intense pain shot through her ankle. Her foot had cracked hard against the footwell. She'd damaged, possibly broken, something.

Another smell wafted over the scent of rain-soaked woods. Gasoline.

"Shit." She limped from the wreckage, bracing her weight on her good leg, both hands clinging to the slick roof of the truck.

She looked up at the road above her and froze. The headlights of the truck pointed into the forest. The person who'd run her off the road was up there, watching.

Gasping against the pain, Nettie limped the opposite direction, away from the road and into the woods. She knew these woods. They sloped toward the deeper forest, but if she went far enough, she'd hit Moon Lake.

Two minutes into her trek, she heard a twig snap behind her.

Nettie stopped and listened. She craned around and searched the dark woods. If they'd followed her, they hadn't brought a flashlight. Like her, they were navigating the darkness.

Nettie did not know how long she limped through the woods. The damp had seeped into her clothes and hair. Her ankle throbbed. When she finally came to the lake, she moaned with relief and waded into the water in her shoes, crying out as the cold water enveloped her inflamed ankle.

She passed three houses along the lake. All were dark. When she finally stood in front of her own, a sudden tremor of fear ripped through her. What if the person who'd run her off the road had then gone to her house and attacked Nathaniel, Celeste, and Adam?

As she approached the house, she saw Nathaniel through the front windows. He stood in the living room, a cordless phone pressed to his ear.

Nettie pushed through the door and lurched into the front hall. "Call..." She struggled to catch her breath. "Call the police."

Nathaniel set the phone down and strode toward her, eyes wide. "What happened? My God, you're filthy. Here, kick your shoes off."

Nettie limped to the table and clutched a chair back, gritting her teeth. She couldn't kick her shoes off. Her ankle had swollen to the size of a cantaloupe. The skin pressed against the edge of her tennis shoe. Putting her attention there for even a moment caused a slick nausea to course through her.

"Mama, Mama." Celeste tugged on her hand. She wobbled and bumped into Nettie's leg. Nettie gasped.

"Here. Let me see," Nathaniel squatted beside her.

Nettie clenched her eyes shut, and Nathaniel rolled up her pant legs and revealed her bulging ankle. He untied the laces and gently slipped the shoe from her foot. She gripped the chairback harder.

"You need to call the police, Nathaniel. Now." She twisted around and peered at the dark hallway. She hadn't locked the door when she came in. If the person was still following her, they could walk in at any moment.

"Let's get this iced first. What happened? Why do I need to call the police?"

"Someone ran me off the road."

"On purpose?"

"Yes, on purpose, and then they...I'm pretty sure they followed me into the woods."

"Well, who was it?"

"I didn't see them. I never actually saw the person. They were driving a truck."

Nathaniel helped her to sit and positioned a bag of ice on her ankle. He grabbed the cordless phone and dialed, explaining to the dispatcher what Nettie had told him.

"Suzanne says the sheriff and both deputies are out on Crescent Road for a domestic. She can pull one of them off if it's an emergency," he told Nettie, covering the receiver with his hand.

Nettie frowned. "Well, it's not an emergency. Not right at this minute, but what if they followed me here?" She didn't want to seem hysterical. The sheriff must have his hands full if they were all on the call.

"I'll get my gun out of the safe and sleep downstairs tonight," Nathaniel said.

"Okay." It didn't feel okay, but she sensed Nathaniel's reluctance to make a big deal out of the situation. "Tell Suzanne I'll call the sheriff tomorrow."

52

It took most of the day for Celeste and Harris to put his plan into place. They drove to Morgantown and bought five surveillance cameras. Nothing high-tech, but good enough. Celeste also bought a new phone and texted the number to Adam and Detective Bowman.

Harris pulled into a beauty supply store and parked.

"What are we doing here?" Celeste asked. "Pedicures?"

"I'm sure I could use one, but no. I'm getting a wig."

"A wig?"

"Yep. Tonight, I'm going to be you."

Back in the car, Harris put the red wig on. "How do I look?"

Celeste burst out laughing. "Great. An exact replica of me."

He tilted the rearview mirror and angled his face down, batted his eyelashes. "Not by a long shot, but it'll do."

As they walked in and out of her childhood home, discussing their plan, Celeste repeatedly looked over her shoulder, squinted into the trees, worried the person who'd stolen the videotapes was observing them, aware of what they intended to do.

They set up cameras pointing at the door in the laundry

room, another in the hallway upstairs and one outside that could capture the driveway. At the rental house, they set up two additional cameras: one outside pointed at the driveway and another in the main room of the house.

After they finished, they picked up a pizza and returned to the rental house.

"Is it okay that you're down here? I can't imagine most detectives can just hop in their car and disappear for a few days," Celeste said.

Harris took a bite of his pizza. "I have a lot of PTO. Vacations haven't exactly been a priority for me for quite a long time. And"—he held up his phone—"between this and my laptop, I can do a lot of work remote. Plus, I got that green light feeling when I thought about coming. So here I am."

"And what about Robin? Is she okay with you coming?"

Harris held her eyes for a moment and then nodded. "I let her know. We're not...I mean, we are dating, but we're not serious. I've told her I'm not ready for that. Right now, she accepts it."

"Right now?"

He smiled. "People like movement, progression. There will come a point when I'm faced with the 'commit or quit' expectation and we'll cross that bridge when we come to it. What I want to know is how you're handling all this. It can't be easy."

Celeste picked up her glass of Scotch, watched the ice cubes clink around, but didn't take a drink. "Sometimes I wonder why I'm still here. Why didn't I just die during the hit-and-run? And I didn't go through an ounce of what you did, losing your wife and daughter. And yet..." Celeste pushed her hands through her hair. "I'm not sure the purpose of my being here. My life has imploded. I need you to explain to me how you keep going. How you've found peace. Alcohol seems like the only salve and even that's not helping lately."

Harris finished chewing. "The meaning of life over pizza,

huh? Okay. Here's what I know. This place—Earth, human life —is a school, a dense, three-dimensional, conflict-riddled school. We're all spiritual beings, infinite, eternal. When we leave here, we'll return to love and peace. Harris," he rested a hand on his chest, "will cease to exist. On the other side, I'll understand that this body was a costume I put on, this life was a part I played.

"But here," he patted the couch, "in this room right now, I struggle to feel that other place. Even though I know it's more real than this, as long as I'm in this body, I am limited in how much I grasp, how much I can remember about the other side, and that's the struggle. Every day I think about checking out of this place and going back. Every day I have to remind myself that I chose this life, this experience, and my eternal self wanted to be here now. And so I am here.

"But I am not at peace. I am not all-knowing. What you're feeling, I feel it too. There's a lot in this life that is good and beautiful, but there's a lot that's difficult. Dying and coming back doesn't free us from being human. For a year after my wife and daughter died, I was so reckless. If we had calls into the station about domestic fights or guys with guns, I'd go running into the heart of the chaos without a second thought. I drank a lot. I wanted to be numb. It was all too much. The near-death groups helped me and it was through that I found an anchor, a way to be here without constantly needing to distract or numb or escape. I'm not opposed to drinking, obviously." He held up his bottle of beer. "But I've done what you're doing. It didn't help. It made things worse."

Celeste sighed and gazed at her Scotch. He was right, but she didn't want him to be. She wanted to hold fast to this new crutch, much the same way she was holding onto the cane she'd bought in the pawnshop days before. The truth was she no longer needed it and yet...

"I haven't been drinking as much down here," she admitted.

"I got sick one of my first nights and ever since"—she shook her head—"I can't stomach more than a couple sips. Which honestly is frustrating because I want to dull it all. I don't want to watch my life fall apart in Technicolor. And when this is all over with Jonathan, with finding out what happened to my mom, then what? No husband, no home, no job, no roots. Even the bit of childhood I thought I knew, the story of my family I thought I knew, is one big lie. Who am I on the other side of all this? What is the point of being here?"

Harris took a sip of his beer. "I have two responses to what you're feeling. Eternal Harris, or not-Harris if you want to be specific, says there is no point, no goal, no grand purpose. This," he gestured at the pizza, the beer, the lake through the front window, "is my non-physical being, getting a chance to feel the joys and constraints of being human. The sensations and emotions of touch, of lust, of wonder, of pain. All the iterations. And that self knows there is no good and bad beyond this life. In the mortal world, there is sensation, there is experience and all those experiences lead to growth.

"The physical me, the Harris who's logged forty-two years on this planet, who has loved deeply and lost deeply and devoted my life to stopping people who hurt others, that me understands fighting for the good, making this version of reality better, is all I need to do. It doesn't have to be extraordinary. Maybe some days all we manage is to give a dog a head rub when we pass him in the park. That's good. That's enough. I know it's enough."

"I haven't given any dogs head rubs lately," Celeste said. She'd barely come up for air since starting her search in West Virginia for her mother.

"And that means what? You're not accomplishing anything? Look at the lives you've changed since your accident. You ended the killing sprees of two murderers. You brought closure to Joanna and River. Is there a greater purpose than that? And guess what? Even if you never did anything like that again in your life, the purpose is in all the little things.

"We've talked about this. Our world is shaped by every tiny interaction. We're always looking for the big picture, but what matters most is the little stuff. Clearly, an injustice exists here. That's why you came to West Virginia. You deserve the truth about what happened to your mother. So does your brother. Every time we shine light into the darkness, expose it, we've changed the world for the better. After this is over, you'll have time again for the doggie head rubs or whatever else makes you feel happy. It doesn't have to be more than that."

53

———————

In the evening, Celeste called Spencer and told him the crazy story about someone stealing videotapes from her car. She added that she'd found several more in the house.

"What did he say?" Harris asked when she ended the call.

"He seemed surprised someone stole them and wanted to talk about my theories on who did it."

"All right, good. If he's leaking information to someone, we'll know."

Celeste and Harris drove separately into downtown Kingwood and left Harris's car in a busy restaurant parking lot. Harris got behind the wheel of Celeste's truck, wig in place. He was wearing one of her oversized sweatshirts and Celeste imagined he'd already started to sweat.

Celeste's disguises included tucking her hair beneath a ball cap and large sunglasses. She wore a shapeless t-shirt and baggy jeans. In the passenger seat, she reclined all the way back.

"I'm going to stop at the rental house to drop you off,"

Harris said. "Stay low. I'll get as close to the house as I can and hopefully, if they're keeping an eye on your rental, they won't see you go inside."

"What if they don't come back tonight?"

"My gut tells me they will."

"Are you going to confront them?"

"Depends."

"On what?"

"If you can identify them without doing that. Either a clear look at their face on the cameras or their vehicle with the license plate. Either of those will do. If you recognize them, text me who it is. If they're in a mask and they walk in, rather than drive, I'll have to confront them."

Celeste rubbed her hands over her arms. "I'm worried."

"Don't be. I'm a detective. I have a gun and I've defused a lot of violent people. I suspect this is not an overtly violent person. If they were, they'd have attacked you by now. They like to operate behind the scenes, in the shadows. Time to put the high beams on them."

"Okay. I'm sorry to drag you into this."

"I wouldn't call my driving to West Virginia uninvited and showing up at your rental house you 'dragging me into anything.'"

She smiled. "All the same. Thank you."

"You're welcome," he said. "Got your cell?"

Celeste held up her new phone.

Harris parked in the driveway close to the door of the A-frame. Celeste muffled another laugh as she considered him in his wig. "Red looks good on you."

He fluffed the top and winked at her. "Yeah?"

She climbed out, squatted low, and shuffled into the door at the side of the house. Harris did not acknowledge her.

Once inside, Celeste locked the door and hurried to the

front room. Her laptop sat on the coffee table, open to all the camera feeds.

Several minutes later, Harris appeared in her truck in the driveway at her childhood home. He parked and, clearly trying to make himself look smaller and more feminine, walked toward the side of the house to enter through the unlocked door.

Harris appeared on the laundry room camera and waved before disappearing into the hall. He emerged a moment later in the upstairs hall and took off his wig.

"Itchy!" he announced, scratching his head.

He pointed toward the doorway at the end, the room that had been locked when she'd first arrived. "I'm going to hunker down in there. You don't have to keep a constant eye on the cameras. They'll ping you if there's motion detected."

He slipped through the bedroom door and out of sight.

Celeste made a pot of coffee and sat in front of her laptop.

Hours passed and nothing moved on the video screens. Tiredness from the previous night's lack of sleep had begun to set in. She blinked, took a sip of cold coffee and texted Harris.

Celeste: *How's it going?*

Harris: *Hot! Have had to remove the sweatshirt. Sitting on the floor trying to get a fresh breath from the window, but somehow the breeze coming in feels as stifling as this buttoned-up house.*

Celeste chuckled and thought of her own sense the night before, that she'd settled down to sleep in a sauna.

Celeste: *Maybe they're not going to come. It's almost midnight.*

Harris: *We're not giving up now.*

Before Celeste could send another message, the motion activator for the camera in the driveway beeped. Celeste enlarged the image and texted Harris.

Celeste: *Are you watching driveway cam?*

Harris: *Yep.*

On the screen, a person dressed in dark clothing moved quickly down the driveway, staying close to the edge of the tree line. She couldn't make out their face and felt sure they wore some kind of mask.

"Shit," she muttered, thinking about what Harris had said about a confrontation.

The person disappeared from view and, a minute later, the laundry room camera beeped.

She clicked that one as the person entered through the side door. They flipped on a flashlight, which made it impossible for her to make out any features at all.

The flashlight moved out of the laundry room.

Celeste texted Harris.

Celeste: *They left the laundry room, using a flashlight. I couldn't see them.*

Harris: *I'm watching.*

Several minutes passed and Celeste imagined the person downstairs searching for the videotapes.

Celeste: *Are you okay?*

Harris: *Fine.*

Maybe the intruder would simply leave when they didn't find the videos.

The third camera in the upstairs hall beeped. Celeste's heart raced as the beam of the flashlight appeared at the end of the dark hall. A shadow appeared from the guest bedroom. Harris. He stopped in front of the camera, momentarily blocking her view.

"Freeze," Harris shouted.

The beam of the intruder's flashlight pointed toward Harris, who stood wide-legged, the gun pointing at the person in the mask. Suddenly, the flashlight flew forward. Harris swore and jumped sideways, disappearing from view. Celeste spotted the person from behind as they fled down the stairs. She switched to the laundry room camera as they rushed past and into the driveway.

Halfway up the driveway, a second person chased the first. Harris. He lunged at the masked intruder and tackled them to the gravel. They were rolling. One of them howled in pain.

Celeste bolted from the couch and out the glass doors. She ran across the spongy lawn and shoved a kayak into the lake, nearly tipped when she hopped in and sent the kayak rocking dangerously to the side. She rammed a paddle into the sand, steadied and started paddling hard across the lake.

She was halfway across when she realized that this had not been part of the plan. Harris wanted her to stay put, to not be seen, to not put herself at risk. Now here she was, paddling madly across the dark lake toward the old house. What if the masked person had gotten the upper hand, had wrestled Harris's gun away and now lay in wait for Celeste?

She fought the thought away and focused, not on her childhood home, which had vanished into the dark shoreline, but on the lights ablaze in the house next door, Rose's house.

Her lungs burned and her mind raced. Lorenzo, her physical therapist, had liked to say *calm breath—calm mind.* 'Breathe deep,' he'd instruct her, 'using the diaphragm, release the exhalation slowly, using the abdominal muscles.' She hadn't done her exercises since leaving Michigan, but she did her best to mimic the breathwork.

Her arms ached, but she didn't slow.

As she drew close, she searched the darkness around her childhood home for movement, but found none. The kayak slid into shallow water, stones scraping the bottom. Celeste jumped out and yanked the kayak onto the rocky shore.

As she started toward the lawn, she glanced back at the lake and froze. In the water, maybe fifteen yards out, a silhouette barely distinct from the lake's surface rose from the water. Long, wet hair clung to the pale contours of a face that gleamed faintly in the moonlight. The woman's head was motionless, yet her eyes—or what Celeste thought must be eyes—were fixed on her.

54

———

Celeste took a step back. Behind her, raised voices broke the quiet, and she whipped around, searched for Harris, but still couldn't see him.

When she looked back at the lake, the woman was gone.

Celeste turned and raced to the back of the house, pressing a hand against her hip as if the pins holding bones in place might snap beneath the impact of her footfalls.

She spotted Harris, cell phone to his ear, gun pointed at a person sitting on the gravel driveway. Slowing to a walk, Celeste stared at the man slumped on the ground.

Spencer Ashman.

His eyes rose to meet hers briefly, then he quickly looked down.

"I was trying to call you," Harris said, tucking the phone in his pocket. "You were supposed to stay at the house."

Celeste focused on Spencer. "Why?" she demanded.

Spencer dabbed at his bloody lip with the black ski mask. "Could you put that away?" He stared at Harris, who still held his gun pointed at Spencer.

"That depends on you, doesn't it?"

Spencer shot Celeste an exasperated look. "You didn't tell me you had a bodyguard."

"Why did you break in? Why did you steal the tapes?"

He frowned, shook his head. "I didn't take the tapes. I swear. I came by tonight because you said you found another one. I thought you might be watching it. I snuck in planning on just, you know, watching it from the hallway then slinking back out."

"At midnight?"

"I'm a night owl."

"Bullshit," Celeste said.

Spencer blew out a noisy breath. "All right, fine. My mother always said I'm a terrible liar. Garth Durand paid me to keep an eye on you."

"Garth, the high school teacher?"

"Why?" Harris asked.

Spencer shrugged. "Beats me. I asked, believe me, but he gave me one of those 'do you want the money or not?' spiels and I need the money. Need, not want. I'm two years behind on the taxes on my house."

Harris slowly lowered his gun, but didn't reholster it.

"When did he ask you to start following me?"

"Just after you met him. Garth called me up. He knew I'd been sniffin' around Moon Lake over the Elliot situation for ages and he said he had a little job, one that could help us both out, but I'd be getting paid. He said you'd come back into town looking for your mother. He didn't have a clue I'd already met you. He asked me to strike up a conversation and get a sense of what you were up to. Celeste"—he held up his hands—"if I'd known you, then I wouldn't have done it. I swear. Now that we're friends—"

"We're not friends," she snapped.

"All things considered, I get that. I do. You're pissed."

"Did Garth pay you to come here tonight?"

Spencer chewed his lip and nodded. "He asked me to come out and look around. If I saw the tapes, to grab them. I've told you before, I've been dying to get into this house for years. Had half a mind to break in a few times, but didn't know if there was some snazzy hidden surveillance goin' on. Apparently, there is now."

"Why did you come in knowing she was in the house?" Harris demanded.

"Garth asked me to come tonight, so I came. I was surprised to see your truck here, but then it was dark and quiet. I figured, you're sound asleep in there, I'll sneak in, grab the videos if I see them."

"You actually expect me to believe you weren't the one who broke into my truck last night?"

"I swear on the life of my beloved cat, Noodles, I was not here last night. That being said," he added, "I drove by once in the afternoon. But that's it."

"Then Garth did it," Celeste muttered. "He was the guy in the Polaroids," she told Harris. "With the other teenager."

"Is it possible this Garth person was involved in your mom's disappearance?" Harris asked.

"Maybe. He and my dad were clearly both sleeping with students."

"They were?" Spencer asked, eyes wide. "Garth Durand? He's married, you know? Married for like forty years."

"If your mom found those pictures..." Harris murmured.

"She might have threatened to expose Garth and my dad."

Spencer watched them, rapt.

"I don't want to talk about this in front of him," Celeste said.

"I don't think Garth stole the tapes," Spencer interrupted.

Celeste and Harris turned to look at him.

"Why not?" Celeste demanded.

"Because I didn't tell him about the tapes until this morning. We caught up over coffee and I filled him on what had been going on. You were looking for your mom, we'd checked out where she grew up, et cetera. I mentioned this morning you'd found videotapes, and he did seem a little twitchy about that, and said if anything else comes up with the tapes to call him. I'm pretty sure he was worried about what was on 'em, which based on your little Polaroid exchange just now I can imagine why. This afternoon I told him you'd found more tapes, and that's when he asked me to come out and maybe snag them if they were lying around."

"Why should we believe you?" Harris asked.

Spencer looked at the sky as if the right answer might be written there. "You've already caught me. What's the point of lying now?"

"To keep your piggy bank out of trouble," Celeste said.

"Can I get up?" Spencer asked. "I've got a rock jabbing into my backside and in about ten seconds, I think it might puncture the skin."

"Go ahead," Harris told him.

Celeste glared at Spencer. "I want you to call Garth on speaker phone in front of us. I want you to tell him you didn't find any videotapes and ask him why he's been paying you to spy on me."

Spencer paled, but nodded. "Right now? You realize it's one in the morning?"

"Right now," she insisted.

Spencer took out his cell phone. A man answered after two rings, sounding groggy.

"Huh? Yeah?"

"Garth, it's Spencer. Have a minute?"

The other man said nothing, but they could hear fumbling through the phone as if he were getting out of bed and leaving the room. Minutes passed.

"Spencer?" the man whispered, sounding annoyed. "Why

the hell are you calling me? I was asleep next to Doreen. Jesus, this is unprofessional, you know?"

"You're paying me to spy on some lady. I don't think business hours apply."

"What do you want?" Garth demanded.

"I went by the house and found some videos."

Celeste narrowed her eyes at Spencer.

"I might pop 'em into my recorder tonight and watch them, but first I'd like to know what I might see."

"How the hell do I know what's on them?" Garth snapped.

"You're the one who asked me to take them."

"I asked no such thing. I was only curious. I figured if they were lying around...it doesn't matter. Watch them, don't watch them, just...if you see anything..."

"Like what?"

Garth sighed. "Like two people skinny-dipping."

"Two people skinny-dipping?"

"Or four. Among other things...Listen, it was a long time ago, okay? I'm a different man now."

"You're going to have to be more specific than that."

"No. I'm not."

"Why are you paying me to follow Celeste? If you want these videos to remain hidden, I want to know what your agenda is."

"Are you threatening me?" Garth demanded.

"Take it however you want. Why am I following her? What are you worried she's going to find?"

"Evidence of an affair from a very long time ago. That's it. Okay? I slept with a student. Nathaniel, her dad, was involved with a student as well. We were both...having sex with students. If it comes out, I'll lose my job, which...I guess is less important these days. I'm planning to retire in a few years, but I'll also lose Doreen and I love Doreen. It would destroy her if she found out."

"What happened to Nathaniel Harrington's wife?"

"Nettie? How should I know? She left him. Nathaniel said she ran off to join a commune or some such thing."

"Did Nettie find out you and Nathaniel were sleeping with students?"

"I'm not sure. It's possible." Garth sounded suddenly fatigued, as if the mere act of remembering exhausted him. "She started to look at me different. I cut it off with Loretta. I told Nathaniel to do the same. We'd had our fun. I wasn't going to throw away my marriage, my career, but Nathaniel...he was in a completely different headspace. He was...in love, I guess. That's what he said, that he was in love. In lust is more like it. How can a grown man be in love with a teenager? But he was ready to get a divorce, whatever it took. He wanted Hannah. And...well, Hannah wasn't going to let him go easily. Loretta told me if Nathaniel tried to cut it off, Hannah intended to tell everyone. The school, the police, and obviously Nettie as well."

"And then Nettie disappeared, and you just assumed she'd left? Never had a shadow of a doubt about Nathaniel's story?"

"Spencer, I can hear what you're implying, but Nathaniel Harrington was a science teacher and a girls' basketball coach. I never so much as heard him raise his voice to a student. If you think he killed his wife, well, that's just preposterous."

"Fine. I'm done though, Garth. No more spying."

"What about the videos?"

"I lied. I don't have them."

"Please, this needs to stay between us. My wife—"

Spencer ended the call. He tucked the cell back into his pocket and looked at Celeste.

55

———————

N ettie

Nettie had been at the sheriff's office for the previous two hours. She'd filled out the report on what had occurred the night before. Her truck, beyond repair, had been towed from the woods.

She wore a large walking boot the doctor had given her that morning. Luckily, she'd only suffered a bad sprain rather than a break.

"I'm going to round up Brice today and question him," Theon explained. "Is there anyone else who might have tried to run you off the road?"

Nettie bit her lip, tried to imagine who would be angry enough at her to do such a thing. For a moment, Hannah's face flashed through her thoughts. No. Hannah didn't even own a vehicle, and she'd never...

"No one I can think of."

"But you don't think it was an accident?"

"That truck bumped into me three times. It was intentional."

"Okay. If Brice is behind this, the front of his truck should be scuffed. I'll start there."

That evening, Nettie was on edge. Rain pounded the roof and obscured the dark night beyond the windows. Nathaniel was out, having committed to refereeing a boys' basketball game at the high school. He'd offered to stay home, but Nettie sensed he didn't want to cancel, so she'd encouraged him to go.

She gave Adam his bottle in the playpen and he lay on his side, watching Celeste on the floor stacking wooden blocks.

Someone knocked on the door and Nettie stood, staring down the dark hallway. She picked up Nathaniel's gun and walked slowly toward the back of the house.

Only a murky silhouette showed through the frosted glass.

"Who's there?" Nettie called.

Her hand was slick on the gun. It was heavy and she couldn't imagine actually releasing the safety, pointing it at someone, firing.

"Please!" a girl's voice called out beneath the pounding rain.

Nettie opened the door to find a soaking wet Hannah. Her blonde hair was plastered against the sides of her face. Rivulets of water ran from the hollows beneath her eyes and one eye was puffy with a startling blueish-purple color mottling the skin. It was impossible to distinguish the rain from Hannah's tears. Her body shivered beneath her thin shirt and shorts.

"I'm sorry. I'm sorry. I know that you don't want me here, but my stepdad hit me and I had nowhere else to go. Please, can I just...I'll sleep in the garage. Anywhere. I just can't go home," Hannah blurted.

Stomach twisted, Nettie quickly set the gun onto a hall table and wrapped Hannah in a hug. Her mistrust of Hannah wanted to shoulder in, but Nettie fought it down. "Here. Come on. Of course you can stay here."

Hannah continued to cry as Nettie ushered her into the house. She froze when her eyes landed on the gun Nettie had set down.

"Oh, gosh. Don't even worry about that." Nettie shoved the gun into the drawer of a side table. She put her arm back around Hannah.

"Do you want to tell me what happened?" Nettie asked after she'd given Hannah a pair of pajamas to change into and they were both settled in the living room.

"I don't want to get in trouble," Hannah murmured, a sheet of her drying hair concealing her swollen eye.

"Hannah, you are not going to get in trouble. The only person who is in trouble here is your stepdad."

Hannah's head shot up and her eyes widened. "Please, no. You can't tell anyone. If Sawyer finds out, he'll beat the shit out of me and my mom, too. Please..."

"Hannah, I work pretty closely with the sheriff. I know him. He's a good man. I can ask him—"

Before Nettie could finish, Hannah began to shake her head no. "My ma's called, and neighbors too, when there's been a fight at our place. They come out, tell Sawyer to settle down and leave. That just makes it worse. I swear it. They can't do nothing to him and they won't."

Nettie wanted to argue, but she wasn't stupid. She'd grown up in her own version of Hannah's life. Though her parents had never abused her, they'd abused themselves with drugs, and on more than one occasion, when deputies had been sent to her trailer when her dad was on a rampage or her mom had been asleep for days, they did little more than leave a pamphlet and a phone number for a social worker who could help.

56

"What aren't you telling us?" Harris asked.

Spencer stared at him. "What do you mean?"

Celeste glanced at Harris, saw the determined expression on his face. Harris's eyes bore into Spencer as if he thought if he stared hard enough, he might see into Spencer's mind. "You're holding something back."

Spencer glanced at Celeste, then shifted his gaze back to Harris. "I don't understand—"

"Spit it out, Spencer," Celeste snapped. "We're all exhausted."

Spencer glanced at the house looming beside them, stared at it for a moment. "All right. Okay," he said. "I've never told this story to a soul. I mean it. Not another living human being, which is maybe a tad hypocritical considering my bread and butter is the *Strictly Supernatural* podcast. But shoot, it's easier to interview people giving these stories than to give my own." He chuckled.

"What are you talking about?" Celeste asked.

"I'm getting there. Okay? Just"—he rubbed his hands

together—"warming myself up to it. I told you I heard about Elliot's case from his grandmother, Sheila, but that's not actually true. I had an, um...an unusual experience. Now that I think about it, you're probably the best person to tell this story to, eh? Considering your..."

"Considering my what?"

He twiddled his fingers near his eyes. "Your ghosty abilities or whatever."

"Just tell the story," Harris said, sounding annoyed.

"All right, all right. I could use a glass of water. I'm parched. Not used to runnin'."

Celeste glared at him.

"Okay. Never mind. But if I lose my voice halfway through..." He cleared his throat loudly. "This happened about twelve years back. Before I ever started the true crime podcast. A few of my buddies rented a camper, and we came here to Moon Lake for a fishing weekend, sort of a bachelor party before I married my second wife. Spent a few days fishing and drinking, the usual stuff.

"One morning, I took the boat out alone. It was spring, ice had only been off for a month, if that, and the water was colder than a snowman's balls. I've got my pole in the water, not getting any bites, and my eye catches on this house across the lake. Your house. I see this kid, a boy, come darting across the lawn and down the dock. He's got a raccoon-tail hat on, but he's wearing nothin' else but a pair of jean shorts. Before I can even make sense of what I'm seeing, that kid cannonballs off the end of the dock and disappears into the water. I'm thinking, holy shit! That is one tough kid. He's obviously doing a polar bear swim or whatever, except he doesn't come up.

"Seconds are ticking by, then a minute, and that's when I start to panic and haul ass across the lake. I get to where he jumped in, but there isn't so much as a ripple in the water. What could I do? I jumped in and that water was even colder than I imagined. Sucked the breath from my lungs. I'm yelling and diving under and screaming for that kid and then for help.

"Finally, I drag myself up onto the dock and run for the house because obviously this kid's parents are inside, clueless that their kid is drowning in the lake. 'Cept when I get to the house, it's as quiet as a tomb. Windows are dark, doors are locked and I notice straight away the leaves on the ground, on the porch, and none of them are disturbed, like no one has walked there all winter. The house is shut right down.

"I go running next door and the neighbor's house is closed up and the one after that. And you've seen the houses, they're not close. I'm about giving myself a heart attack. Finally, my boys come barreling down the road in the van. They heard me across the lake. Sound travels real clear when it's calm and quiet. I yell, 'We've got to get to a phone now and call for help because a kid went into that water.' One of 'em heads to Hobart's store to make the call and me and my friend, Zander, go back to the lake and we're running up and down the shore trying to see this kid, but he's nowhere to be found. Eventually a cop pulls up, hears my story and in no uncertain terms tells me there ain't no kid. I'm seeing things."

"What did you do?"

He shrugged. "What could I do? Nothin'. I went back to Fairmont with my buddies, that's where I was livin' at the time, and I sent out for Kingwood newspapers for a month. I kept waiting to hear the kid's body had turned up or to read about a missing boy. Nope. Never.

"But it stayed with me. Life took its turns. *Strictly Supernatural* was going gangbusters and then I started up *Dark Deeds* and then one day I see a listing for a little house for sale in Kingwood. It's in my budget. I've just gotten divorced for the second time and all I can think about is that damn kid I saw go into the lake. So, I moved here."

"You moved to Kingwood to find Elliot Thacker?" Celeste asked.

"I guess I did. Yeah. I tried to tell myself it wasn't that, but it was an itch you can't scratch. You hear about people with OCD who have to, like, touch certain things every day, run their fingers over some particular doorknob in order to feel all right in the head? I imagine it felt somethin' like that. Once I moved here, I came to this lake every single day for the first year. Every day. I told you I walked the shoreline that's real swampy? I've done it fifty times. I've rowed around the lake, swam in it. I've sat in a boat in front of this house," he gestured at the house, "for hours at a time."

"Have you ever seen him again?"

Spencer scratched his jaw. "I don't know. Not like I did that first time, but a few times I've seen...something. Then one day, about three years ago, I'm reading the local paper and some journalist did a little write-up on Kingwood's longest unsolved disappearance. And whose face is right there on the page? Elliot Thacker's. It was like somebody zapped me with a cattle prod. I knew like this," he snapped his fingers, "that it was the kid I saw jump in the lake that day."

57

———

It was after three in the morning when Celeste and Harris returned to the A-frame.

"Do you want to talk?" Harris asked.

"Not tonight," Celeste said. "I need to sleep."

In the upstairs hallway, Harris brushed his fingers across Celeste's hand. The sensation sent a zing through her arm. She blinked at him and he smiled.

"I'm right through the wall if you need anything."

"Thank you," she told him, holding his gaze for a moment.

Celeste retreated to the master bedroom. She climbed beneath the covers and willed sleep to carry her away.

———

Celeste was surprised to discover she'd slept until nearly ten a.m. She found Harris at the kitchen table, cell phone pressed to his ear, laptop open before him.

"Work," he mouthed at her.

She gave him a thumbs-up and poured a cup of coffee.

"How'd you sleep?" Harris asked after he ended his call.

"Probably the best I have since coming down here, oddly enough. I think knowing I wasn't alone in the house helped."

"Makes sense." He took a sip of his coffee and clicked something on his laptop. "We've got a string of burglaries in Traverse City that I sort of ran out on. I need to sift through some of these tips that came in. I'll probably have to work on this for the next couple of hours."

"That's totally fine. I wanted to run back over to the house. There are a couple of totes in the spare bedroom I haven't gotten to."

Celeste walked into the house and upstairs. She hauled the two totes she hadn't yet searched from the closet and peeled off the first lid. The tote was filled with baby stuff. Onesies and footie pajamas and other tiny outfits. Celeste lifted out a small pink dress, a kitten blowing bubbles stitched into the fabric. Celeste ran her fingers over the stitches and wondered if her mother had made the dress. Also in the tote she found baby shoes and booties. The items had all been neatly folded and arranged. Nettie had likely placed them there, saving Celeste and Adam's special outfits that they'd outgrown. Was it in the hopes that one day she'd have another baby? Or maybe she'd saved the items to give to a grown Celeste and Adam for their own children. It hurt to contemplate Nettie lovingly folding the little clothes, focused on a future she'd never experience.

More photos lay scattered in a second tote. She picked one off the top. It was her dad leaning against the hood of a black Camaro behind the Moon Lake house. He was young, blond hair tousled, blue eyes shining. He wore jeans and a white shirt unbuttoned at the collar.

Her cell phone rang, her dad's number on the screen.

"Celeste?" her dad asked as soon as she answered the call.

She stared at the photo of him in her hand, then set it slowly on the bed, suddenly sure he was about to confront her for breaking into the house. "Yes."

"I've been trying to call you, but your phone goes right to voicemail. What in the world is going on, Celeste? Adam gave me this number, said you're not using your other phone. And Jonathan called me. He said you've had some kind of mental breakdown. Is that what's going on?"

Celeste's body grew cold. Her heart thumped faster. "When did you talk to Jonathan?"

"The day before yesterday. Is that why you're in West Virginia digging up all this nonsense about your mom? You've had some sort of...of..."

"Did you tell him where I am? Where the Kingwood house is?"

"Of course I told him. He's your husband."

Outside, a car rumbled into the driveway. She stood and walked to the window, looked down to see Jonathan's car parked behind her truck. "I have to go, Dad."

"No. Wait—"

She hung up the phone and texted Harris.

Celeste: *Jonathan is here.*

She walked downstairs just as Jonathan began to bang on the door.

"Celeste!" he yelled.

She opened it.

Jonathan looked disheveled, eyes bloodshot, face unshaven. He blinked at her as if shocked she'd opened the door.

"What are you doing here?" she demanded.

His mouth fell open, but he quickly closed it. "What am I doing here? You've stopped answering my calls, my emails."

"Maybe that's because you had an affair with one of our co-workers."

Celeste knew she shouldn't confront him. Now was the time

to play nice, to pretend she knew less than she did, but something twisted in her guts at the injustice of his actions, the injustice of her father decades before having an affair with a student, moving that girl into their lives, getting rid of Nettie. How dare he? How dare any of these men so effortlessly betray the women they'd made an oath to love, honor and protect?

"I didn't...intend for that to happen."

She glared at him, partially surprised by the admission. She'd expected him to lie. Lies had become far more commonplace than the truth in their marriage. "When did it start?"

He swallowed and tugged at the collar of his button-down shirt. She noticed spreading shadows beneath his arms and wondered if he'd been sweating the entire drive from Michigan to West Virginia. "It started not long after ProtoCure failed during clinical trials."

Celeste thought back to that time. ProtoCure had been an anti-cancer drug that had showed promise in inhibiting tumor growth during its inception. Jonathan and Darlene had worked together on the drug for months, but in clinical trials, they'd been unable to replicate their earlier results.

"Darlene and I were both so disappointed. And frankly, when I tried to vent my frustrations to you, you barely gave me the time of day, acted like I should just get over it."

Celeste bristled at his explanation. "It was my fault, then?"

"No. Obviously no. I'm not saying that. Listen, I'm..." He wiped sweat from his brow. "Could we go inside? I'm roasting."

"It's hotter in there. There's no power."

"Just to sit down. I'm feeling a little..." He blinked a few times and reached an unsteady hand to the doorframe as if to keep from falling over.

"Okay, fine. Come on."

He followed her into the house and down the hall into the living room. She opened all the windows.

"So, this is it? The childhood home?" Jonathan murmured.

He stripped off his blazer and slung it over the back of an easy chair. He sat down, crossed one leg over the other, and scanned the room.

A memory swam up. Celeste's dad Nathaniel sitting in the same chair in much the same way. Hannah perched on the edge, leaning over him, her blonde hair brushing his face.

"So?" Jonathan's voice pulled her back.

"So what?" she asked.

"Therapy, Celeste. We can get rid of Gail, find someone more suitable for our specific needs." *We* and *our* still rolling off his tongue as if he hadn't had a different *we* and *our* for nearly two years, as if that woman weren't under suspicion of trying to kill Celeste.

He leaned forward and picked up the coffee-table book, blew the dust off the top. *Mountains of the United States.*

"Remember when we hiked to those hot springs in Utah and found a whole nudist camp out there? My God." He shook his head, laughing. "Ten of 'em at least, just bare naked."

She smiled. Jonathan had been so shocked, he'd tripped and fallen right into one of the springs and had to hike out soaking wet.

"We haven't done enough of that," he continued. "We used to travel more. We could do that again. Remember, you always wanted to visit that active volcano in Hawaii? We could go. Say 'screw it' and just go." He flipped through the mountains book as he spoke, a sort of feverish hope in his face.

It was intoxicating what he was offering. A chance to erase the previous months, to start again, the same but different. To not be alone, to not be facing the uncertain future with no one by her side. And yet, even as she considered the possibility, a bitter heaviness lurked in her stomach. That feeling held the truth. The truth was that there was no turning back in this life. Actions had consequences. Jonathan had had an affair, and that woman had tried to kill Celeste. Even if that most extreme series of events had not occurred, Celeste and Jonathan no longer fit. They'd changed, and that growth had not occurred together.

Still, she bit back the words not only because they'd hurt him, but because a part of her didn't trust him. That niggling in her belly was a warning.

As had happened before, Jonathan's hands flipping the pages were suddenly crimson, as if he'd dipped them in a bucket of red paint.

Celeste stared, transfixed.

Blood on his hands.

The words appeared in her mind and Celeste finally understood what the red meant.

When she looked up, Jonathan watched her.

58

Down the hall, the front door slammed open and Harris strode into the room.

Jonathan jumped from his chair, staring at Harris. "Who are you? Who is he?" Jonathan looked at Celeste.

"This is my friend, Harris. The detective from Traverse City."

Jonathan's eyes bulged. "Why is he down here? What the hell is going on, Celeste?"

Harris scoffed. "You're joking, right?"

Jonathan whirled to face him, a vein pulsing in his forehead. "I'm talking to *my* wife, not you!"

Celeste stood and put a hand on Jonathan's chest. "Stop. Okay? Calm down. He got here yesterday, and he came because he was worried about me because you took off and the police in Grand Rapids think you and your girlfriend tried to kill me."

"I had no idea Darlene was the driver. I didn't know, Celeste," Jonathan insisted. "If it was her, she did it on her own."

Harris's gaze was laser-focused on Jonathan, and Celeste

sensed he didn't believe a word he said. "You have two options, Jonathan," Harris said. "I spoke with Detective Bowman not two minutes ago. They're aware you're here in West Virginia. Either surrender yourself to the local police and get extradited back to Michigan, or I can escort you back to the police station in Grand Rapids."

"Surrender myself? What does that mean? They intend to arrest me?"

"Yes. They have a warrant for your arrest."

"But how?" Jonathan looked at Celeste, imploring her. "I didn't do anything, Celeste. I didn't."

"You have to go back," Celeste murmured.

"I can escort you," Harris repeated.

"I don't need an escort," Jonathan snapped. "I'll go back on my own."

Harris shook his head. "That's not going to happen now. You're a flight risk. Driving down here proves that."

"I wasn't under arrest."

"But you were advised not to leave the state."

"So what?"

"I'm telling you, if you drive away from here, Detective Bowman will alert the local police and tell them to arrest you. You'll be transported back to Michigan in the backseat of a police cruiser. Probably in handcuffs."

"Just let him follow you back," Celeste said. "If you're being honest and you didn't know what Darlene intended, then your attorney's going to prove it. Don't make this worse for yourself."

"Funny how 'innocent until proven guilty' doesn't apply in real life," Jonathan muttered. "Fine. What choice do I have?"

***

It was an awkward goodbye when Jonathan and Harris left Kingwood. Jonathan did little to hide his hostility, while Harris made it clear he couldn't care less how Jonathan felt about being forced to turn around and make the long drive back to Michigan after only just arriving in West Virginia.

"I'll call you when we're back," Harris said as he walked to his car.

Jonathan, sitting in his own vehicle, looked furious but said nothing.

After she'd watched their cars disappear down the road, Harris following Jonathan, she climbed into her truck and drove into downtown Kingwood.

As she had before, Celeste found Garth at the Children's Museum. He sat on a stool reading a book to a group of young children. When he glanced up, the color drained from his face. He blinked at the book, then offered an apologetic smile to the kids. "Seem to have lost my place. Okay. There we are. Grumpy Bear is nearly home."

Garth read the story, a noticeable tremble in his fingers as he turned the pages. Celeste stood near a rack of cartoonish West Virginia postcards and watched him.

After he finished his story, Garth hugged several of the children and chatted briefly with their parents.

He made his way to Celeste. "Um...Hi, Celeste. Is there something—"

"You paid Spencer to spy on me."

He closed his eyes for a moment, a pained expression freezing his features. When he opened them, she detected fear there. "I did. Yes. But please, let me explain." He glanced behind him, made sure the children and their parents had occupied themselves with other things. "A very long time ago, more than thirty years ago, I got involved with a student at Kingwood High. I was in my twenties, and I just got caught up in the attention from the girls. It's no excuse. I understand. What I did was wrong, terribly wrong. Loretta and I have discussed it. Several years after it happened, I visited her and apologized. My wife and I had a daughter, and I realized how... how wrong I was. If I could take it back, I would."

"Why did you steal the videotapes?"

He held up his hands. "I didn't. I swear it. Spencer said they were stolen. I would never...I only wanted him to...keep me in the loop. I knew your dad had taken photos and video. I assumed he'd destroyed them, but I couldn't be sure. Our friendship was over that summer when I broke it off with Loretta. I pressured him to end his relationship with Hannah and he stopped speaking to me."

Garth's voice started to rise and he looked around self-consciously and dropped it. "I suspected your mom had found out and figured it was only a matter of time before she told my wife Doreen. We'd lose our wives, our jobs, but he got pissed and basically tossed me out of the Moon Lake house. After that, I didn't know what happened to the... evidence of our affairs. When you came in the other day, I panicked. I..." He rubbed his temples. "I imagined you going into the house and finding that stuff and exposing everything."

"Don't you think your wife deserves the truth?" Celeste demanded.

He shook his head. "It would kill her."

Celeste stared at him coldly. "It's sickening how arrogant you men are. As if your wives would cease to exist if they knew you'd betrayed them. Let me tell you something, Garth. I don't think you're worried about her. I think you're worried about you. Your precious ego, your persona as the great teacher, all of it shattered."

He blinked at her. Sweat broke out on his brow. "Of course I am. I am, Celeste. But I'm not the man you're saying. I'm not. The guilt after that summer ate me alive. It still does. Why do you think I told you to talk to Nicole? I wanted you to know the truth about...about why your mom left."

"Someone broke the window out of my truck and stole the tapes. Who was it?"

"God...I have no clue. The only other person I could imagine wanting them hidden is your dad, and he's...where is he?"

"Florida."

"And they were his tapes. If he was worried about them, why didn't he get rid of them years ago?"

"What about Loretta? Is she the type of person—"

He shook his head. "No. Well, she and I are not close, but I can't see her doing that. But maybe..." He frowned, chewed his lower lip.

"What?"

"I ran into Loretta a few months ago here in town. She mentioned...that Hannah was back."

"In Kingwood?"

He nodded.

"Where is she?"

"I haven't seen her. You'd have to ask Loretta."

Celeste parked next to Hobart's store.

Inside, Junior stood at the cash register talking to an older woman about why Hobart's General Store would never stock keto products.

"The brain needs glucose," he told the woman. "It's basic science." Junior nodded at Celeste as she passed.

She made her way to the coolers that aligned with the open door into the backroom. She glanced into the room where crates of bottled water sat. No sign of Loretta.

Celeste grabbed a bottle of tea and a package of almonds and walked to the register.

"You see, these are the sweet and spicy?" Junior asked.

"Yeah. I like those."

"Huh. All right. I get the smokehouse myself or the sea salt. The unsalted taste like chewing on wood chips. No, thank you."

"Is your wife here, by any chance?"

"You know Loretta?"

"I think we might have a mutual friend."

"Who's that?"

"Her name is Hannah."

"Hannah, huh? Never heard of her. Prolly someone Loretta went to school with. She's always runnin' into old schoolmates, teachers. She hates that, but I don't mind. I tell her, 'Loretta, those are potential customers, give 'em a smile and wave.' Think she does? Nope, pulls her ball cap down and scurries by like they might try and bite her."

"Is she here or—"

"Oh, yeah, she's around the side of the store filling up the ice."

"Thanks."

Celeste found the woman in front of the ice cooler, face flushed, sweat stains darkening her gray t-shirt as she lifted the heavy bags of ice and tossed them inside.

"Loretta?"

The woman's eyes narrowed on Celeste. She slammed the door to the cooler closed. "Yeah?"

"I just spoke with Garth Durand at the Children's Museum."

Loretta's eyes darkened.

"He said you mentioned to him that Hannah Hawley was back in town."

Loretta crossed her arms over her large chest. "Why are you looking for her?"

"My name is Celeste. My mother was Nettie Harrington."

The woman stared at her. Celeste suddenly wondered if Loretta didn't have a clue who Nettie was.

Finally, she dropped her arms and jerked the cooler door back open, picked up a bag of ice and hurled it inside.

"Don't have to look far," she said. "Hannah's living right next door to your house. Goes by Rose these days."

59

———

N ettie

As Nettie drove Nathaniel's car out of town, she spotted a familiar figure walking into Skinny's Tavern. It was Sawyer, Hannah's stepdad.

Nettie pulled in and parked, hobbled into the bar.

Nettie knew she should just walk out, not say a word to the tall, wiry man with a tattoo of a rattlesnake wrapped around his biceps, but she couldn't force her feet to turn and go the opposite way. "You're Sawyer, right?"

He grinned. "Guilty as charged."

"I'm Nettie Harrington. Your stepdaughter Hannah babysits for me."

He looked confused, then slowly nodded. "Oh, yeah. Okay. The ones with the big fancy house down on Moon Lake. You know, her ma says you guys are spoiling that girl. I told her Hannah was spoiled the day she was born. You know how some apples don't form right, got something wriggling inside of 'em when the seed is planted—Hannah's one of them."

"That's a disgusting thing to say," Nettie snapped.

He raised an eyebrow. "I guess you ain't spent enough time with her yet."

"She came to my house two nights ago with a black eye. I took photos."

He stared at her as if waiting for the punchline. "And?"

"And you hit her. That's domestic abuse."

Sawyer guffawed and slapped one hand on his thigh. "Oh, that's rich. That is rich! I hit Hannah Hawley." He laughed again. "You think I'd be standing in front of you right now if I hit that girl?"

"Are you denying it?"

He shook his head, grinning. "Let me tell you the first ever story I heard about Hannah Hawley. This was about three years back when I was fixin' to marry her ma and my buddy was trying to steer me clear. He said Hannah, only twelve or thirteen at the time, had taken a liking to some boy down the street. Billy something or other. She told him one day and he all but gave her the middle finger and said she was barking up the wrong tree. Well, Hannah, not a girl to be turned down, decided the next best option was the 'if I can't have him, no one can' route and not two days after he snubbed her, his little house burned clear to the ground. The whole family was inside, but they managed to get out. Lost their little dog though."

He shook his head, staring hard at Nettie now, the smile gone from his face. "Now you might think this is a tall tale—God knows Appalachia is dripping with 'em—but I'm tellin' it to you straight." He pointed a finger at her. "I wouldn't lay a hand on that girl. I married her ma, but I steer clear of Hannah Hawley. She is trouble in every way a person can be."

"If I find out you hit her, I'm calling the sheriff." Nettie started toward the door.

"Hold on a sec. How'd you hurt your leg?"

She turned and glared at him. "What does it matter to you?"

"Curiosity is all." He shrugged. "But if Hannah's staying at your place, I'd sleep with one eye open."

As Nettie drove away from the bar, she pondered the story Sawyer had told her. It was possible he'd lied, made up the whole cockamamie yarn to keep Nettie from telling anyone he'd hit Hannah. But she didn't think so. She sensed an honesty in Sawyer. The man might not have been the most upstanding citizen, but he didn't strike her as a liar and she'd seen something else in his eyes as he'd talked about Hannah.

Fear.

As she passed the high school, Nettie eased off the gas, staring into the parking lot. A group of teenagers stood near a large black pickup truck, the front corner scratched and dented. Hannah stood among them.

60

———————

The sun had begun to set across the lake when Celeste made her way quietly through the woods to Rose's house. Through the large windows at the front of the house, she could see the blue light of a television playing.

Celeste crept closer. There were no shades on the enormous lakeside windows and, thanks to the massive television, Celeste could see her father's face on the screen. Rose had stolen the videotapes.

The screen grew blurry as Rose fast-forwarded, stopping every minute or so, watching a bit of the footage and then fast-forwarding again.

Celeste moved around the house, gritting her teeth as she tried to turn the knob on the back door. Locked. At the side of the house, she spotted a window cracked open. She moved toward it and peered in. It was a bathroom.

Biting her lip, she carefully pushed the window up, braced her hands on the ledge, and hoisted herself inside. She wobbled as she tried to reach the floor with her left leg, then finally planted it and, though it shook violently beneath her, she swung her other leg in and stopped, listening. Had Rose heard her enter the house? The only sounds from within were the home videos. A child laughing.

A smell permeated the bathroom, the same cologne scent Celeste had detected in her childhood home.

Celeste slipped into the hall. A video of a child Celeste on a stage played on the flatscreen TV. She wore a blue and white sequined leotard and danced with five other girls to the song *Tainted Love*. A voice whispered, 'We're leaving as soon as this is over.' A man's voice, Celeste's father's voice, shushed the girl who'd spoken—Hannah.

The recital ended and the screen went dark.

Rose put in another tape. The large screen showed Celeste and Adam in the living room. Celeste ran to a table and picked up a white Halloween mask and slipped it over her face. She was pretending to be a ghost, waving her arms dramatically and chasing a laughing Adam around the living room coffee table.

Rose fast-forwarded the tape, and the children were outside now, a bonfire in the pit near the lake. Celeste had again put on the white mask. She and Adam held sparklers as they ran through the yard, laughing. In the background, her father called, "Give Hannah a sparkler too." She appeared on the screen, young Hannah, with her long blonde hair draped over her bare shoulders. She wore a purple tank top and black nylon shorts.

Celeste watched her childhood self veer toward the forest for a moment and flick her hand as if waving to someone. Her stomach clenched as she studied the dark, dense trees. She couldn't see him, but knew who stood in the trees, just out of sight: Elliot Thacker.

Rose stopped the video, rewound it, paused on the flick of Celeste's hand. She stood and walked closer to the television, searching for the child Celeste knew hid among the trees.

The memory was inching in, taking hold of Celeste, pulling

her down those long-forgotten corridors and suddenly she was there again on that autumn night by the lake, catching glimpses of Elliot through the trees as she ran with her sparkler. She wanted to give him one, but couldn't. He would be in trouble, was supposed to be back to his grandma Sheila's by sundown, but Celeste and Elliot had conspired that day for him to stay overnight. They were going to catch nightcrawlers with flashlights and go fishing the next day where the stream fed into Moon Lake. After everyone went to bed, Celeste planned to sneak him into the house where he'd sleep in her closet on a pile of blankets she'd ferreted up earlier in the day.

After Hannah and her dad had settled by the bonfire and Adam had fallen asleep in the house watching *Inspector Gadget*, Celeste slinked into the trees to find Elliot.

He hopped from a branch, landing hard in front of her, the pennies in his pocket jangling. His raccoon hat tumbled off his head. He picked it up and shook it out.

"Want to play tag?" Celeste whispered.

"No. Hide and seek. And the seeker gets the mask."

She took the mask off, careful not to get the elastic band caught in her hair, and handed it to Elliot. He shoved his raccoon hat in the pocket of his jean shorts and slid the mask over his head.

"Smells like strawberry Chapstick. Gag me with a spoon," he said.

"Fine. Give it back."

He shook his head. "No way."

"Count to fifty," she said.

"Twenty."

"Thirty."

"All right. Thirty," he agreed. "And no hiding in the house."

"Okay."

Celeste waited until he closed his eyes, then she ran, light on her feet, further into the woods. She doubled back, hoping to confuse him, and stopped behind a big tree. As she searched for the perfect hiding spot, she spotted Hannah's car in the driveway. Celeste darted forward, released the trunk, and climbed inside.

The cramped trunk was hot and stank of stale carpet and motor oil. Celeste held the hatch open a crack and watched for Elliot. He appeared for an instant, running behind the car and disappearing into the woods on the other side of the driveway. She waited, grinning. He'd never find her. Minutes ticked past.

When the driver's side door opened and she felt the shift of someone settling inside. Celeste's breath caught. Had Hannah gotten in the car? Or maybe her dad? Hannah was parked behind Nathaniel's convertible and he'd said earlier that day she'd have to move it before he left for school in the morning.

The engine rumbled to life.

Celeste wondered if she should hop out, but Hannah would see her and demand to know what she was doing. She'd have to confess that Elliot hadn't gone home, and they'd both be in trouble. She'd wait. Hannah would only move the car to the side. A few minutes and she'd be done.

As Celeste waited, heart hammering, Elliot emerged from the trees, the white mask over his face. She opened the trunk a bit wider and tried to whisper a call for him to hide. Hannah was going to see him. He heard Celeste, but didn't seem to see her. He started across the driveway and paused.

Suddenly, the car shot in reverse, hard and fast. The back end slammed into Elliot. The trunk flopped open and Celeste stared at the sprawled body of her friend. The blood-spattered white mask lay cracked on the gravel beside him.

As Hannah's door opened, Celeste yanked the hatch back down, but not all the way. She watched Hannah pause and stare down at the body. Her expression was cold, her eyes unreadable.

"Oh, fuck. It's not her," Hannah muttered.

The words drifted into the trunk. Celeste heard them, but didn't understand, or maybe she did.

Suddenly, Hannah started to scream.

61

The memory faded and Celeste was back in the present, the video still playing, pointed at the fire pit now, Hannah sitting on Nathaniel's lap, but her gaze had moved to a place behind the house and Celeste understood. She thought she'd seen Celeste back there, running around in her mask.

"I'm going to move the car," she told Nathaniel.

Nathaniel didn't get up, stayed at the fire, eyes fixed on the lake beyond.

A minute passed, two, and then Celeste heard the thump, though Nathaniel hadn't registered anything significant had occurred. Another minute and then Hannah began to scream.

The voices were muffled, indistinct, but Celeste could hear them. Nathaniel saying to call the police, Hannah insisting they not. His question about whether it was an accident. Indistinct arguing.

A red low battery icon blinked on the screen and a moment later it went black. Nathaniel had gotten a video of that night, the night Hannah had killed Elliot Thacker.

Celeste waited for Rose to stand and remove the tape, but

the fuzzy blackness continued. She searched the dark shapes in the living room, but couldn't discern Rose among the furniture. Where had she gone?

A sudden cool breeze whispered along the back of her neck. Celeste spun as Rose crept around the corner, something in her hands.

Celeste jumped back as Rose sliced the air where Celeste had just stood. Rose lunged again, whipped the knife forward. Celeste tried to bat the knife away as Rose thrust it toward her chest. The blade cut the flesh on the edge of her hand.

Celeste snatched a hanging picture from the wall and flung it at Rose, who stepped back as the glass shattered on the tiled floor. Celeste turned and ran through the house, tensed for the knife to suddenly sink into her back. She risked a glance back at the door as she wrenched it open. Rose was not behind her.

Celeste stumbled down the stairs and into the woods toward her childhood home. She shoved her bleeding hand into her t-shirt, gritting her teeth against the sting as the fabric touched the open wound.

Ducking behind trees, she strained to hear where Rose had gone. Minutes passed with no sign of her.

As Celeste neared her childhood house, leaves rustled somewhere behind her.

"Celeste?" Rose called in a singsong voice. "You're bleeding, Celeste. Let me help you."

Celeste froze, pressing her back against a large oak tree, searching the dark trees.

An engine sound came from the direction of her childhood home. She ran towards it, ducking again behind a large tree.

A small white car pulled into the driveway and parked behind Celeste's truck. Hunched behind the tree, unsure of where Rose had gone, she watched her dad step from the car. He squinted at the dark house and then walked up to her truck, put his hand on the roof and peered into the driver's seat as if he expected Celeste might be sitting inside.

He cupped his hands around his mouth and called to the house. "Celeste!"

Celeste stepped from behind the tree. "Dad. Be careful. Ro—Hannah is here. She has a knife."

"Hi, Coach Harrington," Rose said, emerging from a clump of trees closer to the lake.

Celeste could no longer see the knife. Either she'd dropped it or concealed it somewhere.

Celeste's dad blinked at her, clearly not recognizing the much-changed woman before him. Time alone would have dramatically shifted her appearance, but Hannah had taken pains to further modify it.

"What?" she asked, smirking. "Don't recognize me?" She held her arms up and twirled around, her dark silk robe fluttering up and revealing her lacy shorts. Celeste stared hard at the pocket of the robe. Something bulky lay inside it, held that part of the robe down as she spun.

"It was her, Dad!" Celeste pointed a finger at Hannah. "She killed Mom and that little boy, Elliot."

Nathaniel's face paled. He didn't look at Hannah, nor did he look at Celeste. His eyes were trained on the house, on the upstairs window in the spare bedroom.

Celeste followed his gaze and, for an instant, she was there. Nettie with her long, dark hair and pale skin.

Hannah smirked. "Do you want to tell her or should I, Coach Harrington?"

62

Nettie

Nettie woke, alert. She'd not had the drink Nathaniel had given her earlier in the evening and she knew in her gut had she drunk it she'd have been unconscious, out of it, drugged.

A sound emerged in the house, a rhythmic thumping. She wondered if Nathaniel was downstairs, had turned on the radio and a song was responsible for the steady reverberation.

No. It sounded different from that.

Nettie stood and, whisper quiet, eased open the door to their bedroom.

The noise emerged from the room across the hall where Hannah slept. The door was open a crack.

Nettie moved closer, peered into the room, and froze. It was dark, but not black. Moonlight slivered through the blinds and illuminated the bed. Hannah was on top, naked. The golden key from Nettie's necklace rested between her small breasts.

Her eyes were closed, her head tilted up as her hips rocked back and forth.

Nathaniel lay beneath her, his hands on her thighs.

Nettie pushed the door open, reached in, and flipped on the light.

Hannah screamed, rolled off of Nathaniel and bolted past Nettie and out of the room. Nathaniel stared at her, shocked, his naked body slick, his erection rapidly disappearing. He jumped from the bed, snatched a pillow, and held it over himself. Nettie hadn't moved, couldn't. Her heart thundered. Her world was crumbling, sand dissolving into the sea. Gone, gone, gone. It was all gone.

And then the fury came, white hot, an explosion of rage.

"How could you?" she screamed. She darted across the room and pushed him. He sat back on the bed, had not yet spoken. She slapped him. Her hand left a red welt on his cheek, and he reached up and gripped her wrist. She was still screaming, her words incoherent, flooded now with tears.

"Shut up. You're going to wake the kids."

The kids. Celeste and Adam.

"You'll never see them again," she hissed. "You're finished." She whirled away. She'd gather them up, take Nathaniel's stupid little convertible. She was done. She was packing up her children and getting far away from the lying snake. Clem had been right, and Luanne. They'd all been right and Nettie, blind to what he'd been doing, the denial so deep it now seemed to be splitting the earth beneath her, had allowed it to go on.

Before she made it to the door, Nathaniel's hand gripped her hard, high on the arm.

"Don't you dare touch me," she shrieked, trying to wrench away.

He gripped harder, pinched her skin.

She didn't have time to react. Suddenly, both his hands were on her and he hurled her sideways. Nettie lost her footing, stumbled and fell. Her head smacked the corner of the side table. Stars exploded behind her eyes. She landed hard on the carpeted floor, instantly dizzy. Warmth oozed down the side of her face. She tried to get her hands beneath her, get to her knees, but she was woozy. She saw the crimson spots drip onto the beige carpet. Blood. She was bleeding.

Warmth seeped from the side of her head and when she turned, the pain made her stomach roll, but she managed to fight back the bile that threatened to spew out.

There on the floor, knocked off the side table, lay the telephone off the hook.

Nettie reached for it. Her hand was weak, her fingers refusing initially to hit the buttons. She lifted the phone to her ear, and a shadow fell over her.

Rough hands again on her shoulders. Nathaniel. He'd help her. He'd realize he'd done a terrible thing.

"Help," she whispered.

He rolled her over, stared down at her. His eyes were distant, strange.

She watched his hands, those large hands that hers had gotten lost in, that had held her ring as he dropped to one knee and proposed, that had cradled Celeste and later Adam, that had cupped Nettie's face as he kissed her hundreds, maybe thousands of times.

He wrapped them around her neck. The pressure was instant, powerful. He cut off her breath. She tried to gasp, lift her arms, but they were pinned to her sides. She was trapped beneath him.

Terrible pressure built in her head and dark spots exploded behind her eyes. The sounds in the room—her own struggling, Nathaniel's heavy breaths—faded. Nettie could hear nothing.

Darkness edged in.

By some twist of cruel fate, she was awake again. She had been nearly gone, had been in sweet black, but now consciousness had jerked her back once more. Her head throbbed and her throat burned. She opened her eyes and stared at the starlit sky. Ravens, hundreds of ravens circling above her and more on the ground surrounding her.

In the distance, she heard her little daughter, her baby girl.

"Mama?"

"Celeste. No!" Nathaniel's voice and then both of their voices faded. Time passed. Blood trickled from Nettie's head. Had he called an ambulance? Was that what they were waiting for?

Her eyelids grew heavy, her body cool. She closed her eyes and drifted down.

63

———————

"Tell me what?" Celeste asked, studying her father's face, the grooves deepening near his mouth.

"Hannah, please," he said.

"Please?" she mocked him. "My God, you've gotten old. Look at you."

His cheeks grew red. He turned to look at Celeste, his eyes sad. "Are you okay?"

Celeste blinked at him. "It was her, wasn't it, Dad? Hannah killed my mom."

He stared back at her, eyes misting. "I—"

"No, Celeste," Rose spat. "And I'd love to tell you all about it, but time is up. Let's go for a ride, shall we?" Rose reached into her pocket and withdrew a handgun. She pointed the gun first at Celeste, then Nathaniel.

"This is not the answer. Okay?" Nathaniel held up his hands.

She gestured the gun back toward her own house. "Come on. I'm not interested in being out here all night."

Celeste and her dad walked next to each other through the woods. Celeste imagined darting away, disappearing into the trees, but knew she had to wait. There'd be a moment, a right time.

"I told you to burn that place down," Rose told him. "You have only yourself to blame for this."

"Hannah, if you want to burn the house, we'll burn it. Okay? Or I'll sell it and give you the money and—"

"Sell it?" She released a high angry laugh. "Wouldn't that be grand when the new owner decided to pull that old safe out of the crawl space?"

Celeste had searched the safe. There was nothing else inside of it. "What do you mean?" Celeste asked.

"We'll deal with what's beneath the safe first," Nathaniel pleaded.

Celeste stopped and stared at him. "What's underneath the safe? Not Mom?"

"Walk," Rose snapped. "And no, Mommy dearest is not underneath the safe, is she, Nate? Hmm?"

"I'll take care of it," Nathaniel promised her. "Just...don't hurt anyone else, Hannah."

"It's too late for all of that, Nate. Where were you thirty years ago, hmm? When you left me broke, homeless, when you disappeared without a fucking trace? I stood by you after Nettie. Me."

"You...you killed Nettie," he said, his voice trembling.

Rose snorted. "You strangled her, you bastard. I just put her out of her misery."

Celeste's mind reeled with Rose's words. *You strangled her.*

As they passed the large modern house, the tall windows reflecting the moon beyond, Nathaniel turned and looked at it.

"That's my house now, Nate. Do you think I need your money? I've risen so far above you, I'm disgusted with myself for ever having given you the time of day."

Celeste saw her father's jaw tighten, but he said nothing.

Behind them in the forest, something rustled and then

came the laugh, a child's laugh. Elliot, running, and the sound of change clinking together.

Rose swung around, pointed the gun into the trees. Before Celeste could break for it, Rose shifted back, trained the gun on her.

"Don't even think about it," she hissed. Her voice trembled, her eyes were wider.

"Hannah, there's a child in the woods," Nathaniel said. "You're going to get caught. Their parents—"

"There's no child," she snarled.

"But...you heard him. We all heard him," Nathaniel mumbled.

"On the boat," Rose told them. "Go."

Celeste glanced into the woods, saw a fleeting glimpse of white and then nothing.

Celeste walked in front of her dad, climbed into the speedboat, eyes searching the gloomy interior for a weapon. The red and white seats gleamed in the moonlight. There was nothing.

Her dad climbed in behind her, grunting as he landed hard.

"Are you okay?" she asked him.

He looked at her, eyes full of some emotion she couldn't place. "I'm sorry," he whispered.

"Shut up," Rose snapped, quickly climbing in behind them. "Untie the boat and drive us into the lake slow, Nate. You floor it and I'll put a bullet in Celeste's head."

Celeste's dad did as he was told. He loosened the ropes from the dock, started the boat, and drove slowly into the lake.

"I didn't ask for this," Rose muttered. "My life has been fine. I managed to make it despite how bad you fucked me up, fucked us all up. Across the lake," she directed. "Toward the old boathouse."

As the boat sliced across the calm water of the black lake, Celeste imagined bailing over the side, but every escape scenario left her with the certainty Rose would shoot her dad and then come after her.

"Slow down," Rose demanded. "Kill the engine."

The boat coasted to a stop. Nathaniel turned the key. The hum of the motor was replaced by the buzz of insects and frogs from the swampy lakeshore.

"Go to the front. Get the anchor out of the bow," she told Nathaniel.

Celeste watched her dad open a hatch at the front of the boat. Beside her, Rose shifted, widened her stance. She adjusted the gun, was aiming at Nathaniel's head. Her finger was growing tight on the trigger, her eyes focused, unfeeling.

She was going to shoot him.

Celeste screamed and barreled sideways into Rose. "Dad, jump," she shouted.

The gun went off.

64

───────

Rose managed not to fall. She shrieked and swung the gun around, pointed it at Celeste, and squeezed off another shot. The bullet missed her, but Celeste felt the rush as it passed, the eardrum-splitting reverberation. Celeste turned and dove into the lake. Another bullet exploded through the water beside her. She dove deep and kicked away.

Her lungs burned, but she didn't come up for air.

Celeste didn't know if her dad had made it into the water, if the first bullet had missed him.

When she finally emerged, trying to break the surface quietly, she searched the water for any signs of him. The boat was a little way behind her, but not nearly far enough. Almost immediately the gun cracked, and another bullet exploded the water near her head.

Celeste dove back under, swam until her lungs screamed for air, until she thought if she didn't surface now, she'd suck in a mouthful of water.

When she emerged again, a dark structure loomed on the shore in front of her. The boathouse. She turned back and saw Rose scanning the water. Their eyes connected.

Celeste again plunged beneath the water and swam hard.

Her clothes were heavy, sodden weights dragging her down, and she had to stay down now because the motor on the boat had started and whirred closer.

Celeste kicked her legs, lost her shoes, popped up only for an instant, gulped air and went under once more. She'd spotted the boathouse and swam toward it. The weeds skimmed her stomach as she pushed into more shallow water.

Again, Celeste poked her head above the surface. Behind her, the boat engine idled. She didn't think Rose could see her, but still the boat moved toward the boathouse.

Celeste could touch the ground now, spongy, slimy. Seaweed threaded through her legs as she struggled forward. Weeds and cattails slowed her progress. With each step, her feet sank into the silty mud, cool as it suctioned her ankles.

Her bare foot sank into something thin and brittle. The silty ground oozed around her foot, but she wiggled her toes, tried to feel what she stepped on. It was hard and curved, oddly shaped.

Slowly, heart hammering, she crouched, letting her fingers trail into the murky water. The surface rippled as she reached down, searching blindly. Her fingertips brushed over something—a spindly shape, a hollow between. Celeste jerked back so violently she almost lost her footing. A chill swept through her, raising the fine hairs on her arms.

She recognized the shape. A ribcage and threaded through the soft bone a chain. She held the chain in one hand, followed it, tugging it slippery from the mud. It was attached to a boat anchor. The murk swirled with disturbed silt, made it impossible for Celeste to see the submerged remains, but she continued feeling along and her hands grazed something round. The shape of a skull.

A crack of gunfire split the air. The bullet lodged in the boathouse just behind her.

Celeste ducked beneath the water. Her hands and feet brushed the skeleton. Her mother, wrapped in an anchor, dropped in the lake at the old boathouse. Celeste pushed away, didn't emerge until she'd moved fully into the shadowy boathouse. She came up, sucked in the scent of damp rot.

The weathered boards shifted and groaned. Dozens of ravens tittered from the shadowy rafters, their eyes gleaming.

From the lake, the boat motored closer, drifted into the weeds. Rose stood there, searching the gloom. Celeste slipped lower in the water, positioned herself behind a hunk of dislodged dock.

A splash came from the direction of the boat. Rose was in the water.

Celeste searched the surface, grabbed a floating piece of board. It was soft and slippery. Useless.

The splashing drew closer.

"Come out or when I do shoot you, I'll hit you somewhere it hurts. I'll make it last. Watch you bleed out in this disgusting water," Rose called, her voice venomous.

Celeste peeked around the dock and saw Rose waist deep, eyes roving over the dark interior of the boathouse. She looked angry, but also...wary. Her eyes were fixed on the birds.

"Stupid little bitch," she muttered. "Should have killed you already. All of you."

A bird rustled and dropped from one of the wood beams. Rose shrieked and pointed the gun up, but didn't pull the trigger.

Celeste wondered if she could sink low, swim beneath the water and somehow bypass Rose. The air was thick, the humidity pressing in—the buzz of mosquitos, cicadas and frogs a constant drone.

No. The weeds were too high, the bits of collapsed boathouse poking jagged from the silt.

Rose moved into the boathouse, the water rippling out.

Celeste watched her face. Her lips were curled back, her eyes black.

"Fucking migraines. I hate this lake. I hate it!" she shouted.

Two ravens flew down, breezed past Rose. She swatted at them with one hand, but kept the gun trained forward.

She trudged deeper into the boathouse, slowed. From the angle she'd moved into, Celeste was in Rose's line of sight. She had only to look left.

Rose started to turn, but something stopped her.

From the back of the boathouse, another sound emerged. An odd suctioning as if something were pulling itself up from the mud, a scratching as it clawed its way onto the dock.

Celeste tried to see in the darkness. A sudden silence descended. The frogs, the bugs, the birds all ceased their chatter.

Rose shifted in the water, eyes darting around. Celeste stayed put, tried to keep her breath slow and quiet.

At the back of the boathouse a thick raspy moan broke through the silence. Celeste tried to make out what moved back there. The darkness seemed to shift and the birds too began to move, feathers rustling.

The shadow pooled unnaturally, and a silhouette emerged, the blackness knitting together. It was incomprehensible, terrifying, and yet Celeste was not afraid.

The ravens started to chatter and shift. They began to fly into that spreading darkness.

"What is it?" Rose murmured. The fear in her voice caused Celeste to look towards her.

Her usually tan skin had gone ashen and the age lines she'd carefully hidden appeared as deep grooves marring her forehead and mouth. The gun dipped as her hands trembled.

Celeste didn't wait. She lunged from her hiding spot, splashed through the water and shoved Rose as hard as she could. Rose teetered, managed to keep her footing, and swung the gun toward Celeste. She pulled the trigger. The bullet whipped by Celeste's face and grazed her temple.

The dark shape swelled and released a howl of grief and fury. It echoed deep through Celeste's own body and she understood it had been trapped in this place ever since her mother died.

The shadow flooded toward Rose and engulfed her. She screamed and thrashed. For an instant her eyes locked on Celeste's, her terror so raw Celeste's breath caught. Celeste almost stepped forward, reached for her, but the boathouse shuddered, the walls buckling. A rafter broke free and crashed onto Rose's head, forcing her beneath the surface.

Celeste turned and, fighting through weeds, feet sinking deep, she struggled into deeper water. Behind her, the boathouse collapsed.

65

———————

Nettie

Nettie came to and again stared at the stars. Had she ever truly seen them? A billion sparkling fires in the sky. Souls, she thought, billions of souls watching her and her watching them, all unaware.

A breeze blew from the lake, tickled the cool grass beneath her.

The lake. She could get to the lake, slip into the water, hide.

Nettie shifted, her body protesting, her head swollen, pulsing. Onto her hands and knees, then her feet. She took a staggering step toward the dark water. The stars glittered, expanding and contracting. Dark splotches hopped through the grass beside her. Ravens. Nathaniel had not killed them all. She thought she saw Popeye, his one bulging eye catching light from the moon.

She took another step, tasted the metallic stickiness of her own blood at the corner of her mouth.

Celeste and Adam. She had to survive for them.

Another step, another. Soon she felt the cool stones of the beach, the water lapping her bare feet. To wade into it, that cool perfect embrace.

Yes.

Almost there.

Grass rustled behind her. Movement.

Nettie turned.

Hannah stood in the center of the yard, eyes gleaming cold and hard. Slowly she lifted Nathaniel's gun.

Nettie never even heard the shot.

66

———

"Celeste?"

The voice called across the water. She squinted at the aluminum fishing boat. A man stood at the back, waving his arms.

Spencer.

"Celeste! Is that you?" he yelled again. "I think I have your dad. He was in the water."

"It's me," she yelled back, started to wade into the lake as Spencer sat and pushed the oars, gliding the boat closer.

"I stole this boat from your neighbor's house," Spencer called. "I heard the gunshots...holy shit. Are you okay?"

Blood seeped from Celeste's hairline. She put a hand to the warmth running down the edge of her face. "I'm okay."

She climbed into the boat. Her dad lay curled on his side, his skin a grayish color.

"Oh, my God. Dad?" She put two fingers to his neck, felt the weak pulse. "We have to get help. We have to call the police."

"I already did." Spencer rowed hard back across the lake. "I called them when I got to your dad's house."

"But...how did you know to come?"

"I tracked down Hannah tonight online, realized who she was."

"Rose," Celeste murmured.

"Yeah. And you know what's crazy? I had that itch again. I told you I had it back when I first moved here—this need to come by the house all the time, come to the lake. I felt it again and totally tried to talk myself out of it. After last night's debacle, I figured you wouldn't appreciate me showing my face again, but I could not ignore it. Look at my fingernails. I chewed them down to nubs. I'm pretty sure Noodles has a bald spot from how much I brushed him. Finally, I said 'screw it' and here I am. Where's Rose?"

Celeste looked across the lake to where the white speedboat floated as a ghost ship, empty on the calm lake, and beyond, barely visible in the darkness, what remained of the boathouse. "In the boathouse. It collapsed."

"Frickin' A."

"How did you find my dad?"

He slowed for a minute, eyes a little wider. "I almost didn't, rowed right by him, and then I heard…a voice, a woman's voice say my name. I swear, I expected to find her sitting beside me. I turned and there he was floating in the water."

In the distance, the sound of sirens filled the air.

Harris burst through the double front doors at the sheriff's office. Celeste sat shivering in a hard-backed chair. She blinked at him.

"How are you here right now?" she asked.

"I went to the house to the Moon Lake house and talked to a detective. They said you'd be here. I tried to call you about a hundred times."

"My phone is…I don't even know where it is. How did you

get back here so fast? You and Jonathan already drove to Michigan?"

Harris's face fell. "That's why I was trying to call. I lost him or…" An angry expression flitted over his face. "Or he lost me."

"How?"

"He pulled into a gas station, said he'd driven all night to get to West Virginia. Needed to sleep for a half hour, was getting groggy. I said fine, went into the gas station to get some coffee and use the restroom. I came out to find him gone."

"He ran," she said, unbelieving.

"Yeah. Detective Bowman has a BOLO out on his car, but… Who knows where he went. I turned around and drove back here. I was afraid he was coming after you and then I got to your childhood home and it was crawling with police." He closed his eyes for a moment. "That scared me half to death."

"Did they tell you what happened?"

"No. I'm not sure most of them knew what happened."

"Rose, the neighbor, was Hannah. She's the one who killed Elliot Thacker, and she shot my mom."

Harris sat heavily beside her.

"My dad showed up tonight. He had a bad feeling after Jonathan called and grilled him for the West Virginia address and then my brother confirmed that Jonathan had gone off the rails. My dad booked a flight and showed up at the house. Rose forced us out in her boat. She was going to kill us both."

"Your dad got shot?"

Celeste nodded. "But he's stable. A shoulder wound. He's at the hospital. Spencer saved us."

"He did?"

Celeste nodded. "Yeah."

"And where's Rose?"

"The boathouse fell on her. The police are out there now. I don't know if they've found her." Celeste's teeth chattered as she spoke.

Harris wrapped an arm around her and pulled her close, rubbed her back. "You need dry clothes." He leaned forward, studied her face. "What happened?"

She pressed her fingers lightly to the bandage on her head. "Grazed by a bullet."

Harris rubbed his jaw, his face troubled. "She came that close?"

Celeste nodded, closed her eyes.

"Let me talk to the detective." Harris stood. "We need to get you out of here."

67

———————

ettie had fallen once when she and Keith were scrambling up the face of a steep rock in childhood. They were barefoot and dirty, laughing, and she'd leaped for a boulder. When her hand caught it, the surface crumbled and broke away. She was in a free fall.

Nettie felt that now, falling faster than she could comprehend, and then suddenly she was jerked upward as if some giant in the sky had reached down and caught the invisible string attached to the center of her chest.

That was how she left her body.

She rose then, a dizzying ascent into those brilliant flaming stars and then...stillness.

A rich darkness settled around her and a bit of light, first a pinprick, then brighter and closer and it was her mother and from her poured a warmth and light that Nettie had not known in life, but knew just the same. She remembered this mother, this soul who'd traveled with her so many times in and out of bodies, centuries passing as a blur of light.

And this life, the one she'd only just left, flashed before her and she felt her love for her babies and for a thousand other souls who slipped in and out of her orbit. She saw Hannah, and she felt Hannah's longing for Nathaniel and her desperation to be chosen, to be seen and loved. But she did not only see her, she felt the painful void that lived in the girl, a void that had started in childhood and expanded until it could not be filled. She saw Nathaniel, his story playing out alongside hers. She experienced the conflict within him, his own yearning for Hannah, his guilt at turning his heart away from Nettie. All the emotion, the love and pain and grief and desire, flashed through her consciousness, there and gone. Nettie had only love for them both, and for everyone who'd chosen in the time before their lives began to go together and share in the experiences of the world.

The woman who had been Nettie's mother in the most recent life, but so much more in the eternal life, beckoned her to come now. It was time to go home. And somewhere down that tunnel of light was her father. She heard his voice and his laughter.

For a moment Nettie thought of her children in the house somewhere far beneath the stars.

A piece of her would remain with them, with the house, with the dark shadows that had consumed their brief happy lives.

EPILOGUE

It was nearly time to go, but Celeste watched from the tree line as a forensic team carried the black bag from the house. Inside were the bones of Elliot Thacker buried in the crawl space, covered by the safe, hidden for more than twenty-five years. The divers had not gotten all of her mother's remains and her identity would not be confirmed until a DNA test was done, but Celeste knew it was her and her dad had confirmed it.

Also in the boathouse, they'd discovered Hannah Hawley, Rose, dead from an apparent drowning.

As Celeste stared at the house, she felt the tear, the split somewhere deep in her body, and it was an odd pain—an old pain, because she was only just learning of her mother's death and yet she'd lost her mother a long time ago.

This pain perhaps was more from the loss of her father, the sudden dawning that the man who'd been so distant had committed the ultimate act of betrayal—not only against Celeste and Adam, but against Nettie, the wife who'd adored him, and he'd done it all for his own selfish lust—his desperation for a teenager.

That realization cut deep and tasted acrid. He had taken from his children the person who loved them most, who would have comforted Celeste during those difficult years of moving schools, of breakups with friends and boys, of periods and pimples and the ever-lingering question of who she was and who she was meant be. The woman who, with deft hands and gentle words, would have helped Adam when he struggled to tie his shoes, or when anxiety caused panic attacks in high school. The woman who would have cried at their graduations, at Celeste's wedding, who would have comforted Celeste now as she faced the certainty of divorce.

How would their lives have been different had her mother been allowed to live?

Even as the thought rumbled painfully through her mind, a memory surfaced. Celeste in kindergarten sitting on a cold bench in the too-bright cafeteria, biting into her ham sandwich then shrinking away in horror when she saw the shock of blood on the soft white bread, a tiny tooth poking from the center. The boy seated across from her, whose name had long vanished from her mind, had yelled 'Eww!' And a fire of shame had rushed into Celeste's face. She'd had a moment where her entire body prepared to bolt from the table, the cafeteria, the school. But there'd been a touch—feather-light, as if someone had rested a hand on Celeste's shoulder and somehow lifted the pain and embarrassment up and out and carried it away.

And she knew now her mother had been with her. She'd been the calm Celeste had found amidst her darkest hours. She'd been the presence who'd welcomed Celeste into the world between this one and the next and the gentle force helping to send her back.

Celeste now understood that she had always known her mother was dead, and the memory that had evaded her for so long slid into place with stark clarity. A toddler Celeste waking to the sound of that beeping phone, fumbling down the stairs and out of the house. Rushing into the yard now only feet away, driving on pudgy legs towards her mother, but a crowd of ravens blocked her. They were gathered around her mother's corpse, not feeding on her, but standing guard over the woman who'd rescued their babies, who'd sat on the porch and tossed them bits of bread, who'd talked to them as she drank her coffee, who might have confided in them that she'd begun to dread the night.

Now Celeste watched a raven drift toward the surface of the lake, then cut toward her. It swooped so close she could have reached out and touched its inky feathers. Another reminder the world was truly that magical, that connected, that impossible to comprehend.

Her eyes trailed back to the house, little more than a mausoleum now. Had the house become haunted by what her father and Hannah had done? With the lingering laughter and later sobs and not long after the screams of Nettie? Was that why Nathaniel been so distant with his children? Driven deeper and deeper into himself by the guilt of what he'd done, made all the crueler and more pointless when his young lover turned out to be more nightmare than dream girl and he realized it had all been for naught?

Fingers brushed against her own. Harris smiled.

"Ready to go?"

Celeste nodded, cast a final glance at the house, and followed him toward the road.

***

Celeste pulled into the driveway at her house in Grand Rapids just after ten at night. She'd driven from West Virginia, Harris tailing her, and they would only stop here long enough to grab a few things. He'd made them each a hotel reservation for that night and in the morning, they'd drive north to Traverse City.

Eliza, Harris's friend from the Memento Mori group, had a mother-in-law apartment she'd offered to Celeste for a couple of months or longer if she chose.

"I'm going to do a quick sweep of the house," Harris said when she stepped from her car. "Is that okay?"

She nodded, though she doubted Jonathan was hiding inside. He'd fled from Harris somewhere in Ohio. Celeste didn't know where he'd gone, perhaps to hide at his parents' for a few days, though they claimed not to have spoken to him in weeks. They sounded shocked to hear that police had issued a warrant for his arrest.

Harris appeared several minutes later. "All clear," he told her. "I'll wait downstairs while you get your stuff."

Celeste followed Harris through the front door, paused and took a moment to feel the house. She had once loved their house in Grand Rapids. How many nights had they come home after a long day in the lab, kicked off their shoes and relaxed on the couch? Breakfasts and dinners and lazy Sundays. It held years of memories and yet no longer felt familiar.

"Harris."

He shifted his gaze from a framed photo next to the door. It depicted her and Jonathan at their college graduations, each in dark caps and gowns.

"How did they get the arrest warrant for Jonathan?"

Harris studied her. "Darlene talked. She admitted everything. In her version of the story, Jonathan was the mastermind."

Celeste frowned. "Meaning he...?"

"Was the one who first proposed the idea of murdering you."

Celeste nodded slowly. "I see." She turned and started up the stairs. "I'll just be a few minutes."

Celeste walked into the master bedroom, stomach sinking at the sight of their king bed unmade, the comforter rumpled.

More evidence of Jonathan's spiraling psyche. She couldn't remember a single time in their years together when he'd left the house without making the bed.

Immediately, the thought felt absurd. She'd learned seconds before Jonathan had been the driving force behind her attempted murder and Celeste was noticing an unmade bed. She might have laughed, but feared if she started, she'd fall to the floor, laugh until Harris had to come upstairs and cart her off to the mental hospital.

Focus.

Celeste pulled two large suitcases from the closet and filled the first one with clothes. She picked up a black cashmere sweater Jonathan had gotten her for the previous Christmas. She'd never even worn it. She returned it to the closet.

After adding a pair of tennis shoes, snow boots and an extra pair of sandals, she zipped it shut.

She slipped into the bathroom, closed and locked the door, and took the pharmacy bag from her purse. For a moment she didn't open it, fingers tight around the crumpled bag, and contemplated how to face what it might reveal.

Swallowing the thickness in her throat, she drew out the little white box. A pregnancy test.

She inhaled through her nose, deep into her belly, counted to four, then exhaled through her mouth. *Calm breath—calm mind.*

It was just chemistry.

Hands steady, she followed the steps on the test and set the little plastic strip on the lip of the tub. In the shower sat Jonathan's sandalwood shampoo, his antibacterial soap, his razor. Nothing more than inanimate objects and yet her eyes lingered on them.

She moved away, glanced at herself in the mirror, but that too was an emotional landmine.

Stopwatch set to three minutes, Celeste watched the seconds tick by and then the first minute and the second.

Heavy, hip suddenly singing, she moved toward the tub, cast her eyes down and picked up the plastic stick.

Two little pink lines sliced through the white box.

Positive.

THE TRUE STORY THAT INSPIRED DREAD THE NIGHT

Lynette Dawson was a 33-year-old mother of two from Sydney, Australia, who disappeared in January 1982. Her husband, Chris Dawson, a former professional rugby player and high school teacher, claimed she left their home voluntarily, but her family and friends never heard from her again.

Suspicion grew over the years as reports surfaced that Chris had been having an affair with one of his teenage students, whom he moved into the family home shortly after Lynette vanished. Despite multiple police investigations, no trace of Lynette was ever found, and the case remained unsolved for decades.

In 2018, the true-crime podcast *The Teacher's Pet* brought renewed public attention to the case, leading to fresh investigations. Chris Dawson was arrested and charged with Lynette's murder in 2018, and after a high-profile trial, he was found guilty in 2022.

For a more in depth look at the story, check out my blog at www.jrericksonauthor.com.

ALSO BY J.R. ERICKSON

Dear Celeste Novels

Come Home, Katie

The Worst Kind

Dread the Night

She Writes in Red

Troubled Spirits:

Where paranormal fiction and true crime meet.

The Northern Michigan Asylum Series:

Ghost stories inspired by a real former asylum.

You can find all my novels and join my reader team to find out about new releases, book giveaways, and more at www.jrericksonauthor.com

ACKNOWLEDGMENTS

Many thanks to the people who made this book possible. Thank you to Team Miblart for the beautiful cover. Thank you to RJ Locksley for copy editing *Dread the Night*. Many thanks to Emily H. and Saundra W. for finding those final pesky typos that slip in. Thank you to Hannah Hawley for offering up her name as a character in this novel. Thank you to my amazing Advanced Reader Team. Lastly, and most of all, thank you to my family and friends for always supporting and encouraging me on this journey.

ABOUT THE AUTHOR

J.R. Erickson, also known as Jacki Riegle, is an indie author who writes ghost stories. She is the author of the Troubled Spirits Series, which blends true crime with paranormal murder mysteries. Her Northern Michigan Asylum Series are stand-alone paranormal novels inspired by a real former asylum in Traverse City.

These days, Jacki passes the time in the Traverse City area with her excavator husband, her wild little boy, and her three kitties.

To find out more about J.R. Erickson, visit her website at www.jrericksonauthor.com.